EXHUMED INNOCENT?

Other books by Howard Hodgson:

How to Become Dead Rich, Pavilion, 1992

Six Feet Under, The Book Guild, 2000

EXHUMED INNOCENT?

Howard Hodgson

The Book Guild Ltd
Sussex, England

First published in Great Britain in 2002 by
The Book Guild Ltd
25 High Street
Lewes, East Sussex
BN7 2LU

Typesetting in Baskerville by
SetSystems Ltd, Saffron Walden, Essex

Printed in Great Britain by
Bookcraft (Bath) Ltd, Avon

A catalogue record for this book is
available from the British Library

ISBN 1 85776 696 2

For Howard, Jamieson and Davinia

Acknowledgements

I salute the help and support given in the writing of this book by every single member of my family. In addition, I am bound to acknowledge the City and the people of Birmingham for providing yet again such a colourful backdrop for my story. I thank you all.

1

The Radio 4 *Today* programme was giving the news and obviously rejoicing in Mrs Thatcher's mid-term difficulties. The presenter, Brian Redhead, could hardly contain his glee at the latest opinion polls. It was eight thirty-three on a Monday morning in January, 1981. Stillion Sloane, displeased by the news, was further angered at what he believed to be the political bias of this programme – a view, no doubt, shared by Conservative Central Office.

As he listened he stood before his wife's dressing table, which was situated in the bay window of their large bedroom at the rear of the house, overlooking their spacious gardens and those of the neighbour. He glanced into the mirror and put the finishing touches to the immaculate Windsor knot in his tie. He cut a smart figure. Now aged thirty he was a successful professional, but his fair hair, swept fringe and boyish looks made him appear younger. His tanned face, brought about by a combination of a Christmas skiing holiday and the need to stand around in cemeteries, made a sharp contrast to his starched white shirt, black waistcoat, black and white corporate tie and pinstriped trousers.

He adjusted the double cuffs on his right sleeve and was resetting his cuff-link when something caught his eye through the window and off to the right in the next door neighbour's garden. The dull grey early light of this cold winter's morning was opening up to reveal gardens covered in snow, their features hidden by its depth. Stillion was dressed, as usual, as if he was off to Buckingham Palace, but as usual he would be working in

1

the snow. His eye had been attracted by the sight of young Julian Ripley, his neighbour's youngest. The four-year-old was galloping down the garden through the snow in his school uniform, without a coat and almost certainly without the permission of his mother. For some reason this spectacle held Stillion's attention and the tones of Mr Redhead faded. The boy was heading for the iced over and snow-covered swimming pool. Stillion's eyes squinted as his total attention locked into place. Any sound of the news had vanished before the boy disappeared and Stillion was off across the bedroom, leaping down six stairs at a time, skidding over the polished wooden hall floor, tugging at the great oak front door and racing into his front drive. He, like his little friend before him, was now galloping through the snow. His left arm clung to his driveway gatepost as he flung himself left onto the pavement before turning left again into the Ripley's drive and racing up. He threw himself at the five-feet-something fence that divided their front garden from their back. Amazingly, he hit the top just below his ribcage and was therefore able to roll over and down the other side in one easy movement before he was off again, following Julian's virgin steps across the snow.

He crashed through the ice into the freezing water. He didn't feel the cold. He was only conscious of what he could see, and he couldn't see the boy. He sat down so that his head sank below the water. He stared. In front of him, Julian, eyes and mouth wide open in an almost expressionless gaze, stared back. Stillion grabbed him and in one movement threw both of them from the water and onto the side of the pool. They rolled over in the snow. What should he do? He knew little about life-saving procedures despite having sailed all his life. He now cursed his cavalier abandon. However, this time God was to smile on him. The weight of his body rolling over Julian had got the boy spluttering, coughing and now crying. He picked him up, threw him over his right shoulder and raced for the Ripley's kitchen door, bursting in on the usual humdrum atmosphere of a typical domestic scene – the rushing around of a family gathering items for the day while grabbing at toast or

2

cereal and being ordered about and given time checks by mother.

The Ripleys hadn't missed Julian. After John Ripley had left for work, Julian had been sent to get his cap and coat from the cloakroom off the large hallway. He had only got as far as the glass door that led from the rear of the hall into the back garden. The tempting sight of all that virgin snow had obviously been too much for the boy. All of this had happened in the last three minutes. 'In the midst of life we are but in death.' But happily, not this time.

Now the table jarred and the tea spilled as Elizabeth Ripley pushed Julian's two elder brothers aside in an instinctive lunge to take her screaming youngest from Stillion's outstretched arms. Julian was rushed before the Aga, his school clothes ripped from his trembling little body and his thin little frame quickly cloaked in a big towel. She vigorously rubbed his back, his chest, his hair, his legs, his hands, his fingers and finally his toes. Half the time she was talking comfortingly to Julian, half the time barking orders at his brothers who were now rushing here there and everywhere in an attempt to obey.

Finally the emergency was deemed to be over and Elizabeth turned her head back over her right shoulder towards the still open kitchen door. There Stillion still stood, dripping, slightly stooped, and with his eyes and mouth wide open. His only movement was the heaving of his chest and shoulders caused by his gasping for breath.

'Stillion how can we ever thank you enough?' she exclaimed as she noticed him for the first time since she had grabbed her baby from his arms and motherhood's automatic pilot had taken over.

'No need. You'd have done the same. Christ! I must go – it's only half an hour until I'm due at my first house, and look at the state of me.'

Suddenly he felt very cold, a feeling that became more acute as he trotted back to his house.

'What the hell have you been doing?' asked an amazed Stephanie as she ran her eye over his bedraggled appearance at the front door having taken, as it seemed to Stillion, an age to answer the bell.

'Oh I've been for a swim next door. What the hell do you think I've been doing?'

'I don't know, which is why I'm asking,' she shouted as he ran up the stairs. Typically such wifely banter was followed by the comment, 'Oh Stillion look what a mess you've left behind you,' as she surveyed a trail of water and melting snow which was left in the wake of his progress. 'Stillion!' she repeated. There was no response. He was already in the bedroom peeling off soaking clothes and diving into a steaming shower for the second time in an hour.

It had been thirteen months since Stillion's week of funeral wars with Sydney Gridley. At that time he had added 500 funerals per annum to his total by the acquisition of Richards & Gridley and a further 300 by taking over their proposed acquisition of Higgins & Co. These annual totals had then been added to Sloanes' 600 funerals per annum, Burton & Sons' 150 and A. Kemp's 50. Thus the total number of funerals that the growing Sloane Empire conducted at the beginning of 1980 was 1,600 a year.

Since then Thomas Baldwin of Winson Green had been bought which added a further 300. This all meant that Stillion Sloane had made remarkable progress. It was less than four years since he had inherited his father's mantle. During this time Sloane & Sons had been transformed from the respectable but failing funeral company of North Birmingham, trading largely on its past due to Stillion's father's ill health, to the largest private firm of funeral directors in the city. Indeed it was now only second to the Birmingham Co-operative Funeral Service in size.

Stillion raced through his washing and dressing chores. Time was short. He barked an order downstairs for Stephanie to phone either John Palin with the news that he would drive to the first funeral address directly in his own car. This would save valuable time. Would John please ensure that the staff put the right coffin in the right hearse before leaving Sloane House as

4

Stillion would not be there to ensure the same. Luckily, this first Monday morning funeral, the first of five on the 'A' fleet, three of which he would conduct personally, and the first of fifteen overall, was in Harborne, which was only two miles away. Thus a timing disaster was averted which would have inevitably punished, in turn, all the later funerals scheduled on that fleet for the day.

Stillion descended the stairs looking pretty much the same as he would normally have done, except that his hair remained wet and had been combed back. 'Steppie, I forgot to ask you to tell J.P. to put my top hat, gloves and tailcoat in the hearse along with the green burial cert and cem gratuities. Could you—'

'—Yes darling, you little hero.'

'Hero?'

'Elizabeth just phoned to see if you were OK.'

Stillion swept through the kitchen door leading to the garage, leapt into his XJS and with the garage doors already open, courtesy of Stephanie, knocked the transmission into reverse and hit the accelerator pedal with his right foot, but not before blowing his wife an affectionate kiss and giving her a wink of his right eye.

Stephanie watched the blue Jaguar bump, slither and slide down the drive before skidding backwards towards the right and then powering off to the left, churning up a snowstorm behind it as it went. She smiled. She was indeed a contented girl. Yes it was true that her husband might not always be everyone's cup of tea. He could be grumpy, intolerant, single minded, precise, vain and, on occasion, flirtatious. But he was strong, protective, good, kind, knew the difference between right and wrong and loved her. Moreover, in her eyes he was bewitching and she loved him.

She lingered in the cold garage for a second contemplating all of this, a cup of black tea in her right hand, her left resting on her expectant bump. The pregnant Mrs Sloane was due to give birth any day now to their first child, a baby conceived in the happy months of reconciliation following the regrettable

5

episode with Lottie Wilkes. She returned to the kitchen to phone John Palin as requested.

Naturally there had been stressful times in the months following Stillion's affair. It might have only been a one night stand but the play, however short, had run to the final act. It had thus taken a long time for such a picture to dim in her head. In the early days just the briefest glimpse of them together in her mind made her tummy turn and the actual sight of Lottie – one lunchtime at the tennis club – had made her physically sick. Their eyes had met for a second before both had turned away in shame. One the shame of the robber, the other the shame of the robbed. Initially Stephanie had, with Stillion's mother's blessing, giving Stillion a hard time. Indeed, so hard that her mother who knew nothing of the affair, feared for the marriage on the grounds of her daughter's attitude. Stephanie even had to put up with one of those 'Now listen to me my girl . . .' lectures, and although tempted to do otherwise, had kept her secret and taken the blame.

Stillion for his part had been attentive, romantic and even patient – a virtue not normally associated with him. There had been an autumn break in Paris, many flowers, some jewellery and dresses. At Christmas he had given her an XJS of her own and they had decided to start a family. The pregnancy had been the biggest healer of all. It had pulled them back together, closed the wounds and now even the scars had faded. The wrong had been his, the forgiveness hers, the recovery theirs.

As Stillion sped away along the slushy, suburban roads of palatial Edgbaston towards the Quinton end of Harborne and his first funeral, his thoughts turned to his latest acquisition target – Frank C. Williams Limited. This firm conducted 1,000 funerals a year and had a virtual monopoly on the Bilston area of the Black Country when it came to funerals. Consequently, as soon as it had become known on the grapevine that Charles Williams wished to retire, competition for his signature on a sale agreement had become fierce. The natural front runners were the Birmingham Co-op, Frederick Gilbert & Sons, where the dislodged and embittered Sydney Gridley had found employment as a funeral conductor following his departure from Richards & Gridley, and of course, Sloane & Sons. The stakes were high. A victory for Sloane & Sons would increase their size by over 50 per cent, pull them closer to the Co-op in size, and leave Gilberts way behind in their wake. Moreover, and perhaps more importantly, success would enable much rationalisation of labour and capital equipment to take place, which would enhance profits and as a result build a war chest for further acquisitions. On the other hand, failure would mean either the Co-op moving further ahead or Gilberts catching up, and whichever victor gaining the spoils that Stillion knew he needed.

Stephanie had said that to lose would not be the end of the world. Stillion knew she was right. But he also knew that to lose might mean he may never win again. He had thus determined early on to win every acquisition contest and to date he had. He did not intend this one to be any different. In the end money always sang the final song and Stillion would outbid the opposition. They would then appease their feelings of failure with the thought that he had overpaid. He would know he had not. He believed he could bid more because of his ability to operate the economies of scale better and thus, by rationalisation, extract more profit per funeral while remaining price competitive. And facts showed he was right. Acquisitions had grown Sloanes' profits faster than they had its size – the ultimate acid test.

However, not everyone in the Sloane camp was happy. Stephen Bellamy, the Company Secretary, and accountant, had become increasingly concerned about Stillion's desire to spend so much time conducting funerals. Stillion *had* cut down. He now only conducted Sloane funerals, as opposed to those of the acquired firms. Nevertheless Bellamy insisted this was still too much and that Stillion should spend more time behind his desk controlling and tending to the needs of his growing business. Stillion knew that he was right and that a successful bid for

Frank C. Williams would require him to hang up his top hat and cut that final link with his father and those cherished childhood memories.

More importantly, Stillion's love affair with his bankers, and theirs with him, was starting to wane. They had supported him robustly from day one, but as the acquisitions grew so did the cash required to make them happen and increasingly proposals had been referred to the regional office. Those faceless people had never met Stillion and were therefore immune to his charms, to his enthusiasm and to his passion. As a result the cautious regional HQ had started to voice their desire to see a period of consolidation. Stillion disagreed. He was in a hurry. He had determined not to miss any acquisition opportunities and wrote off the bank's thinking as a lack of understanding. He understood that if he did drop an acquisitional stitch then all he had to do was sit tight and let the death rate do the rest. The bank had not been impressed with this argument and there were now growing tensions. However, mainly thanks to the support of his branch, the bank would grant him the 1,000,000 pounds sterling he needed to win over Charles Williams. Nevertheless there was to be a condition. Namely that, once Frank C. Williams had been bought and the overdraft raised to £1,500,000, Sloanes must reduce it to £750,000 before a further deal could be put before them. Stillion had agreed, but at the same time made up his mind to replace them as soon as possible following the deal's completion. It was a case, he rather arrogantly perceived, of the 'Jesus of Nazareth theory'. Jesus might have been the Son of God around the world, but to the folk of Nazareth he was just the local carpenter's boy who had developed ideas beyond his station. It was the same, according to Stillion's law, with banks and their clients. Little clients who became successful outgrew their bank's perception of them, and so the bank had regrettably to be replaced. Stillion wrestled with such problems of high finance as he drove.

*

To the north and east of the city, in the very different climate of the poor Lozells area, a very different person wrestled with very different financial problems. She was Theresa Field, Terri to her friends. She had milky white skin with freckles, deep red, long and wavy hair, was eighteen years of age, hung out with Rastafarian pimps, was a part-time whore and had an expensive drug habit.

Her Rasta pimp, the dreadlocked, drug pushing, sometime boyfriend Jimmy 'Gimme', had given her drug credit in exchange for sexual favours. He could probably have had the sex without the credit if he had threatened to beat her if she didn't earn enough from the usual punters. However, he had two problems. Jimmy Gimme liked to think he was tough, when in reality he might have been bullied at a soft middle-class prep school, and more to the point he couldn't help but fancy her. She was, for all her inner failings, very desirable, with her milky skin, sweet features and natural red hair that fascinated him so much – especially that soft clump in the forbidden place.

Jimmy pretended to be tough. He worked a good con act. Most believed him. Terri didn't. She was close enough to know otherwise. She was smart enough to manipulate him as a result. All had been going well until Jimmy got more frightened of his drug suppliers than he was infatuated with her. Harry Wilkes, Lottie Wilkes' husband and Stillion Sloane's sworn enemy due to his wife's sexual indiscretion with Sloane, not only controlled the city's scrap metal but also his growing interests were now well developed in narcotics.

Harry was neither a patient nor an understanding man. He didn't mind 'casting a little bread on the water to get the business going' but he had no time for people who didn't pay their debts, especially if the money was owed to him. Jimmy, thanks to Terri, was now behind in his payments and the pressure was starting to tell. The threats of what would happen to his manhood if he didn't pay up had, understandably, scared the shit out of him. There was nothing for it, he must put all thoughts of 'soft pussy' to the back of his mind and threaten the bitch with a good slapping if she didn't pay up. However, there was a problem. The crazy boot couldn't pull enough tricks in the time he had been given to redeem his debt. There was nothing for it. If the whore wanted to escape his backhand across her face and his shoe up her arse then she would have to steal the amount needed.

As a result he had summoned her to an early morning meeting at the coffee and pool bar in Lozells Road opposite the Villa Cross. The meeting had been set for nine-thirty. A reasonable time of day for most, but outrageously early for both of them. He had done this in order to make a point. Terri arrived fifteen minutes late and in a defiant mood. She made the early running with her complaints and threats of no more sex. He said nothing. He appeared to listen and was still appearing to listen as he approached her and gently stroked her hair before grabbing it and violently slamming her head down on a pool table.

'Listen, bitch, and listen well. You owe me two grand. That's the amount I got in my book, bitch. Do you think d' money comes to me? Do you think its mine t' give? I got people who want to feed my laughing tackle to the dog. I will only let that happen over your dead body bitch. You 'as taken me for a fool. Now tell me when I get zur money or zur next screwin' you get mon is with the pool cue.'

'Where am I gonna find two gees from? Yow're 'urtin' moy – arsehole.'

'Arsehole, why yur . . .' He raised his fist and the look in his eyes indicated that he meant business.

'OK! OK! I 'ear yow. Give us a chance Jimmy. Let moy up. I won't run 'onest,' she said, attempting to sound seriously concerned, sincere and submissive.

'Just make sure yer just do Terri. I'll meet you 'ere at eight tonight and I'll expect answers. Don't even think about doing a runner. I'll find yer and I'll mark yer face,' he said firmly, and left.

'Fuck yow,' she shouted after him pushing up one central

10

finger at the door he had just passed through, safe in the knowledge that he couldn't hear her.

'What a fuckin' mess,' she thought as she sat on the side of the pool table and surveyed the room for ideas. It was as bereft of people as her head was of solutions. She was alone. Oh there was bound to be some flunky in dirty white overalls somewhere round the back, but for the moment, in the actual café, she was alone.

'What a dump,' she mused, looking round at the pool tables with torn baizes, the old fashioned pinball machines against the far wall, the old chairs surrounding the dirty Formica-topped tables, the grubby floor and in the corner the little bar with a battered tea urn and a plastic sandwich display housing stale and curled up sandwiches.

'Yes, what a dump. The only thing that's missing is the bloody sterilised milk and I bet some bastard has just gone out for that. A good looker like me deserves better than this,' she told herself as she inhaled the stale cocktail of damp and last night's second-hand dope.

She made up her mind to phone her elder brother John. He had had big problems with debt for as long as she could remember. His money problems, caused by an addiction to gambling, were big and the Brummie bookie could be as violent as the Brummie drug dealer when deprived of his addiction – cash. Such big problems must have been balanced by some big solutions at some point, or he wouldn't still be around. He would have become a statistic of the funeral trade rather than a worker in it.

At twenty-seven, John Field was nearly ten years old than his sister. She, like all others, knew him as Elton. He had adopted this traditional first name in order that he might identify with Elton John. He had done so in the hope that it would increase his desirability. It hadn't. He was the eldest, she was the youngest, of four. The middle two, along with their father, had drifted away from Birmingham, all drawn to different places in search of a better, richer and easier life – probably at someone else's expense. Their mother was dead.

11

Their parents had shown little moral fibre and had been disdainful of the work ethic. Their father had hardly ever worked other than for a brief period in the car industry at Longbridge. There, he had quickly allied himself to 'Red Robbo' and for a time seemed to work quite hard at ensuring that his fellow workers did not. However, this new communist phase was short lived and he was soon back 'on the box' due to a mysterious back injury which prevented him from working but never seemed to trouble him while propping up the bar at the Nag's Head – his local watering hole situated nine terraced house doors down from their unkempt house. His two topics of conversation were 'the plight of the working man' and the 'pitiful state of my back'. And of course, in his mind, these two issues were the reasons why he didn't work. It was his stand against capitalist exploitation of the workers that had caused him to be a virtual cripple. He never seemed to be too much of a cripple while knocking their mother about. It was no contest really. He, with much of his large seventeen-stone fighting weight out front in a beer belly, she a fourteen-stone dumpling stuck on a five-foot frame that could often be smelt before it could be seen. She was stale. Stale sweat, stale fried food, stale beer, stale cigarettes. She rarely washed, never seemed to brush her hair and would wear the same clothes for days. She only cleaned the house if the 'social' was coming. She fed herself out of greed and her husband out of fear. She did not bother to feed her children and therefore most of their nutrition came from school, when they went, or stealing, when they didn't. She had always claimed that her husband had kept her short of money, which he had, but not short enough to deprive her of the forty or so cigarettes that she dragged on daily, leaving the fingers of her right hand darkly nicotine stained.

In truth there was little to choose between the Mancunian Eric Field and his Brummie bride Carol. Neither should have begat children. Indeed neither should have been permitted to keep animals. Perhaps he was worse as he abused all – the two boys violently and the girls almost sexually – just dropping short

12

of overstepping the mark. She only abused herself but neglected the children to the point of their non-existence. At least abuse was a form of attention.

In their sparsely furnished and dirty hovel, where all the children had shared a bedroom, queued for the outside loo and had often hidden from the irate rent man, the parents had been set an example for their children's future conduct. Hardly surprisingly it had not turned out well.

Elton, who was certainly no over-achiever by any stretch of the imagination, had probably fared best. He had at least managed one 'O' Level, surprisingly in religious knowledge, and had succeeded in becoming an embalmer after being apprenticed to the Birmingham Co-operative Funeral Service. He had married young and had two children whom he loved but not enough to kick his gambling habit which had brought him much grief, including beatings at the hands of the bookie's men, gas and electric cut-offs and house evictions for the non-payment of rent. It had also reaffirmed him as a thief and a con man and cost him a good job as embalmer for Sloane & Sons just over a year ago during the 'funeral wars' between Sloane & Sons and the then independent Richards & Gridley. This sacking had probably cut off the one chance Elton had of moving away permanently from his appalling beginnings. It had confirmed that he simply did not have the willpower to distance himself from the standards set by his parents.

The other children, Terri included, hadn't even done that well. They all had juvenile criminal records.

In 1974 Carol died after a short illness. Not long after the funeral, payment for which was never made, the family quickly dissolved. Elton got married, Eric disappeared back to Manchester, and the other two children escaped to different parts of London, cutting their ties with each other as well as Birmingham. Terri went to live with her maternal grandparents some four roads away. They weren't rich. Indeed they were quite poor. But the house was clean and she was fed. Moreover they were old and couldn't bring about much control, which suited her comings and goings up and down the Lozells Road and in

13

and out of its pubs just fine. Then in 1978 the grandmother died and Terri, faced with having to look after her grandfather, chose to move out and throw in her lot with the Irish alcoholics and Rasta pimps and druggies of the Lozells' twilight zone. Such an existence had led her to the problems she now faced – and face them she better had, without delay.

She dropped off the side of the pool table and wandered out of the front door into the Lozells Road. She meandered round the pedestrians and passed the Asian fruit and vegetable stalls until she found a telephone box that wasn't broken and rang her brother's work number.

Elton, following his demise at Sloanes and subsequent beating by Sydney Gridley's foreman at Richards & Gridley, had spent some time out of work, dodging his bookie. He had only managed to avoid a serious second beating, this time at the bookies' hands, by landing a job as embalmer and occasional limousine chauffeur at Frederick Gilbert & Sons and then promising to give the bookie a cut of his wages each week.

To his surprise and certainly not his pleasure, his arrival at Gilberts coincided with that of Sydney Gridley, who having been vanquished during that December week in 1979 had been left with little option but to accept Stillion's offer for his remaining 20 per cent of Richards & Gridley's shares and clear off. This had not left old Sydney penniless but it had meant that the sixty-one-year-old still had to work to avoid cutting into his savings. Therefore he had been grateful to be offered a funeral conductor's post by Fred Gilbert, who disliked Stillion only a little less than Sydney did himself – the base reasons being the same that had originally attracted Sydney's sentiment: fear and jealousy.

Neither had Sydney been pleased to see Elton at Gilberts. He would never forget Elton's role in the events of that dreadful week. He even somehow managed, in his own mind, to blame Elton for the loss of Richards & Gridley. Sydney had not realised, and perhaps would never realise, that the loss could be laid fairly and squarely at his own door due to the treatment he meted out to his wife and son. After all, Elton played no part in their decision to sell the business from under Sydney to his hated rival Stillion. Indeed, they had made such a decision as the only possible escape route from a life of insufferable tyranny at his hands. This was obvious to all but Sydney, who could only dream of a day when circumstances would provide an opportunity for him to get even with both Stillion and Elton. Such a day would surely come but until it did Sydney and Elton would have to remain uncomfortable workmates.

A receptionist at Frederick Gilbert & Sons answered Terri's call. Elton wasn't there. He had been sent to fetch a body from a nursing home in Herefordshire and was not expected back until after 4 p.m. Terri banged down the receiver at her end half in anger and half in panic. She was angry because, as ever, Elton, like any other member of her family, wasn't there to help her when she really needed it and she was panicking because without him she hadn't got a clue how to raise two grand over the next ten hours, or even ten days for that matter. Sure she was pretty and men would pay for her services but she didn't have access to a client base that would pay big money for her tricks. Her price list was £5 for digitally organised relief, £10 for a blowjob and £15 for the full works. At those rates it would take forever to raise two grand, especially as she had to live while she earned and that meant food, drink, rent and drugs, which would have to be bought for cash secretly now that Jimmy was cutting off her credit. No, there was nothing else to do but visit grandfather and see what could be squeezed out of the tight old git. She reckoned that was a better choice than attempting to steal the amount as she only knew how to shoplift and the shops which she frequented did not carry goods to that value. Even if they did, where would she fence them?

Stillion had met the cortège at the first house, conducted the funeral without incident and on time (which was no mean feat given the state of the roads) and returned to Sloane House in his car. He made straight for John Palin's office to see how many removals had come in over the weekend. He found John looking pale and shocked. Stillion immediately knew something was wrong. They were very busy and John could look flustered at such times, but John did not look flustered now – he looked shocked, the way the bereaved look shocked. This was impossible. John was good at his job, professional, efficient, polite and even considerate but he never became emotionally involved. He left work each night, went home, had a steak and never gave a thought to the misery he had witnessed that day. Something must be very wrong. Stillion asked the question and couldn't wait for John to spit out the answer. When it came Stillion was also shocked. Something had happened that had really got to John as it now did to Stillion.

'No. Nothing's wrong. We've had fourteen house removals and nine "first call instructions" over the weekend and I've just taken another four over the phone from the Coroner.'

'John, you look like you've seen a ghost old man. What is it?'

'It's the last four. They're all kids from one family. Burned alive in a house last night in the bottom end of Lozells near Wheeler Street. Two were pronounced dead on arrival at Dudley Road Hospital and the other two died there later. Various colours and sizes. One, three, four and six. Obviously not the same fathers. Mother was down the pub with her current boyfriend. She left the kids on their own. They knocked a paraffin heater over. The mob will string her up if they get their hands on her.'

'Yes, they will,' confirmed Stillion slowly, now as deeply horrified as John. 'I bet that poor cow wishes she could turn the clock back one night,' he thought to himself before asking John, 'Who told you all of this?'

'Sergeant Wilson, the new coroner's officer. Apparently you conducted the mother's aunt's funeral a couple of years ago and the family asked for you by name. What about payment?'

'Let me think on that,' answered Stillion.

This reference to the account came about because most funeral directors gave credit on adult funerals but all demanded payment in advance for children. This was not because funeral

16

directors were callous. Far from it. Indeed the costs involved in a child's funeral were virtually the same as an adult and yet most funeral directors charged only for their variable costs and therefore a child's account was only a fifth of the amount of an adult. No, the reason lay with the public for it was the public who always failed to pay for a child's funeral unless the money was collected in advance. Stillion had on occasions bent this rule and on each occasion his faith in human nature had been misplaced and all monies lost. However, just at this moment money and funeral accounts were far from his mind. Last night four little innocents had been taken whereas this morning little Julian hadn't. Sure 'the Lord giveth and the Lord taketh away' but how the hell did the Lord maketh his choice?

Both men had worked with death for years. Sometimes tragic death, nearly always sad death, but like all funeral directors they couldn't swallow a child's death as part of their daily working diet, and now they were confronted by the deaths of four children on just one throw of life's dice.

'When are the family coming in to make the arrangements?' demanded Stillion in an attempt to snap both of them back into 'business as usual' mode.

'This afternoon,' replied John.

'OK. I'll back your judgement. If you think they haven't any money then we'll conduct all four funerals free of charge, provided they're held at the same time, which the family will want anyway. So, only charge them the fees to be collected on behalf of the cemetery and minister, which they must pay in advance. Oh, and see if the minister will provide his services for nothing, like us. Freddie Price would, most of the other bastards won't.'

'Right you are,' nodded John and the two men moved on to discuss other pressing, if less tragic, arrangements: removals and funerals. Both would now have to put the tiny quartet to the back of their minds, but found this impossible. John wondered what his three children were doing at this moment, even though they were all adult. Stillion phoned Stephanie to see if she was

OK before leaving to conduct a large Sikh funeral. 'In the midst of life we are but in death' seemed to ring true, as did 'there but for the grace of God'.

Lozells Road runs east to west and slightly north. It connects Aston in the east with Handsworth in the west. To the north is also Handsworth. To the south and down the hill is Hockley and further south is Birmingham's city centre. Aston Road North, Hockley Hill, Soho Road and Lozells Road had been the main shopping and social areas of the inner North Birmingham since the city's incredible expansion during the industrial revolution of the eighteenth and nineteenth centuries. Such streets had provided the big pubs, shops and music halls of the nineteenth century. In the twentieth century the music halls gave way to cinemas, which in turn gave way to bingo halls. Following the Second World War, the slums of Hockley gave way to the socially disastrous tower blocks of the fifties, and by the sixties the working-class English and poor hard working Irish had been joined by thousands of immigrants from either the Indian subcontinent or the West Indies. Initially, and perhaps understandably, the communities did not sit well together. Indeed it would take much effort by the good, race riots by the bad and the mingling of two further generations before race relations, if not crime rates or moral attitudes, would improve in this area. In 1981 this boil was developing a head, which would erupt in the summer of that year with the now famous '81 race riots. Local property prices had plummeted in the sixties and seventies as English racism meant low demand and high supply. The immigrants weren't rich enough to create demand and join the house-owning classes until they had enough time to make enough money – and until the arrival of Mrs Thatcher who wanted them to become home owners, whatever their colour, and encouraged them by the cheap sale of council houses. The two events were to occur at approximately the same time. Initially the English who could afford to go went, leaving a poor and old population behind to become ever more resentful of Asian introspection and trading success, and fearful of a violent Afro-Caribbean youth that saw itself as cultural outcasts and at the back of every queue. The Irish also felt diminished and overtaken by the Asians and were shocked by the kind of violence that a drug culture brings. So this was the cauldron that bubbled uneasily along the Lozells Road and down the lines of terraced houses which ran off it, south towards Hockley.

As Terri walked into the street where her grandfather lived she noticed a group of people gathered on the pavement. On the other side of the road there was a clear-up operation going on. There had obviously been a fire some hours earlier. She did not have time to stop and stare. She stepped into the road and passed the people and the house without a glance or a thought for either. Moments later she rang her grandfather's bell. Eventually it was answered by a short, fat old man.

Bill Woodall had given his only child Carol his looks but not his character. Unlike his daughter's cluttered, dirty life, he led a precise, clean existence. With the exception of the Second World War, in which he fought as an infantryman, his whole life had been spent in the area. He had been to school in Wheeler Street and brought up in a damp, gaslit tenement, which had opened up onto a courtyard not five hundred yards from where he now lived. His working life had been spent further down the hill at Joseph Lucas, where he had put in forty-five years despite his six-year absence in the army. He bought his current home in 1946 with savings, a little money he had been left by his father and an inheritance his beloved wife Betty had unexpectedly received upon the death of a spinster she had been in service to since she was a girl. Betty had received cash and some personal effects.

Neither Bill nor Betty had liked Eric Field but Carol wouldn't listen. Bill had blamed Eric and his way of life for Carol's habits and eventual death. This had broken his wife's heart and in Bill's mind led to her death four years later. After his daughter's death he had welcomed Terri into his home. His initial sympathy soon turned to dislike when he realised what

19

sort of a girl she was and how neither he nor Betty could influence her to climb up to a higher moral plane. He had been neither surprised nor displeased when she had run out on him only two days after Betty's funeral. Since that time, now nearly three years ago, he had seen her only twice and on each occasion the purpose of her visits had been to borrow money.

Terri smiled sweetly. ' 'Ello granddad.'

'Oh it's yow,' he responded sternly. 'Yow had better come in. Been up to no good I suppose. Still runnin' around with those no good darky boys I'll be bound. Need somethin' do yow?'

'Yow shouldn't be so anti black granddad. It's against the law nowadays. Yow know.'

'I ain't anti black. I'm anti violence. I'm anti drugs and I'm anti all the thieving that goes on to pay for it all. And I don't need a lecture from yow about it and all neither,' he said over his shoulder as he led the way into the back room. He offered her a seat.

'Granddad. Yow are moy only 'ope. I need some money and I need it now.'

'I bloody knew it! I bloody knew it! Yow is no bloody good is yow? 'Ow bloody much this time?'

'Two grand.'

'Two what?'

'Two thousand pound.'

'Two bloody thousand nicker! Yow mad! I ain't got that sort of dough!'

'Yow gotta 'elp moy. There'll kill moy or somethin' if you don't.'

'Well they'll bleedin' well have to 'cos I ain't got it. And it's no good turning' on the water works,' he added as she began to cry. 'Any road, who's they and 'ow the bloody 'ell do you get to owe them two bloody thousand nicker in the first place? I'm an old man and I could do without this sort of thing.'

'Please,' she pleaded.

'I already told yow, I ain't got it, all right? Yowa grandma would turn in 'er grave if she could 'ear all of this.'

20

'Grandma loved moy. She would 'ave 'elped moy. She weren't tight.'

'Yowa grandma never 'ad two thousand nicker in her life and nor do I.'

'Yeah. But she 'ad jewellery and other stuff left by her that rich old bitch.'

'Yow wash yowa mouth out young lady. She were a good 'un. Yeah, she did leave yowa gran some things and yowa gran loved 'er for it. I 'ad 'er favourite ring buried with her along with the ring I gave 'er on the day we was wed. There was two more. They were identical. I lost one, but you can 'ave the other if yow like. I was gonna give it yow one day any road. Then go 'cos I'm an old man and I don't need all this bother.'

He went upstairs and returned with a gold ring with one small diamond set in it. She took the ring, hardly looking at it, and slipped it into her front right jeans pocket.

'Thanks granddad,' she said with as much sincerity as she could muster.

'Just repay yowa grandma's memory by livin' right or at least betta. Don't bring any more problems 'ere and don't bring them on yowa own 'ead neither. Just think of those poor nippers up the road.'

'What nippers?' she replied.

'The ones that were burned in their beds last night of course. Yow must 'ave heard. Yow bloody passed the 'ouse on the way down 'ere. It's been on all the news all mornin'. Even the national news. You ain't 'eard?'

'No, I ain't,' she replied without interest. She left for the jewellers on the Lozells Road with an ungrateful goodbye to him and a 'sod the tight arsed old bugger' to herself.

Over at Gilbert's the receptionist who had taken Terri's message had written it down, placed it in an envelope, sealed it up and written 'Elton – Urgent' on the front. During the late morning Sydney Gridley crossed the reception on his way to one of the arrangement rooms. The receptionist caught his attention with,

'Oh Mr Gridley, could yow please give this to Elton 'cos 'e won't be back until after I finish. Monday is moy 'alf day yow see.' Sydney, small, dapper and supercilious, stopped and turned to face the girl. The loss of Richards & Gridley to that bloody boy Sloane and the humbling financial hardships it had brought about had done nothing to soften his attitude to those he considered to be inferior to him. This girl, who hailed from Chelmsley Wood, a huge estate built in the sixties which ran down the side of the M6 motorway and housed the fleeing English from the immigrant invasion of Hockley, Lozells and Aston, was no exception.

'Maureen, you take messages from other people and give them to me if they are for me. You also take messages from me and give them to the people I want you to give them to. That is your job. It is what you are paid for. You are not paid to take a message and then get me to do your job for you. Are you, you stupid girl?'

'I'm sorry Mr Gridley, I was only tryin' to be 'elpful. Elton's sister said it was urgent – a matter of life or death.'

'I don't give a—'. Suddenly Sydney smelled trouble for Elton and thus perhaps an opportunity for him to drop Elton in it, or even better get him the sack. 'OK. You can leave it with me,' he said, grabbing the envelope from her hand, slipping it into his inside jacket pocket and proceeding into the arrangement room.

There he introduced himself to a family from Dudley, the father of which had lost his sister, a widow from Yardley. This man wanted to sort out the money side of things before anything else. ' 'Ow much am they?' he enquired about the cost of a funeral.

'How much *are* they,' replied Sydney disdainfully, rudely correcting the man's English.

The fellow looked surprised. 'Well I don't know – that's why I'm asking yow.'

'Oh God' thought Sydney. Death might even be preferable to dealing with these Black Country half-wits. He couldn't wait for these particular idiots to be on their way in order that he might open Elton's envelope.

The middle of Stillion's day was taken up by a large, no, enormous, Sikh funeral. Stillion's father, Arthur, had welcomed the Asian and West-Indian immigrants in the fifties and sixties as fellow members of the Great British Empire. They had fought with us in two world wars and for centuries we had taken our customs to their countries. Now, he had felt, they should not be denied their customs while living in his country. This had been in stark contrast to the bigoted attitude of most of his rivals who, like Sydney Gridley, gave out the 'When in Rome do as the Romans do' speech in answer to special ethnic requests. Consequently Sloane & Sons had built strong ties with the West-Indian, Sikh and Hindu communities. The Moslems tended not to use Sloanes because the Sikhs and Hindus did, and not because of any racial attitude on behalf of either Arthur or Stillion Sloane.

Now the head of a Sikh sect had died while visiting relatives in Essex. These relatives had instructed a local Dagenham funeral director. However, the service would take place at the sect's temple on the Soho Road in Handsworth, just opposite Reverend Price's St John's Anglican church. The Sikh elders there had insisted that the cortège be led into the temple and out again before proceeding on foot the six miles to West Brom Crem by Stillion himself. This would take a great deal of time and the weather was bitterly cold with slush and snow everywhere. Stillion didn't really want to do it. On the other hand how could he refuse? He couldn't afford to offend the Sikh elders and risk undoing all the good work his father had done. There would be perhaps as many as 10,000 local Sikhs present who would certainly wonder why he wasn't leading the cortège. What's more, there was the promise of heavy media coverage which might even include *News at Ten*. No, there was nothing for it, he would have to do it.

If Stillion hadn't really wanted to spend a lot of his day

walking some six miles in the freezing cold then this was nothing compared to the feelings of the funeral directors from Essex, who believed it was their funeral and were strongly opposed to any interference from another firm. Indeed, last Friday they had phoned John Palin to say they would not co-operate with Sloanes. Palin had informed the temple who had in turn denied them access unless Stillion walked at the head of the procession. In the end Palin had negotiated a settlement that allowed their conductor – a Mr Brian McGigan – to walk alongside Stillion.

Stillion should really have been paying attention to winning the Williams acquisition but he was there to protect Sloanes' interests and felt no need to either command or be unpleasant to Mr McGigan. Not so Mr McGigan. It was plain from when Stillion first clapped eyes upon this shortish, bald and plump man of fifty-something that he was just a couple of degrees away from throwing his teddy out of the pram. Stillion's attempts to explain Sikh customs were brushed aside without a word, just a face of thunder and the wave of a hand.

Then as the 10,000 or so mourners arrived at the temple, which would only accommodate 1,500 at most, and the thronging and surging mass was blocking not only the Soho Road but the Villa Road and Hockley Hill traffic-lights as well, Stillion again attempted to help McGigan.

'Do what I do,' he said as the only two white men stood in the eye of the storm. Stillion put his top hat on and took his shoes off as they entered the temple. He then pushed them very close to the main front door pillars on the right in order that he might easily find them again. McGigan looked round but could see nothing but the tops of turbans as thousands of Sikh men bent forward to remove their shoes. He turned back to Stillion. 'You do what you bleedin' like. I ain't taking my shoes off for some bleedin' punkah wallah to run off with.'

So Stillion let McGigan make his own mistakes: he left his shoes on but took his hat off inside the temple and then put it back on for the long icy walk to the crematorium. Then he had almost shaped up to hit Stillion as the latter had steadied the coffin as the Sikh bearers took it from the hearse.

'I'll bleedin' stick one on you in a minute,' he whispered hoarsely to Stillion, his temper now at breaking point. Perhaps only the presence of the TV cameras actually prevented him from taking a swing.

Stillion stepped back and waited. The elders flocked to him and would not allow the procession to proceed into the chapel until Stillion took his place.

At last the foolish Mr McGigan got the rewards his ignorance so richly deserved. At the end of the committal he tried to lead the main male mourners outside when he should have been escorting them to the furnaces, so that they could see the great man set on fire and watch the early stages of the cremation. There was uproar and McGigan became flustered and confused. The more he tried to steer them to the garden of rest exit the more they pulled back towards the door on the other side of the chapel. Stillion stepped forward and resolved matters. A deflated, humbled but still seething McGigan was left to lead the 'Mrs Kaurs,' as Sikh ladies were referred to locally, into the garden of rest and wait for the smoke to go up the chimney. His role had become, much to his annoyance, but to all others' relief, very secondary.

The rest of the funeral passed off without incident. McGigan left for the long hearse journey back to Essex, which would give him ample time to lick his wounds and perhaps learn that you don't take on a real pro, especially not in his own back yard, unless you know what you're doing. It might not have been a contest that Stillion had sought, but it had been none the less an unfair one. McGigan had been a second-hand car salesman for most of his working life. Stillion had been born into the business. His childhood toys had been made from coffin offcuts and his early memories had always contained a backdrop of funerals and his father's business which had arranged and con- ducted them. Indeed, despairing at Stillion's poor school reports, his father had once asked him: 'Who said "I come not to praise Caesar but to bury him"?' 'I don't know daddy,' the five-year-old Stillion had responded, 'but did we get the funeral?'

Perhaps if the unfortunate Brian McGigan had known any

of this he would have enlisted Stillion's help rather than push up his own blood pressure to gain an end result that only made him look a fool. On the other hand, history shows that small, bald men in their fifties with big egos and even bigger insecurities tend to ignore the logical route.

For Stillion's part, the whole exercise had all been in a day's work and by the time he was back in the warmth of his office and giving dictation to his long serving secretary, Victoria Thomas, McGigan had almost slipped from his mind. Almost, but not quite, as Stillion had a lasting impression that McGigan really should tend to his eyebrows, whose unkempt state starkly contrasted with his shiny bald head. However, the image quickly disappeared as he concentrated on the Williams acquisition and tomorrow's garage orders.

Terri left her grandfather's house and strode up the road. She passed the burnt-out house without a glance or a thought and continued up to the Lozells Road. Sure she was sorry some kids had died. She would have preferred it not to have happened, but it had and it had nothing to do with her. She might show some emotion about it all when the time was right and the same was expected of her, but for now it was merely an unwelcome distraction from her main mission which was to look after herself.

She was only frightened because Jimmy was frightened. Jimmy, himself, did not frighten her. Why should he? She knew she could manipulate Jimmy all over the place. But she also knew that Jimmy's weakness could be turned against her. He might think he loved her but she knew he loved himself more, just like all his mates did, and if threatened he would betray her. She had seen it in his face that morning. She had known then that she was on her own. She didn't know where Jimmy bought his stock from, but if he was supplied directly or even indirectly by the Wilkes family then he was in deep trouble on her account and that meant she was in it up to her armpits, with the danger of going deeper.

26

At the head of the Wilkes family was Harry, a scrap-metal dealer who had a finger in most unsavoury pies in and around Birmingham and was known to be the head of the Brummie mafia. Ironically he, like the self-righteous Sydney Gridley, hated Stillion Sloane. Sydney's hate was because Stillion had his business; Harry's was because Stillion had had his wife. This fact was not generally known and certainly not to the likes of Terri. All Terri knew was that Harry was supposed to have had anybody who had crossed him inserted in the concrete that held up Spaghetti Junction. This was clearly not true but Harry did nothing to dispel such stories as it made the controlling of the Jimmys and Terris of this world that much easier. A point proved by the lazy Terri's hard working efforts so far that day.

She arrived at the jeweller's shop and was confronted by the sign in the window which read 'Gold, Silver and Jewllery Bought. Enquire Within'. She did. A young Indian in a dark-blue turban smiled and said, 'Can I help you please miss?'

'Yeah, I want to sell this ring. Fetch the owner,' commanded Terri as she retrieved the ring from her pocket and placed it down on the glass counter.

'I *am* the owner,' smiled the smart handsome Indian, his white teeth almost sparkling.

'Well bugger moy. They bloody own everything nowadays,' thought Terri to herself as she displayed the same sort of racism to the Indians as her grandfather had earlier to the West Indians. 'I bet this little brown bastard will try to jip me,' was her second thought as she said, ' 'Ow much will yow give moy for this ring?'

The jeweller, whose name was Singh, put in his jeweller's glass and picked up the ring. 'Hmm,' he said after a few seconds. 'It's not worth much.'

'Yow bloody would say that,' said Terri, now sure that her initial distrust of him was correct.

'No, no that's not right,' countered Singh, offended by the remark and his smile now suddenly missing. 'I assure you this ring is not worth more than £50, I have seen it before. I cleaned it and had it valued for a lady about three years ago. She was

27

one of my first clients when I bought the business from Mr Smith. She brought in three rings, this, one identical and one very lovely ring.'

'What were 'er name?' interrupted a disbelieving Terri.

'I cannot be remembering for so long miss, but a moment and . . .' He reached for an old receipt book and flicked over a few pages. 'Mrs Bette . . . Woodall,' he said, a broad smile returning to his face.

'She's dead now. I'm her granddaughter. Moy mum is dead too. I'm her only living relative. 'Er jewellery is mine now. 'Ave you a copy of the valuations?'

'Oh most certainly, in my records,' purred Singh.

'Show moy,' demanded Terri before adding a belated 'please.'

Singh caught the eye of his assistant that said 'Watch her' as he disappeared into his back room before returning triumphantly with three pieces of white paper. He placed them down on the glass counter facing her and then gently pushed them towards her.

Terri hadn't attended school that much and when she had in the latter years more time had been spent looking into boys' trousers than into books. Consequently hers had not been a fine education and she now struggled to read. However, she did understand numbers and pound signs, both of which interested her when added together. She pretended to read the pages.

'Rhubarb, rhubarb, rhubarb £50,' she thought as she glanced at the first page. 'Rhubarb, Rhubarb, Rhubarb £50' for the second page. 'Blah-blah, blah-dee-dah £18,000 . . . what!! 18,000 nicker, 18 grand. No!' She couldn't believe her eyes. Bloody hell. What did all these words above that magic figure mean? For the first time in her life she wished she had spent a little more time learning to read and a little less time extracting boy's willies from their trousers for the then going rate of 50p a time in the school toilets.

'This valuation 'ere.' She pointed to the £18,000 valuation. 'Are you sure? and couldn't this be the eighteen grand ring?' She added pointing to the ring on the counter.

'No. Not at all. Not this ring nor its twin but the other ring was certainly worth eighteen thousand pounds. A most wonderful ring. Eighteen carat gold ring with a seven diamond setting. The centre diamond is large, flawless and gives the ring a very big value. That is why I am remembering the ring you showed me. I remember all three rings and the lovely lady. I never have anything like it since. She didn't want to be selling it. Anyway I couldn't be buying it after the valuer said the price. Too much money. I tell her "Lady pay insurance or put it in the bank." You have ring now?'

'No,' responded Terri, whose brain was moving into overdrive.

'Well it may be in her bank I expect,' smiled Singh.

'I expect so,' said Terri, her thoughts now miles away, before returning with the words, 'Can you make moy a copy of this?'

'Not right now, but you can be borrowing that one if it pleases you. But please be returning in due course.'

'Thanks,' said Terri as she turned to leave.

'What about the ring?' asked Singh as he pointed to the forgotten ring on the counter.

'Maybe later,' replied Terri as she turned back, collected it and returned it to her jeans pocket.

Once outside she didn't know whether to roll around on the pavement screaming, throw herself under the first corporation bus that passed or go straight round to her grandfather's and kill the stupid bastard. Surely the silly old fool would never have buried Grandma with that ring on her finger if he had one inkling of its value. No, he wouldn't have. Sure he had loved grandma but he also loved money and comfort in his old age far too much to make such a barmy gesture. No. She must never have told him. Yes, for whatever reason the silly old cow had never told him or anyone else. And now, more importantly, something that she could have got her hands on one way or another and was probably worth as much as a whole Hockley tower block was six feet under in Handsworth Cemetery. She could hardly wait for four o'clock to roll round so she could speak to Elton. They had to do something. That bloody ring could solve all their problems, his as well as hers. He would have to help her now.

Harry Wilkes had spent the morning sitting behind his big desk in his large, plush and warm office. His big frame looked expensive in his hand-made shirt, but the thick gold ID chain around his right wrist and his loud tie told you where he really came from. Nevertheless, long gone were the days when he dressed for work in denim and went straight to his scrap metal yard.

He surveyed the books; things looked good. Metal trading up. Second-hand car dealings up. Protection up. Gambling up. And his growing little narcotics empire was going like a train. However, one thing had caught his eye that didn't please him. He had outstanding monies around the Villa Cross District. Initially this had not been his patch and he hadn't minded casting a little bread on the water in order to catch a few fish and of course put the opposition out of business in the process. But now the time had come to pull in the credit and the best way to do that was to make a couple of examples of what people could expect if they got behind with their payments. He picked up the phone to the lieutenant of his 'heavy brigade'. 'Alf, who's Jimmy Gimme?'

'Oh 'e's a freelance pusher we supply on the Lozells Road. 'E's a Rasta, likes reggae music and is not too bright.'

'According to the figures I've got in front of moy 'e's bleedin' bright. 'E's flashin' red to the extent of two fuckin' gs. Get Frankie and some of the boys and lean on him. Now. OK? Phone me back with good news. OK?'

These instructions were sufficiently clear for Alf to get cracking at once and not honour the two days he had previously promised Jimmy. Instead, Jimmy, sooner or later that day was going to experience a rather unpleasant time.

*

No sooner had Sydney Gridley seen off the wondrously stupid bereaved family from Dudley than he had ripped open the envelope that the receptionist had left with him for Elton. It read: 'Elton, please telephone your sister Terri at the Calypso Coffee Bar – 554–8427 between 4 p.m. and 5 p.m. today. She says it is very urgent. Extremely urgent'. That was good enough for Sydney. He was convinced this was the moment he had been waiting for. He had known about Elton's gambling problems for some time. Indeed, it had been such knowledge that had led him to bribe Elton to betray Stillion Sloane and trigger the December '79 funeral wars. Elton must now have got himself into even greater trouble than normal. Sydney couldn't wait to exploit this. He had been watching Elton these past few months. He knew Elton had been slipping behind with his old gambling debts and had been paying half, or even less, of the agreed weekly sum to the bookie who had scared him so much before Christmas in 1979. Moreover, he knew that the reason was that Elton had been betting for cash with a betting shop down the road from Gilberts and not buying essentials for his two streaming-nosed, unwashed and non-toilet trained kids, as he had told the bookie. On the other hand, Elton's long-suffering and somewhat dim wife, who definitely needed a lesson in domestic science, thought she and the kids were going without due to the fact that he, now reformed, was using his wages to pay off his past misdemeanours.

Obviously such economic use of the truth laid Elton open to attack and painful damage one way or the other. Sydney now intended to have Elton's balls chopped off in a perfect pincer movement that would supply great pain from both directions – physical, like broken legs, and mental, like the loss of his children. It was, to Sydney's mind, no more than Elton deserved.

Sydney placed the note in a new envelope and when Elton returned just after four p.m. gave him the same with the words, 'Maureen left this message for you.' The gormless, spotty, seedy, little blond pushed his thick jam-jars back up his nose and stared at the back of the retreating Sydney. Elton did not like

Sydney and he knew the feeling was mutual. Anything else would have been impossible given what each had attempted against the other in the past. Therefore Elton was now surprised Sydney had bothered to take the message and even more surprised he had delivered it rather than throwing it down the toilet. However, such thoughts were pushed aside as Elton read the message and raced to the garage foreman to beg use of his phone. He didn't like the message. Terri might be in trouble. That was bad. On the other hand, she could be trying to warn of impending trouble for him. That was worse. He dialled the number and hung on while Terri was brought to the phone.

'Elton, that yow?'

'Sure sis. What's the problem?'

'I owe Jimmy Gimme two grand.'

'Well don't look this way our kid. I owe nearly a grand to the bookie and another in back rent and stuff. I can't 'elp you can I?'

'I suppose you don't care if 'e kills moy.'

' 'E won't do that. Yowa the boss there our kid.'

' 'Arry Wilkes or someone like that will nobble 'im if he don't nobble moy, or pay, or both.'

Elton started to see that this was more serious than he had originally supposed. He, like everyone else who had 'a bit of a gamble' knew what happened if you didn't pay the likes of Harry Wilkes. He knew that it had been a blessing that he hadn't started an account with a Harry Wilkes' betting shop in the first place, or perhaps he wouldn't have been here now.

'OK. It's serious our kid, but what can I do?'

'Listen, granddad gave moy a ring today from grandma. It was worth shit. But the jeweller gave moy a valuation for the ring which must have been buried with her, which says that ring was worth eighteen grand.'

'Wot, eighteen grand? Nah. You got it wrong.'

'I don't get things like that wrong! I got the valuation with me. Look, yow gotta 'elp moy. I need that bread now and by the sound of it, so do yow.'

'The ring's gone. Dead. Buried. OK? And I told you I got no bread. I owe what yow do and I got blokes on my back too, OK?'

'Couldn't we claim on the insurance?' Terri asked.

'Wot insurance? And anyway yow can't claim on insurance when granddad 'ad the bloody ring buried with 'er in the first place.'

''Elp moy! 'Elp moy!' Terri turned on the waterworks as everything else seemed to be failing.

'Look. There probably ain't insurance sis, and even if there were then yow can't claim on it when you bury the ring of yowa own free will. Sorry kid.'

'But it weren't my free will, it were granddad's,' sobbed Terri.

'Don't cry our kid, I think I know a road out of this,' said Elton, more softly.

'Do yow?' sniffed Terri, now attempting to pull herself together.

'Yeah. Reckon I do. Maybe get us both out of debt. What time could you meet moy bookie and moy with that Jimmy kid?'

'I gotta meet 'im at the Villa Cross Coffee Bar at eight,' answered Terri in between sniffs.

'Right. Meet up round the corner in the Nags Head at eight-fifteen,' said Elton. They both knew that neither Elton nor his bookie could enter the Coffee Bar. There was a colour bar in place. No whites allowed and the only exceptions were young whores like Terri, the underworld enforcers employed by the likes of Wilkes and the occasional visit from the men in blue who always turned out in force on the rare occasions they visited the joint.

With the appointment made and the conversation concluded they both felt a sense of renewed hope. Maybe the family had a real asset after all. They just had to get their hands on it. They replaced their telephone receivers, as did Sydney who had monitored the call via the Gilbert switchboard.

*

33

Stillion, having pushed his case for Williams by making a 'hale fellow, well met' call to Charles Williams himself, had blasted his solicitors into action with a tweaked offer to the Williams' solicitors and had completed the Tuesday garage orders. He concluded his day by returning to the cold to conduct his third funeral. This funeral was a hearse and two limousines, from a council house in Kingstanding at four p.m. to Perry Barr Crem for 4.30. Kingstanding, named so as a result of Charles I standing there during the seventeenth-century's Civil War, was a high point looking down towards Aston where Charles' Cavaliers were skirmishing with the Parliamentarian Roundheads for the control of Aston Hall. This beautiful Jacobean palace was later to be trapped inside the nineteenth-century industrial expansion of Birmingham which engulfed Aston and thus the beautiful building was left surrounded by row upon row of terraced houses. The ground at Kingstanding was reputed to be the highest going east until the Russian Ural Mountains. This may or may not be true, but the people who lived there believed it and their belief seemed to be supported by the tremendously bitter cold that chilled to the bone when an easterly wind blew in the winter. Consequently the area was nicknamed 'Little Moscow'. This name was born solely as a result of the weather. However the dour hard-line trade union and Old Labour attitude of the inhabitants made it even more apt.

Sloanes were as stretched as they expected to be in a cold, snowy January and the post-Christmas death rush was well and truly underway. This meant that all three fleets were packing in five a day, five days a week and, as a result, the cash was rolling in, as expected. However, such use of labour and capital equipment caused problems. Hearses, limousines and ambulances (a polite name for removal vehicles) all needed to be free from either bumps, bangs or mechanical breakdowns, and the chauffeurs and bearers and their commanding funeral conductors all needed to be free from illness and on top form.

Funeral wages were low and what's more the job was not considered to be attractive. Therefore Stillion, like other busy funeral directors, had to keep a constant eye on his staffing, its

34

quality and the availability of part-timers drawn from the police, ambulance and fire services. By and large the part-timers did not present a problem. They were drafted in to be the fourth bearer or third chauffeur and therefore tended to play 'follow my leader' which they were more than capable of, given their need to absorb training, have discipline and a certain 'nous' in their full-time jobs. These men worked for Stillion or his competitors when there was a demand and their work shifts allowed. They did so for extra, and often undisclosed, cash. It was thus a second line of income for them when they were on 'nights' and a quality source of part-time labour for funeral directors when the need arose. No, such men presented no problems, other than they were, due to the poor price of a funeral being charged at that time, unobtainable as full-time staff and therefore the funeral profession was stuck with full-timers of a lower quality who needed lots of attention when first employed, which should be during the quiet summer months and never, hopefully, during the busy winter ones.

Unfortunately for Stillion, an old and long-serving driver, Andy Black, whom Stillion's father had employed some twenty years ago, had been taken ill suddenly in November and had, just as suddenly, retired in December, leaving Sloanes with a gap to fill. Graham Stone, the Sloane senior conductor had, after some effort found a replacement, one Ian Hurst. This young man seemed to fit the bill. He was big, strong, willing and very polite. On the other hand, he looked a little like Joe Bugner the boxer, spoke as if he had a cleft palate when he didn't and perhaps, upon reflection, appeared to be a little simple.

In order to share 'the experience' around the fleets and to train up Mr Hurst as soon as possible, Stillion and Graham Stone had decided to transfer Stillion's long-time and trusted lead chauffeur, Walter Warburton to Graham's 'B' fleet and put Ian Hurst in as an 'A' fleet driver under the guidance of the Sloane garage foreman and 'A' fleet hearse driver Arthur Kemp, whom they agreed would not carry passengers and therefore train the new recruit quickly.

Hurst had started on the previous Monday, and true to the form he had shown at his interview, had seemed very willing. However, Arthur Kemp, who expected great patience for his own shortcomings but displayed little for those of others, was already lobbying for Hurst's replacement saying that he was 'Thicker than pig shit and about as smelly'. Sloane and Stone had taken this with a pinch of salt, both knowing Arthur like the back of their hands. However, this last Monday 'A' job might just put the issue to the test as the way things had worked out meant that the novice Ian Hurst would have to be the lead limousine driver.

As usual the vehicles travelled from Handsworth to the house in Kingstanding with the hearse at the back. This was always a Sloane feature. It was done in order that the general public might realise that the speeding vehicles were on the *way* to a funeral rather than actually on it and in some disarray. The hearse would then be called through once in the road of the funeral and would thus sedately pass the limousines whose drivers would respectfully doff their caps and add to the 'theatre' of the occasion for Brummie women in the street, who could then be heard to say, 'Nobody does it like Sloanes. Co-op is cheapest. Sloanes is best.'

As the hearse passed, Stillion, sitting in the lead limousine's front seat with top hat in hand, said to his attentive recruit, 'Ian, this is Kingstanding. When built in the nineteen-thirties it was the biggest housing estate in Europe. Note all the houses are the same. After the funeral I'll guide you back into this road. All you have to know is where the actual house is, so pick a recognisable landmark now.'

'Right yow are Mr Stillion,' snorted Hurst down his nose.

Once at the house Hurst made his choice and then proceeded to help the other chauffeurs arrange the flowers in the hearse before returning to his limousine. Eventually Stillion loaded both limousines separately, before thanking the assembled audience and walking the cortège to the end of the road from where it glided through the January twilight to Perry Barr Crem. There the service passed off with the usual precision despite the normal hymned up rock 'n roll classics of organist Michael Russell.

Then the hearse took the flowers to Old Soldiers' Park old people's home at the family's request while the limousines took them home. Stillion precisely guided Hurst there with a Birmingham *A to Z* on his lap and one eye on the nearside wing mirror to ensure that the other limousine and private cars were still in tow.

Finally they pulled back into the family's road. It was five-twenty and too dark to read the house numbers.

'Drive to your landmark and that will be where the house is,' commanded Stillion. There was silence. 'You did pick a landmark?' questioned Stillion in a hoarse whisper, not daring to raise his voice in case the family heard him through the partition window.

'I did Mr Stillion,' came back Hurst's reply.

'Well?' queried Stillion earnestly.

'It were a big black dog sitting on the pavement outside the 'ouse.'

'What!'

Arthur Kemp was an old pro. Perhaps Stillion and Graham should have listened to him after all.

During the afternoon, Alf, Frankie and two of the boys had earned their money by cruising the streets of Aston, Lozells and Handsworth looking for Jimmy Gimme. They had stopped at every known pool bar, coffee bar and café. They had seen most of their clients and half of Birmingham's CID and drug squad's wanted list but they hadn't seen Jimmy. This was a game of cat and mouse. They did enquire of his whereabouts but did so in order to frighten who they asked rather than believe what they were told. Indeed they went to where they were told he wasn't in the knowledge that eventually their paths could cross. Whereas, if they went where they were directed, perhaps they never would.

However, this policy, although logical, did not bear fruit and by the time it was dark Alf decided to phone Harry for further instructions.

'Hi boss, we been all over. 'E's disappeared from the face of the earth. Vanished into thin air.'

'Crap!' spat back Harry.

' 'Onest boss. Been everywhere. Should I send the boys 'ome for their tea and meet yow in the pub later?' went on Alf, rather unwisely.

'I told yow I wanted bloody good news yow bloody incompetent fool! No bloody wonder 'alf the fuckin' nignogs think they can steal from moy with 'alf-wits like yow enforcin' moy will. Now bloody find the bastard if yow know what's good for yow. Or would yow like moy to put someone else on the pissin' job?'

'Leave it to us boss.' Alf had clearly got the message but Harry was no longer on the end of the phone to hear the answer. His receiver had already been slammed down safe in the knowledge that this would be the case.

Alf returned from the phone box to the old sky blue Mark Ten Jag, parked his bulk in the front seat and commanded, 'OK boys back to the Lozells Road.'

'What!' was the reply in unison.

'Shut it, OK? We go 'ome when we finished work. All right?'

Stillion had guided his charge of vehicles back to the right house despite the missing landmark. Once he had taken his leave of the bereaved family he and the two limousines returned to Sloane House where Palin and Stone were only just managing the pandemonium.

The garage was full of hearses and limos in various stages of cleaning. One or two were finished and covered. Three, or perhaps four, had been sprayed only, while several had not even been started. The reason for this was that the garage was empty of men, ambulances and even one hearse. Stillion knew immediately what this meant. There must be an epidemic of house removals. Stillion commanded Hurst and bribed the second limo part-timer with extra cash to spray, sponge, spray and leather all unfinished vehicles before leaving both men in the large, well-lit but bitterly cold garage, where the water would freeze on the vehicles if the leathering wasn't done fast, and where Hurst and his mate would lose all feeling in their fingers within minutes. Little wonder then that old pros like Walter Warburton and Arthur Kemp had raced out on house removals safe in the knowledge that much of this painful work would be completed by the time they returned. It was always preferable to sit in a warm ambulance, pick up a stiff and the out of hours removal fee than stand in a freezing garage, pick up a freezing leather and the pittance of overtime that went with it.

Stillion bounded through reception and up the main staircase, making straight for John Palin's office.

'It's gone crazy again,' said Palin, his desk completely covered with 'First Call Instruction' sheets and completed arrangement forms. 'We had twenty-six in over the weekend as you know. Today we've taken a further twenty-three and eight of those are house removals which have to be done now. I need those two in the garage to go out and fetch a sudden death in Handsworth and take it to the coroner's mortuary in Newton Street. A policeman is already waiting at the house.'

'No,' countered Stillion.

'Oh no. This means he's going to send me out on a removal,' thought John, horrified at the prospect. John was good at his job, but in his mind that did not include the sight of the dead let alone actually having to touch them.

'But everybody else is out already. Even Graham is on one and I've got to make sense of all this,' he complained, pointing to the paper nightmare on his desk.

'Don't worry old man, not you,' reassured Stillion, who would have loved to send John out on this removal but realised how important it was to re-establish order on his normally tidy desk. Confusion there could lead to wrong bodies going in the wrong coffins or to the wrong chapels or even the wrong funerals. 'Not you. You sort this out. The guys in the garage must finish the vehicles before the temperature drops further, so I'll go with Jones and you'll have to cover the evening viewing for him until some of the others get back.'

'No problem,' said a relieved John, who didn't like doing viewing duties either but it was better than going on a removal and a bit of him was humbled by Stillion's 'lead from the front' approach.

Stillion rang the bell of the caretaker's flat and called out Keith Jones. Together they loaded a hearse, which would have to substitute as a removal ambulance, with an old removal shell in which they placed a 'cricket bag' – a latticed body bag which resembled the bag used by cricketers to carry their gear around in. Inside the cricket bag they placed two clean, white sheets and a rubber mat.

As they pulled off the forecourt of Sloane House the front doorbell went and, much to his annoyance, John Palin had to leave his precious administration and descend. He answered the door. A small old lady stood before him. It had started to snow again and the flakes were gently landing on, and mingling with, her ruffled grey hair.

'Do come in. What can I do for you?' said the tall, thin and balding Palin with as much genuine good feeling that this good but hardly openly caring man could muster at the end of a long hard day that had started so badly with the news of the four-child fire.

'I've come to see Horace Buggins please,' said the woman timidly before stuttering out, 'the family ain't s-s-said I can't g-g-go in 'ave they?'

Palin referred to the viewing book in the reception. There were no special instructions so he was able therefore to confirm that they hadn't. He then asked her to take a seat before disappearing to put the chapel lights on and check that he'd got the right body. Soon he returned and escorted the woman to Chapel Five, hoping as he went that Mrs Jones, Keith's ancient old hag of a mother, would have the sense to answer the phone if it rang while he was downstairs, as all other staff members were either out on removals or departed for the

40

evening. Palin opened the chapel door and motioned for her to enter.

'Could yow please come with moy? I ain't see a dead body before, see,' pleaded the woman.

Palin could hardly contain his displeasure but somehow he did and they entered together. She moved apprehensively to the coffin, while he stood respectfully a pace behind. Eventually she clasped the desceased's cold hand. Her eyes welled with tears as she uttered a few words which were audible enough to Palin for him to realise that what he had suspected by virtue of her question in the reception was indeed true. She had been a sometime and probably a long-time mistress of the object of tomorrow's ceremony.

'Oh just look at 'im,' she whispered finally. She appeared to be cheering up a bit. 'Oh yes, just look at 'is face.' Palin reluctantly obliged. 'Yow can see that week in Majorca at Christmas did 'im good,' she smiled.

'Well I don't think it did,' thought Palin to himself as he led the woman away.

Meanwhile Stillion and Jones had made their way through the dirty slush of the Soho Road before turning left just past the old school to negotiate the more treacherous side roads. Finally they came to rest outside the three-storeyed terraced house, where there was, just as Palin had said, a policeman waiting.

'Yow've taken yowa time. We all got a tea to go 'ome to yow know,' was the arrogant young copper's greeting.

'Sorry but we came as soon as we could. Every ambulance is out,' said Stillion pointing behind him to the hearse as proof.

'Well that's yowa problem. Let's be 'aving yow,' was the response. Stillion bit his lip. He, like Palin, and indeed all his staff, had had a long hard and at times cold and stressful day but it didn't do to get on the wrong side of the police, even if sometimes their local 'pig' nickname seemed most apt.

Stillion checked the name of the deceased. The young

bobby confirmed the same and added that she was a thirty-something West Indian woman who was very large. Perhaps even eighteen stone or more. She was to be found right at the top of the house, first door on the left, next to the last flight of stairs.

Stillion knew these houses well. The copper's information meant that this poor, unfortunate woman had died three floors and therefore six flights of stairs up. Oh shit. Six flights to descend with a big West Indian mama who should be handled with care and respect. And he only had the slightly-built Jones for help.

'Would you like to give us a hand?' enquired Stillion politely.

'Nope. Not moy job mate. I'da become an embalmer if I'da wanted to work with stiffs,' was the aggressive reply. Then the copper added, 'Oh and the electric ain't workin' neither.'

'Well do you think you could possibly come up with us and shine your torch around?' asked a still polite but slightly more clipped Stillion.

'I don't 'ave to go up there mate.'

'Well then just lend us your torch.'

'The torch stays with moy. Yow make yowa own arrangements and sort yowaself out mate.'

Stillion stared at the young policeman. An icy-cold superior stare, packed with moral indignation and disgust that only a British public schoolboy can deliver so well. The working-class bobby recognised the look and yielded a little. He might be a policeman but Stillion was a toff after all. 'I'll come in the hall and flash moy light up the stairwell.' They went in.

The stairs were very steep. Indeed so steep that having left the shell coffin in the hall, it was tough just going up with the cricket bag which only contained two white sheets and the rubber mat. Eventually they climbed the sixth flight and located the room. What little light there was from the copper's torch three floors below soon faded as they advanced. The room was situated at the back of the house and therefore they couldn't even rely on any lighting from the street. They stumbled about in the pitch black, talking to each other to relay their discover-

42

ies. Jones stammered, half due to the cold, half out of fear. Stillion's voice was assured. He was as cold as Jones and perhaps a little unsure but it did not show.

The room was very cold, obviously dirty and seemed to have no furniture. Eventually Jones located a pile of rough old blankets in the far corner to the right. He pulled the top one away and felt about. He squealed. He had located the body when the first two fingers of his right hand had slipped up the deceased nose.

'Steady,' commanded Stillion.

'She's 'ere Mr Stillion,' said Jones, who felt almost winded from the shock.

'OK Keith. Well done,' said Stillion reassuringly as he edged in the direction of Jones' voice, dragging the cricket bag with him. This disturbed something and Jones squealed again as suddenly the black floor seemed full of dancing red lights which squeaked as they darted about. 'Bloody hell – rats,' thought Stillion. He said, 'Don't worry it's only a couple of rats. They won't harm us.'

'A couple?' enquired Jones with disbelief in his voice. He didn't wish to contradict Mr Stillion but he failed to understand how what seemed to him like a hundred pairs of eyes could be described as a 'couple'.

'Yes, a couple,' repeated Stillion, now bending down beside the body. The woman was huge. Her body appeared to be only scantily clad and wrapped in a large ex-army overcoat. Obviously the police didn't suspect foul play. If they had the place would have been lit up by lamps and crawling with pigs rather than rats and that ignorant little shit downstairs. Stillion soon discovered why. As they struggled to put the woman on her back before lifting her into the white sheets inside the now open cricket bag, Stillion noticed her body wouldn't lie flat. He put his hand down to investigate. It came across a growth attached to her back, every bit as large as either of her breasts.

'Bloody hell, this poor cow has died from cancer in agony, penniless, cold, without clothes or food and alone.' He was pleased for her it was over. He was angry that the great British

43

welfare state had let her down so badly. Nobody deserved to die this way.

With great difficulty they got her into the cricket bag and managed somehow to do it up. This would have been some feat in the light – in the dark it was almost impossible. They started the long and painful trek downstairs. Stillion had decided to send Jones down first with the feet end. The man at the head end would have to take nearly all the strain and therefore had to be the stronger. Stillion was a stronger man by far and Jones was grateful for the governor's decision even though it clearly meant that if Stillion's strength failed them Jones would be in the line of fire as the West Indian woman thundered down the stairs like a runaway express train.

'Take your time Keith and be as gentle as possible,' said Stillion as they started down the first flight.

'Wot yow blokes doin' up there?' came up the copper's voice from below.

'Ignore him,' Stillion told Jones quietly.

'I said wot . . .'

'We are coming as fast as possible. Please shine your torch up here again,' shouted Stillion.

As they passed the second floor landing Stillion, despite the pain in his back and the ringing in his hands, became aware of a presence. He was sure he heard movement and maybe even someone quietly crying. He didn't stop. To stop Keith now might mean he didn't get started again. So he just noted it as they continued on their black, cold, eerie and dangerous journey.

At last they were down. Stillion didn't bother to ask for a lift into the shell. He already knew the answer. The large woman only just squeezed in. Jones and Stillion put the lid on and secured the clips.

'Come on then, let's be away from 'ere,' said the young policeman. Jones bent down to lift the shell. Stillion did not.

'Who found the body?' Stillion asked.

'That's nowt to do with yow,' came back the response.

Stillion ignored the provocation and continued. 'Who confirmed this building was empty?'

'That's nowt to do with yow either.'

'Look here I've just about had enough of you. I think there's someone else upstairs. Maybe they're ill. You can suit yourself I'm going back up,' declared Stillion. He grabbed the torch from the officer and headed back up the stairs.

'Yow come back with that torch now! Get this body out of 'ere now. I'm going to lock this 'ouse up now. Come back. I'm warnin' yow.'

There was no response from Stillion. He was now going to do what that little wet should have done but had been too fearful to as darkness fell: make a proper search of the building. He went back to the third floor and started where the body had been found. The torch caught the rats in the act of searching through the blankets and set them off again, scrambling for any bolthole they could find. But there was no one there besides them. Neither was there anything or anybody in any of the other three rooms on that floor. He descended to the second floor, where he had been almost certain that he heard someone. There was nothing in the two rooms on the right of the stairs that he had just come down. Nor was there anything in the front room to the left. Then he tried the room whose door was just before the descending stairs – the one directly below the room where the body had been found. He went in. Nothing. He was surprised. He had expected to find someone. He must have been mistaken. He went to leave, then he noticed a slight recess between the chimney-breast and the outside wall. A little nook for someone to hide in perhaps? Stillion advanced further into the room and shone the torch directly into the recess. There, huddled on the floor and pushed tight into the corner, was a small black boy, his head pushed against his chest, his right arm covering his face.

'It's OK old chap, I won't hurt you, I promise, and I won't let anyone else either,' said Stillion softly. There was no movement or response from the boy.

45

'Come on old man. You can't stay here alone. You'll freeze to death. How would you like a burger and chips? What's your name? Mine's Stillion.'

'With tomato ketchup?' a small voice asked.

'Lashings of it old man,' promised Stillion, who was now on his haunches in front of the boy. 'What do they call you?'

'Me mam called me Luther,' said the boy, who still had his arm thrust in front of his head.

'Where's your mam?' asked Stillion, half expecting the answer he got.

'She were ill, she couldn't work, she couldn't get money. We woz kicked out of our digs last week. We broke in 'ere. Today she were bad, badder than ever. I called an ambulance from the phone box but when they came they just left her on the floor and then the pigs came and I 'id. I don't like pigs.'

'Well Luther, I'm not a pig – policeman, I mean. I won't hurt you and I will feed you and make sure you are properly looked after in a nice warm house with lots of food.' With this Stillion swept the boy into his arms and took him downstairs.

'Where the 'ell 'ave you b—?' demanded the young copper before Stillion interrupted. 'Searched the building did you? This is Luther. Luther this is Keith and PC . . .'

'Harris,' said a shocked PC Harris.

'. . . and PC Harris,' continued Stillion. 'And neither of them are going to do anything but be friends with you.' He stepped down the last steps into the hall. PC Harris was glad it was dark. He did not fancy another of Stillion's stares. Sloane could get him into serious trouble for this so he had better try and make amends.

' 'Ere give moy the boy. I'll 'old him while yow put the coffin in the 'earse,' he offered politely now. Luther clung onto Stillion's neck.

'I'll take Luther, you give Keith a hand,' commanded Stillion politely. PC Harris obeyed and did a little undertaking after all.

*

46

It was seven fifty-five p.m. when Terri arrived at the Villa Cross Café. She was on time and keen to collect Jimmy so that they could keep the appointment she'd made with Elton and his man from the betting trade. She didn't notice the Mark Ten Jag or more importantly its occupants parked just inside the side street by the entrance. Unfortunately for her, they clocked her.

Alf, Frankie and the boys had been sat there, watching the entrance, since six-thirty. Frankie blurted out, 'A result Alfie. A result. That's 'er. The redhead going in now. That's Jimmy's property. Let's go.'

'Sit tight,' growled Alf.

'But she's . . .'

'Wait. The boss wants Jimmy not 'is bit of stuff, OK? Wait 'cos I'll lay money she's gone there to meet 'im. 'E'll be along any second . . . Wot did I say.'

Jimmy arrived in a rush with his coat's hood up against the cold and to prevent identification. Word was out that the Wilkes' army was after him. He would have preferred not to be here. He knew that to keep off the streets just now was the smart thing to do. But he also knew he needed to keep the meeting with Terri if she was going to get him the money she owed and he needed. The disguise was pathetic. The hood was up and, true, his face couldn't be seen, but the coat was his and he was the only guy to own one like it in those parts.

'Wot 'ave yer got mon?' was Jimmy's opening line. She didn't reply. She seemed to have gone even more white than usual and was looking beyond him. Then he noticed that the buzz in the room had suddenly vanished. Only the reggae track on the juke box remained. All else was silent. Instinctively he knew he was now the centre of attention and that he must turn around and face the entrance. He did. There, facing him, standing shoulder to shoulder, toe to toe, feet apart, were Alf and the boys. If any ordinary four white guys had just popped into the Villa Cross Café for a cup of coffee and a quick game of pool they would have been lucky to leave again without having had pool balls inserted up their arses. But these whites were not

47

ordinary whites. They were Wilkes' whites. Ordinary white men got violence. White policemen got silence. White Wilkes' men got respect. In a second the room had been filled with fear.

''Allo Jimmy mate. We got a message for yow from Mr Wilkes. It's a kinda private. Best talk outside eh?' said Alf, whose friendly tone failed to disguise the threat. This was only to be expected; he was after all a long-time pro at this game and nobody in the room misread the real meaning behind his innocent words.

Jimmy looked back to the little bar and the back exit beyond. He would never make it. Then he glanced towards Terri, his terrified eyes pleading for help. She looked away. She hoped not to be noticed and anyway what could she do to help him? She might owe him but he owed them and she didn't – well, not directly, so that was that. It was his fault really because he shouldn't have allowed her the credit in the first place.

'Let's not keep Mr Wilkes waiting Jimmy, there's a good lad,' smiled Alf through clenched teeth. Jimmy moved slowly towards the door.

'Oh and Jimmy, bring yowa white trash with yow,' added Alf almost as an afterthought, and then remarked directly to Terri, 'Yes darlin' that means yow.'

''E's nowt to do with moy,' complained Terri.

'Oh wot touchin' loyalty,' replied Alf softly before barking out, 'Move now!'

She joined Jimmy, now suddenly relying on him for protection. Then, in a flash, the Wilkes soldiers and their two guests were gone. Once outside Jimmy was kneed in the balls and thrown into the back of the Jag and Terri was grabbed by her curling red hair and thrown head first after him. A guard then got in either side of them. Alf resumed his seat in the front. Frankie drove off slowly.

'Where yow takin' us? I done nothin'. Why moy?' blurted out Terri.

'Look darlin', lover there owes Mr Wilkes two big ones. 'E's been tellin' moy blokes it's down to yow and yow is good for the dough. They told moy. I told Mr Wilkes and Mr Wilkes trusted yow. But lover ain't made the payments. Now Mr Wilkes 'as got the idea that yow two 'ave been laughin' at 'im. That's no way to treat a kind man like Mr Wilkes is it? So yow 'ave to pay a little forfeit tonight and then find all the money by the weekend or it's bye bye sambo and it's bye bye whore.'

'But I done no business with Mr Wilkes!' cried Terri, hoping that the old waterworks trick might work.

'Not directly you ain't perhaps, but two people's efforts is better than one and two bye byes is a better lesson for your friends and easier to disguise as a lover's tiff. Good ain't it?' replied Alf, now even impressing himself and really warming to the evening's work.

Terri now knew that talking would do no good. Jimmy had always known this and thus had not breathed a word since leaving the café.

Alf now turned fully back in his seat so that he could see the whites of his captives eyes.

'First it's yow Jimmy. Yowa forfeit is this.' Alf held up a pair of pliers and waived them in Jimmy's direction. 'Yow is goin' to drop yowa pants and Frankie 'ere is going to reshape yowa left or perhaps yowa right ball. Find somethin' to bite onto sambo, 'cos the bad news is big pain, but the good news is that yow get to choose which ball gets tweaked. Course you won't be able to spurt any sambo juice for a bit, but then yow may be dead by Sunday any road.' Alf laughed and was immediately joined in his merriment by the other three.

Alf turned to Terri and the laughing stopped. 'Now for yow, whore.' The others did not know what the punishments would be but they could have guessed Jimmy's. Ball trimming or willy snipping were common punishments à la Wilkes & Co. Either was painful. It was humiliating and it didn't show unless the recipient was willing to walk into a police station and drop his trousers for photographs to be taken and subsequently pro-duced in court. Logic had told Harry that a guy was more likely to show the police a mutilated hand, foot or toe than his seriously damaged manhood. So Jimmy's bad news was entirely predictable. However, nobody could remember a woman being

49

punished before, let alone a pretty girl. Therefore there was silence for her sentence.

'We'll deal with Jimmy first. Then in order that 'e might recover a bit and give us more room we'll put 'im in the boot. Then yow is goin' to strip. Then the boys and moy will do wot we want to yow and yow will do to us whatever we say. That's just a little bonus for the boys from Mr Wilkes.' This last statement was not true. Alf and Harry had not discussed Terri let alone a punishment for her. But Alf guessed that Terri was more likely to crack than Jimmy and probably had a better idea of how to get the money. And if she didn't, they could all have fun. Harry wouldn't mind that and rape could never be proved. It would be the word of a whore against theirs, and theirs would be backed up by all the usual Wilkes network of alibis.

Alf, egged on by the others who were all experiencing a certain swelling of the old Y-fronts at the prospects laid out by him, was enjoying his work. Fantasy sex was taking over. The high and mighty attitude of an eighteen-year-old whore, who clearly did not fancy his fifty-six-year-old hulk, had to be crushed. She had to be brought down. He would enjoy her humiliation. She would beg to be allowed to give him yet another blowjob before he had finished with her.

'Then,' he continued, 'when we've finished with those games, we got another one. Frankie will drive round the streets and I will drop yowa clothes out of the window one at a time. Yowa shoes, stockins, coat, pully, jeans and of course yowa bra and knickers. Then we will drop yow off. If yow find 'em all then you can dress and go 'ome. If yow don't, we'll drop yow off naked at Mo-Mo's. Either way yow, just like lover sambo, have till Saturday to produce the dough. Right?'

Jimmy reluctantly nodded. There was no point in doing anything else. Terri's brain was racing. The last ten minutes had been the most terrifying of her life. That morning she had been frightened by the prospect of this happening. Now the reality was worse. To be delivered naked to a secret club in Aston for drinking and drug taking Moslems was more frightening than death itself. Sure she was a whore. Sure she did tricks. She could even cope with these old bastards. She hated the idea but she could cope. But to be a naked white girl pushed into a room of perhaps of one hundred seriously drunk, drugged and sexually oppressed Asian men would be like dropping a pound of prime fillet into a cage of lions. She was terrified.

'I can get the money. I can get it and more for Mr Wilkes,' she blurted.

'Yeah, course you can bab,' sneered Alf.

'I can and if yow don't let moy Mr Wilkes won't like that,' Terri snapped back.

'Go on then,' replied Alf slowly, seeing the unfortunate logic of her statement.'

'Shit,' thought the others as the prospects of a great evening's entertainment started to diminish.

'We got to meet moy brother in the Nag's Head. I'm due there now. I made arrangements to see 'im to get Mr Wilkes 'is money. Moy brother knows how we can get the money now and more for Mr Wilkes' trouble so.'

'Why yow not said this before?' queried Alf.

''Cos yow never gave moy a chance did yow?'

'Nag's Head Frankie, and yow'd betta be right, whore.' Alf was as disappointed as the others but he daren't run the risk of her being right. What's more if he did deliver the money in total this week then his street cred with Harry would rocket and keep him secure at the top of the Wilkes empire where he had been slipping recently, mainly due to Harry's brothers wanting a bigger say. No, business must come first. He was, after all, a pro.

The Nag's Head was situated, like most pubs in the area, on a street corner. When the rows upon rows of terraced houses were constructed in Aston, Lozells, Hockley and other similar areas at the end of the nineteenth century they provided huge areas of inexpensive homes which were densely populated by the factory workers needed to fuel Britain's industrial revolution. Birmingham had grown enormously at that time. It had become

51

known as the workshop of the world. It made anything and everything. In particular its jewellery and gun quarters became famous.

Then the men worked, if times were good, and hung around in gangs on the street corners if times were bad. The Depression of the 1930s brought an extended bad period and the gangs grew and became infamous. One from Hockley called the 'Peaky Blinders' became a household name across the city. They were so called because the members had this pleasant habit of placing razor blades in the peaks of their flat caps. A flick of the head could produce a result which diminished Liverpool's 'Kirby Kiss' to a mere bump on the head. Therefore it was not the young Afro-Caribbeans or even the Wilkes family that had first introduced violence into the area. No, Aston, Lozells and Hockley had always been violent places since they had first been built.

In those days the women did not go out to work. They stayed at home, had children, cleaned the house, especially the front doorstep, dressed in pinafores and headscarves and spent much time gossiping with the neighbours.

There were no televisions and no one in these areas owned cars, and wouldn't until after the Second World War. Therefore each street became a tight community and life took place in the street. If a boy married a girl from more than four streets away then he was marrying a foreigner. Much of the land, and the houses on them, was owned by the breweries. They very sensibly ensured that public houses were constructed on virtually every street corner and thus made sure that each adjoining street drank only their beer. These pubs were the centre of street life and with no television to keep you at home and no car to take you away, the local was the social nerve-centre. Of course people did visit relatives, take a tram, go to the music hall or cinema occasionally, and in good years they might even go to the seaside. But those things happened only now and again. The visit to the pub was at least a daily occurrence, with a big session on Saturday, and weekly sex later if Villa won and a black eye for the wife if they didn't.

The Nag's Head was in every way a typical Brummie pub of this order. It was owned by the Butby Brewing Company whose brewery was situated in Aston and who owned most of the alehouses in Hockley, Aston, Lozells, Nechells, Handsworth and Winson Green. The entrance was on the building's corner and the building itself was attached to the houses which ran back up the hill to Lozells Road on one side. Inside there was only one public room. The bar itself was tall and ran along most of the left-hand inside wall. There were no bar stools. Behind the bar, sparsely filled shelves hung in front of a large mirror, which ran the length of the bar. The pub did sell spirits, but not often. Most customers either preferred or could only afford Butby's bitter or mild. There was no other beer on tap. Bottled beer could be bought and a selection was kept on the shelves below the mirror. The floor was a dirty dark colour and wooden, and there was a permanently lit fire burning in the grate of the fireplace, which was situated on the far wall. Running down the centre of the room were two neat lines of round tables, each with three stools whose wooden legs were topped with well-worn cheap red leather seats. Either side of the entrance both outside walls contained long, high windows which bore both the name of the pub and the owning brewery in stained glass. Underneath both windows ran bench seats which were covered in the same badly worn leather. Here and there were more round tables in front of the bench seats and some of these also had stools. Beyond the bar and at the fireplace end of the room there was a door. It was stained the same chocolate brown as the bar, the shelves, the picture rail and the skirting boards. The door led through to the landlord's stairs to his flat, a small pantry for washing the glasses, an inside lady's toilet, which had been added in the 1950s and the door to the yard where the outside, primitive and foul smelling gents could be found. The walls of the pub were covered in a faded and often ripped brown paper. The ceiling was painted cream. Both were badly discoloured by nicotine as were the white, plastic ashtrays which were placed on the bar and each table. The pub did not sell food other than

Smith's crisps and then it was more than likely that it had none if they were asked for. It did sell cigarettes but normally only Park Drives or Woodbines.

The couple who ran the place as the brewery's tenants had been there for some time. He was younger and trimmer than her, probably queer and smelled like a woman overdosing on cheap perfume. She was fat and smelled permanently like a pub always smells first thing in the morning. She was the boss. He was always threatening to leave but never seemed to get round to it, which was a shame as he didn't tend well to his beer.

Now, in 1981, thanks to cars, television, better living standards, better pubs and many of the old families gone to be replaced by Muslims who didn't drink, business was much slower but not yet slow enough for the brewery to be awoken from its complacent sleep. Yes, the Nag's Head was in every way a typical working Brummie pub.

It was eight twenty-seven p.m. when Terri, Jimmy, Alf, Frankie *et al.* entered. The pub was less than half full and therefore a glance around by Terri quickly located Elton who was sitting with his bookie, one Nick Smith, on the bench seat half way down the room under the window on the right. She, followed by her pusher and her gaolers, strode across to him, pushing past an old man engrossed behind his *Evening Mail* at the next table as they arrived.

'Yow're late!' said Elton angrily, having only initially noticed Terri and Jimmy. His anger was produced to impress his bookie. He immediately regretted it as he realised they were not alone. 'N'er mind eh?' he instantly added meekly and sprang to his feet. 'Take a seat. I'm Elton and this is Nick Smith.' He thrust his hand out to shake Frankie's. Frankie did not respond.

'We know that,' said Alf coldly.

'This is Mr Wilkes' representative,' added Terri, pointing at Alf. Elton needed to be told, because luckily for him, given his poor record of paying off racing debts, he had never dealt with the Wilkes. Nick Smith didn't need telling. He knew the Wilkes well. They knew him well. Indeed the Wilkes and he could be said to be business partners. The relationship worked like this.

He paid them 33 per cent of his takings and in return they allowed him to keep his three betting shops open. Indeed he had even met these four very gentlemen previously when he didn't like the idea of the then 25 per cent being raised to 33 and he said as much. As a result these friendly guys had arrived at his house at one in the morning, demanded entry into his posh Edgbaston home and having gained it relieved him of his pyjama trousers in front of his hysterical wife before placing the helmet of his penis in the jaws of a large pair of kitchen scissors and enquiring about how much of a circumcision he would like. He had quickly seen it their way and they left without damaging his willy but wrecking his and his wife's nervous system. Since then he would have loved to have sold up and moved on, but who would buy such a business? He wasn't soft. He was good at bullying the likes of Elton but he was no match for the Wilkes and consequently he had never given Harry Wilkes a reason to send his boys round to see him again. This was the first occasion they had met since that night and just the sight of them had his stomach churning. For their part they made no reference to the event as they took seats on the bench either side of Nick and Elton, and on stools borrowed from the old man who was so absorbed by the Villa team news on the back page of his *Mail* that he never bothered to lower the paper while granting his consent.

'Right, this 'ad betta be good young lady,' commented Alf once they were all seated.

'W . . . e . . . ll,' started Elton slowly as he and Terri looked at each other for inspiration.

'Well,' interrupted Terri, 'we own this ring and its worth a lotta money. 'Ere is an official valuation. See,' she exclaimed triumphantly, and placed the valuation on the table for all to see. 'As it says,' she went on, now dropping her voice, 'it's worth eighteen grand.'

Frankie and the boys looked impressed. So did Jimmy who was both amazed and relieved. Nick Smith even relaxed a little at the prospect of collecting Elton's debt, even if 33 per cent of it would go to bloody Wilkes. Only Elton still looked nervous as

Alf spun the paper around and studied it. After some time Alf, who was hardly a better reader than Terri, exclaimed 'OK, this is the deal. You can sell the ring tomorrow and we'll take fifty percent of the proceeds and forget about the punishments. My God, Mr Wilkes will be pleased that his two grand has turned into eleven overnight.'

'Eleven!' blurted out Terri, who understood enough about arithmetic to know that half of eighteen was nine.

'Yes eleven. Nine for half the ring and two that you owe,' purred Alf who was now feeling very pleased with himself.

Terri felt outraged. She only owed two grand. To have to give half the ring was bad enough but to then have to pay the two grand out of the other half was really twisting the knife. But she wasn't in a position to negotiate and anyway once the eleven had gone and Elton had paid off his two they would have five left to split and at least this nightmare would be over. Wasn't her thinking just a little premature?

'Well that's a deal then,' said Alf smugly before adding with menace to Terri, 'Don't yow even think about double crossing us kid. If yow did, everything I've said earlier would be a picnic by comparison to what would 'appen to yow and sambo 'ere. We'll collect you from the Villa Cross Café at ten tomorrow and take yow to these sales rooms in the jewellery quarter.' He finished by pointing to the address on the valuation which he then folded up and put in his pocket with the words, 'Mr Wilkes will want to see this.'

Nick Smith felt that while the Wilkes' percentage remained crippling at least for once they had done something for their money. At last he might collect his long outstanding debt from Elton.

Elton was by now looking very nervous. Finally he moaned 'T-e-r-r-i, ain't yow forgettin' somethin?'

'Oh that. Well,' she turned to Alf. 'I ain't going to make tomorrow 'cos I got to get the ring first, ain't I?'

'Wot yow mean? Got to get the ring? Where is the fuckin' ring?' asked Alf angrily.

'With my grandma,' came back Terri's reply.

56

'And where the fuck might she be?'

'In 'andsworth cemetery.'

Well talk about uproar. Frankie and the other boys looked at each other in disbelief. Nick Smith glared at Elton, his patience finally exhausted and spat out words to that effect. Jimmy Gimme rolled his eyes and threw his head back with a loud moan, his balls already tingling again with expectant pain. Elton stared at the floor and wished to be somewhere else while Terri let out high-pitched squeals as a result of Alf yanking her to her feet by her hair. Mine host, his wife and the other drinkers ignored all this. Everybody knew these men worked for Harry Wilkes and everybody knew it was best not to get involved if you wanted to hang on to those important little bits of your anatomy. Even the old man next to them didn't lower his newspaper.

'Right boys, bring sambo, we're off. Goodnight Mr Smith. I'll leave the brother to yow,' said Alf as he started for the door, his right hand still attached to the screaming Terri's hair.

Just in the nick of time Elton looked up and caught Alf's eye. 'Wait! I'll get yow the ring.'

'Oh yeah, 'ow? Yow can't just walk into the pissin' cemetery with a pissin' shovel and say "Excuse moy I've come to dig up Grandma",' smirked Alf, but at least he had stopped.

'No yow can't, but there are other ways,' answered Elton.

'Yeah? Wot?' asked Alf in a manner which suggested he didn't expect a serious answer.

'If yow take a pew and give moy just two minutes I'll tell you 'ow,' answered Elton in enough of a serious tone to make Alf think. The prospect of delivering the boss eleven grand and thus reigniting his own star within the organisation was a powerful incentive. 'Two minutes,' he grunted as he released Terri and they both sat down again.

'There are two ways of getting moy gran's grave opened. First, wait for granddad to snuff it; 'e's due to be buried with 'er.'

'Well forget that it might take months or even years unless yow want to bump the old bastard off,' interrupted Alf, to whom a little mutilation was an everyday occurrence but murder was something more serious.

'The other way is exhumation,' went on Elton.

'Wot the fuck is exhumi . . . whatever?' demanded Alf.

'Yeah. Wot the 'ell is ex whatever 'e said?' repeated Frankie.

Alf stared at Frankie, who then knew that his verbal contribution was not required.

'Exhumation is a kinda court order that allows yow to dig up bodies.'

'But surely yow would need yowa granddad to apply for it as yowa grandma's nearest relative, and then it might take months even if he agreed to do it,' threw in Nick Smith.

'Sure would,' replied Elton.

'I've 'eard enough of this shit. Take 'em out,' barked Alf. He made to leave.

'We could get an exhumation order before the week is out if we go another route,' continued Elton, ignoring Alf's threatened departure.

''Ow's that then?' Alf retook his stool and Terri and Jimmy started to breathe again. Alf's desire to do the great deal for Harry meant he wanted Elton's idea to work almost as much as Terri and Jimmy needed it to. Consequently he listened intently as Elton explained that the police could apply for an exhumation order themselves if they believed that by so doing it might solve a murder or make a big drug bust.

'Yeah, but why would the police do that? I mean why would they believe yowa gran did drugs or was done in?' asked Nick Smith.

'They wouldn't, 'cos she weren't. But if the pigs was led to believe that inside 'er coffin was placed loads of seriously red 'ot coke and perhaps even the murder weapon for the Rider killin' in seventy-eight, then if the story were convincin' enough they would 'ave to act wouldn't they?'

'Yeah, yeah, yeah, but even if yow could convince 'em to get a bloody whatever order and they bloody go and dig the old boot up, they ain't goin' to take the ring off and return it to madam there are they? And they ain't goin' to be too pleased to find no gun nor drugs neither.'

'True they won't be 'appy to find nowt but the pigs daren't be too pissed off with informers or folk won't bother coming forward in the future. What's more, moy plan won't let 'em point the finger at anyone. Yow'll see. As for the ring itself, that's the easy bit. An exhumation normally takes place at first light, before the punters are about. That means the grave has to be reopened the day before down to a couple of inches of dirt above the box. Jimmy and moy will break into the cemetery overnight, scrape away the dirt, lift the lid, nick the ring, replace the lid and dirt and scarper. Simple.'

'I ain't goin' in any cemetery at night, let along jumping down a bloody grave,' blurted out the usually silent Jimmy.

'Yow'll jump where I say,' growled Alf. 'That is unless yow want to be pushed in to find yowa balls. All right?'

'Right,' nodded Jimmy reluctantly.

Elton leaned forward and lowered his voice still further. 'If Jimmy were to phone the drug squad . . .'

'Oh it's fuckin' me again is it?' Jimmy couldn't help saying, despite Alf's threat.

'I shan't warn yow again,' snapped Alf before turning to Elton. 'Go on then.'

'If Jimmy were to phone the pigs tomorrow and give them an anonymous tipoff that 'e 'appens to be a drug insider . . .'

'I ain't givin' them my fuckin' name!' bleated Jimmy.

'Oh for fuck's sake you silly jungle bunny that's wot anonymous means. I've seen more intelligent dog turds on the pavements of Handsworth than yow,' growled Alf.

''Appens to be a druggie pusher,' continued Elton, 'Who 'as information that thousands and thousands and maybe even more than a hundred thousand quids' worth of coke with fingerprints on all the packets and all, has been buried in one Elizabeth Woodall's grave in Handsworth Cemetery, and what's more, he has reason to believe that the gun that killed George Rider in '78 is also buried there.'

'Why bring all the Rider shit up again?' asked Alf, who knew that Harry had been very nervous about the police handling of the George Rider murder nearly three years ago. There was nothing to link the Wilkes to it and as far as Alf knew the Wilkes had had nothing to do with it. But the police knew that George Rider had been a Vance henchman and with Vance being the other big Brummie crime gang it hadn't taken them long to come knocking on Harry's door.

'It'll add weight to the story, and anyway wot are they goin' to find when they open the grave? Nowt, 'cos it ain't there,' answered Elton assuredly before continuing. 'The pigs will then ask Jimmy 'ow 'e knows all of this and Jimmy will say 'cos 'e woz given the job of deliverin' the coke and the gun to the funeral directors – Sloane & Sons Limited. That 'e 'as already told moy about it 'cos I'm a relative and that they should call moy at moy work as I 'ave even more information 'cos I used to work at Sloanes when moy gran kicked it. Jimmy should finish by sayin' that 'is understandin' is that the drugs was to be placed in her coffin, which was thought to be a safe and recoverable place until the heat were off. And that Mr Sloane agreed to it to avoid either payin' protection or getting 'is funeral 'ome burnt down.'

'Why Sloanes?' asked Alf.

' 'Cos they did moy gran's funeral and I used to work there. The pigs will probably ask Jimmy why 'e's tellin' them all this and Jimmy mate, yow'll reply that yow 'as got yowa reasons. Then don't 'ang around on the phone 'cos the pigs will trace the call. Naturally use a phone box. The pigs will then phone moy or I'll even phone 'em 'cos Jimmy 'as told moy about the drugs and all and I will confirm that Elizabeth Woodall was moy gran and that I woz a Sloane employee but I 'ad nowt to do with the funeral 'cos I was a mourner. When pushed I'll tell 'em that George Brown, the old Sloane night caretaker told moy 'e thought 'e 'ad seen Mr Stillion Sloane put some black packets in the coffin before it were closed. Those waterproof black bags, and a lotta 'em. I'll say Brown 'ad asked moy if it were a special last request of my gran. I'll tell 'em that I told him nah. Probably then they'll ask moy if I mentioned it to Mr Sloane and I'll say nah. I just thought old Brown were mistaken.'

'Yeah but when they ask Brown,' interrupted Alf.

'They can't. He died last summer. Good one uh?'

Now there was silence. Jimmy, Terri and even Frankie and the boys had been told not to talk, and Alf and Nick Smith were thinking hard to see where the flaws might be, while Elton's brain was doing overtime running through the same and trying to remember if he had left anything out. Finally Alf spoke. 'And the pigs could get one of those exey things quick?'

'I'm told in less than forty-eight hours if it were important,' replied Elton with confidence.

'And if none of this works . . .'

Elton finished Alf's sentence for him. 'Yow can always beat the shit out of Jimmy.'

'And yowa sister and perhaps yow,' continued Alf, before Nick Smith chipped in 'Oh most certainly yow,' to Elton.

Nevertheless both Smith and Alf were impressed. Smith enough to dare to think he might get his money back and Alf enough to postpone the beatings for that night.

'I wanna be kept informed at all times and I want it done this week. Yow phone moy Jimmy and yow Elton at all times, startin' with ten o'clock tomorrow mornin'. Jimmy, yow give Elton the number. All right?' With that Alf swept out of the pub and into the cold night air with Frankie and the boys in tow. Frankie turned as he left to point a finger at the rump of the meeting and uttered the Wilkes' words: 'Yow 'ave been warned. All right?'

The remaining four sat in silence not even looking at each other. 'Do yow want another drink?' Elton eventually asked Nick.

'Nah thanks. I'm off 'ome. Just don't screw this up 'cos if yow do I'll be there, with the Wilkes, kicking shit out of you and laughin' as they cut little bits off.' With that he left.

So now there were only three. The three that had debt, danger and damnation in common. They were pleased to be on their own and grateful to be left alone. Elton and Jimmy didn't really know each other, indeed Terri was their only real link, but now they would have to strike up a relationship if only for this week, and they would – fear would see to that.

Things looked a little better now. For sure all three were still in deep shit and perhaps, by attempting to help his little sister, Elton was in deeper than he had been before, as he had now been introduced to the Wilkes mob who wouldn't forgive any failure. But, on the other hand, he couldn't have put off his problems forever and at least Terri had found out about the ring which could now save both their hides and Jimmy's as well, not that he cared much about that. Moreover, all had escaped a fearful beating or worse for the moment, thanks to a plan which if executed properly could indeed work and by so doing not only clear all slates but leave £5,000 between Terri and him.

'Wot's my share of the five grand left over?' asked Jimmy once he had completely recovered his composure for the terror of the previous hour.

'Get lost mate. The money will be split between Terri and moy. The ring belonged to our gran and yow ain't the Wilkes and yow don't frighten moy,' responded Elton.

'Quite right Elton. You and your sister need that because you are going to give me three thousand of it,' said a familiar clipped voice to Elton from behind the *Evening Mail*. Terri and Jimmy looked more surprised than threatened by the intervention of this unidentified old man whose posh tones meant nothing to them. Not so Elton. He knew that clipped voice. He didn't have to peer around the newspaper to know that the speaking face had thin lips, large yellow false teeth, a grey moustache, thinning grey and black hair, sunken brown eyes and hollow cheeks, all of which sat upon a puny if smartly dressed body.

'You must introduce me to your sister and her friend,' continued the old man as he at last appeared from behind his newspaper, which he folded neatly and placed on the table in front of him.

'Who the 'ell is this?' said Terri who clearly couldn't take much more.

'Terri, Jimmy, this is Mr Sydney Gridley, late of Richards & Gridley and now a funeral director with Gilberts. Mr Gridley, yow appear to already know about Terri and Jimmy.'

'Indeed I do. What an enterprising little bunch you are. Three thousand pounds towards my pension and a chance to see that bloody public schoolboy twit Sloane receive the most horrendous dose of damaging publicity. Delicious.'

'We ain't givin' you one penny,' countered Terri who had been genuinely terrified of what the Wilkes gang had planned for her but was certainly not going to be bullied by a solitary, small and frail looking old man.

'Oh but you will. Firstly because I will have an old friend of Elton's, Rolley Brown, break a few fingers if you don't. Elton remembers Rolley. Don't you Elton? He would love to see you again. He has wanted to see you so badly ever since Stillion Sloane kicked him out of his flat at Richards & Gridley within a month of taking over.'

'I had nowt to do with that.'

'Of course not, but Rolley can't quite get that straight in his head.'

'Why the fuck is there so much bloody violence about? Every fucker wants to beat my 'ead in nowadays,' whined Elton.

'It's clearly the company you keep. Secondly and more importantly, I know all about your little plan. One word from me to the police and it won't work and then you can add the police to the bookie, Rolley Brown and the Wilkes on that growing list of people who will be looking for you and you had just better pray that the police find you before the Wilkes do. I would say that your predicament warrants three thousand pounds. Wouldn't you?'

'What if we tell the Wilkes about yow? They'll fix yow,' answered Terri, still determined not to give any more money away.

'I could get to the police before they could get to me and

what is more the Wilkes daren't touch me. Your brother will confirm that I am a councillor, JP and Rotarian. The Wilkes of this world can sit on little guttersnipes like you my dear, but they would never dare attack a man of my standing. That would be far too risky.'

Jimmy said nothing as it was not his three grand in the first place and therefore he had nothing to gain and everything to lose by arguing with this Mr Gridley. More significantly, Elton had also fallen silent.

'Tell 'im Elton,' demanded Terri.

'Tell 'im wot?' responded Elton.

'Tell 'im to fuck off for fuck's sake,' whined Terri.

'Is that your answer Elton?' said Sydney calmly.

'No it ain't,' replied Elton before turning to Terri. 'Look. We ain't got a choice gal.'

'Quite,' said Sydney before continuing. 'Now that's settled, I want you to tell your grandfather about the rumour that there are both drugs and maybe a gun in his wife's coffin.'

'Why?' asked Elton.

'Because he'll be so stirred up by the story that he'll put the police under a lot of pressure to find out what actually happened and that will help them to decide to apply for the order. Jimmy, you should call him after you've told the police and then Elton, you phone him a few minutes later saying that you have been contacted by a person from within a drug gang and told the same story. Oh yes and Jimmy, when telling the police the story in the first place, ensure you lead them to believe that the packets of drugs and the murder weapon could be reclaimed at any time. They will ask you for names but say nothing. Refuse to give names, just say that the fingerprints will be on the black packets. This will all help them to act urgently.'

Jimmy nodded. He wasn't really sure who this Gridley bloke was but he made sense and appeared to know what he was talking about. 'Right boss,' he replied.

Elton looked across at Jimmy with disdain but said nothing.

64

Terri felt she should be saying something more but now that Elton and Jimmy had given up she realised it would be pointless.

'Good evening,' said Sydney as he got up before adding, 'and don't even think of . . .'

'. . . double crossing yow,' finished Elton wearily.

Stillion had kept his promise to little Luther. Once he and Keith Jones had delivered Luther's mother to the public mortuary in Newton Street where she had had to be laid on the stone floor, there being no more trolleys available, he had rejoined Luther at Handsworth police station where the latter had been dropped off by PC Harris. Initially Luther had demanded to go with Stillion in the hearse, but Newton Street was no place for a child, especially when the purpose of the visit was to deposit his dead mother. So Stillion had persuaded the boy to go with the young policeman who was by now very co-operative, on the understanding that Stillion would go straight to the station himself and wait with Luther for the social worker to arrive and personally ensure that he was to be well looked after, just as he had promised upstairs in that cold, dark room.

When Stillion arrived at the police station it was with a burger and chips and lots of tomato ketchup. Luther, despite having just finished egg and chips from the police canteen, polished the lot off in seconds. Now that the boy was in the light Stillion could see just how undernourished and ill-kept he really was.

They talked. It was clear that this child had had a very rough time. Life had never been good and had got worse. He knew his mother was dead. He had been expecting it. She had been in great pain and had had no help, no medicine or pain killers, just the honest but nonetheless pathetic efforts of this little lad who had provided her final nursing in that bare, cold rat-infested house. And yet despite this and his obvious grief at the loss of his mother and perhaps only friend, Luther could not suppress his overwhelming hunger, for it had been a long time

65

since he had eaten anything and a very long time since he had eaten well.

Eventually an arrogant but well-meaning young woman arrived from social services. It became immediately apparent that her self-confessed goodness had to be balanced against the fact that she was obviously very inexperienced but believed she knew it all, having just come down from university. To deal with the issues which would now confront her in her working life she believed she only needed two things: a university degree, which she had, and to be a true red flag socialist, which she was. Consequently the job at hand was made much harder for all concerned as her remarks to the police revealed her belief that they must hate the boy or at least not care about him at best, as all police were racist fascists who didn't care about anybody's children other than their own or those who belonged to the well-off, and certainly not one whose skin was black.

Stillion fared no better. What was a funeral director doing there in the first place? What did funeral directors know about children? Indeed what did men know about children? Worse, as a man who owned his own funeral directing business he was obviously a capitalist who made his money from other people's grief. Funerals in her opinion should be provided free by a local government department that in turn should be funded from the rates. A man such as Stillion could not possibly care about the boy even if the boy insisted he did and appeared to like him.

Worst of all was her attitude to Luther. After all, Stillion and the police only had to put up with this self-righteous saint for a matter of minutes before, hopefully, she would disappear from their lives without trace. On the other hand, Luther was going to be stuck with her for a little while at least. She talked to him in a very kind and pleasant way, however it was a way that assumed that he was a backward four-year-old rather than the bright six-year-old he actually was.

For Luther's sake everybody bit their tongues and after some sad goodbyes and a five-pound note being slipped Luther's way without the woman's knowledge and a promise to keep in touch, Luther was whisked away to become another statistic in the nanny state that left-wing local government wished to preserve and right-wing Mrs Thatcher wanted to demolish.

Stillion stood in the snow-covered road waving until the car carrying Luther away disappeared out of sight. He then trudged back to where he had parked his Jag. To his pleasure it had not been broken into. Well of course not. It was after all outside a police station, but in 1981 Handsworth such a parking space gave no guarantee of safety.

From there he drove back to Sloane House to check all removals had been completed and all hearses and limousines were ready for the morrow. He bid Jones good night, left for home and arrived at nine-thirty, just about the time when the Wilkes & Co. meeting had been breaking up at the Nag's Head.

As Stephanie welcomed him into the warm, friendly and expensive kitchen he knew how lucky he was. Lucky to have her. Lucky to have been born the son of his father. Lucky to have been, as a result, well educated. Lucky to have inherited such a business. And lucky to be shown daily down in Lozells and Handsworth just what other people didn't have. It was only by seeing this that he could appreciate how lucky he really was and thus never lose sight of it and keep his feet upon the ground, his head right and his heart good.

He piled into a piping-hot mushroom risotto. Stephanie pushed hers around her plate. She was due any day now and her appetite was waning. They shared a bottle of claret. She sipped half a glass while he finished the bottle off as he told her of the horrors of the day. She sat there, so pretty, so demure and so vivacious that he hardly noticed her pregnant state. He kicked off his riding boots, which he wore beneath his pinstripe trousers in order that his feet might stay both warm and dry while still appearing smart, and slid across the bench seat before propping his back up against the warm wall by the Aga. They often spent hours talking like this and tonight was no exception. He did not tell her about the four children who had been burned to death. It had been on the news all day. Maybe she knew about it. If she mentioned it they would discuss it. If she didn't, they wouldn't. Stillion did not believe it sensible to bring the subject up. He had felt the pain when John had told him about it. He had seen it upset the normally unemotional John. If it could have such an effect on them then he was certainly not going to discuss it with a woman who was pregnant and at full term.

They retired to bed. She bathed in oil. He showered the grime of Lozells away. She rubbed prenatal cream onto her tummy while he lay on the bed in his boxers ready for the late movie to begin. He glanced through the door into the *en suite* bathroom. She had her back to him. She was naked. She was so very beautiful. Her ash blond hair tumbled down her back and she was carrying her bump so much to the front of her that he found it hard to believe that she was pregnant at all.

In time she emerged from the bathroom in a long, white cotton nightshirt that had originally been bought by her mother for Stillion, though he had never worn it. It now made a perfect sleeping garment for the full-term lady of the house. She had to take care as she made her way to the bed. The shirt was far too long for her and as a result at least four inches were trailing along the ground, ready to trip her up the moment she forgot about them. She got on to the bed beside Stillion and took his hand before placing it on her lower belly. There he could feel the bumping and banging of a very active baby. He sung McCartney's 'She's My Baby' to it as he did every night, only changing the words to 'He's My Baby' as he was convinced that their first born would be a boy. Indeed he wanted a son and heir as did Stephanie, but she erred on the side of a boy mainly for his father's sake. And in the final analysis neither cared that much as long as the baby was delivered fit and well.

They had enjoyed a good sex life throughout their marriage. She had quickly understood Stillion was quite different from other men she had either read about, seen in films, or had described to her by her friends. She had quickly learned how to please him while at the same time ensuring her own pleasure. She had a good libido and was the one who usually made the first approach. Stillion would normally respond although he could, when a dark mood took him, turn his back with the words 'Good night darling'. Stephanie did not understand or like these moods. Happily they were infrequent and therefore she had not felt the need to mention them either to Stillion or 'the mothers'.

However, in the last few days as her pregnancy was drawing to a close, she had not felt the need for sex and therefore her mood this night took them both by surprise. She opened his legs and knelt between them. She ran her fingers lightly over his nipples and down his ribcage. His breathing quickened, his chest went out, his stomach in, his buttocks tightened and as his hard piece bulged in his boxers she knew he was ready to respond to the craving which had come so suddenly upon her. She massaged his stomach with her fingers before dropping her thumbs inside his shorts by each hip-bone and then gently easing the boxers over his raging engine. He lifted his buttocks from the bed and the shorts were quickly dispensed with. He was now on his back, naked before her. She continued to kneel between his legs assuming the position of control with one hand teasing his stem, the other gently tickling his balls and probing his rather feminine hairless crack. At this moment she always felt that she had the upper hand, that she was, for once, the boss and had the elusive mind of Stillion under control. This excited her. It excited him.

She leant forward to lick the straining purple helmet but instead met his mouth as he sat up and kissed her delicious face. 'Let me just make love to you tonight. Sex tomorrow or whenever but just passionate love tonight. I have a desire for you right now that hurts. You're taking my breath away. I could eat you,' he said breathlessly, as he continued to kiss her eyes, forehead, cheeks and nose. He pulled her up and over his hips. He gently entered the tent of a nightshirt feeling for the moist canal which would be the route to the physical explosion which sometimes expresses lust but tonight would express a great and mutual love. When it was over they slept contentedly in each other's arms.

69

2

Sydney Gridley rose at six, a man with more purpose than had been the case these past thirteen months since his wife and son had conspired to sell his business from beneath him to that bloody public schoolboy twit. Losing his wife, son, mistress, business and home in one day and in such a public and humiliating fashion had been painful. He may have treated his wife like a servant and his son like an idiot but that did not mean that he didn't miss them. He certainly missed being waited on hand and foot. He certainly missed having them around to blame and bully. And in his own way, he actually missed their company. He was now a lonely little man in a rented flat. An employee and not an employer. A man who would have to work on past sixty-five in order to preserve his savings. All a far cry from the Rolls-Royce, the Rotary lunches and the days spent either on the bench or in the council chamber. To date he had retired from neither but it was only a matter of time, as it was employers and not employees who could commit the time to the higher circles of public life and thus the network of private gain. In any case, up there his former high-octane colleagues would either be laughing at, or feeling sorry for, him. He hated the idea of either. Birmingham might be Britain's second city in size, but in high society terms it had always been a village and therefore Sydney knew there was nowhere to hide.

The pain of all of this had aged him. The grey hair that used to mingle with the black upon his head and moustache had now largely defeated the black and wiped it out. And, although he still dressed smartly, the clothes now covered a slightly stooping

70

frame. Otherwise he hid his pain. However, on the inside his motivation and confidence had been ripped apart and it was perhaps only the prospect of getting even with Elton and more importantly with Stillion that held him together. Now that faint hope had become, since yesterday, a very real possibility. He therefore intended to grab such a chance with both hands and rock the House of Sloane to its very foundations.

There was a certain spring in his step for the first time in over a year as he arrived at work. He studied the garage orders for the day. Oh good, he had been put down to conduct the Gilbert second fleet and noticed that Elton Field was down to drive the hearse on the first funeral. Elton was an embalmer and rarely went out on funerals. However, this was January and they were very busy and everyone had to lend a hand.

Sydney and Elton, although they worked in the same firm and at the same location, did not see much of each other. Sydney was usually arranging or conducting funerals while Elton could normally be found in the mortuary. Given that Sydney did not harbour any good thoughts to Elton, the prospect of sharing a hearse with him would have, in the normal course of events, not pleased the aged funeral director. Today, however, was different. Sydney was pleased by the prospect. He could keep an eye on Elton and ensure he followed the exhumation plan to the letter.

But first he had some calls of his own to make. He phoned Charlie Williams at his office. He phoned Fred Gilbert at his home and he phoned the editor of the Birmingham *Evening Mail* at the paper.

Obviously Charlie and Fred knew who he was. He made the call to the editor anonymously. The content of all three calls was the same. He had been told by a very reliable source that Sloanes had agreed, instead of paying Handsworth protection to whoever, to bury drugs and perhaps even a murder weapon inside an old lady's coffin. That an insider of the drug circle, with a grudge, had squealed to the police, who would have to order an exhumation, and when they got one, and up the old lady came, the shit would really hit the fan.

Sydney would have loved to have been able to soak up a few quid from the *Evening Mail* – after all this sort of scoop was worth good money to a news-hungry editor, but he realised that that would mean having to identify himself to the paper, thereby giving them the chance to run, 'Broken old JP and Councillor Demands Cash for Scandal Details' or worse in a few days, '. . . for lies', as Sydney knew that the eventual exhumation would find no drugs or gun. Nevertheless a lot of mud would stick to Stillion, unless at that time a story was printed suggesting that it had all been made up by a vindictive old man who had lost his business to Sloane just over a year ago. So Sydney resisted the temptation and remained anonymous.

Charlie Williams, a timid man by nature, was panicked by the tale. He couldn't possibly be associated with such a scandal or the people in it. He knew nothing of drugs, guns, murder or protection and the only contact he ever had with the police was when they called his firm out on coroner's removals. He had never even got himself a parking ticket and could not remember going into a police station these sixty years, man or boy, even to report a missing dog. Sydney could almost feel Charlie move Frank C. Williams Limited away from Stillion's grasp as they spoke. A fine feeling.

Fred Gilbert, a pompous man who pretended to be pious and hard-working when in reality he was neither, was not pleased to be disturbed at home. He liked the staff to think he was often out on an appointment first thing in the morning. He would let it be known that he had to go 'to so and so first thing' before leaving the office at night. He could then have a lie in while his staff got the early funerals out of the way. When the weather was cold he seemed to have more of these early morning appointments. Sydney knew all about Fred. He knew he would catch him at home. Naturally Fred did not like being caught there but quickly forgot his displeasure once Sydney started to tell his tale. This could help Frederick Gilbert & Sons acquire Frank C. Williams. Fred became quite excited and enthused at the prospect of that and the downfall of Sloanes. He would not forget Sydney if this all came off. After all, Frank

C. Williams would need managing. Who could be better suited than Sydney? A Sydney with a healthy pay rise and more status. A warm feeling.

Johnny Titmarsh, a brash young editor, who saw the *Evening Mail* as a mere stepping-stone from his native Yorkshire to a London national, was an ambitious man, keen to be noticed. That meant controversial scoops that could find a wider audience than that provided by those who bought the *Mail* for its Villa write up or what was on TV that night. He had no love of Birmingham or its people and therefore its problems were there to be exploited for his gain with no thought for responsibility. Moreover, he was never going to let the truth stand in the way of a good story and believed the odd lie could even make a good story great as long as the lie remained undetected. He loved Sydney's story and feverishly took down all the details, asking lots of questions as he did so. These were parried by Sydney with the continual repeating of 'You'll have to ask the police about that when they eventually have as much information as you've got now'. Titmarsh loved the idea that he was ahead of the police. My God, he had got the bit between his teeth. He was going to expose the story in a very big way. Hold the front page. A great feeling.

Stillion arrived at Sloane House in time to fit a couple of telephone calls in before spending the day out on another five 'A' fleet funerals. He wanted to ensure Charles Williams was a happy man and that the bloody solicitors were getting on with it. He phoned Williams on his direct line first. He got him. Charlie was nervous, evasive and very non-committal. Quite a different man to the one Stillion had spoken to yesterday. Stillion asked if everything was all right and didn't really succeed in getting a satisfactory answer. More worryingly, Williams couldn't wait to get off the phone and before Stillion could do anything about it he had stuttered his excuses and was gone, leaving Stillion holding the receiver next to his ear and worrying about whatever it was that had clearly upset the delicate Charles.

He replaced the receiver and walked slowly round his desk so that he could warm his behind in front of his office fire while he thought. The phone rang to disturb his concentration. It was Victoria Thomas, his secretary. She announced, hardly disguising her dislike of the woman in question, that Joyce Higgins was on the phone. Stillion was surprised. He had been miles away, worrying about his conversation with Charlie and hadn't really been concentrating when he picked up the receiver and answered Victoria. Now the words 'Joyce Higgins' made him take notice. What on earth did she want?

He had bought her business by honouring the deal Sydney had agreed with her once he had obtained a controlling stake in Sydney's business. She had intended to move to southern Spain once the sale had gone through and rumour had it that she had now found the right location. Stillion had allowed her to stay on in her flat above Higgins & Co. for a nominal rent while she had searched. He had forgiven her for her trickery and his stripped humiliation. After all, he had acquired her business in the end, even if not by the route he had expected. Since then they had spoken rarely and on the occasions they had, had not mentioned his ordeal at her hands. Moreover he was grateful that she appeared to have kept their dark secret to herself. Gillian Weston might know about it as the two women were close friends. Victoria Thomas had guessed that something improper had taken place but wouldn't realise what in her wildest dreams. She didn't like Joyce, for sure, and for all the right reasons, but she would have no knowledge that sexual sadism could beat so feverently in the breast of a woman.

For Stillion's part, he avoided both Joyce Higgins and Gillian Weston like the plague. Not only was he deeply ashamed of his two brief encounters with these women, but was most fearful that one or both of their stories would get out and find their way to Stephanie's doorstep. Such news would certainly most seriously damage his marriage and would probably wreck it beyond repair. No more than he deserved? For sure, because although he had struggled hard ever since with his sexual problems, due to his great love of Stephanie, he had after all committed the crimes in the first place. Yes, probably no more than he deserved, but a lot more than she deserved at any time and especially now that she was about to give birth.

These two swords of Damocles had hung over his head for the past thirteen months.

'What a bloody morning. First an odd call with Charles Williams and now her,' he thought as he braced himself and told Victoria to put her through. 'Hello Joyce. How are you?' he said in a friendly way, designed to hide his fear.

'I'm fine. I'm almost ready to bugger off to Spain. I've got myself a pleasant little apartment in Estepona which overlooks the marina there. Marbella and Banus are close by and I move in next week. Look, the reason I'm ringing is that I'm having a few people in for drinks at six forty-five tonight. I'd like you to come.'

'Is that such a good idea?' enquired Stillion.

'Yes it is. There's nothing to be frightened of you know,' she taunted.

'No. No. It's not that. It's just that Stephanie is due any day now and—'

''You must be there for her. I understand. However, you'll be gone by seven-fifteen, and I'd so like you to meet a friend or two of mine before I leave. Remember, our secret is safe with me,' she finished pointedly, which meant it wasn't if he didn't go.

'OK, I'll be there.' The words left his mouth while his mind wrestled with the dangers of going versus the potential damage of not.

The conversation finished and he couldn't dwell on it for long as he had to grab his tailcoat, top hat and gloves and make for the forecourt. As he raced through the reception he came across his own doctor.

'Hi Stillion. How are you? Well I trust? I'm here to collect some ash cash doing a second part for Doctor Jones.'

As he spoke Victoria arrived with the BC & F papers for Doctor Jones' now deceased patient, and the doctor's fee – in cash of course.

'Would you like to see the deceased now?' she asked the doctor.

'No, that won't be necessary. If old Jones says it was pneumonia then it was I'll be bound,' he replied.

Stillion waved a 'Goodbye' and continued on outside. He couldn't condone such behaviour. Part B was completed by the deceased's doctor. Part C was completed by a doctor from another practice, who was supposed to given an independent view to ensure that the first doctor was not getting away with incompetent medical care, or worse mass murder.

In reality doctors from different practices formed cosy little twosomes and always signed each other's papers, very often, as in this case, without even examining the deceased. A quick flick through the first doctor's comments, a couple of strokes of the pen, an occasional written word, the signature, grab the cash, which was probably never recorded on a tax return, and scarper. A fairly accurate picture of the average general practitioner attending a funeral home in his capacity as second doctor.

Stillion knew this was wrong. So did other funeral directors. But who could afford to blow the whistle on a group of people who could help or hurt you so much by whether or not they recommended you or your competitors when asked?

Stillion went to the rear of the hearse and compared the details on his funeral envelope with the ticket which he took from the handle, while Arthur Kemp read the same details from the garage orders. They all checked out. They had the right coffin, in the right hearse, going on the right funeral and with the right number of limos. Good. Just as well really. Elementary? Perhaps, but you could never be too careful especially as it was possible to conduct as many as a dozen Mr Singhs or Mrs Kaurs in a week, never mind all the Browns, Smiths and Joneses.

Stillion was about to close the tailgate when Arthur noticed the old barber from Handsworth Village.

'Oh, look Mr Stillion, your friend,' Arthur pointed out with a mischievous twinkle in his eye.

'I see him,' replied Stillion in a flat voice. He waved to the barber.

A couple of years before, Stillion had returned from holiday in need of a haircut and having taken leave of his first family at the crem so that the trusted Walter Warburton could take them home, had asked Arthur to drop him off at any hairdressers they could find for a quick trim before the second funeral.

The only one that could be found open on that Monday morning was a little old-fashioned barbers in the line of shops known as Handsworth Village. Stillion had entered with some apprehension. The shop was dark and old and resembled those seen in films of the 1940s. There was a line of old wooden chairs under the window for the comfort of waiting clients. The opposite wall had some dark old shelves erected on it, on which were some faded white jars of Brylcream along with an advert for the stuff featuring a young Denis Compton. To the right was an old-fashioned 'sit up' dentist's chair, complete with a small headrest, facing an aged mirror. There was no washbasin. The room was void of people.

Stillion could just about remember places like this from the recesses of his mind, which flickered over his childhood's earliest memories of the 1950s. Instinctively he knew this was a mistake. He was about to leave when a tall, thin, balding old man, who was dressed like an old-fashioned dentist, walked through from the back room and welcomed him. 'Mr Sloane what an 'onour.' And before Stillion knew what was happening he had been shown to the dentist's chair and was being asked how he liked it.

'Only a little off please,' Stillion responded cautiously.

'Right yow are sir,' said the dentist or barber (or perhaps butcher), and proceeded to walk round the back and sides of Stillion's head with a comb in one hand and scissors, which he continually clicked, in the other. To Stillion's relief he didn't appear to be cutting much off, and perhaps this was just as well as he seemed to be concentrating more on his conversation than on Stillion's haircut.

'Are yow a Christian Mr Sloane?'

'I am.'

'Church of England?'

'Yes.'

'I used to be yow know. In the war I got some shrapnel lodged in moy back. Very painful yow know.' He started the electric clippers, to Stillion's horror.

'Er I don't think . . .' Stillion attempted to interrupt.

'Never got any betta,' went on the inspired barber. 'Until a friend took me to Hockley Pentecostal Church. They laid hands on moy back and I never 'ad the pain again. Praise the Lord,' he shouted exuberantly as his right hand, with the electric clippers attached, shot up the back of Stillion's neck sending a shower of fair hair all over the room.

What a nightmare. The clippers had left a line up the back of Stillion's head as if they had been a lawnmower going across an unmown lawn. As a result everywhere else had to be cut the same. So, within minutes, the blond Beatle had been transformed into a First World War soldier complete with pudding-basin haircut.

When finished, the barber proudly showed Stillion the back of his head by holding up a second mirror while saying, 'Very smart, sir,' and then adding in a lowered voice, even though they were the only two in the shop, 'Anything for the weekend sir?'

Stillion surveyed the disaster before quietly replying, 'No. I don't think so. I don't suppose I'll be needing anything for the weekend or for a few weekends.' His reference to how unattractive he felt went completely over the barber's head, which was evident by his response.

'Oh dear, yow're 'aving problems down there are yow Mr Sloane? Why not let them lay hands on it at Hockley Pentecostal . . .'

'No. No, I'm not having problems *down there*, thank you very much,' interjected Stillion curtly, wishing he had used as much force to interrupt the barber ten minutes ago. 'Anyway, how do you know my name?'

'I saw you pull up in the 'earse with Sloane & Sons on the plate in the window and I've seen yow walk the funerals off down the road.'

'I see,' replied Stillion as he paid the bill and left a tip, telling himself that the fault lay with him and not the butcher barber who may be a religious crank but seemed a friendly and sincere man.

Stillion put his top hat on and returned to the waiting hearse.

'Wot the . . .' exclaimed Arthur who could not see what little hair Stillion had left as it was concealed by his top hat.

'Don't say a bloody word if you know what's good for you Arthur. Let's get back and pick up the second funeral.'

Stillion's new look wasn't a complete disaster. Indeed the eighty-five-year-old widow on the very next funeral looked at him with a little gleam in her eye and when he went to say goodbye to her she took his hand with the words, 'Can I give yow a little kiss?'

'If you would like to, I would be honoured,' he replied genuinely.

'Yow see, I 'aven't seen a boy with an 'aircut like that since I were a girl.'

'Oh bloody great,' Stillion had moaned to himself, and now two years on Arthur was enjoying the sight of the barber as a fond memory of an embarrassing time for the boss.

The barber waved and shouted, 'I'm going to Hockley Pentecostal on Sunday. Yow should come. They would lay hands on it if yow were still 'aving trouble with yowa . . .'

'No, I'm fine,' shouted Stillion, keen to prevent Arthur from having any more mess-room material.

The first Gilbert funeral of the day, that was to pitch Sydney and Elton together, was leaving from one of the isolated little slum areas still left standing in Aston. Elton, in the hearse, had to be there fifteen minutes before Sydney who would be arriving with the limousines, as the family wanted the deceased home for a quarter of an hour. This meant that the coffin would be placed on trestles in the front room with the lid off in order that friends and family alike could pay their last respects.

79

The house was in a terrace. Its front door led straight onto the pavement via three steep steps. It was old, built in 1831, damp, dirty, lousy and rotten. Even Elton noticed how dirty it was and neither he nor his assistant could fail to realise how rotten it was as the assistant's leg disappeared through some bare floorboards in the hall, which nearly sent him crashing into the cellar and the coffin being dropped in the process.

In the event disaster was averted and once the coffin was lying in state, perilously close to the raging coal fire in the hardly furnished front room, Elton enquired if the family might have something to cover up the hole which had appeared in the hall. They did – it was a piece of carpet. Elton, without much thought, placed the carpet over the hole. Certainly there was an immediate visual improvement, but could this be a case of out of sight out of mind? Elton and his assistant then returned to the hearse and waited for the esteemed conductor, one Sydney Gridley, to arrive with the limos. They were too busy talking to notice the cars pull up behind them and Sydney get out.

Sydney proceeded to the house. The front door was ajar despite the cold. Sydney knocked on it and proceeded in. 'Good morning my name is . . .' said Sydney, right arm outstretched to shake whoever's hand as he advanced. 'Sydney Gridley of—ah ah ah!' Crash! Sydney disappeared from sight. He reappeared about thirty seconds later via the door at the rear of the hall that led to the cellar. His black bowler hat and overcoat were covered in a combination of dust, dirt, whitewash and cobwebs. At that moment Elton, having by now noticed the limousines and their drivers, had arrived at the front door.

'Who put that ruddy carpet over the hole in the floor?' demanded a furious Sydney with little politeness or goodwill to the open-mouthed bereaved family.

'He did,' they replied in unison, and pointed at Elton.

Sydney would have liked to have wrung Elton's neck but even he realised that this was neither the time nor the place and therefore such matters would have to be dealt with later. Despite Elton's continual and consistent assertions that the episode had been an accident Sydney would eventually go to his grave believing that Elton had contrived it to happen on purpose, as he could not believe anyone could be that stupid. Not even Elton.

Jimmy had stayed the night at Terri's place. Something that had rarely happened before. Oh, they had had sex there many times, but after sex he had either wanted to move on or she had to get back on the job either in her room, which meant he must go, or occasionally elsewhere, which naturally meant she would have to leave herself. But last night their shared horrors and how close they had come to serious physical damage had taken their toll on both their nervous systems. Therefore it had been physical presence rather than sex that had motivated them to fall asleep in each other's arms. Two babes in the wood with Harry Wilkes' wolves just waiting to pounce.

In the morning Jimmy awoke and lay in the rather tatty, unwashed and never ironed sheets that made up Terri's bed. He ran through the supposed conversation he would have with the police and tried to cover every angle and remember all the tips and instructions he had been given by Elton, Alf and that Gridley bloke.

Eventually Terri awoke. She snuggled up to him with the words, 'Jimmy, yow want a hand job or maybe a blow job or give moy a massage or even straight sex?'

'Yer offering?'

'I could be. I was thinking if yow were to knock off ten quid for every time we did whatever yow fancied it would 'elp moy, yow know.'

'Why yer cheeky bitch! I'm in charge of yer. Yer is supposed to be earning for me! I'm supposed to be living off yer immortal earnings.'

'Immoral,' she corrected.

'Yes it is. Bloody immoral. Now get the 'ell out of my way. I've got to get ready to have my little chat with the police.'

He got dressed and looked for a cup in which he could

make himself a coffee. They were all half full of old milky tea that had mildew floating on it. Yes, Terri might be much better looking than her mother on the outside, but on the inside it was very much a case of like mother like daughter. He decided the chore of cleaning one of these cups was greater than his desire for coffee so he gave up on the idea and left to find a phone box on the Lozells Road.

The morning was dull, grey and bitterly cold. Occasionally it tried to snow and a flurry of white flakes would blow around in the wind before joining the dirty slush and ice underfoot. Jimmy made his way to the Lozells Road. He was still not used to being up at nine o'clock, despite having been unusually on the street at that time two mornings running. He felt both cold and tired as his old and dirty sneakers attempted to find the driest route and therefore minimise the amount of water getting into them.

Over his dreadlocks sat his 'tea cosy' hat. He had a cigarette between his teeth and his hands were rammed deep into his coat pockets. He passed the chapel of his youth. What a difference a few years makes. Who would have guessed that the small little boy with an open face and flashing smile, so clean and proper in his white shirt and short grey trousers, would lose his way and mind behind five-day stubble and a curtain of unwashed hair. He reached the phone box. He did not call the local police. He called the drugs division direct and asked for Inspector Hooper by name.

'Hello inspector. It's Mr Anonymous 'ere.'

The next hours saw the heroes and villains of this tale heat up the phone lines of Birmingham. Fred Gilbert phoned Charlie Williams to confirm that he had heard the news about Stillion Sloane and went on to push up his offer to £800,000 for Williams' business. Williams promised to get back to him before the weekend. Williams then phoned his solicitor and asked for advice. There may be a problem at Sloane's end. He wasn't prepared to say but the solicitor would hear soon enough if the story he had been told by two different sources was true. If it was he might not want to sell to Sloanes, and what's more Sloanes might not be in any position to buy. On the other hand, Sloane's offer of £1,000,000 was still better than the improved offer from Fred Gilbert of £800,000, which was in itself better than the £750,000 currently on the table from the Co-op.

What should he do? He wanted the best price and had been of a mind to sell to Stillion Sloane but he did not want to run with a party who might get embroiled in a scandal and fail to complete the deal. After some thought the solicitor advised that both Williams and he should avoid Sloane and his solicitors, keep the other two bids alive and see what happened over the next couple of days.

While this was happening, Jimmy, having finished with the police, phoned Granddad Woodall, Elton and then Alf as promised.

While the Aston slum family's service was in progress, Elton phoned the police, saying that he had received an anonymous call and then repeated the same to Granddad Woodall before phoning Alf as arranged.

Sydney then, anonymously, phoned the *Evening Mail* editor, Johnny Titmarsh, to confirm that the police drugs division was now in possession of the facts. The editor phoned the inspector who had just put the phone down from a call from Granddad Woodall who had phoned to report the story he'd been told by both Jimmy and Elton.

The inspector then phoned his paymaster to report that half the city had suddenly got it into their heads that scores of packets of coke and the Rider murder weapon were buried in Handsworth Cemetery inside the coffin of one Elizabeth Woodall.

'Look I can't 'ang around long on the blower, but I thought yow ought to know. Forewarned is forearmed and all,' whispered the inspector.

'Listen 'Oopy, I don't know wot yow is on about. We never 'ad nothing to do with Rider or any coke and who the fuck is

83

Elizabeth Woodall?' roared Harry at his end. 'Just keep yowa little piggy mates' snouts out of moy business all right?' The bad man of Brum and his payroll cop finished their conversation.

'Alf!' screamed Harry through his open office door. Alf came rushing in, just as everybody did when Harry screamed.

'Yes boss?' he smiled breathlessly, half from the run up the stairs and half from the fear that a Harry scream conjured up.

''Oopy just phoned to warn us that this Rider murder thing is blowing up again. Apparently a pusher in 'Andsworth tipped off the pigs that there were a gun and 'alf a ton of coke buried with some old bat in the cemetery. I mean, we control all the fucking pushers. So who is this "see you next Tuesday" and wot's 'is fucking game then?'

Alf's mouth would not obey. His jaw locked. His tongue stuck to the roof of his mouth. He had been struck down by blind panic. What should he do? Should he pretend to know nothing and offer to look into it? If he did, he wouldn't look very good at controlling his area and if Harry was to find out that Alf had helped put the little wheeze together and given permission for it to take place, having denied any knowledge of it now, then he could expect the sort of trouble that was normally reserved for the likes of Jimmy. On the other hand, it would take courage to explain the plan to Harry while he was in this mood and in any case, suddenly the plan didn't seem quite so good. Nothing ever did if Harry didn't like it.

He had wanted to execute the plan, get the money and present it as a *fait accompli* to Harry by the weekend deadline. He had hoped to then get great glory for his success and had also hoped that Harry would never hear about the ring at all if it wasn't there or if they didn't get it. In that event he and the lads would just have to give Jimmy, Terri and Elton the best thrashing ever on Monday.

He hadn't reckoned on the police tipping off Harry. This was make your mind up time and Alf chose to come clean. He told Harry the story. '. . . and so they won't find any drugs or a gun but you'll get nine grand plus yowa two grand and there's

84

nothing to point anything at us,' he finished, and nervously waited for Harry's reaction.

''Ow do I know yow weren't going to keep the dough for yow self? If yow weren't going to tell me about it? I mean wot was to stop yow giving me moy two gees and yow keeping nine?'

'The boys all know and any road I never done anything but be loyal to you Harry.'

'That's true Alf.' Harry drew breath and then exhaled before saying eventually, 'Yow did OK. It's OK. I like it. Two gees paid off, nine extra gees for me, that fucking public schoolboy twit gets a load of bad publicity and in the end the pigs look like shit. Right. I like it. No. I *love* it.'

Alf smiled the smile of relief and gratitude he normally reserved for a magistrate or judge who had just fined him or given him a suspended sentence rather than the few months inside he deserved.

And Mr Sloane? Hadn't he wished to avail himself of the General Post Office telephone services also? Of course. His first funeral had been in Father O'Rourke's St Mary's Roman Catholic church. Unusually, the deceased hadn't lain in church overnight, but no sooner had the coffin come to rest on the trestles in front of the altar that morning, than Stillion had beat a dignified retreat out of the church and while the chauffeur bearers warmed themselves in the hearse and limousines he walked towards Hockley Hill in order to find a phone box.

He had a compulsive need to speak to Charlie Williams. He must find out what the problem was. He was sure there was a problem and he instinctively knew he was within an inch of losing the deal. But he didn't know why and he had to find out if he was going to prevent that from happening.

He waited by the phone box for ages for some old Irish fool to finish his conversation. The man had a bottle of whatever in one hand, the phone in the other, a half smoked but now unlit Park Drive in his mouth and a vacant look upon his face as he kept repeating the same comments at the top of his voice through a mouth half filled with rotten and decaying teeth.

Stillion wished he could drag the alcoholic from the box or at least ask him to hurry up. He couldn't. He was dressed for work and had the Sloane corporate tie around his neck. This was his badge and even his tension would not have him betray that.

Eventually the drunk fell out of the box having finished the call. Stillion, in his hurry, dialled incorrectly twice before getting it right only to be told that Mr Williams was not available. Time and luck seemed to be running out as he hurried back to the church. He got there in time to lead the procession back into the dull daylight, reload the cars, capture the elusive Father O'Rourke, complete with committal service book and holy water, before he could dive back into the presbytery for bacon and eggs and walk the cortège off in the direction of Witton Cemetery.

The cortège eventually came to Birchfield. Here an underpass had been built in the early 1960s. Arthur Sloane had decreed that it was not to be used by Sloane cortèges on the grounds that it was not reverend to use such passages and therefore they should travel on the departing side road, go straight round the island which ran above the centre of the underpass, join the connecting road to the underpass and thus arrive at the end of the underpass without having travelled upon it. Stillion, as usual, had decided that his father's knowledge and taste in such matters were sacrosanct and consequently the rule remained.

As a result, on this morning, the funeral was taking the more sedate route above the underpass. As it was about to rejoin the main road, Arthur Kemp looked to his right and down to see what traffic was coming through the underpass as he, being on the connecting road, would have to give it priority.

'Wot the . . .' he started and then paused. Stillion, alerted by Arthur's expression looked off to the right as well. Together, they saw, as the connecting road descended and the underpass rose to meet it, that a Frederick Gilbert cortège had come through the underpass and was now attempting to overtake them.

The levels equalled and ran parallel for a hundred yards

before the roads met. Stillion and Arthur could clearly make out the funeral conductor and hearse driver. Their opposite numbers were Sydney Gridley and Elton Field.

The two cortèges were now running side by side, neck to neck, coffin to coffin, head to head. Something had to give.

'Increase speed by ten miles an hour and hold your course,' ordered Sydney through his moustache as his mouth hardly opened and he stared straight in front of him.

'What shall I do?' questioned Arthur in the other hearse.

'Give way,' responded Stillion.

Both hearse drivers obeyed. ''E's going to nick owa time at the cem,' complained Arthur.

'He'd better not,' replied Stillion. But he did, and Sloanes' family were kept waiting ten minutes as a result.

Stillion complained bitterly to Tom, the Witton Cemetery foreman. 'It ain't moy fault. Sydney arrived first and told moy 'e'd seen yowa fleet still outside the church.'

Sydney enjoyed this little victory as '*un petit hors d'oeuvre*' to the main course, which would be, like all perfect revenges, according to the French, a dish to be eaten cold.

Terri eventually dragged herself off the old mattress she called bed and staggered across the originally fawn but now dirty grey carpet that appeared to have a brown fleck, except upon closer inspection these marks were not part of any pattern but just burns caused by hundreds of cigarettes being put out underfoot or even just left to burn by Terri, her clients and previous like-minded tenants.

She was not only, as the best looking Field, a lot prettier than her mother, but she also had one further saving grace, namely that while her domestic science skills were no better, her personal hygiene certainly was. Therefore while her room, her bed and her kitchenette may have come straight out of the 'Carol Field contented pig bible', she did not.

In the corner of the room was a typical early 1960s bedroom shower unit, complete with powder-blue base, a crooked rail and a torn curtain. The water, which was never too hot, mostly missed the base and soaked the filthy carpet, which had, as a result, rotted away in places. Next to the shower was a discoloured white hand-basin, where her toothbrush resided along with a tube of paste that had already had every nook and cranny explored for the last trace of cleaning material. Above the basin was a mirror, crudely stuck to the wall without a frame.

Terri stood before the mirror and wearily pulled her grubby sweatshirt over her head and flung it to the floor. Now, in just a pair of skimpy white knickers, she surveyed herself. She was more beautiful naked than dressed. Indeed, clothes hid her beauty because her beauty was contained in a pure and almost virginal understatement. She was five-feet-five or maybe five-six. She was thin. As she raised her arms she could clearly see her ribcage. Her breasts were small but exquisitely formed. Her tummy was flat, her bottom taut, her legs long and wonderfully shaped and her arms slender. Her tousled red hair hung over her boney shoulders, blending with her white and slightly freckled skin.

She pushed her knickers over her pert buttocks and let them fall to the floor, thus revealing to the mirror a red and surprisingly well-kept pubic crop. As a whole, most men didn't turn her on. Men could turn her on but she never met those men. She just met all the lousy shits who paid her crap money for her services, and Jimmy wanted a lot of that. But she was sexual. She hadn't yet been on the game long enough to either hate herself or sex. She could still distinguish between the atrocious sex of work and a sexual desire that flickered deep within her. She could turn herself on, and often did before this mirror, taken by her mind miles from this place.

She licked the thumb and forefinger of her right hand. She rubbed them together. She repeated this several times until they were moist enough to insert to where she knew it was right and where the bastards who rogered her daily never even asked about let alone got close to.

She closed her eyes. One day she would be taken by a caring man. A rich man. A strong man. A good looking, rich, strong and caring man. He would carry her up the stairs of his big house in the posh Edgbaston district. He would gently remove her clothes before lying her on his huge bed, open and defenceless and to be taken like a virgin. Her mind raced away as did her finger. She came. And then it was back to reality and that awful room. Time for a shower.

She dressed, closed her room for business and crossed the Lozells Road to visit her granddad for the second time in twenty-four hours.

She deemed another bloody boring visit with its possibilities of countless lectures as essential, as it was obviously important to get granddad stirred up enough to cause the police some grief and therefore put them under extra pressure. She passed the burned out house, now mainly hidden behind a green tarpaulin, without a glance or a pause but a little shudder did hit her mind. Those kids must have been so frightened. She could identify with that. After last night she knew all about fear but they must have had it far worse. Threatened with gang rape at Mo-Mos was bad but it didn't compare to being burned alive. But that was enough of that. She had no time for such sentiment. She wasn't out of the wood yet and she must stay focused. She rang granddad's bell.

'Oh bloody 'ell, just like a bad penny ain't yow?' was his welcome.

'Oh charming I'm sure. Wot a way to welcome yowa granddaughter.'

'Well if it's money yow want I ain't got none. But yow had better come in any road.' He led the way to the back room and said, 'Take a seat.' She obeyed.

'Look granddad. Of course I need money. I told yow yesterday, but that's not why I'm 'ere now. Elton 'as phoned moy this morning and very distressed 'e were. 'E was brief 'cos 'e were on a funeral, but 'e told moy that loads of drugs and a gun were in grandma's coffin. Some bloke 'ad contacted 'im saying as much.'

'I know. Elton 'as already phoned to tell moy. But not before some bloody nignog did.'

89

''Ow do yow know 'e were a darky?'

''Cos of 'is voice, silly. Mon this and mon that. I already phoned the police. I told them I wanted them to investigate. I mean if this is true I want those black bastards caught.'

''Ow yow know they're black?'

''Cos 'e were and they always are any road.'

'Well Mr Sloane was in on it and 'e ain't black.'

'Who said that? 'E wouldn't. 'E were a gent. 'E gave Elton a big discount off the bill and 'e did a lovely job.'

'Yeah, well, that's wot I 'eard from Elton,' replied Terri, quickly moving on as she didn't like talking about her gran's funeral, mainly because granddad had given the cash to Terri before the funeral to give to Elton so that he would take it with him to work at Sloanes. In fact she had given half to Elton, who had used it as gambling stake money, and kept the other half which she had then used to feed her drug habit. Elton had then had Sloanes send him the account after the funeral and had hoped to settle it when his luck changed. The same old story of course. Naturally his luck hadn't changed, well not for the better, and then he had got the sack and Stillion, unbeknown to Elton and Terri, had told the accountant to write off the debt rather than approach old man Woodall for the money. So as they sat there granddad thought the bill had been paid whereas she knew it hadn't and even she wasn't proud of that.

'Anyway,' she quickly continued, 'the pigs will sort it out. Yow should call them.'

'As I said I already 'ave. Don't yow worry, I told them it were bloody disgusting an old man like moy being upset like this.'

'Quite right granddad. Yow tell them. Then they'll 'ave 'er dug up in no time.'

'Wot?'

'Dug up. Exhe-whatever. Yow know.'

'No I don't know and I don't want 'er dug up. She should rest in peace.'

'Well they got to exe-whatever the word is her to investigate ain't they?'

'Oh no doubt yow'd like to get yowa 'ands on wot's in there. Wouldn't yow?'

She went cold with shock. What did he know? And how did he know it? 'I don't know wot yow mean,' she replied defensively.

'Oh yes yow do. Yow'd like to get yowa 'ands on those bleeding drugs, I'll bet.'

'Nah. Don't be silly granddad, 'ow could I with all those pigs about?' she said, relieved. 'Got to go. Just thought I'd warn yow. Yow being family and all.'

'Don't make moy laugh gal.' He showed her out.

As the day wore on Elton and Harry had the conversations they wanted. Stillion did not.

When Elton arrived back at Gilbert's funeral home he received a message to telephone Inspector Hooper. He did. Hooper told him that he was following up on Elton's complaint of that morning and that he, Hooper himself, had received an anonymous call, probably from the same man. But this man might not be telling the truth. It could all be a hoax. Could Elton shed any light on the subject? Slowly, bit by bit, Elton let his information drip-feed the inspector. The reluctant inspector remained reluctant but no longer showed it. He promised Elton action even if he had no real intention of doing very much. However, not long after that conversation finished the inspector's day was again interrupted, this time by Johnny Titmarsh who read his proposed front-page lead article over the phone to Hooper before asking Hooper's comments.

The article ran under the headline 'Handsworth Cemetery – Arsenal and Drug Warehouse for Brummie Mafia'. It started: 'It has been a well-known fact in Birmingham's mafia circles for some time and commonly believed by many funeral directors as well that both guns and drugs are stored in the coffins of the dead and then buried in Handsworth Cemetery for safe keeping.' It then went on to cite the Woodall case. It named her and

91

the month and year of her funeral. It mentioned the Rider murder weapon and the packets of coke. However, there was no mention of any mafia names and the funeral directors were not mentioned either.

Hooper had been initially panicked by the gleeful readings of Titmarsh but he quickly regained his head and remained silent. He picked up on the fact that even the brash Titmarsh had shied away from naming certain names.

'Naturally we're looking into this,' he told Titmarsh professionally, before asking: 'Do yow want to be on the inside track or wot?'

'What do you mean?'

'I mean give moy twenty-four hours. Hold this for twenty-four hours and thereafter I'll share all future developments with yow and no other press. Promise.'

'No. But for the same deal I'll hold off from tonight's *Evening Mail* and will publish in tomorrow morning's *Birmingham Post*.' This was the Machiavellian Titmarsh at his best. He had realised that printing in tonight's *Evening Mail* would mean that all tomorrow's nationals would have it and the power of a great scoop was to run it when other papers did not run it, even though they published at the same time.

'Deal,' Inspector Hooper responded. The conversation closed with a promise from both to keep the other informed.

No sooner than Hooper had put down the phone it was up again as he dialled Harry Wilkes.

'Look, 'Arry, I'm very sorry about this but this Woodall thing just won't die. I've 'ad the 'usband, the grandson and now the editor of the *Evening Mail* on to moy. The pressure is building to get an exhumation order and bring up the coffin. I know you 'ate 'aving the police crawling around but I can't . . .'

'Stop it. Of course yow can't. I already told yow. It 'as nowt to do with us. I'd get an exhumation order if I were yow. We don't give a monkey's shit, 'onest. 'Oopy, yow do wot yow think is right. But if Vance killed their own man and 'id anything in that coffin then be sharp about it and get the order and nobble them. The Wilkes would like that.' He laughed.

Hooper laughed also. 'Thank God for that,' he thought. He had been worried sick that everyone would want an exhumation order *except* Harry. Whereas as it turned out, everyone wanted an exhumation order, *especially* Harry. Well, nearly everyone. The husband had phoned that afternoon to say that while he wanted the black bastards strung up he didn't want his wife disturbed. He had been told that in the event that it became necessary it would be done with every respect but that it would have to be undertaken. Inspector Hooper was happy about having to upset Mr Woodall if it meant that he didn't have to upset Mr Wilkes.

While everyone else had been giving or receiving the phone calls necessary to make their day, Stillion had failed miserably to connect. He had attempted, while each service had been underway, to phone Williams and he'd attempted to do the same in-between each funeral also. He had phoned the main number so many times that there was now a mutual embarrassment between him and the Williams receptionist. Charlie Williams' private line, which had been given so happily only a week or so ago, just rang out.

At lunchtime Stillion had instructed his solicitors to get hold of the Williams' solicitor and fish for a problem. The senior partner, James Steel, had phoned back saying that, strangely, nobody on the other side seemed to be returning calls.

No, there was nothing for it. Stillion would have just to sit tight and wait until tomorrow. Nevertheless it troubled him and it was with a heavy heart that he climbed into his XJS for the ten-minute drive over to Higgins & Co. and of course Joyce Higgins' flat.

It was six forty-five p.m. precisely when Stillion parked in the car park. He had visited Higgins & Co. many times since acquiring it from Joyce Higgins via Richards & Gridley. Indeed he tried to visit each of his establishments at least once a month to ensure that the standards of service and facility met with his requirements, and naturally Higgins & Co. was no exception.

93

However, he had not visited the place at night and neither had he visited Joyce Higgins' flat at any time since that cold Friday December evening in 1979, when she had tricked him and stripped him of both his clothes and his pride.

He was ashamed and a little fearful. Ashamed of what he'd allowed to be done to him while he was supposedly a happily married man, and fearful that he could now be blackmailed into allowing it to happen again. Moreover, he was also ashamed because, at that time, he had found it wonderfully exciting and was therefore also fearful in case he might weaken if put to the test again.

Joyce had correctly guessed that her sadistic sex drive could unleash a masochistic tendency in him. Indeed she had, by his capture, brought him to five shattering explosions in one hour and every bit of him had tingled with the excitement of his state and her power. When it was over he had escaped into the night having lost, as he then thought, her business and much of his own self-esteem.

However, worse was to follow. Stillion, who had previously experienced the problem of relating love to sex, now found himself craving this form of sex. He didn't want to but he did. The loving husband, good son and likely excellent father, who worked hard and showed much endeavour had this dreadful flaw. The despair. He couldn't love Steppie more than he did and yet he couldn't help himself. He had a need for older women. He did not have a passion for them. He loved their passion for him. He wanted to be taken, stripped, paraded and crucified at the altar of their desire.

He never lusted after other women. He was as in love with Stephanie physically as he was mentally. Indeed it was her cleavage and the backs of her legs alone that brought out a desire for womankind in him. His love and his physical desire for her were in tune. He had only ever loved one woman and that was her. Therefore he hated being this way. He didn't understand why he was. Was it in his genes? Or perhaps a flaw in the maternal relationship of his youth? Maybe it was an illness that just afflicted British public schoolboys like him? He

94

didn't know, but everything within his moral fibre told him that in the end it was his fault and he must take the blame and keep the unhappy secret. Given his love for Stephanie, his rising position and his pride in himself, he couldn't confide in anyone.

No, he had decided that it was his problem and therefore he would have to deal with it himself. If he could not have sex without it being sustained by the mental picture of a middle-aged hen party raping him, then sex must stop until he could manage without such perverted predilections.

Perhaps he was a little hard on himself. After all, all these orgies had only been going on in his head. He had committed no physical indiscretion since walking from Joyce's flat that night. But Stillion was a driven man, an idealist who tended to see things as black or white, right or wrong. And this was wrong.

However, his self-imposed sex ban without any explanation had caused pain to the pregnant Stephanie as she wrongly, if somewhat understandably, took his 'Good night darling' responses to her sexual advances as rejection due to her growing size. Therefore he had relented and now lived with the orgies in his head.

The shame of this was Stillion's middle-class inability to talk things through when they showed him up in a less than perfect light. He had been brought up at his father's knee an 'Empire Boy'. He always wanted to play the British matinée idol in real life. He never really realised that such people did not exist.

Of course he would have been foolish to have confided in Stephanie about the night with Joyce Higgins or his encounter with Gillian Weston for that matter. He shouldn't have been with either, but he had and telling her about it would hardly undo the wrongs, would hurt her very badly and probably wreck their marriage forever.

On the other hand, he could and should have introduced her to his fantasies. They were not terrible after all. He didn't wish to harm anyone. He didn't want to become either a paedophile or a rapist for example. Moreover the highly sexed Stephanie enjoyed controlling Stillion in bed and could have

95

told him blockbusting stories if she had been given the chance but to date, she hadn't. So he was accordingly sentenced, by himself, to suffer in silence.

He rang the doorbell and waited. His mouth was dry. He believed it was wrong to be here, but he knew it was dangerous not to be. Eventually the door was answered and the same old man whom Stillion had retained despite his eighty-seven years and who had welcomed Stillion on that fateful night, welcomed him again but, as Stillion was now the owner of the business he pointed politely to the stairs and Stillion made his own way up to the top floor. He hadn't forgotten the way. He knocked on the flat door.

It was opened by a smiling Joyce Higgins. She looked radiant. Her dark hair tumbled softly and naturally down and just reached her shoulders each side of a well-tanned face. Her eye make-up, lipstick and fragrance all said 'party'. She was wearing a brilliant white cotton blouse, which was immaculate and just transparent enough to detect a white bra beneath which covered the shapely breasts that Stillion had been denied sight of on the night of her victory. The top three buttons of the blouse were undone so as to expose the start of her cleavage, all of which was tanned like her face and neither showed the ageing which her love of the sun and her forty-eight years should have created. Below the blouse was a black, straight, knee-length skirt, which was smartly cut and obviously expensive. Beneath it, dark stockings covered her well-proportioned legs. She was not wearing shoes.

Behind her the hall and the drawing room were as smart as he remembered, beautifully lit and warm. He could hear a Frank Sinatra tape playing and noticed a bottle of Moët et Chandon on the coffee table in the drawing room. But the atmosphere was not of a party. There was something missing – people.

'Am I too early?' he enquired nervously while making a conscious effort to look her in the eye.

They had hardly seen each other since that night. Even the acquisition had been handled by their solicitors without the need for principals to be at meetings and they had eventually signed in separate places, she at her solicitor's office, he at Sloane House. They had occasionally met briefly and by accident when he had visited the Higgins funeral home for its monthly random inspection. They had always been polite but distant. Nothing personal had ever been said from that Friday night to this Tuesday evening.

'No. You're bang on time. Come in,' she replied.

He entered and wandered through the hall and into the drawing room beyond. She followed behind him. The drawing room was as he remembered: blue carpet, magnolia walls, the oil paintings underneath individual wall lights and antique furniture. He was aware of another presence. He turned round. Standing in the doorway was Joyce and next to her was Gillian Weston, the second sword of Damocles, the one time lover of Stillion and best friend of Joyce.

Stillion hadn't seen the matron of Old Soldiers' Park nursing home since Councillor Martin's funeral. A funeral he would like to forget about as he would the manner by which he had obtained it. He had continued to make generous donations to the nursing home. She had continued to recommend his funeral services to her bereaved families. They had exchanged Christmas cards and small gifts but they hadn't spoken, both being acutely aware of their own dangers. His, lest he plunged or was plunged back into something which could destroy his rebuilt marriage; hers lest a second dose became an addiction or worse, lust became love.

The two friends were dressed almost identically. Gillian was also wearing a white cotton blouse, except it was worn outside her black skirt, which finished two or three inches above the knee. Like Joyce, she also wore dark tights and no shoes. Her brown hair was lighter and a little longer than Joyce's. Unlike Joyce she had remained a dedicated worker and therefore had no tan. But like Joyce the three undone buttons of her blouse exposed a hint of the bosom that was cupped in the white bra and which, unlike Joyce's, Stillion was familiar with.

Both women were in excellent shape for forty-eight and

97

forty-six respectively. Both had a glass of champagne in their right hands. Both were leaning against the doorframe in a pose which barred his way. Both were smiling and from those smiles, he surmised that both had been drinking. Joyce, who looked as in control as ever, perhaps not very much. Gillian clearly more, which seemed to be confirmed as she left her post and walked in an uncharacteristically slinky way up to Stillion, went up on the tip of her toes and planted a kiss on his cheek while she ran her left hand in a poorly disguised accidental fashion across the front of his trousers.

'Hello pretty boy,' she giggled.

Stillion's mind was spinning. He had to control everything at once. He had to control them and do so without them wreaking the most wicked revenge on him, and he had to control himself because he remembered, only too clearly, that his raging zizi had been only too happy to participate with both of them, even if initially his mind had not.

'Where are the others?' he asked Joyce, who remained in the doorway as Gillian slipped her arm around Stillion's waist and turned back to face Joyce a little unsteadily.

'What others?'

'Your other guests. The other people coming to your party.'

'I never said anything about other people.'

'Yes you did. You said you were having a party and wanted me to meet some people.'

'Quite right. I did. We are the people that I wanted you to meet and we are all going to have one hell of a party.' Joyce raised her glass to Stillion.

'I don't think you understand . . .'

'No, I don't think *you* understand Stillion, darling boy. We two girls have kept our little secrets so well. Gillian has never uttered a word about how you came to get Councillor Martin's funeral.'

'No, I haven't. I've been totally shush,' interrupted Gillian as she put a finger up to her lips.

'Neither have I said a word about how you were so willing to drop your trousers in order to secure the acquisition of my company. Over the last year we have watched your star rise, read about you and your wife as the golden couple in every other addition of the *Birmingham Sketch* and we have never uttered a word. And now it's payback time.' This last sentence was said more slowly, more deliberately and more coldly. Joyce knew she was gaining the upper hand. She felt the control which excited her so much. Her sexual juices started to flow and her body tingled in anticipation of what the two of them were going to do with him.

She continued in a more friendly vein. 'It's only a little going away party. My best friend, me and our mutual toy boy.'

'But my wife's pregnant. She is just about to have our first baby. You know that I find both of you attractive. I've proved that. But you can't in all good conscience expect me to repeat those actions. I was wrong then, not because of what we did but because I shouldn't have done it. I'm not saying that I didn't enjoy it with either of you. I did. It was brilliant with both of you. I physically proved that but I was married and I am married now and Stephanie deserves better than this.'

'Well you should have thought of that the first time round,' continued the relentless Joyce. 'Anyway, I never said we were going to repeat anything. We'll have a few drinks, play a couple of games of dice and then you can be on your way home to wifey. I'll be away next week to Spain. You and Gillian can make any arrangement you want and I promise that after tonight the subject will never be brought up again. Will it Gillian?'

'Nope,' hiccupped Gillian, now starting to lean a little more heavily on Stillion.

'So what's it to be, pretty boy?' asked Joyce.

'And if I say no to this party?'

'That's for me to know and you to find out.'

'I don't believe you would . . .'

'There's the door. Try me.'

'A drink and a dice game?'

'Yes.'

'OK.'

'That's better,' smiled Joyce, before moving away from the

drawing room door and into the room where she poured
Stillion a glass of champagne and then led the way to the small
dining table in the far right corner. The other two followed.
Joyce sat to the left, Gillian in the centre, with her back to the
room, her desire to get on with the game allowing her to take
an unusual position for a woman, while Stillion reluctantly took
his seat to the right.

All three placed their bubbly on the table and the other two
looked to Joyce, who having leant back to lower the volume on
Mr Sinatra's 'Come Fly With Me' produced nine dice from the
top of the stereo unit. Three blue dice were pushed Stillion's
way, three white were handed to Gillian and three red were
retained by Joyce.

'The game is called Plan de la Tour dice. I learned how to
play it in Plan de La Tour last winter. Plan de la Tour is a small
village in the mountains behind St Maxime in the Gulf of St
Tropez. It's very small with just one restaurant and only a couple
of bars. One bar is favoured by the British expats. A group used
to take a back room there a couple of times a week in the winter
and play this game, along with others, in order to while away
the hours when the rain fell or the mistral blew. The Côte
D'Azur climate can be pretty awful sometimes out of season you
know.' Gillian nodded in an exaggerated fashion. 'Anyway,'
continued Joyce, 'this is how you play. We all start with an equal
number of clothes. Gillian and I have five each so Stillion you
must take off your jacket, tie and shoes, but you can leave your
waistcoat on. We then throw our dice. The player with the
lowest total loses an item of clothing. The player in the middle
does nothing. The player with the highest total can, for each six
thrown on their dice for that go, either retrieve an item of
clothing, if they have lost any, or demand an item to be removed
from any of the other players. Clothes are removed in the strict
order of outer garments first. If a player is down to their last
item of clothing they can chose a forfeit three times before
having to lose it but then they have to face a naked forfeit as
the loser and that's supposed to be more difficult if you use up
all three forfeit lives than if you surrender after one. Got it?'

'I thought you said we weren't going to repeat anything,' exclaimed Stillion as calmly as possible.

'Correct. I did. Because you and I never played this game before. I only got to hear about it when I was away last March. Anyway, you made a deal to play a game of dice and who said you were going to lose?' answered Joyce calmly, confident she had hooked Stillion by her earlier threats.

Her story about Plan de la Tour and the game were true in so far as she had been there, the back room did exist, as did the game and the expats, and she had played. But the game stopped well short of what she had in mind for this evening's entertainment, which naturally was to be mostly at Stillion's expense.

In Plan de la Tour the expats, even in their most inebriated state, never forced ladies to take their knickers off, and if a man lost he had only to give a quick flash of his willy. It was all designed just as a bit of fun for the 'a little rich retired early brigade' who had loved the South of France in the summer, went to live there and then discovered the winter. Indeed, the only raunchy forfeit Joyce had seen was when a worse for drink guy had used up all three lives and was then asked to serve beer dressed only in a little white waitress apron. The girls had all giggled as they had slapped his arse, but she had felt underneath the apron and discovered that he would be incapable of sexual stimulation and so lost interest.

Her plan for tonight would yield the most wonderful entertainment if she executed it in the right order and with skill. She had got Stillion to play and now she must make him want to stay. An erect penis knew no morals and therefore control must be transferred from his head and heart to his willy, which must be excited first. Then he would be theirs. They would have his clothes and thus effectively he would become their prisoner. He would then serve them champagne clad only in one of her studded neck collars with lead attached, which would be used on his pert little bottom if he didn't please them. They would gorge themselves on caviar, especially bought for the occasion, which would be smeared over his purple straining helmet before being licked off by them while he provided the occasional protein and salt that added so much. Then he would be taken to the bedroom. The place of his previous imprisonment. Once secured to the bed, they would work on him and have him work on them until he pleaded, begged or even cried.

She could hardly wait. She had laid awake in bed for months planning this night. She had told Gillian, whom she knew not to be quite in her sadistic league, only half the story and then ensured her compliance by getting her a little the worse for drink. Now it was time for it all to happen. Her body shivered in anticipation as she waited for Stillion to lose his jacket, tie and shoes.

'Throw the dice,' she commanded.

'Oh I do love games. It's so exciting isn't it Stillion?' slurred Gillian.

'Hmmm,' Stillion managed. His mind was trying to find a way around Joyce's plan while not surrendering any control to his own animal lustings.

They all threw their dice. Stillion's finished four, four and three giving him a total of eleven. Gillian's gave up a lower yield. She had only managed, one, three and five, a total of nine. The two of them, having seen each other's scores, looked across to Joyce's. Six, six and six – a full house, just fancy that. Sillion physically shuddered as he suspected his thinking time had now run out.

'Gillian, you're last so that will be your skirt, I'm sorry to say,' said Joyce.

'That's OK,' smiled Gillian. She got up and undid the hook and zip at the back of her skirt causing it to fall to the floor. She stepped out of it before kicking it away into the centre of the room and raising both her arms above her head as she twirled around. As she did so the hem of her blouse rose to expose her buttocks and some skimpy white knickers beneath her tights. Stillion's eyes caught this sight and try as he might he couldn't prevent it from starting a stirring in his loins. Everything there was now growing at an alarming rate. Blood and mental control were deserting his head for the other place, as he had feared they might. Gillian went to sit down again.

'Don't sit down dear girl. You haven't finished. You forget I've got three sixes,' smiled Joyce, who knew that the exposing of Gillian would tip the balance towards Stillion's willy and thus vanquish his mind and with it his resistance. Very soon now he would be once again in her power.

'What?' questioned a surprised Gillian.

'I have three sixes and therefore I would like you to take off your tights, blouse and, I'm afraid, dear girl, your bra,' replied Joyce very politely.

'But you said we would gang up on Stillion. You told me if we used all our sixes on him we would be able to strip him in no time,' said Gillian in a confused voice.

'Well I've changed my mind. You can see that pretty boy is in a shy mood. You'll have to show him the way. Come on then. Rules are rules.'

'OK. I know,' was Gillian's response. She sat down and removed her tights, before starting to undo the buttons on her blouse.

'Stand up. Rules say that with the exception of socks, shoes, tights or stockings, all other clothes have to be removed while standing,' ordered Joyce.

Gillian stood up again and undid the last two buttons of her blouse. She was warming to her work now that she knew what was expected of her. She had never stripped in front of another woman before. It felt naughty and that was nice, but not as naughty or as nice as the feeling that Stillion's eyes were burning into her again as they had just over a year ago.

The blouse fell open, exposing as it did a white bra that held her ample breasts in place above her flat stomach. Below this was just a pair of brief white pants, which covered her soft brown crop. At the lowest point the cotton clung to her, held in place by her moist excitement.

She undid each of the blouse's cuffs and pushed it off her shoulders. It fell to the ground. She flicked it with her foot so that it joined her other garments in the middle of the room. Now she wiggled her hips the way 1960s beauty queens did, raised her arms again and did another twirl.

Stillion couldn't help but watch her. Electric shocks ran through her as his eyes explored her. Joyce studied Stillion studying Gillian before commanding, 'And now your bra please.'

Gillian turned away to face the room so that only her back was visible to her audience. Then her hands reached round and undid the clasp before flicking the straps off her shoulders and allowing the bra to fall to the ground, where by the courtesy of her right foot it also found its way to the centre of the room. Stillion now had a highly sexual woman whom he had once enjoyed about to face him topless while another whom he'd allowed to abuse him to the fulfilment of her sadistic pleasure held him in the power of her blackmail.

His head was thumping as he fought for control.

'Turn around please dear girl,' purred Joyce.

Gillian obliged but hid her breasts behind her hands as she did so.

'Oh, come now, what modesty. You won't be able to throw your dice like that will you? And just before you sit down, feel the front of Mr Sloane's trousers and do tell if he is, in your opinion, having a good time.'

Gillian moved her hands away and her neck and face flushed with excitement as Stillion's eyes glanced at her stiff nipples. Her shoulders heaved with the force of all the exquisite sensations that she was experiencing as she leant forward, her breasts now only inches from his face, and ran her hand up the full length of his swollen flies while her eyes locked into his. Without losing his gaze she answered Joyce. 'The Rock of Gibraltar, I'd say.' Then she sat down. 'They're not bad for my age are they?' she enquired as she gave her breasts a little shake.

'Indeed no,' commented Joyce, who fancied that Gillian's were slightly bigger than hers but that hers were slightly better. She might even let Stillion be the judge of that later. But if she did it would be on her terms and only if she felt like it.

'Ready? Throw your dice,' she said with the smugness of a woman who expected to win.

Stillion threw four, two and one and was last with a total of seven. Gillian fared better this time. She had no sixes but she did score eleven. Unbelievably Joyce pitched in with another maximum eighteen – three sixes.

'Stillion, you're last and because of two of my sixes, that will be your waistcoat, socks and trousers, and Gillian my third six means your knickers please.'

'Why not Stillion's shirt?' demanded Gillian, who suddenly felt vulnerable again and the one being picked on.

'Because the choice is mine. Anyway you can always play your first forfeit,' replied Joyce.

'Well what do I have to do then?'

Joyce pondered for a second. The time seemed right. 'Take off pretty boy's waistcoat, socks and trousers for him and then bring me his boxers.'

'With pleasure,' smiled Gillian, who felt reassured that the game might now be going her way after all.

The pounding in Stillion's head became unbearable. Words spat out of his mouth and the first thing he could really remember was walking across the Higgins' car park with his tie and jacket in one hand and his shoes in the other. His state was such that his stockinged feet did not feel the snow and ice beneath them. He unlocked his Jag and got behind the wheel. He was panting. He was totally out of breath. Adrenalin was almost pouring out of his ears, but his erection had gone and he had defeated both Joyce Higgins and his own dark side. He had won.

He started the engine. It was now seven-thirty and the last three-quarters of an hour had nearly blown his brain. But he had won and he felt elated. Well, he did until he remembered why he had gone and then stayed in the first place. What if Joyce phoned Stephanie or got someone else to do it? He had always believed she could, which is why he had gone there. He didn't think Gillian would. But he knew Joyce could.

As he drove, his mind cleared a little and he could recall screaming at Joyce: 'Enough! I'm sorry but this is going no

105

further. Two wrongs don't make a right. I'm off and if you must tell Stephanie you must. But I shouldn't be here. I'll take my chance.' And with that he had grabbed his things and left.

What a bloody awful day. First some unaccountable problem with the Frank C. Williams deal. Charlie Williams had evaded him and his agents all day and now, by at last doing the right thing, he might have consigned his marriage to the domestic dustbin just when his wife was going to bear him their first child. A time which should be so happy and a time when she should not be put through any upset, let alone become aware of these dark secrets.

Perhaps he should have stayed and let Joyce, with Gillian's help, sacrifice him at her sexual altar. At least it would have meant that there was no chance of Stephanie finding out and maybe that would have been the end of it. After all, Joyce was going to live in Spain. But deep down he knew that Joyce living in Spain was only half the story. He had had to win against himself as much as her blackmail. Indeed that had been the real battle and in the end, and against his own expectation, he had won. As a result he didn't feel like he had expected to feel. His inner self had assumed he would lose the battle and therefore like any other person with such a problem, be it drink, drugs or sex, he would crave his fix, as indeed he had as Gillian turned to face him topless. Then, by the end, he would have despised himself, once all the hot cream had gone. But it hadn't happened. His mind, helped by his heart, had beaten his willy for the first time in his life.

It was with great trepidation he left his car in the garage and entered the kitchen. He was greeted by the great smell of chicken chasseur, and the sight of a laid table, complete with bottle of claret and best of all a smiling woman.

'Hi darling. Good day? Oh before I forget, Joyce Higgins phoned.' Stillion's heart sank. 'To say,' continued Stephanie, 'that she will be leaving next week and needs to see you about the flat before she goes.'

'Oh, I see. When was that? This morning I suppose,' asked

106

Stillion in as much of a matter of fact way as he could possibly manage.

'No. I only just put the phone down. She seems to be such a nice woman. Do you know her well?'

'Er, not really,' replied a relieved Stillion. What on earth was the woman playing at? Obviously cat and mouse, but at least she wasn't going to wreck their lives tonight.

They had dinner and retired to bed. For Stillion it was the end of a bad day. He had no notion that worse was to follow.

Once Stillion had left in such an emotional state, Gillian had dressed. She had enjoyed the little party. Of course it would have been better if he had stayed longer and she could have done to him whatever she had wished, which she had been promised would happen by Joyce. But she could understand his point. His wife was, after all, having a baby. Moreover she didn't feel slighted by him. She had felt the rock in his trousers, which meant she still had pulling power, and in any case, and unlike Joyce, she didn't want to force anybody to do anything against their will.

Joyce on the other hand felt totally let down. Her plan had not worked. She liked Gillian a lot. She was her best friend but she would never be turned on by a naked woman alone. Gillian's nakedness had been the bait to catch the big fish. What's more she had caught the man that she had wished to strip, parade, tease and humble, but the bastard had somehow got away this time. She had lost this battle and that surprised her. She did not intend to lose the next.

They had decided, as it was still early, to go out for a meal and perhaps on to a club afterwards. Their hormones were up for it and they both felt they should enjoy every second. Joyce retired to freshen up and make her call to Stephanie which would indicate to Stillion that he might have escaped tonight but that he had a whole week to negotiate before she left for Spain.

Gillian waited for Joyce in the drawing room. Having finished dressing she sat down at the table and replaced the finished Sinatra tape with The Beatles' *Abbey Road*. She sipped what remained of everyone's champagne just in case that nice feeling wore off. Idly she rolled Joyce's dice. Six, six and six. She did it again. Six, six and six. She did it a third time, and then a fourth, fifth and sixth. The result was always the same. Six, six, and six.

'Joyce,' she called out.

'Yes?' came the reply from the bedroom.

'I'm rolling your dice and each time they come up six.'

'I know. They cost a fortune.'

So as the heroes and villains either slept or played their way through the night, Stillion was troubled, Joyce was frustrated, Gillian a little drunk and Sydney a bit happier, even if he had fallen through a floor. Jimmy was relieved, Elton hopeful, Harry, Alf and Nick Smith expectant as was Johnny Titmarsh. Inspector Hooper was confused and Bill Woodall was worried, while Terri, as you might expect, was high. Only Stephanie slept as someone who had not been affected by the last two days. But how long would that last?

3

Wednesday

The *Birmingham Post* front page screamed out: 'Handsworth Cemetery – Arsenal and Drug Warehouse for Brummie Mafia'. John Palin had read it and the accompanying story on the train into work. Stillion had read it over a cup of coffee in his kitchen. Both had started the story out of idle curiosity before being stabbed by the realisation that the coffin referred to had been supplied by them. The article did not mention them but the next surely would, as both of them knew that they had conducted the Elizabeth Woodall funeral.

As the funeral directors, both the police and the press would be asking questions as to how a gun and a large quantity of coke could have got into a coffin in their charge.

'I don't bloody well believe this,' thought Stillion. 'Whatever upset Charlie Williams will be small beer compared to this.'

Stephanie could see he was concerned. 'But what's it got to do with us?' she asked.

'Well, it was Elton's grandmother's funeral, and we conducted it.'

'But you didn't know anything about a gun or drugs did you?'

'Of course I didn't,' snapped Stillion angrily before quickly adding in a soft voice, 'No of course I didn't, but it looks bad because the only way they could have got into the coffin, if indeed they are in there, which I don't believe they are, is if someone put them in just as the lid was being screwed down. And that implicates either Sloanes or a member of our staff. You know what? That bloody Elton Field is a bad penny. He wrecked the Martin and the Griffiths funerals, was a thief and a liar, and now just as you're having a baby and we're supposed to be buying Frank C. Williams, a story turns up in the *Post* saying that his bloody Granny has been buried in a sea of coke with a bloody pistol to blow the head off any worms which might disturb her. And it all sort of links the funeral directors to the mafia by asking how it all got there. I'd better get off darling. Take it easy and phone me if anything starts. Are you going to see John Johnson this morning?'

Stephanie replied that she was due to see Mr Johnson, her gynaecologist at eleven. They kissed and then Stillion was gone.

Once at Sloane House he and Palin met on the main staircase. Short exchanges between them quickly communicated that both men had seen the same article and reached the same conclusion.

'You don't think Elton could be behind this do you?' asked John as they stepped into his office.

'Yes I do. With that little shit anything is possible. Anyway, I'm going to take the bull by the horns now, before I'm out on the first funeral.'

'What do you mean?'

'I'm going to phone the drug squad and find out what they know and what they're going to do about it.' With that Stillion left for his own office.

Inspector Hooper struggled to understand this case. It had been raised by an anonymous drug pusher and sort of confirmed by a relative of the deceased who had worked at the funeral home where the woman had been taken. The drug pusher said he delivered the drugs and gun to the funeral home. The relative said another member of staff saw the owner of the funeral directors put them in the deceased's coffin. For some reason Harry Wilkes, who was never keen to have the police round and never encouraged them with anything was now almost demanding that he seek an exhumation order, whereas the widower

110

seemed angry at the prospect. 'There's more to this than meets the eye,' he thought. But what?

Normally such circumstantial evidence would not be enough to take such a story seriously and certainly not enough to warrant applying for an exhumation order. But these were not normal circumstances. Race and drug-related issues had meant the Lozells Road area had become a powder keg, and one spark (which would eventually come later that year in the now famous 1981 Handsworth riots) could blow the whole area up.

On the one hand the West Indian youth believed that the police only stopped *their* cars and that if you were a Rasta then you were guilty before even a question was asked. The police and the Rastas had had poor relations for some time but now the open drug culture of the Villa Cross area made things almost impossible. The police needed to appear to be fair and act in a way that could not lead to accusations of bias and racism. This was easier said than done as many were both biased and racist. People like Hooper had to keep a kind of peace that allowed business as usual. He couldn't bust a drug baron like Harry Wilkes because he was on his payroll, and if he overdid it with the Rasta pushers he would have a riot to contend with.

On the other hand he was coming under increasing pressure to do something by the West Indian Federation and their churches. They had accused the police of being cowardly, complacent and were forever pointing out that the police would never have allowed such drug addiction to affect the white children of Edgbaston.

He needed a result. To recover the gun that killed Rider and a large quantity of coke would be a good result. If the packets really had fingerprints that led to convictions that would be a great result – unless, that is, the fingerprints belonged to Harry Wilkes or any of his gang. He had better speak to Harry again.

''Ello Harry, that you? Look, wot if your fingerprints or the boys' fingerprints is on these packets we spoke about?'

111

'I already told you. It got nowt to do with us. Ain't you applied for that order thing yet?'

'No.'

'Why not? Come on, look lively for fuck's sake mate.'

That was enough for the inspector. The easy course of action for him was to apply for the order. The West Indian Federation would want him to. More importantly, Harry Wilkes had told him to. He determined to apply without further delay. Just then his phone rang and the police telephonist announced that a Mr Stillion Sloane was on the line for him. 'Bloody hell,' thought Hooper. 'This case gets more queer by the minute. I should be phoning *him* not the other way round.'

'Hello Mr Sloane, Inspector Hooper here. What can I do for yow?'

'Inspector Hooper, thank you for taking the call. I won't keep you long. I've read the story in this morning's *Post* which claims that a murder weapon and a large amount of cocaine were stashed in the coffin of a late Elizabeth Woodall. The story implies these items were put there while her coffin lay in a chapel of rest. Naturally, as we were the funeral directors and neither my staff nor I have any knowledge of either gun or drugs, and would never have agreed to place them in anybody's coffin, I would be grateful to know who told you this story.'

'We never divulge our sources sir, but I can tell you that our informant is certain that he delivered both the murder weapon and the cocaine to Sloane House. What's more, an ex-member of yowa staff says that he was told by another staff member that yow personally placed the items in the coffin.'

'Me? Now look here, that's ridiculous. I've never heard such rubbish in my life.'

'I'm sure you 'aven't sir,' said the inspector with a slight air of sarcasm.

'Have you spoken to this staff member, the one who apparently saw me do this act?'

'Not yet sir.'

'Well don't you think you should?'

'All in good time. We got to trace him. Apparently he retired a couple of years ago.'

Stillion's heart sank. This week was becoming a nightmare. A week from hell. Every bit as bad as the 1979 funeral wars week. 'The name you were given wasn't George Brown was it? asked Stillion hardly able to contain his disappointment.

'And what if it were Mr Sloane?'

'Well there's no need to trace him. I can tell you where he is. He's dead. He died last summer down in Bournemouth and his name is in the Bournemouth crematorium book of remembrance. Check it out.'

'Oh dear. Doesn't look good for yow, does it sir?'

'What the hell do you mean? Some nameless person tells you that he gave me cocaine and a gun to hide in a deceased's coffin, and another nameless person who was on my staff says that he was told by a person who is now dead that they saw me do it. Please? I mean what a heap of shit. Anyway what would be my motive?'

'Money?'

'Money! Now look here. I make my money by running a respectable funeral business. I am not and never have been involved in drugs.'

'I didn't say yow were. But I was told yow agreed to do this to avoid 'aving to pay high protection money.'

'Nonsense. I have never paid protection money to Harry Wilkes or anyone else for that matter.'

'I never mentioned Mr Wilkes.'

'No, but I did. It's people like Mr Wilkes you should be talking to about protection, guns, drugs, prostitution and the rest.'

'What are yow inferring?'

'Nothing. Just get a bloody exhumation order and let's see what's in that coffin shall we? And when you find there's nothing there perhaps you might consider apologising to me and spend some time looking for the real villains. The drug barons. And you know as well as I do who they are.'

113

'Just one further thing Mr Sloane,' said the inspector, as if he had been conducting the interview, 'you won't leave Brum without letting us know will you?'

Stillion was furious. In the last twenty-four hours his main acquisition prospect seemed to be disappearing down the toilet, he had had his two swords of Damocles dangled dangerously over his head and then a funeral which he had conducted and never been paid for had come back to haunt him with a charge in the city's main newspaper that the coffin was stuffed full of drugs and a murder weapon. And now a police inspector had just told him that he had been told third-hand from a dead man that Stillion had put the drugs in the coffin himself, and that he shouldn't leave the city.

'Oh I'm not going anywhere. I've got a business to run. Please tell me when the exhumation will be. Thank you. Goodbye.'

'I bet he'd like to know,' thought Hooper, who was nevertheless still no further down the road in his own mind.

No sooner had Stillion put the phone down than Victoria Thomas rang him to say the editor of the *Post* and *Mail*, a Mr Johnnie Titmarsh, was on the phone. Stillion told her to put him through.

'Good morning Mr Sloane,' said Titmarsh in his Sheffield dialect.

'Morning,' replied Stillion as politely as possible, given his temper.

'Mr Sloane, you may well have seen the story in the *Post* this morning.'

'Indeed I have.'

'What comment would you like to make?'

'About what?'

'About the fact that the police are investigating an allegation that a Mrs Elizabeth Woodall was buried some two years ago with a murder weapon and pounds of cocaine in her coffin in Handsworth Cemetery and that you were the funeral directors that the family used,' said Titmarsh with a hint of aggression.

114

'Mrs Woodall was buried in Handsworth Cemetery on the date quoted in your paper. She was buried by this firm. However, neither my staff nor I are aware of anything being placed in her coffin. None of us was asked by the family or anyone else to place anything in the coffin. The day book record shows there were no special requests other than two rings were to be left on at her husband's request. This request was adhered to as always. Other than that I can't help you.'

'But an ex-member of your staff said that he had been told by another ex-member of staff that he had seen you personally place items in black bags in the coffin. What have you to say about that?'

'Absolute nonsense. The person who was supposed to have seen me do this thing is dead. And nobody seems to know whom he told,' said Stillion calmly as he realised that losing his temper would not help.

'Oh, I do,' smarmed Titmarsh. 'It was a relative of the deceased. One Elton Field I think.'

'Oh, I bloody knew that little shit was in this somewhere,' thought Stillion. He replied, 'Look, if the police feel there should be an exhumation then they will apply for an order and then we'll all know won't we? In the meantime you'll receive a letter from my solicitor today making it quite clear what our position is and what I have told you. I would be very careful not to report anything else and not to misquote me. Do you have any further questions?' The conversation finished.

'What's that little toerag Elton up to now?' thought Stillion, who would have loved to have told the Yorkshireman that Field had been sacked but hadn't dared to for fear of opening up the can of worms concerning the funeral wars.

Stillion put his top hat on, adjusted his tie and went downstairs to conduct his first funeral. He had thought about calling Charlie Williams first but had decided against it until he had some answers. At least he now knew where to start. He needed to talk to an embalmer first – one Elton Field.

*

115

Meanwhile, over at Gilberts the mood was light. The pious Fred Gilbert was confident that he would be able to get Frank C. Williams without having to raise his bid. A belief that seemed to be confirmed when Sydney arrived in his office with a copy of the *Birmingham Post*. Sydney had been allowed to stay and hear Fred phone Frank C. Williams, be put straight through by the receptionist and then enjoy Fred's assertions that he had always wondered where that bloody boy had got his money from. Well now everybody knew; the *Birmingham Post* had exposed obvious links with Birmingham's underworld. Charlie Williams said he had been surprised, that he hadn't thought of Stillion like that, that Arthur would have been so shocked had he been alive, but that he was grateful for Sydney's tip-off.

Fred invited Charlie to meet him for lunch. He hoped to cement the deal there. Both men, as comfortable owners, could afford the time, Sydney as an employed conductor could not. He would be out in the cold directing funerals. But things would change once he was installed at Williams. He wouldn't own it, but it would be his domain. A bit more like the old days. And what's more the idea of Stillion's discomfort would keep him warm as he stood at the graveside today.

Down in the mortuary Elton read the *Birmingham Post* with pleasure before he surveyed the line of stiffs on trolleys and under white sheets. There were five to do. He would have preferred two. Not because he was lazy, but because, while he was a first rate shit at everything else, he took great pride in being an embalmer. It was his one island of discipline. The only thing he did where self-esteem was involved. The problem with five was that he wouldn't be able to devote enough time to any of them. A squirt of embalming fluid in through an artery, draw the blood from a vein, concentrate on the head and hands, close the eyes and sew up the mouth.

Elton often wondered if there was a heaven, if it had betting shops with extended credit and if he would be greeted by hundreds of silent people, shaking their fists at him due to the fact that he had sewn up their mouths.

He surveyed the line and thought, 'I'll deal with that fat cow

116

on the end first.' The reason he had chosen the dumpy Mrs McBride was because she had turned – gone green – and was starting to stink the place out. Oh the joys of preserving rotting flesh.

Embalming gives a life-like appearance, prevents purging, post-mortem staining and horrid smells. More importantly it kills most known germs dead. It also gave Elton a living and a little sanctuary away from the outside world. The stiffs didn't talk much, other than the occasional belch as trapped air escaped from their bodies as he moved them around. On the other hand he didn't get into debt with them and thus they didn't chase after him with threats of beatings.

He turned on another bar of the electric fire. Of course Mrs McBride would smell all the more but he was used to that and hated being cold. He had grown up cold.

Jimmy had shown Terri a copy of the *Birmingham Post*. It was not a paper he normally bought, but its lead headline screamed good news as did billboards advertising it. He had noticed the billboard outside the newsagents in Lozells Road and had run inside to buy a copy which he eventually managed to purchase after rummaging through his pockets to find enough change among old dog-ends and cigarette papers. He had managed to make enough sense of the article to understand more or less its meaning and had then made for Terri's flat.

A tousled-haired and sleepy Terri opened the door. Jimmy pushed the paper at her. She pushed it back and asked him to read it while she made them coffee. He remembered the cups and declined but read the article all the same. She didn't care either way. She didn't really want coffee, she just didn't want him to know that she couldn't read.

He made a fairly decent stab at it and if it didn't quite flow like the BBC news then at least he did well enough for both of them to get the general meaning, and that meaning was good. It told them that their story was being taken seriously and that could mean action and a result.

Once he had finished reading they giggled excitedly, just like children. They rolled around in fits of laughter on the bed and then rolled into each other's arms. The contact swelled the engine in the front of Jimmy's jeans. She was compliant and surrendered on her back, her outstretched arms bent upwards at the elbow, her legs slightly open. They stopped laughing.

He took the invitation. He removed her knickers while commanding her to remove her floppy, outsized T-shirt, before ripping the metal buttons off his jeans to expose a throbbing, black spike which longed to pass between her milky, freckled thighs and the beautiful red crop before plunging into the joys of her inner self.

His continued desire for her, despite the fact that the trouble he was in was totally her fault, overcame him quickly and soon he was finished and thus mercifully the experience was short lived for her. Sex without desire should be paid for, and he didn't pay.

Stillion's first funeral of this miserable Wednesday was from Hockley Tower, a high-rise apartment block in Hockley, to Perry Barr Crem. There, one Michael Russell, the mischievous organist, had hymned up 'It's All Over Now' and the rest of the service passed off as one might imagine and the six elderly lady mourners all returned in the single limousine to the apartment block where the flat was situated on the fourteenth floor.

Once the diligent, professional, but nonetheless preoccupied Stillion had unloaded the limousine he escorted its occupants to the lift, which ascended upon command. The six old ladies smiled at Stillion as they rose. Stillion attempted, despite his distraction, to smile back. His thirty-year-old frame towered over all of theirs, most of which had been constructed at the turn of the century or even before.

The lift seemed to take for ever. Stillion was mindful of the time. He had to be at his next house in twenty minutes. His thoughts switched back to the story in that morning's *Post* when they were immediately and rudely interrupted by a sharp jolt as the lift came to a sudden halt between the eleventh and twelfth floors. The ladies looked at each other and then at Stillion. Stillion smiled reassuringly at them. He told them that the lifts in these tower blocks broke down all the time and that the caretaker would have it going again in no time at all.

'Not 'ere 'e won't,' replied one of the elderly ladies. 'The caretaker is a useless drunk. His wife is worse. The only time they come to see any of us is when they want a gift at Christmas. The lift breaks down all the time and often we're stuck inside for more than an hour at a time.'

'Well at least we've a nice young man to keep us company,' said another before asking, 'Anyone got a pack of cards?'

'Why?' queried a third.

'So we can play strip poker of course,' came the reply.

'Oh Ethel!' went the other five in unison.

Stillion gave little thought to the threat of gang rape by six old ladies. They were the least of his problems right now. He was stuck in a lift. He had to be at the address of his next funeral in eighteen minutes. Somehow he had become embroiled in a drug protection racket with murderous overtones. And his wife was about to give birth to his first child. Nevertheless an escape from the lift was essential if what had been said about the caretaker was right, and therefore they would have to play strip poker without him.

He gave his top hat to one old lady and his tailcoat to another. He located the exit hatch in the lift's ceiling. He jumped up and punched it open with his left fist. He jumped again and clung onto the hatch opening's rim with both hands. The ladies huddled in the opposite corner as he struggled to lift his own weight through the hole. Eventually he managed this without the assistance that was so freely offered by Ethel, to the amusement of her companions.

He hauled himself to his feet on the lift's roof. He did so with great care, not because of his delicate position, but because he was concerned to keep his pinstripe trousers, shirt and waistcoat clean. His father would have been proud of him. He was indeed a Sloane gentleman and a most professional funeral

119

director. He might be late at the next location but he had no intention of adding to his embarrassment by turning up covered in either dust or, worse, axle grease.

It was pitch black in front of him. He steadied himself and gently turned to the right. There, from about the height of his waist running upwards for approximately eight feet was a thin line of light. Stillion correctly understood this to be light that was entering the lift shaft from the crack between the lift doors on the twelfth floor. He put his hand into his right trouser pocket and produced his Zippo petrol lighter. He flicked it open and spun the flint wheel. It lit and immediately gave him a generous and wind-proof flame, which was as well as the draft fairly whistled down the lift shaft. He was able to find his way across the couple of feet of lift roof to the thin line of light. There he placed one hand on each door and forced them slightly apart. He was then able to place both hands into the gap created and slowly push open the doors to expose the landing on the twelfth floor.

Stillion called back over his shoulder to the ladies, 'I'm going to get the caretaker, which floor is his apartment on?'

'The ground floor,' came the response.

Stillion clambered from the lift to the dirty twelfth floor, stood up, dusted off his waistcoat and then lurched through the fire door to the service stairs before leaping down flight after flight until eventually he reached the ground. There he quickly located the caretaker's flat and rang the bell.

A rather greasy man of some forty-five years answered. He was overweight and stood only about five-five. He was dressed in old red carpet slippers, dirty grey flannel trousers and a (once upon a time) white string vest. He also had braces on but these hung down from his trousers as they were not currently employed. Either he, or his flat, or both, smelled of stale, fried cooking. A lined and fairly toothless hag stood to the side and slightly behind the greasy man's right shoulder. From the ladies' description Stillion immediately understood this to be the caretaker and his wife.

120

'Good morning. Sorry to trouble you but the lift is stuck between the eleventh and twelfth floors,' exclaimed a breathless Stillion.

'All right. All right. Calm down mate. The place ain't on fire is it? I'm just going to shave. You wait 'ere and when I've finished you can tell moy all about it.'

'No, it's not all right.'

'Well too fuckin' bad mate.'

Stillion, who had come across many ignorant Brummies in his life and usually dealt with them with passive disdain, suddenly exploded. His left hand grabbed the caretaker's greasy, unkempt hair and smashed it along with the attached head against the open door. At the same time his left knee scored a direct hit on the Brummie's balls and the lard parcel, which was held together inside the string vest, fell to the floor.

'Get up, you pathetic excuse for a human being,' shouted Stillion.

'I can't. You've fuckin' crippled moy,' panted the collapsed grease ball, who was paying for all of the other things that had happened to Stillion so far that week. Stillion could rough it. He wasn't bad for a public schoolboy. But he wasn't a violent man and such behaviour while on duty was unthinkable. Well, unthinkable that was until the greasy caretaker's comments proved to be the straw that broke the camel's back.

'Get up,' repeated Stillion as he bent down to assist the lump of lard to his feet. Just in the nick of time his left eye picked up movement and his brain registered danger. He raised his left arm and his hand clasped a china vase which the hag was just about to bang down on his head. He rose to his full height as the hag attempted to lunge at his face with her dirty fingernails. His right hand grabbed her hair as his left threw the vase behind him onto the entrance hall so that he could have two free hands to defend himself. The vase smashed into a thousand pieces. At the same time the hag's hair became detached. It was a wig and now the fairly toothless and fairly bald hag, who was perhaps only ten years older than Stillion, beat a hasty retreat into the depth of the flat, covering her head with her hands and screaming. Her husband remained on all fours in the entrance.

'Are you going to get up?' enquired Stillion with some menace in his voice.

'That vase has been in the family for years yow know.'

'Yeah? Too bad,' responded Stillion flatly before adding, 'If you don't get up now . . .'

'All right mate, give us a chance. You just fuckin' beat me up, OK.'

'I'll show you what a beating is if you . . .'

'OK. OK.'

'Look, there are six old ladies locked in that lift.'

'Oh dear, what can the matter be? Six old ladies locked in the lavatory,' chuckled the lump as he clambered to his feet.

'Move it or your head will be going down a lavatory,' responded Stillion with a poker face that told the caretaker that this wasn't a good time to crack jokes.

'I'll reset the circuit breaker switch. That may work. Sometimes it does. Sometimes it don't. If it don't then I'll have to call the engineer out,' said the caretaker as he crossed the stone entrance floor.

Stillion followed behind. 'Don't you have a manual winch or something like that?' he enquired.

'Na. You don't know much about lifts does yow?'

'No I don't. But I do know you are going to do everything within your power to get those ladies out of there.'

'Don't worry mate. They don't care. They're used to it, see? Often they is stuck there for an hour or more.'

'While you have a shave no doubt. Well not this time my friend because I have to be at my next funeral in less than quarter of an hour.'

'Well you won't be if this switch don't do the trick mate,' replied the lump of lard as they arrived at the locked door to the side of the lift shaft. He unlocked the door, turned on the lights, pulled the switch and yes, sweet Jesus, the lift motor burst into life.

Stillion bounded back up the stairs without further comment to the caretaker. It was a lot harder work going up than it had been coming down, but he was fit and in any case the adrenalin kept him going.

Neither the ladies nor the lift could be found on floor twelve. He eventually caught up with them in the flat on the fourteenth floor. He recovered his top hat and tailcoat and thereafter he took his leave of them and trusted that everything had been conducted to their entire satisfaction, which it had for all except Ethel who was sorry that no game of strip poker had taken place.

Stillion departed down the stairs. He did not trust the lift and had no desire to get stuck in it again and be at the mercy of the lump of lard and his bald wife, while his next family was kept waiting.

'God I thought you weren't comin' out of there gov,' said the reinstated lead limousine driver Walter Warburton as Stillion leapt into the limo's front seat.

'Nor did I. I'll tell you about it later,' responded a breathless Stillion as he grabbed the radio telephone mic. 'Sloane Two to Sloane Control. Sloane Two to Sloane Control. Come in Sloane Control.' He looked at his watch; they should now be arriving at the next house.

'Sloane Two this is Sloane Control. Go ahead,' came back Victoria Thomas' voice.

'Control this is Sloane Two. We have been held up due to a broken down lift. Ask the other two limousines to meet us directly at the house and ask J. P. to ensure they know where they're going. Also please confirm that Sloane One is already at the house and has taken the deceased inside.'

Walter drove as fast as the snow would allow as they made their way through the back streets of Hockley and Lozells before joining the Birchfield underpass and racing towards Great Barr where the home address of their next funeral was located.

'It's more like the *Dukes of Hazard* than funerals ain't it?' joked Walter without a laugh in his dry voice or a smile on his serious Black Country face.

'Right,' smiled Stillion anxiously, still waiting for Victoria to come back to him. He had heard her call Sloane One but could not, as with any two-way radio, hear Arthur Kemp's response. He was just about to call her again when, 'Sloane Two, Sloane Two this is Sloane Control,' came across the airwaves.

'Come in Sloane Control. Sloane Two receiving you loud and clear. Over.'

'J. P. has despatched the two limousines which will now make their own way to the house. Sloane One is already there. The deceased is in the front room and the Reverend Winston Wylde has arrived and will say prayers in the house before the casket is closed. Arthur would like to know your ETA. Over.'

'Tell him another ten minutes and ask him to close the casket when the prayers are concluded and supervise the family's bearers to reload the casket. Also ask him to identify the family flowers for the casket, place them on and load the rest onto the hearse with cut flowers on top and wreaths inside. I will arrange the seating in the three limos when I arrive. Over.'

'Sloane Control to Sloane Two message received and Charlie Wilco, over.'

'Sloane Two standing by.'

Stillion listened intently as Victoria passed the message on to Sloane One. It was word perfect and she was able to come back to Stillion quickly with the news that Arthur Kemp had understood and would carry out the instructions without a problem.

'If Arthur does that, we don't get stuck and the other two limos have fair passage then we should be able to pull back the time and run to church on time,' Stillion told Walter who vaguely nodded as he continued to concentrate on both the road ahead for danger and the road behind for police cars.

They made good time, as did the other limousines. Arthur had loaded both the casket and the flowers. Stillion arranged the seating in the limos, which were then loaded one at a time, pulling into place outside the front drive in turn, before he walked the funeral off down the road.

Eventually Stillion stood to one side and slipped into the hearse's front seat as Arthur glided it past him. It was still bitterly cold, but at least the sun was trying to poke its head around the clouds for the first time in days, and as Stillion glanced at his watch he was able to say, 'Put it on eighteen Arthur' confident in the knowledge that they had caught up the lost time.

In all the excitement he had almost forgotten about the two swords of Damocles, this morning's *Birmingham Post*, Charlie Williams' refusal to speak to him and the fact that at any moment his wife was due to give birth. He could do little about any of these things as he sat in the hearse, except worry. But at least he could enquire after the health of his wife.

'Sloane Two to Sloane Control, come in please.'

'Sloane Control, receiving you over.'

'Vicky, phone home and see if Steppie's OK, over.'

Bill Woodall had risen at nine-fifteen a.m. on that Wednesday morning as usual. He put his heavy, grey woollen dressing gown on over his blue and white striped pyjamas, as he did each morning to protect him from the cold, and descended the steep and narrow stairs to his tiny hallway. There was no post, which pleased him because the only post he ever seemed to receive was bills and they didn't please him. He continued on through his back room into his small kitchen. Once there he lit the gas stove and filled a kettle in order to make himself a brew of tea and draw a bowl of boiling water so that he might shave.

At nine-thirty his old Bakelite phone rang. It was Elton.

''Ello granddad. Yow're famous now. Yowa story is all over the *Birmingham Post*. It's all there, how grandma was buried with drugs and a gun and all.'

'What? Where?' queried the bewildered old man.

'In the *Birmingham Post*. On the front page. It's great.'

'No it ain't. It's bloody disgraceful. Yowa beloved grandma should be left in peace and our family shouldn't be shamed this way. Hopefully folk round here won't see it. Most don't take the *Post* and they're all occupied with the funerals of those nippers who copped for it in that fire last Sunday.'

125

'Well I thought yow'd like to know any road.'

'Leave 'er in peace is what I say. She 'as 'ad enough shame brought on 'er 'ead by yowa mum and dad, let alone yow kids, without all of this,' whined Bill as Elton at the other end wished he hadn't bothered to phone.

As the conversation finished Bill's front doorbell rang. 'I bet it's that bloody Terri again. Making a bloody habit of calling nowadays,' he said to himself as he shuffled in his slippers to the front door, his razor in one hand and his cup of tea in the other. He placed the razor in the teacup's saucer and opened the door with his free hand.

Bill opened his door and peered out bleary eyed from his dark hallway. It was hard to focus straight away as the sun was in his eyes but instantly he knew that this was no visit from Terri.

'This way Mr Woodall.'

'Over here Mr Woodall.'

'Mr Woodall I'm from the *Daily Express* . . .'

'*Daily Mail* Mr Woodall . . .'

'The *Mirror* will buy your story Mr Woodall . . .'

'The *Sun* will pay more for your exclusive . . .'

'The *Daily Mail* will pay the most . . .'

'Tim Johnson-Smythe, *Daily Telegraph* . . .'

Flash bulbs were popping from every angle, dictaphones, microphones and note pads were being thrust in his face as some twenty or so reporters and photographers jostled for position. There was even a film crew. And Bill gave them such a photo opportunity. An old man in his pyjamas and dressing gown with half his face covered in shaving soap, a cup of tea in hand and standing on the front doorstep of a working-class terraced house. Great. What a victim.

This pack of dogs had been hunting him down since their editors had picked up on the story from the first edition of the *Birmingham Post*. It was no accident that they had arrived altogether. All were too frightened to let the others out of their sight for fear of missing the story.

126

Bill stood there blinking for several seconds. He found it hard to take in what was happening.

'Mr Woodall, what do you think about the article in today's *Post*?' called out one reporter.

'I ain't seen it,' answered Bill, still blinking and now putting a hand up to shield his eyes.

'Are these drugs in your wife's coffin?' yelled another reporter.

''Ow the 'ell do I know?' blurted out Bill.

'You didn't see anything in the coffin then?'

'Course I didn't yow bleedin' idiot.'

'Who were the funeral directors?'

'Sloane & Sons. Now bugger off the lot of yow. Leave 'er in peace and moy, an old man, who fought for this country. Leave moy be all right?' And with that he retreated and slammed the door.

He took a swig of his tea. Yuk, it was cold and tasted of shaving soap. The doorbell rang again and again, which prompted Bill to shout through the letter-box. 'I said bugger off and I meant it. Be off or I'll call the police.'

The pack of newshounds took off to Sloane House. Where else?

Not many West Indian widows lived in one of the better roads of Great Barr. In actual fact none did, but the funeral that Stillion was now conducting had an interesting story attached to it.

Jessie Nicholls had arrived in Birmingham in 1952 from Jamaica. She was then thirty-five and she and her husband of the same age had come in search of work. He got a job at Joseph Lucas and she became a nurse at Dudley Road Hospital. They settled in a little flat just off the Lozells Road. They had wanted children but never had them for reasons that they never understood. Other than that they were a typical couple of that time. West Indian immigrants coming to get work and perhaps

127

a better life by doing the many jobs that the indigenous population had rejected on the grounds of either being too dirty or too poorly paid.

Then, tragically, the husband died from bronchitis in the spring of 1954. West Bromwich Albion brought the FA Cup home as she prepared to bury her man.

She considered returning home to Kingston. She had family there and few real friends in Birmingham. Then one day she met a frail asthmatic as she nursed the private wards at the hospital. He was a kindly man in his fifties. He was well-off, had a private income, which was as well given his poor state of health, and lived alone in a smart five-bedroomed house in Great Barr.

She teased him as she propped him up in bed and made him laugh. He looked forward to her coming in to see him. He was a lonely soul and she brightened his day.

Eventually he confided in her that he was worried about what would happen to him when his housekeeper retired later that year. He had an active mind but his health made it impossible for him to look after himself. How would he cope? Then he shyly asked, 'You won't consider?' She didn't need to be asked twice. She resigned and became his new housekeeper when the post became vacant.

They made an odd couple as she pushed him in his wheelchair down to the shops on warm days, his pale and balding head poking out from beneath several layers of blankets, happy to be there, happy to be alive. She, big, strong, buxom and black with a flashing white smile, also happy to be there, happy to be alive. He was the master, she was the housekeeper, and they were friends. She cleaned, cooked and washed for him. She bathed him and she sat up at night with him when sometimes his asthma nearly suffocated him.

She had been content with her husband. They had had sex and he had been her husband. She had been loyal. She had wanted children but they did not come. She doubted if she had truly loved her husband and she knew there was a large emptiness created by the absence of children. Now this man Peter

Baker gave her so much. A roof, a job, security, a home, a sense of purpose, friendship, even companionship. He had taken away the loneliness. He had filled the emptiness. She loved him. Oh, there was no sex. That would have been impossible due to his condition. But more importantly there was no thought of sex. It never entered the equation.

Then in the spring of 1957, just as Aston Villa brought home the FA Cup, Peter Baker slipped away in his sleep and she felt empty all over again.

A few old school friends turned up for the short service at St Michael's church. There were only seven mourners including her. She wore her housekeeper's uniform out of respect. He wouldn't have wanted her to but she did it all the same. She wasn't going to give anyone the chance to gossip.

One of the other mourners was Peter's solicitor. He was the only one to return to the house with her after the funeral, which he had arranged according to Peter's instructions. She gave him a dry sherry in the drawing room. She went to leave. He told her to stay and take a seat. He opened his briefcase and took out a file.

'This is Peter's last will and testament,' he said as he opened the file. He proceeded to read the will. Peter had no relatives, she knew that, but the next line so shocked her that she had to ask the solicitor to repeat it several times. Peter had left all his worldly goods to her. His private income, his home, his furniture, his silver, his everything. There were only two conditions – one, that while she lived in England she remained there, even if she remarried, and two, he would consider it an honour, if, when the time came she would rest next to him in the family vault at St Michael's on the Hill, Great Barr.

She lived on in the house for nearly twenty-four years until her death in this January 1981. She never married and preferred mostly her own company in that large house which she kept immaculately, almost as if Peter was expected to return at any time.

She had made her own will and, having no relatives either, left her considerable estate to Reverend Winston Wylde's Baptist church on the Handsworth, Lozells border, which she had continued to attend for nearly thirty years.

Now her funeral was to take place, but unlike Peter's it would be a huge affair. A very grateful Reverend Wylde had seen to that. He had announced her will as arranged upon her death and he had devoted much of last Sunday's sermon to her. He might have devoted all of it but some had to be held back for today. Winston Wylde was too good a man to place a three-line whip on a funeral service attendance but he had made it plain that the congregation should show its gratitude. They respected him so they would take time off work to be there, and Jessie Nicholls would not be sent on her way as she had lived much of her life – alone.

The friendship between Stillion and Winston Wylde was well known. Moreover, Sloanes were nearly always chosen by the West Indian community due to their non-racial acceptance of ethnic customs. But the main reason why it was a Sloane fleet gliding down from Great Barr to the Lozells Road Baptist church was that Arthur Sloane had conducted Jessie's husband's and her best friend Peter's funerals with such calm, kind, professional care that she, learning from Peter, requested how her funeral should be conducted in her will, and the funeral directors were to be Sloanes.

The money left to the church upon the winding up of Jessie's estate, along with the ongoing income, was to be used by Reverend Wylde not just for the church's upkeep but for the salvation of its members. Its use and direction was left to him and his successors.

The cortège arrived at church on time. Jessie Nicholls, despite her fifteen stone, was shouldered across the slippery forecourt to meet a full 1,500 congregation – the largest since the funeral of Charles Nelson Griffiths in December 1979, and he had been the leader of the West Indian Federation.

The choir, men in their black dinner jackets and women in their royal blue choir gowns, belted out 'When the Roll is Called Up Yonder' as the casket came to rest on the trestles and Arthur and Walter opened it up while Stillion sat the mourners, who were all church elders as there was no family to fill the three limousines Jessie had wanted.

As with any decent West Indian non-conformist funeral the service was long, emotional and highly charged and by its end religion and faith had intoxicated the congregation to such an extent that there were many cries of 'Jesus' and 'Oh Lord' and 'Jesus Saves' from around the church. Naturally the infamous drunk of the Lozells Road, Thomas Griffiths, brother of the saintly deceased Charles, was in the congregation. As ever he produced a bottle of vodka from the pocket of his battered dinner jacket and every few minutes saluted either the deceased, the reverend, the choir or the congregation, before taking a large slug of it. Eventually his long-suffering sister and sisters-in-law removed him after he had responded to one cry of 'Jesus Saves' with 'Yes but the devil scores on the rebound'. The singing of the 'Old Rugged Cross' drowned his cries as he was physically removed from the church and given a good handbagging outside.

The service concluded with the choir chanting 'When the Roll is Called Up Yonder' for a second time as the mourners all filed passed the open casket. Everybody joined in. They sang, they rocked to it, they rolled to it, they repeated it endlessly. The men threw their carnations into the casket as they passed. Many women stopped to touch Jessie's hand, which was clothed in a white net glove to match her white wedding dress that had been bought for the occasion. They were quickly waved on by Reverend Wylde, much to Stillion's relief as the cortège had some way to go for the committal service.

Jessie Nicholls had decided to be laid to rest next to Peter Baker in his family vault. She didn't have to. No solicitor could punish her now she was dead. But Peter had wanted it and so did she. She hoped her husband, and more importantly God, would understand. So instead of the short journey to Handsworth Cemetery the cortège would have to slowly make its way back up to Great Barr and St Michael's on the Hill.

St Michael's was located on top of a hill some two miles north of the M6 motorway and next to an old nineteeth-century

131

mental hospital. Although surrounded by the towns of the Black Country and the City of Birmingham, the area was really quite rural with sheep, cattle and horses grazing in the fields next to the church.

The church had been there since the sixteenth century but had been enlarged and developed in the early nineteenth. It had prospered during the industrial revolution because successful merchants and industrialists moved away from the smoke created by their work in Birmingham, Walsall and Wolverhapton to build new homes on the high levels of Great Barr. Thus the churchyard was a maze of vaults and headstones to their memory. Indeed, Peter Baker was the last of one of these well to do families.

As the cortège arrived the vicar, one Paul Burke, was waiting at the church gate. Stillion approached him in order to give him the green burial certificate and pay him the burial fee, which had been requested in cash, naturally.

Stillion was convinced the Reverend Burke was mad and had perhaps escaped from the mental hospital next to the church. In addition he was a middle-class snob and despite his own insanity, which had probably prevented him from being anything but a vicar, he looked down on the 'lower classes', as he referred to them. Obviously West Indians and Asians were beneath his contempt.

'Good morning sir,' Stillion said.

'But they're black,' said Reverend Burke, looking over Stillion's shoulder at the occupants of the limousines and other following cars.

'Yes they are sir.'

'Well your firm never mentioned that to me when they booked the reopening.'

'Should they have?'

'Yes they should. I am not at all sure my parishioners would approve of this.'

'Why ever not sir?'

'Well the deceased is clearly not from this parish.'

'But she is. She has lived no more than a mile from where

132

we stand for the last quarter of a century. Anyway, as you know sir, she was not the purchaser of the grave. The grave was purchased by the Baker family in the last century, as the deeds state, and it was the wish of the last Baker, Mr Peter Baker, that she be buried here sir.'

'Well I don't like it. I expect to be told in future.'

'Told if a black person is coming to your church?'

'I didn't say that.'

'Well then sir, what is it you wish to be told?'

'Don't be impertinent Mr Sloane.'

'I have no intention to be sir.'

'Good,' the Reverend Burke snapped as he grabbed the certificate and the fee envelope, turned on his heels and disappeared towards the rectory.

'What was that all about?' asked Winston Wylde as he approached and just caught the tail end of the conversation.

'Oh nothing,' said Stillion, who was ashamed of his fellow countryman's racism.

'You OK Stillion?' enquired Wylde. 'You look tired and worried.'

'I'm OK, but perhaps we could have a quick drink after work, I need to ask your advice about something?'

'Sure.'

The procession then made its way through the snow which hid much of the uneven and in part overgrown churchyard to where Arthur Kemp had positioned himself next to the open vault. Arthur had gone on ahead, as usual, to check where the grave, or in this case vault, was and that it had been opened correctly.

'That's funny,' thought Stillion. 'Where's Horace Picton?'

Horace Picton was the local gravedigger who dug new graves or opened old ones for all the churches around North Birmingham and the Black Country. Stillion had noticed his van in the lane outside the church but now there was no sign of him.

The six West Indian bearers had struggled manfully across the rugged terrain behind Winston Wylde and Stillion Sloane. Now the Reverend and the funeral director stood to one side to allow them to have direct access to the vault. But where was Horace Picton? He should be there to take one end of the casket while Arthur Kemp took the other. Stillion looked around again. He was not there. The bearers came to rest in front of the hole in the side of the vault. Stillion would have to act. He placed his top hat on his head in order to give himself two free hands and moved towards the top end of the casket. He was stopped in his tracks as the following mourners gasped, one or two screamed, the bearers' legs seemed to turn to jelly and nearly all present crossed themselves. Arthur Kemp had taken the head end of the casket in his hands. The foot end, which always leads, was almost over the vault's open entrance and was now being clasped by two dirty hands at the end of muddied forearms that had suddenly appeared out of the black from within the vault. Time stood still for a second or two as Winston's congregation, intoxicated by the occasion, believed that Peter Baker had woken to greet Jessie Nicholls.

The shock, reverend respect and holy fear were heightened as a voice which apparently belonged to the hands said in a stage whisper, 'All right, pass it to moy gently.' Then a head appeared out of the black. Stillion instantly recognised its owner. Horace Picton had been waiting inside the vault. Stillion continued forward and assisted the trembling bearers to pass the casket to Horace. It, with poor Arthur Kemp nearly bent double as he clung onto the head end, then disappeared inside the vault. At the end of the committal service Horace emerged and climbed out of the vault. Most had worked out what had been happening but some hadn't and they stopped singing the farewell hymn and watched him mix cement a few feet away for the closing of the vault, convinced that he was the real Peter Baker.

The passing of Jessie Nicholls had crossed the great black and white divide, as had her life, and both had brought out the best in some people as they had the worst in others. However her legacy was to prove to be vital for the salvation of many – one of whom was to be a surprise beneficiary within the week.

*

After the joy of reading the *Birmingham Post* article in the morning and the pleasure of being allowed to join in the plotting of the Frank C. Williams acquisition, Sydney had spent a long, cold and uneventful day conducting funerals, but anticipation kept him warm.

Fred Gilbert and Charlie Williams hadn't noticed the cold. They had spent a long time enjoying the gastronomic delights of the exclusive Midland Twenty One Club, which they washed down with two bottles of excellent claret. Most of this had been drunk by Fred as the timid Charlie hardly ever drank, and when forced to, such as today, he made a little go a long way. On the other hand the pious and somewhat hypocritical Fred enjoyed his drink and was only too happy to keep the lion's share for himself, especially as he was paying the bill.

The more Fred drank the cosier the room appeared to become to him and the more chummy he became in his efforts to close a deal with Charlie. The more Fred drank the less inclined Charlie was to do a deal and the more inclined he became to keep all channels open, at least until the weekend as his solicitor had suggested. Thus Fred became more persistent and Charlie, although polite, more distant. Their meeting concluded at four-thirty p.m., much to the relief of the waiter who had been assigned to remain behind and look after them.

Elton Field, other than one bearing job, had spent his day embalming his stiffs. Like Sydney he was excited by the prospects of success, but unlike Sydney, who did not have to bother about such things, he was worried about executing his part of the plan – the actual robbing of his grandma's grave. Oh, he didn't mind the robbing bit but he didn't fancy groping around inside the coffin of a woman who had been dead for nearly four years in the middle of the night and with just that unreliable Jimmy for a companion. He put such thoughts behind him as he turned the pages of *Sporting Life* with a mug of piping hot, sweet tea to hand.

Bill Woodall, when he had finished shaving and dressing, made sure the pack of press dogs had gone before leaving home. Then he headed by bus into town and made straight for the offices of the drug squad. Once there he demanded to see Inspector Hooper. He was told Hooper was busy. He said he would wait. He was told Hooper wouldn't be able to see him for an hour. He repeated he would wait. Eventually after an hour and a half Woodall's will won out and Hooper, realising that Woodall would not just go away, presented himself in the reception.

'About bloody time too,' said Bill without so much as a 'Good day'.

'I'm sorry to keep yow waiting Mr Woodall but I'm a busy man yow know sir,' responded the inspector.

'Doing what is what I'd like to know. Thanks to yow allowing that story to go into the *Post* I've had the bloody world and his wife round at moy place. It's not right. I'm an old man. I fought for this country yow know. Gave six years of moy life and this is all the thanks I get.'

'Mr Woodall I can assure you I did not give yowa story to the *Birmingham Post*. I am very sorry the press and others have been bothering yow but I can't stop them. What's more the allegation is serious and must be looked into. Any road all should be plain in a day or two. I've applied for the exhumation order and asked for it to be issued urgently.'

'Yow've done what? How dare yow, she was moy missis not yowa's.'

'I'm aware of that Mr Woodall but the serious nature of this case – involving illegal drugs and murder as it may – overrules that. I'm sorry.'

'No yow ain't. Just want yowa bloody mush in the press I bet. Let 'er be is what I say. Let 'er be. Good day to yow. I've been wasting moy time comin' 'ere I can see.' And with that Bill Woodall pulled his flat cap down on his head, stuffed his hands into his old mac's pockets, and left.

Hooper watched him go with little sympathy. He was an old man for sure but he was also a cantankerous old git and it was much better that he be upset than the explosive Harry Wilkes.

Harry Wilkes' day had been business as usual. He sat behind his big desk and rubbed his hands with glee as he surveyed the

136

returns from gambling, protection and narcotics. He should have gone into these fields years ago, he told himself almost daily now. It wasn't that scrap metal and second-hand cars were doing badly, and they did give him a legitimate front, if not a respectable one, after all. But the muscle needed for those two businesses lent themselves so very well to his three newer divisions which in turn produced much higher profit margins as they involved little extra capital outlay. His next big target was to break into gaming and nightclubs. He had nearly amassed enough cash. He already had enough muscle.

As for his thoughts about the Betty Woodall business, he was pleased with Alf on the whole. It would be neat to get his two grand back with a thumping bonus of an extra nine. But his real excitement was the pain and embarrassment that public schoolboy twit Stillion Sloane must be feeling. Harry had chuckled as he read the *Birmingham Post*. He knew this would be only the tip of the iceberg for Sloane and that much worse was bound to follow over the next few days.

Sloane's possession of a baseball bat with his blood on it and Harry's fingerprints, a relic of the 1979 funeral wars, insured Sloane's safety for now, and therefore until that could be recovered Harry would have to enjoy revenge by this kind of second-hand route.

Life had never been better. Harry's wife Lottie was back under his thumb. The kids didn't cause him too many problems. His staff, his clientele and even certain police officers feared him. His business was expanding and becoming more successful by the day. Yes, life had never been better but it could never be perfect until Stillion Sloane was disfigured, ruined or better still dead. He simply could not live happily with the knowledge that Stillion had had his wife, and worse, for whatever Lottie might say to the contrary, his wife had wanted it.

In a funny sort of way this Betty Woodall business had opened old wounds and brought Lottie's affair with Stillion back to the front of his mind. But then he could have a drink tonight safe in the knowledge that Sloane would be worried to death about all the bad publicity.

137

People might not admire Harry or his business, and they might only do business with him out of fear. He was aware of that. He was no fool, but at least his business only relied on fear, and scandal usually increased that fear and therefore helped his business. On the other hand a toffy-nosed, upper-class, public school glamour boy like Sloane would be crippled by scandal and thus had a long way to fall – and may he fall long and hard over the next few days. Harry could drink to that and bank the eleven grand at the same time.

Joyce spent her day plotting and packing. Gillian spent hers at work nursing a sore head. For Alf, Frankie and the boys it was business as usual. Jimmy concentrated on the pimping side of his business as he could not buy for the pushing side until he had repaid his debt to the Wilkes, and he dare not buy from any other source in case they found out. Stephanie had spent her day at home trying to get things done but really she was just waiting, with bag packed, for the big event.

And what of John Palin and Victoria Thomas? Well they had enjoyed a very busy but perfectly normal morning until the rat pack of squeaking pressmen along with their flash-bulb popping sidekicks arrived *en masse* at Sloane House.

They had originally burst into the reception firing questions and flash bulbs as they went only to be driven back onto the forecourt by the strong minded Victoria Thomas who had informed them that they had entered a funeral home and that meant that the place was full of deceased people and their grieving relatives and that they must be shown some respect. Initially this had not impressed the hard bitten riff-raff that makes up the majority of the British press core. However she then cleverly gave them a choice.

'Mr Stillion Sloane is the only one who can speak to you and he is currently out conducting a funeral. He will speak to those who leave this reception now, on his return. I promise he will not speak to those who remain, mainly because they will be removed by the police.'

They all trooped outside. Some regrouped in their cars, which were parked in Holyhead Road and Booth Street, while others stamped their feet in an attempt to keep warm on the forecourt, which had largely been cleared of snow by Jones the caretaker.

Victoria, having repelled the boarders from the reception, returned upstairs and asked John Palin if she should call Stillion at once.

'No, just keep your eye on them and warn Mr Stillion when he's on his way back from the Nicholls funeral. There's no point telling him now. There's nothing he can do until he's finished that funeral and he could do without the distraction,' said John wisely.

Victoria duly waited until she was confident that the Nicholls committal was over before calling Stillion on the radio telephone. Her message was short and discreet, because Sloane & Sons shared a channel with several other commercial operations.

Stillion was not that surprised by the news. He had been expecting it. However, he had equally been dreading it. A gaggle, a posse, a rat pack, a whatever of press outside a funeral home was a bad sign. He had survived the 1979 funeral wars without commercial damage because there had been no press involvement. Now there would be big time. A story that involved murder, drugs and graveyards was bound to be irresistible to the press, and if a funeral director could be shown to be at the centre of it then all the better.

No sooner had the limousines pulled onto the forecourt and the young man in his top hat and tails stepped from the lead car than he was surrounded by spotty men in anoraks, some with note pads and some with cameras. Worse, they were joined by more smartly dressed men in overcoats who were accompanied by film crews.

Stillion knew this was an important moment and that he must rise to the occasion. Questions quickly rained down on him just as they had on old Bill Woodall earlier that day. Stillion ignored them and raised his hands for silence.

'I will only say the following at this time. We conducted Mrs Elizabeth Woodall's funeral in April 1978. There is an article in

139

this morning's *Birmingham Post* which refers to this funeral and in particular the fact that a large quanity of cocaine and perhaps even the gun that killed someone could be buried with her. No one currently working for the firm or to the best of our knowledge anyone who isn't any longer with us knows anything about this. No one known to us put anything into the coffin while it was lying in the chapel of rest or thereafter. There was at no time any discernible change in the weight of the coffin. It was sealed in the chapel before going home where it remained in the hearse. I understand Inspector Hooper of the Birmingham drug squad is considering applying for an exhumation order. This is his right, and provided that it is granted we will all know soon enough what, if anything, other than the deceased, is in that coffin. I suggest we wait until then. I am prepared to be quoted on what I have just said and nothing else. Thank you gentlemen.' With this Stillion turned on his heels and ignored the barrage of questions and flash bulbs that demanded his attention. He went inside and the rat pack dispersed to marry up pictures and copy in the most gruesome way.

Stillion had done very well and yet he knew that it would not prevent a rash of tasteless stories in tomorrow's papers, no doubt attached to even more tasteless photographs which would sit beneath even worse headlines.

Hopefully the inspector would get on and obtain an exhumation order. This was the only way to kill the story – that is, if there was nothing in the coffin that shouldn't be there. Stillion had to play the innocent because he was innocent. On the other hand he was very nervous because Elton Field had been an employee at the time of the funeral. He had also been a relative of the deceased and now had apparently been telling the police that an old, conveniently deceased, caretaker had seen Stillion put black bags into the coffin the night before the funeral. Elton was trouble and something told Stillion that there was a lot more to this story than some pusher who had decided to squeal to the police. He was sure Elton was probably into it

140

up to his neck. How and why, Stillion had no idea and no easy way of finding out.

Stillion phoned James Steele, who hadn't heard from Charlie Williams' solicitors. Stillion, given the events of the day, wasn't surprised. He brushed the Frank C. Williams acquisition to one side and asked James to advise him on the laws of slander and libel once he had told him the Elizabeth Woodall story. James' answers didn't please Stillion. Not only would he have to prove inaccuracy but also establish what damage had been suffered by either Stillion himself or his business. Moreover any retraction won was bound to be small and on page fifteen of any given paper, and not given the same prominence as the original offending piece. In addition, any legal action would inevitably be lengthy, could cost hundreds of thousands of pounds and libel trials by jury were a complete lottery.

Stillion slammed the phone down at the end of this conversation, a very frustrated man. He and his business were being accused of something which he knew didn't happen but he was powerless to defend either himself or his company against the innuendo until an exhumation took place, if indeed one did, and if it did and there were drugs and a gun inside the coffin then all fingers pointed at him even though he knew he hadn't done anything wrong.

This was a nightmare yes, but a fluke no. He swung back and round in his big executive chair, faced the electric fire and thought. Then the pieces of the jigsaw started to fall into place. Charlie Williams had been happy to sell to him. Stillion had given Charlie no reason to change his mind. Charlie had suddenly dropped out of Stillion's world just 24 hours before this Elizabeth Woodall story broke. There must be a good chance that Charlie had been tipped off. But by whom? Well, Fred Gilbert wanted Charlie's business almost as much as Stillion but wasn't prepared to pay for it. And Elton Field worked for Fred Gilbert, as did Sydney Gridley who hated Stillion. Then there was the drugs and protection element to the story, and protection and drugs were run by Harry Wilkes who hated

Stillion almost as much as Sydney Gridley. Here Stillion's thesis came unstuck. Harry Wilkes may hate Stillion, he may even have agreed on some joint action with Sydney. It was Sydney after all who had tipped off Harry about Stillion and Lottie Wilkes. But why would Harry promote a story that pointed a finger at him regarding both the drugs, as the stronger Birmingham drug business, and murder, because the Rider murder was likely to be down either to the Vance gang killing one of their own or the Wilkes' gang doing it over some gangland dispute? Stillion was still trying to work through this when John Palin came in.

The day's funeral bookings were heavy. Stillion expected them to be. It was January, the weather was atrocious and there was an Asian flu epidemic running. Whether all the other funeral directors would still be busy booking funerals by Friday while Sloanes went quiet was another story, and the end of that tale hung in the lap of the gods, who were editors of newspapers in this case.

John and Stillion maintained discipline. They went through the new bookings, the day book and tonight's viewing list, before going through tomorrow's garage orders with Arthur Kemp. They spent several minutes discussing the four children's funeral which would take place tomorrow thanks to an early release by the coroner which was only made possible by the fact that they were to be buried as opposed to cremated.

When they had finished and Arthur had left, Stillion turned on the television in his office so that he and John could catch the national and local news on both the BBC and the independent channel. As they ran at the same time this could only be achieved by constantly switching from one channel to the other and back again.

To their relief the story didn't make either of the national newscasts which were much more interested in Mrs Thatcher's latest tussle with the trade unions. Unfortunately and inevitably such joy was short lived as both stations' local news ran the story and showed Sloane House. The BBC even showed Stillion's statement, which came over well, but perhaps not well enough

142

given the narration of the story by the reporter which alluded to all the gory details.

Stillion had known since first thing that morning when he had read the *Birmingham Post* story that this time might come. The time when he would have to watch his business, his creation, his baby being dismantled, damaged and even raped before him on television. He had tried all day not only to concentrate on the funerals to hand but also to steel himself for this moment. But nothing could prepare him for this. He felt pain. He felt sick. He felt numb. He was in a state of shock.

When he had got up that morning he had been concerned about Stephanie having the baby, about finding out why Charlie Williams wasn't returning his calls and what could be done to stop Joyce Higgins blackmailing him into bed. All of these things were urgent and important to him but as soon as he had read the article in the *Birmingham Post* he knew he was in for a serious fight which could destroy his business.

He tried to hide his hurt from John and keep morale up. He said goodnight to Victoria in her office. She told him not to worry. He smiled tiredly. Then Stephanie phoned to tell him that she had seen the local BBC news, as had both their mothers who had phoned her immediately. Stillion told her not to get upset and not to answer the phone to anyone who didn't ring three times first, then ring off and ring again. He told her to phone their mothers and others and tell them to use that technique. He said she mustn't worry about this, it was just a storm in a teacup and that the baby was the important thing now. He said he had to see Winston Wylde for a few minutes and would be home within the hour. He said he loved her. She said she was proud of him. He went downstairs and checked the chapels with Keith Jones and left to keep the appointment he had made with Wylde.

'You only realise how many people watch the local news when you're on it,' thought Stillion as he became conscious of the eyes in the bar following his progress through it to join Winston.

They had agreed to meet in the King's Head, a pub situated in Lozells Road where it met Villa Road. Winston didn't drink much. In fact Stillion had only seen him have the odd glass of wine with a meal. But Winston liked to visit the pubs. That way he could keep an eye on his flock. He went to several in his parish at different times each week. He drank orange juice, found out what was going on and perhaps just by his mere presence stopped problems before they had a chance to start. Certainly his less dedicated members found it harder to get drunk, fight and buy drugs while he was around, and by going to every pub but in no strict order he was doing his bit to prevent a rotten apple pub from developing. The nearest thing to a rotten apple pub was this one. It was frequented by the jobless, the thieves, pushers, pimps and prostitutes. There were small groupings of Asians, English and Irish but the majority were West Indian. Most of them had chosen a different route through life to Winston. To them he was a nuisance because some of their clients feared him and thus his presence slowed down business. Winston was a good man and he fully intended to save the souls of these men as well as their foolish clients.

'I saw the local news before coming out,' he said in a matter of fact sort of way.

'Did you?' replied Stillion in a flat voice. 'It seems to me the whole of Birmingham did.'

'Is that what you wanted to talk about?

'Yes it is. I need your help. We never put anything inside that coffin. You must know that.'

'Of course I do.'

'But it's crazy. I don't think anything will be found in the coffin because there was no opportunity for anyone to put anything in it, and in the unlikely event they did, then what has been described would weigh at least two stone. We would have noticed that when bearing to the graveside.

'Sure.'

'But Winston, it just doesn't make sense. If there's nothing in it then why did this apparent drug pushing informer say there was? He's got nothing to gain. And then there's Elton Field.'

144

'The bloke who used to work for you?'

'Yeah. Elizabeth Woodall was his grandmother. He worked for us at that time, and the editor of the *Birmingham Post* told me that Elton has told the police that he had been told by the old caretaker George Brown that he had seen me putting large black bags into the coffin once the family had finished viewing.'

'Well, ask George Brown.'

'I can't. He's dead. Elton, like Sydney Gridley, works for Fred Gilbert. All three don't like me and Gilbert wants to buy a business I'm after. On the other hand, what would be their gain when nothing is found in the coffin, and to create a story which points the finger at the Wilkes family as much as it does the Sloanes could be a dangerous game, unless the Wilkes are in on it. But why would they be? What would they have to gain?'

'Nothing. And what's more I can't imagine the likes of Fred Gilbert and Sydney Gridley associating with the likes of the Wilkes, even if they both hate you.'

Stillion knew why they could and why Sydney had, but he wouldn't mention that to Winston.

As they struggled to unravel the plot against Stillion, if indeed there was one, they were unaware that they were being observed from the other side of the room by a girl. She knew all about the Reverend Wylde. He had taught her pimp and sometime boyfriend at Sunday School. Jimmy had often talked about him and indeed she had seen the handsome West Indian preacher in this and other pubs on many occasions. But it wasn't him that took her attention.

Terri had met Stillion Sloane when he had conducted her grandmother's funeral. She had thought him to be tall, blond and very good looking. That was nearly four years ago and she had been but fifteen. Now she was nearly nineteen, a woman of the world or of the underworld to be more precise, and her experience made her appreciate his clean charm and obvious wealth which stood out in this room packed with the city's dregs.

The more she looked at him the more she knew who he was. He was the man who came to her in her head as she admired her own body and brought herself sexual satisfaction in front of

145

the mirror in the mornings. He was the man from Edgbaston. Yes, he was the man who was to be her father, husband and lover. Of course it was clear now, at last she could see the face of the man from Edgbaston. She wanted him for security, for money, for love, for sex and for the fairy tale she had never had. She must have him and therefore she must do whatever was necessary, even if it meant betraying Jimmy and her brother to get him. And what of the Wilkes? The danger? There could be no danger with a man like that and a life in Edgbaston. The Wilkes didn't terrorize people there. She would be safe and away from this terrible life. And what of her new love's wife? She didn't give her a thought. Why should she? She had a goal. Now she must make a plan and take it slowly. She knew she mustn't rush her fences.

She wandered over to where they were sitting. She coughed quietly to break their concentration. Both men looked up. She smiled.

'Good evening Reverend Wylde.'

Winston knew the face. He had seen her in many of the pubs he visited. 'Good evening,' he responded. He could not use her name as he didn't know it.

'Good evening Mr Sloane.'

Stillion had no idea who Terri was. He conducted hundreds of funerals a year and had only met her the once, four years ago when she looked very different. 'Good evening,' he replied as politely as he possibly could given the events of the day. Yet he might have tried that bit harder if he had known what a little mine of information was standing next to him and bidding him 'hello' in such a friendly way.

'I'm Terri Field. You know, the granddaughter of Betty Woodall. Elton Field is moy brother.' Stillion must have looked a little shocked because she immediately continued, 'I just came across to say I saw the news tonight and want you to know that granddad and moy know you would never get involved with drugs and guns.'

'Thank you,' said Stillion before asking, 'And Elton?'

146

'Well yow'd 'ave to ask 'im yourself but I expect so,' she replied softly.

'I will. I'll phone him at work tomorrow. Anyway, thank you for what you said and you're quite right – we put nothing in your grandmother's coffin and I don't believe anybody else did either.'

Terri didn't like the suggestion that there might be nothing in the coffin. After all she was desperate to see an exhumation order issued. She could only abandon that plan once she had captured her prince and at the moment that was but a mere dream that she was drawn to.

'Oh I think yow'll find the police is convinced there is stuff in there all right. It's just that granddad and moy know yow is a gent and wouldn't be involved.'

'We'll see, and the sooner the better for all our sakes. I must be off. I promised Stephanie I'd be home. Very nice to meet you Miss Field and keep your ear open for me, Winston.'

'Sure. Give my love to Stephanie now,' replied Winston.

'Please call me Terri. Would yow mind escorting moy a little way down the road? It's just very rough round these parts and moy boyfriend ain't 'ere yow see.' They left Winston to finish his orange juice.

Once outside Stillion walked Terri to his car which was parked in the safest place available – the main Lozells Road under a street lamp.

'Can I drop you off at home?' he enquired.

She wasn't going home and certainly never wanted him to see the dump she lived in and the style that went with it.

'Oh no. Could you drop me off at moy granddad's? 'E's very old and today 'as been a terrible strain you know. I often stay with 'im. 'E gets very lonely you know and 'e likes moy to stay.' She wiggled her bottom into the luxury of the Jaguar seat. She had never been in a car like this before. She liked it a lot. She intended this to be the first of many times.

As he pulled away into the traffic she looked at him. He was gorgeous. His car was gorgeous. His world was gorgeous and all

147

she had ever dreamed about and she was so busy noticing him she never noticed Elton walking down the Lozells Road noticing her in Stillion's car.

Within moments they were outside the old man Woodall's house. Stillion stopped and despite his total preoccupation he got out and opened the door for Terri. She knew she had to get out and back into her world of the dimly-lit, cold terraced street. How she wanted to stay in that car for a life ticket to Edgbaston.

She got out. She had left her old anorak open, hoping that he would notice her pert braless breasts through the cheese-cloth blouse that was worn within. Her bra was in her pocket. She had been to the ladies in the pub and removed it before approaching his table.

He didn't notice. It was dark and sex with anyone, let alone her, was not on his mind right now. However, he did notice as she stepped from the car her white sneakers and blue jeans. He liked that. Very studenty. He never for one moment suspected she was a whore. He knew nothing about her and she didn't dress like one.

She pressed a piece of paper into his hand as she thanked him for giving her a lift. 'Naturally I'll contact yow if I hear anything. This is moy home number. Please contact moy if yow find out anything or if yow think I could do anything for yow. Anything.'

Then to his complete surprise she kissed him on the cheek and without a further word turned towards her grandfather's door. Stillion got back into his car and she heard it pull away. She remained looking at the door until she was sure he had gone. She had no intention of seeing that mean old git she called granddad, and she started back up the street once the car had disappeared out of sight.

She was quite surprised to meet Elton coming down as she walked up.

'I saw yow bitch. I saw yow,' he whispered with venom.

'What?'

'I saw yow with Mr Stillion. I ran down the street as I saw yow

148

turn into it in 'is car. What the fuck were yow doing with 'im? If yow done anything to put moy in the shit with the Wilkes or the pigs after I thought this up to 'elp yow, I'll fucking swing for yow. I swear I will.'

'Calm down. What yow take moy for? 'E were having' a drink with the Wylde preacher and I thought I'd see what was in 'is 'ead now the news is out.'

'And?'

'And 'e's dead worried. Tries not to show it but 'e's sick. 'E's really 'urtin' and 'e reckons that there will be an order but nothin' will be found.'

'Course nothin' will be found yow stupid cow.'

'I know, but he reckons there'll be an exy-whatever any road.'

'Is that all? I mean how come yow was in his car and coming 'ere and then yow don't go in to see granddad?'

''Cos 'e offered moy a lift 'ome and I didn't want 'im knowing moy address so I got 'im to bring moy 'ere instead, OK Sherlock?' she said sarcastically.

They were standing outside the fire-damaged house and Terri drew Elton's attention to that as a way of changing the subject.

Harry, Alf and Frankie enjoyed the local news. Harry was happy to see Stillion at the centre of so much controversy. Alf was happy that his plan appeared to be working. Frankie was happy because the other two were.

Jimmy took the local news to be another step towards his safety while it had given Sydney his happiest moment since his dethronement. God, revenge felt great.

Inspector Hooper enjoyed it too. He still felt that there was something he hadn't understood. He didn't know what and he didn't know why, but what the hell? His superiors seemed to think he was doing a good job and he was doing what they and Harry wanted. For once serving two masters wasn't that difficult as they both wanted the same thing: a high-profile exhumation.

Harry hadn't spelled out why for the first time in his life he had wanted the police to do their job properly but Hooper suspected that the drugs and murder weapon inside the coffin would point the finger at the Vance gang and thus allow the police to round up Harry's main competition, leaving the city to be run by Wilkes.

Naturally all Stillion's staff, friends and family hadn't enjoyed the coverage and to most of them it had come as a complete surprise. A bolt out of the blue. Sloane & Sons had been established in 1850 and since then the firm had never been hit by such a scandal. They all knew that no one at the company would ever get caught up in drug dealing or concealing a murder weapon. There was no question of that but scandal was scandal and thus could wreck the good name of Sloane unless it was sorted out, and quickly.

Obviously Stillion's competitors were delighted if somewhat surprised by the news. The *Birmingham Post* article had got the old grapevine going in the morning but now the telephone lines were red hot as they phoned each other with the news. No one was more pleased than Fred Gilbert. The one exception was Charlie Williams. He felt genuinely sorry for Stillion and the lunch with Fred Gilbert had done little to further Fred's case. Stillion's offer was still the best on the table. Charlie decided to bide his time. In a few days all would become clear. He was in no hurry. He only had one bite at the cherry and therefore he shouldn't make any hasty decisions.

Old Bill Woodall had caught the news, and himself on it. He wasn't at all happy. Why couldn't they leave her in peace?

Stillion was home within minutes of dropping off Terri. He tried to put a brave face on the events. Stephanie knew it was most serious and that he was worried to death about it. She admired his thoughtful courage.

The Birmingham *Evening Mail* had run the story on its front page and unlike its morning sister, the *Post*, it had named Sloanes and hinted at Stillion's personal involvement. Stillion could hardly bear to read the story but he did and tried to hide both his anger and his fear.

150

At about nine-thirty the phone rang. Stillion answered. It was Stillion's mother, Mary Sloane.

'Hello Stillion. I thought I had better give you a ring to let you know I've had a letter from your brother. His ship docks at Portsmouth next Monday. I thought we could all have dinner next Tuesday. Of course Stephanie may well be in hospital by then.'

'Yes, that would be great. Next Tuesday, your place at eight, with or without Stephanie,' he repeated, and the conversation finished. Neither mentioned the Woodall funeral, the *Birmingham Post* article or the local television news. His mother's call was made to show support of her son. Stillion understood that. It was the contact that was important. My goodness, the Sloanes were a well trained, upper middle class British Empire family.

4

Neither Stillion nor Stephanie slept well. For hours both lay in bed quietly fearful of disturbing the other. Eventually they had realised that each was awake and had talked.

An exhumation order must prove Sloanes' innocence unless somehow Elton had put something in the coffin. Only time would tell and in the meantime they must keep their heads and their dignity and look forward to the birth of their baby.

At five-thirty Stillion gave up on the idea of sleep and decided to get up, shower, dress for work and go into the office via New Street Station in the centre of Birmingham, where he knew he could find all the national and local newspapers on sale.

It was yet another cold and icy morning. The sub-zero temperatures of the night ensured that the city remained enveloped in snow and driving conditions were, as ever, treacherous on the side roads where the corporation gritting lorries did not venture.

At six-forty he walked through the station entrance and left minutes later, laden down with newsprint, having bought an edition of each newspaper on sale. He returned to the warmth of his car and started the engine. But he did not drive away. The temptation to look for headlines was too great so he turned on the interior light and started to sift through them.

First he just looked at the front pages. Only the *Birmingham Post* had the article on the front page. It was basically a re-run of the previous night's *Evening Mail*. Then he hunted through the insides of the others. All but the *Guardian* had run the story

152

in some form or another. By and large the broadsheets had given little space to the story and most just recorded the facts as known, without speculation or comment. Not so the tabloids. The *Sun*, the *Mirror* and the *Star* all gave at least a page and all carried photographs of Stillion, Sloane House, Bill Woodall, the dead Rider and in the case of the *Sun*, Inspector Hooper as well.

All of these articles speculated how the drugs and gun came to be in Mrs Elizabeth Woodall's coffin and all alleged that it had been achieved with the compliance of the funeral directors. They did in part report Stillion's denial but it was really too little too late.

Stillion felt sick. A bit of him wanted to slam the car into gear and make for the nearest port. How could he face the clients? What must they think of him? But Stillion was made of better stuff than that and he slammed into gear and headed for work. He was not going to expect his staff to face this without him being there with them and setting an example.

He pulled into Sloane House by seven-thirty and parked the Jag at the rear. To his surprise Arthur, Walter and most of the drivers were already in the garage, taking off the dust-sheets and dusting the hearses and limousines. They were very early. He bid them good morning.

'Morning boss,' they replied in unison. Stillion went up to his office. The administration girls, Graham Stone, John Palin and Victoria Thomas were all there, and like the lads in the garage they were an hour early.

They were demonstrating their support for the company and its owner. They were not going to let Stillion down and nor was he going to let them down. They would conduct the day's business together with pride.

'We've had three removals in overnight and a further first call instruction. So not everybody hates us,' said Palin.

'Good man, John,' smiled Stillion as he made for his office in order to change for the first funeral of the day. This funeral would also attract much attention, and however sorry Stillion felt for himself he knew that his pain was nothing compared to

153

the pain, guilt and despair that the mother of those four children must be feeling.

Once he was ready he picked up the telephone and dialled Frank C. Williams. He announced who he was and asked the receptionist to give a message to Charlie Williams.

'Please inform him that the reports in the newspapers are wrong and that Sloanes would never be involved in anything like that. Furthermore please tell him that this will become apparent once an exhumation has taken place. Tell him I will not trouble him further until Sloanes' good name is cleared but that I would be grateful if he would give a few days' grace.' He daren't say more as he was not aware whom Charlie had told of his plan to sell the business.

Then Victoria called him and announced Gillian Weston was on the phone. He told her to put the call through.

'Hi Stillion, it's me Gillian. I just wanted to phone to say I know you're not involved with drugs and cover-ups and that I'm feeling for you right now. Moreover, I'm sorry about the other night – I was drunk. It was wrong, especially as your wife is expecting. I'm truly sorry. Forgive me.'

'You're forgiven,' he replied with equal sincerity.

'Old Soldiers' Park will continue to recommend Sloanes. Now, you keep your head up, and don't worry, it'll turn out all right. You'll see. In a week, you'll be a father and this matter will be over.'

'I hope so,' said Stillion, and then bade her goodbye.

As he went to go downstairs to check the four little coffins, two each to a hearse, one in front of the other, Victoria stopped him.

'Stillion, the phone's been ringing again and again – old clients sending their best wishes and saying they know Sloanes would never get involved in drugs. I must have taken at least five calls already. It's going to be OK.'

'Of course it is,' he replied. Then said softly, 'Thanks Vic Vesta.'

Stillion went downsatirs, through the hall and reception and out into the cold. There before him on the forecourt was the cortège. Two hearses, two limousines and four liveried chauffeurs. The vehicles sparkled, their black bodies making a sharp contrast to the snow which lay around them. The chauffeurs took up their positions as Stillion went to the rear of the first hearse. There, Arthur Kemp read out the breastplate details of the two eldest children, checking the same against his garage orders as he did so. Stillion also checked the same against his funeral envelope and the labels on each coffin's back-right handle as he removed them.

Stillion then moved to the second hearse and repeated the exercise. Walter Warburton had moved up from the lead limousine driver to drive the second hearse. 'Ironic ain't it? On the very day that the whole country is being told what a bunch of bad guys we are, our first funeral is being given away. All of this supplied free of charge. Why ain't that in the newspapers?' asked Walter.

The cortège pulled off the forecourt and headed down the Soho Road towards Lozells. The funeral was to leave from the grandparent's home in the next road to the children's house which had been too badly damaged by the fire to be considered.

The cortège approached the house from the Hockley end of the road so that it was facing the right way for Handsworth Cemetery. Sloanes had offered, as Stillion had instructed, to conduct the funeral free of charge. Reverend Freddie Price had offered to take the service without charge. The corporation cemetery had charged the full amount for a new private grave for four internments.

The family, well the mother's dad actually, had accepted the kind offers of Stillion Sloane and Freddie Price, found the money for the cemetery, which he had paid to John Palin yesterday as arranged, and had decided to deal with the florists directly himself.

As the cortège pulled up the hill towards the house, which was approximately halfway up on the right-hand side, the limousines slowed and the hearses were called through. The road was packed with people. More than a thousand of them lined

155

both pavements several deep and spilled off into the road so much that Stillion worried whether the hearses would have enough room to pass by the limos. The crowd parted silently so that the vehicles could get through and then crowded in behind them as they came to rest at the house so that the muster now completely blocked the road.

It was a bitterly cold morning and only just light. The crowd wore black and their faces seemed grey. They remained silent. Stillion introduced himself to the children's grandfather who would be dealing with Stillion as his daughter was in no state to.

Together they arranged the family flowers for the four little coffins. Stillion then pointed the same out to Arthur and Walter who dealt with them while the two limousine drivers took the numerous other floral tributes to the hearses. Their wreaths were placed inside and cut flowers wired on top.

Stillion and the grandfather arranged the seating in the two limousines before going inside so that Stillion could explain the procedure to the other family members. Once all the flowers were arranged the chauffeurs returned to their vehicles.

After five minutes or so Stillion reappeared at the front door of the old terraced house, which opened directly onto the pavement, and nodded. This was the sign for Arthur and Walter to move their hearses at least two car lengths up and over to the left. Then, as the front limo pulled into place, Arthur walked back and opened the door just as Stillion led the family through the front door. Usual Sloane precision. A scene that could normally be watched several times a day then suddenly changed as the crowd erupted as it caught sight of the children's mother. Still became jostling as silence was replaced by a hail of insults. In a second the mourning gathering had become a mob. 'Look at 'er the slut!'

'Ang the bitch!'

'String 'er up!'

'Leave 'er to moy!'

'No, leave 'er to us!'

'Whore!'

'Burning is too good for 'er.'

156

'Sterilise 'er with a poker.'

These cruel taunts came mainly from middle-aged mothers who had sacrificed most of their lives to bring up their children and couldn't forgive a girl who had had four children of various colours by different fathers, had never married, didn't work, got most of her money from the social and the rest from sleeping around while neglecting her kids, who were now dead – burned to death while she got drunk down the road in a pub with a man.

The older women nodded their approval and some of the young girls joined in. Most of the men said nothing but some booed. Then a man shouted out, 'She wanted a collection. Give 'er money lads!' And suddenly a hail of pennies rained down on the mother and her family. Stillion tried to protect the girl with both his top hat and his free hand. She was incapably drunk and didn't seem to notice this biblical stoning. But her parents did. It was not so much the physical pain that added to their grief but the pain of their neighbours' hatred and the shame of having parented such a child. Their daughter was their daughter – they would not deny her but they had lived with these people all their lives and they knew if it had been another family they would have been out there in the crowd, members of this lynch mob.

Stillion got the six mourners in the first limousine seated in double quick time as the missiles continued to rain down on the limos and kicks and blows aimed at them tended to connect with either his back or Arthur's. He ordered the limo driver to lock the doors before returning to the house for the mourners for the second limousine. Meanwhile the first limousine pulled up the hill and over to the left so that it came to rest behind the second hearse as the second limo pulled into place in time for Stillion to reappear.

The lynch mob element of the gathering had pushed its way past the others and were now banging on the roof or bashing the windows of the first limo with their hands. A woman kept screaming out, 'Get 'er out of there! Strip 'er and shave 'er 'ead. Let 'er go to the cemetery like that.' She meant it, and

157

Stillion had no intention of hanging about to see if the crowd would obey her instructions. He cancelled the long walk out of the street, leapt into his front seat in the lead hearse and said, 'Arthur, let's get these vehicles out of this street while we still have any to get out!'

'Too fucking right Mr Stillion,' replied Arthur, and then responded with an acceleration that would have earned him a good bollocking from Stillion under normal circumstances.

Once they were clear of the street and the danger had diminished Arthur turned to Stillion. 'Yow know what boss?'

'What?'

'Those folks weren't too concerned about us or drugs was they?'

'No,' mused Stillion, who had now seen more in three days than most funeral directors do in a life time.

As the cortège had pulled away it had left behind two journalists. Both were from the *Post* and *Mail*. One, a junior, had been sent to cover the funeral, the other had been covering the buried drugs story and had been assigned to accompany the first when it was realised that it was a Sloane funeral.

They walked back to their car in order that they might follow to the cemetery. As they went among the dispersing crowd they heard several comments praising Sloanes, their professionalism, Mr Stillion's kindness, and more than one alluded to the fact that Sloanes had not charged for these four children, and several obviously mentioned that morning's press. Naturally some added cynical comments but the senior journalist, who was covering the potential Sloane involvement with the buried drugs, could not help but be surprised by how the makers of such comments were outnumbered by others who rushed to the firm's defence. He was surprised because he had been given a completely different picture when he had been briefed by his editor Johnnie Titmarsh.

Alan Bater was from the old school. He had always wanted to be a journalist and had joined the *Picture Post* from school when times were hard in the 1930s. He was a small and cultured man of good education, which had been improved at his own

158

hand in adult life. He had a smart, clipped voice rather like Sydney Gridley's, which he had developed over the years and which suited him better now that he was older. He liked golf and he liked a good story, like all journalists, but unlike his more ambitious younger colleagues, it had to have one compelling element – the truth.

As the two men began their journey to Handsworth Cemetery Alan Bater had an uneasy feeling in the back of his mind. He had witnessed an incredibly brave and professional performance from a man and his firm a few minutes ago that sat a lot easier with the comments of the mob than did his editor's brief.

He decided to tread carefully. Not only did he not wish to wrongly accuse Mr Sloane but he also had no desire to make himself or his newspaper look foolish if the story Johnnie Titmarsh had been told turned out to be rubbish. Perhaps his colleagues did take care not to write anything which could bring the newspaper into court, whereas he always took care not to write lies, even if they were legally safe. This story would be no exception.

The mob, having made its point, made no attempt to follow the cortège. They had had their say and now even that harlot deserved some peace to bury her dead. But not all in the crowd were mob and therefore about thirty followed the cortège in their own cars to the cemetery.

Reverend Freddie Price took the service in his usual quiet way. He read from the service book in the splendid gothic chapel and made no attempt to give an address and thus have to explain away these deaths as either being the work of God or the carelessness of an unloving mother.

Eventually matters proceeded to the graveside and the committal service. All four tiny coffins were lowered into the grave, one after the other in order of age.

The poor wrecked mother. She was drunk from alcohol given to her to get her through this awful public pain, for despite her selfishness she was a mother – or had been. A poor mother perhaps, but a mother whose pain, hurt and sense of loss were very real indeed. She might still be incapable of feeling shame but she did feel the pain and her parents and family also felt it for her, as perhaps would have the hardest heart in the mob if they had witnessed her fainted body held up at each elbow by her father and a brother as her knees buckled. She became silent.

Her screaming finished, the crying of the women and the sobbing of the men became audible as did the words of Freddie Price. 'Man that is born of woman hath but a short time to live. He groweth up and is cut down like a flower ...' It was now mid-morning but such was the combination of fog and gathering snowclouds that the time could have been easily mistaken for either dawn or twilight. If weather be a barometer of God's feelings, then these deaths had displeased him.

Through all of this, as he had been at the house, the cemetery chapel and would be on the return home, Stillion Sloane was there. Just quietly *there*. Never obtrusive but always on hand to steady, to advise and to help. And what's more the family saw kindness and not judgement in his eyes; nor did they notice distance, a distance one might expect to be caused by the distraction of this morning's press.

Alan Bater stood at the back of the gathering with his note book in his old mac pocket. He observed, pondered and resolved to meet Mr Sloane.

It was only to be expected. Harry, Alf, Frankie, the boys, Jimmy, Terri, Elton and most of all Sydney were delighted with the morning's press. As of course was anyone else with a vested interest in either the exhumation in question or the bringing down of Stillion Sloane.

Now the news had made the tabloid national press, and in the case of the *Sun* had appeared not too far from page three, the world knew the story, so even Mr Brian McGigan had read it and was able to say to his Essex colleagues, 'I fuckin' told you that boy was too big for his boots – well he's got his comeuppance now.' To be young, good-looking and professional didn't make you popular with your competitors in funeral directing.

160

But then nor did it in hairdressing, dentistry, stockbroking, sport or anything else. Such is human nature.

Bill Woodall remained very angry that his wife was to be 'bloody dug up' as he put it, and Mary Sloane continued to pretend that the press did not exist even though she had them camped outside her house, annoying her neighbours and either consistently ringing the front doorbell or attempting to get through on the phone. Luckily for Stephanie, she and Stillion had only just moved to their new home and the press didn't know the address yet.

Inspector Hooper was also delighted. Yesterday he was getting good local press, today it was good national press and there was a lot of it. Buoyed by his immediate celebrity status he decided to take matters further.

He was convinced that the drugs and gun were in the coffin. Why? Well not because of the tip-off or Elton Field's story, but because Harry Wilkes was convinced they were there. He must know more than he was letting on. Clearly the Wilkes gang had nothing to do with either the drugs or the gun or Harry wouldn't have been pushing him to get an exhumation order. Therefore, it was almost certain that the Vance gang had been behind the drugs, and the Rider murder, and for whatever reason Sloanes had helped them secure this ingenious hiding place.

However, Hooper had a problem. He could easily go from hero to ordinary cop, if not foot cop, if at the end of this he discovered the drugs and the gun but could make no arrests, bring no charges and thus get no convictions. And this would be the case if there were no fingerprints on the gun or the drug bags, or there was no other incriminating evidence inside the old girl's coffin. Problem? Yes, big problem. Hooper could do without that sort of problem if he was to grab this golden opportunity with both hands and perhaps turn Inspector Hooper into Chief Inspector Hooper.

Then Hooper hit on an idea, and he believed it was a good one. He telephoned the Home Office department and got confirmation that the emergency order was to be issued tomorrow, Friday, and that the exhumation could take place at first light on Saturday. Next he telephoned Sloane House and asked for Mr Stillion Sloane. He was told by Victoria Thomas that Mr Sloane was out conducting a funeral. Hooper asked her to get Sloane to return his call when he came in.

This she did, once Stillion had returned from taking home the collapsed, broken and reviled family from Lozells. There had been no mob waiting for the family's return, only Bill Woodall and he wanted to speak to Stillion rather than them. He had waited until Stillion had taken his leave and was thus departing the house before introducing himself and demanding to know if Stillion knew anything at all about the drugs. Naturally Stillion said he didn't and to his surprise Mr Woodall immediately accepted this without further comment. Obviously his daughter had been right when she had said that her father did not believe Stillion had anything to do with the matter. Then Woodall asked Stillion to prevent the exhumation from taking place. Stillion informed him that this was not within his remit and that Mr Woodall should speak to Inspector Hooper. Woodall explained that this was a waste of time and finished with, 'Let 'er be is what I say.'

Back in the office Stillion called Inspector Hooper. He was put through. 'Hello inspector. Stillion Sloane here. I'm returning your call.'

'Ah, Mr Sloane, many thanks for calling back. I know how busy you are. The reason for my call is to tell you that the exhumation order has been granted and it will take place at first light, nine a.m. to be precise, on Saturday morning. Unfortunately, due to the suspicious circumstances concerning this case and the fact that your firm were the funeral directors, I will not be asking yow to assist but will instruct another firm to provide their services.'

Although the cemetery staff would reopen the grave in the case of an exhumation it was necessary for funeral directors to provide a large outer coffin for the original to be placed in, for transportation to the city mortuary and eventual reburial.

'However,' continued Hooper, 'I am an open-minded and fair man.'

162

Stillion could not for a second take this self-assessment seriously and would have broken into a fit of the giggles if the moment was not so crucial and his position not so serious. Instead he replied, 'Of course you are inspector.'

'That I am, and therefore I have phoned to invite yow to attend and see for yourself the contents. Yow can attend the exhumation at Handsworth and then accompany moy to Newton Street for the opening of the coffin. But keep it to yourself. We don't want the press there do we?'

'That's very good of you. Subject to my wife not giving birth, then I'll see you at the grave at five to nine. Thank you.'

Stillion put the phone down, surprised. He was surprised because over the last twenty-four hours his dealings with Hooper had been both infuriating and frustrating. He hadn't liked Hooper one little bit. It had seemed to him that Hooper had a preconceived notion that Stillion was involved, and guilty. And what's more Hooper seemed to be enjoying Stillion's predicament. After all, Hooper was a Brummie boy made good who liked it when the high and mighty from school's like Harrow lost their way. Stillion had been so sure he had been right about Hooper. Indeed so right that he nearly burst out laughing only a few minutes ago at Hooper's assertion that he was 'an open-minded and fair man'. Now he was surprised by the inspector's thoughtfulness. He could not argue against that. Perhaps he had got the inspector wrong.

Hooper put the phone down, pleased. He said to himself, 'Got yow Mr Sloane. Got yow and hopefully your chums in the Vance gang.' The inspector's act of kindness had been born out of his idea. Now Sloane knew there was to be an exhumation and he also knew when it was to be. No doubt that meant Paul Vance, head of the Vance gang, would also know shortly. All Hooper had to do was to put the grave under surveillance and hopefully one or both would do something incriminating by trying to recover the evidence before Saturday morning. The inspector rubbed his hands together gleefully.

*

163

For Sydney Gridley today, Thursday, was the highlight of the week. Naturally for Jimmy and Elton's willies, Alf's future, Harry's pocket, Terri's questionable virtue, Hooper's promotion and Titmarsh's scoop, either the night before the exhumation or the exhumation itself were the important times. But not so Sydney. For sure he looked forward to recovering his share of the proceeds and he would enjoy taking the money off that little urchin Field, but he knew by then the world would know that there was no gun, no drugs and no scandal involving that ghastly boy Sloane.

My God he had enjoyed the morning's press. Indeed, he had enjoyed it more than he imagined he would. He had read every article several times and rejoiced in the obvious pain they would be causing that arrogant public schoolboy. He had even found it hard to tear himself away from them in order to go out on funerals. But tear himself away he had to and so he left them with Fred Gilbert for his enjoyment, as Gilbert wasn't down to conduct any funerals – not surprisingly as it was cold, grey and more snow had been forecast for later.

'Thank you very much Sydney. After going through them all I'll give Charlie Williams a ring and quote any he hasn't seen himself over the phone. It looks very bad for Sloane doesn't it?'

'Yes it does. But Sloane's a tricky customer. I'd tie up the Williams deal quickly. Look at what happened to me. My father-in-law and old man Higgins were fishermen and they always said that a fish was never caught until it was on the bank.'

'You don't think Sloane can recover from this do you?' sneered Fred.

'Unlikely. Indeed impossible if there's an exhumation and it's all there. On the other hand if an exhumation was to bear no fruit then Mr Sloane is a victim and not a villain and people like Charlie Williams may feel guilty and act accordingly.'

'But you told me . . .'

'I told you what I know and I know exactly what I told you, and to date it's turned out to be right, hasn't it? But I don't know what's actually in that coffin any more than you do, do I? I'm just pointing out what might happen if things turn out differently.'

'Of course you're right Sydney. Good thinking. I'll push old Williams hard for his decision today. Now run along or you'll be late for your first job,' smiled Fred.

Sydney was right to hurry up Fred, obviously because unlike Fred he knew that no drugs or gun would be found in Betty Woodall's coffin. He wanted Fred to win because he wanted the promotion and a place of his own to run, and because he wanted Stillion to lose. Moreover, by explaining the downside risk to Fred now he not only showed himself to be intelligent and diligent but also closed off any possibility of Fred blaming him for bringing him the original story and thus nursing his hopes in the first place.

Sydney didn't really like Fred. He certainly didn't respect him, but he was stuck with him thanks to bloody Stillion Sloane, so he would do anything to help Fred beat Sloane.

His first funeral took him to Yardley Crematorium. It was a small uninspiring and uneventful affair. A funeral quickly forgotten. His second took him to Perry Barr Crematorium, a place he didn't like. The crematorium still seemed to favour Sloanes, and always had as long as he could remember. On top of this they had a cheeky young organist there who often wore shorts or less under his cassock in the summer and would come out of the service to brown his legs in the sun while rolling his cigarettes and joking with Sydney's drivers. Sydney could never recognise anything he played on the organ. Sydney, when still the managing director of Richards & Gridley, had often urged James Loftus, the crematorium's manager, to replace the lad.

Loftus had obviously failed to take Sydney's advice as there was Michael Russell behind the organ playing away as the duty minister, a Welshman named Alan David, read the opening sentences and the procession went down the aisle.

Sydney couldn't be sure, but there seemed to be something more familiar about this tune. He thought he recognised it but it wasn't a hymn or a psalm. No, it was something played *like* a hymn but more contemporary. What was it? He was sure that Russell shouldn't have been playing it, whatever it was.

The procession arrived at the catafalque, the minister peeled off to the left, Sydney stepped to one side in order to let the coffin pass, and the bearers continued on and placed the coffin down. Then Sydney sat his mourners to the right. Still the music played and still Sydney was sure it was something he knew and also that it was not appropriate for a funeral. Sydney started his walk to the back of the chapel and then one chord gave it to him. It was 'Smoke Gets In Your Eyes'.

'Right. That's it. I'm going to have that little shit,' thought Sydney. He couldn't wait for Michael Russell to appear from within the chapel so that he might enjoy a smoke.

'What was that tune you were just playing?' asked Sydney aggressively.

'Oh just a little something by Holbein,' answered Russell as he licked his cigarette paper.

'No it wasn't,' spat back Sydney.

'Why do you come on so negative man? I said it was Holbein and I know my music, man.'

'And I say you're a liar, that Holbein was a painter and that the tune you were playing was "Smoke Gets In Your Eyes".'

'And I say Holbein had a cousin who wrote music and shared the name, and sometimes smoke does get in your eyes.' With that he exhaled his first drag accidentally into Sydney's face.

'Now you've done it. I'm reporting you. You're a slovenly disgrace. I hope you realise you'll be sacked for this.'

The argument continued in whispers just outside the glass crem doors before being postponed when Sydney noticed the minister and congregation stand for the committal. This meant Michael must return in order to play as the curtains closed.

Michael, although angry, was not foolish enough to play any of his variations of 'Come On Baby, Light my Fire', 'He Ain't Heavy, He's My Brother', 'Carry That Weight' or 'It's All Over Now'. He played a verse of 'Abide With Me'. Not that it mattered. It was too little too late. Michael might have been able to get away with 'Smoke' – it was after all his word against Sydney's, and no one had witnessed the argument that had followed. But now he was undone by his own forgetfulness, and undone in public in front of scores of witnesses.

166

As Michael played the minister pressed the button on the dais which started the electric motor that closed the curtains at the point of committal. 'And so we now commit our brother John Anthony Michael to the fires, ashes to ashes and dust to dust, in sure and . . .' the minister's Welsh tones trailed away and the congregation gasped.

As the curtains moved towards each other to conceal the coffin they exposed the end chapel wall either side of the catafalque. This was painted white, contained a few inscribed plaques that dated back sixty years, and had old large black tubular radiators either side of the catafalque. These radiators were part of the central heating system, which ran off the heat generated by the furnaces.

Nothing wrong with any of that on any other day, but today was different as the curtains today exposed two old, large, black tubular radiators that were covered by drying, even steaming, washing. There were old greying, moth-eaten Y-fronts, some string vests, a few large collared, floral shirts, odd socks and two pairs of blue jeans.

The stunned silence was only broken by the stumbling minister's voice and the audible sniggers of two young girls at the back of the congregation. Michael's shock at the sight of his own laundry had been so great that 'Abide With Me' had died on his fingers.

Behind his left shoulder and on the other side of the glass door, this fiasco had been watched by Mr Gridley. His initial disbelief, followed by blood-bursting anger, was quickly replaced by the realisation that this laundry must belong to Michael Russell. Nobody else on the crem staff wore floral shirts. All the others were at least middle aged and married. There was only the pot smoking organist who was young and single. At last he had the ammunition to kill off another of his enemies and one whom he knew to be fairly chummy with Stillion Sloane. So this would be the end of the laid-back hippie organist. And who could say that he did not deserve as much? Nobody could possibly complain about Sydney reporting *this*. Sloane, even though he apparently liked the pot-smoking keyboard player,

167

would not have put up with *this*. James Loftus, who had so far turned a blind eye would have to act now.

The service concluded. As Sydney brought the family back down the aisle with some looking over their shoulders at the laundry, his gaze was fixed on Michael. Michael did not stare back, but instead preferred to watch his fingers lightly combine the ebony and ivory notes to make 'The Day Thou Gavest'.

Sydney took the family to the garden of rest to see all the floral tributes and ordered his chauffeurs to follow in the limousines. Then, while they were busy thanking friends and acquaintances for their attendance, he strode over to the crem office to confront Loftus.

Meanwhile, Michael, once the chapel was empty, had sped down the aisle, lifted the front of his cassock and held it up with one hand while he grabbed the bits of laundry with the other and chucked them into his home-made sack as he went. When all were collected he clutched them tight to his tummy with both hands and thus looked for all the world like a pregnant nun as he arrived in the vestry. There he stashed them in the wardrobe provided for the changing clergy.

'Those were yours were they?' questioned the Reverend David.

'Er, yes,' replied Michael in a surprised voice as his desire to get the laundry hidden had prevented him from noticing the minister still changing out of his robes.

'Well I'm afraid it did notice, you see. Look, it's not my business mind, but it did notice all the same. Best not happen again.'

'Right,' replied Michael firmly.

'I mean, I wouldn't want to be telling, like, you see?'

'Of course not man.'

'But . . .'

'But don't worry, because Mr Gridley will be reporting me before the day is out.'

'Well then I won't add to your troubles.'

'No. That's good of you,' said Michael, knowing that the

Reverend David was the last person ever likely to report him for anything.

This was because about a year ago he had given the Reverend Alan David a lift back from St Peter's church youth dance in Small Heath on the south side of the city. He had also given a young West Indian girl a lift at the request of the reverend. Michael didn't know the girl and couldn't remember seeing her at the dance, where he had played with his band.

Strangely, the Reverend David had climbed into the back of Michael's van and sat among the keyboards and speakers. Even more strangely so had the girl. Therefore they were sitting on the van's uncomfortable metal floor while no one sat in the passenger seat next to Michael.

Very soon Michael had come to understand all. It was obvious by the noise of a zip, her whispered but audible encouragement, before his quickened breathing led eventually to muffled groans and his embarrassed explanation.

'I didn't put it in her see, Mike. I mean I didn't actually do it, see.' Then the Reverend David, a pillar of the Anglican community in North Birmingham and a seventy-year-old grandfather to boot, slipped the girl a fiver and asked Michael to stop and let her out of the van. This he did and declined her offer of 'A quick hand job for the same price' saying that it might prove fatal while he was driving.

Michael had not told a soul and now this could be payback time.

As the two men looked at each other knowingly but without a word being spoken, their private meditation was broken by a knock on the door and the immediate entry of James Loftus.

Loftus stood in the doorway, flustered, flushed and breathing heavily. He was a tall man, over six foot. His balding, white, flyaway hair had been blown out of place as he had crossed the driveway from the offices to the vestry's side entrance.

'Ah, there you are Michael,' said Loftus, who was in his early sixties and had been a major during the Second World War. More pompous men would have gone to their graves by the title

169

'Major Loftus'. He didn't. He was a kindly man, with a fairly weak personality. This meant he probably hadn't been great major material, and his lack of man management skills, as displayed at the crematorium, bore this out.

Loftus was shaking. Sydney had already seen him rather than take his family home first. Michael hadn't counted on that.

'You had better come to the office immediately. Mr Gridley has made some very serious complaints against this crematorium in general and you personally in particular.'

The Reverend Alan David grabbed his robes and slipped away without a word. Michael wasn't really sure whether to be happy or not, given their shared secret. In any event he hadn't time to dwell on the point.

As he and Loftus walked briskly back to the offices Michael noticed that most of Gridley's family were getting back into the limousines. He took comfort from that. At least this encounter would have to be brief, as Gridley would have to take them home.

In addition he noticed the Reverend Freddie Price's three-wheeler Robin Reliant coming through the crematorium gates. He was arriving in order to take the next funeral, which meant that the Sloane cortège wouldn't be far behind. Indeed, it was six minutes to the hour, which meant he could put money on the fact that Arthur Kemp and Stillion Sloane's faces would appear in the Sloane hearse in about two minutes so that their procession could go down the aisle bang on the hour.

Michael followed Loftus into the office. There the thunder in Gridley's face told Michael that the next time he got behind the organ there would be a good chance he could be doing so as an employee on notice. Loftus opened the court-martial proceedings with, 'Perhaps Mr Gridley, you would like to repeat to Michael what you told me a moment ago.'

'I haven't time. I've a family waiting outside and I have to go. Anyway there's no need. Mr Russell here is well aware that he played "Smoke Gets In Your Eyes" as my family went into the service and that laundry which I believe to be his became exposed on the radiators when the curtains closed around the catafalque. Moreover, Mr Loftus, you are perfectly aware that I have continually warned you to get rid of this slovenly drug addict. He has obviously been dragged up and must have lacked any form of parental control when young. The result is a rude, insolent waster who should not be employed here. You have refused to take my advice in the past, and this is the result. On my return to my office I shall contact your head office to report these facts to them and request both of you are relieved of your positions. You on the grounds of not being capable to manage, and you as an unemployable lout who is damaging the reputation of this crematorium. You could always apply to Sloanes for a driver's job. They'll employ anything and your obvious drug association means you would be well suited.' Sydney was standing with his back to the door and hadn't noticed Stillion enter halfway through his triade.

'I beg your pardon. What did you say?'

Sydney spun round. The two men were facing each other for the first time since that December morning in Sydney's office in 1979. They stared into each other's eyes. In Stillion's there was distrust. In Sydney's there was hate.

'Oh! it's the drug dealer himself! You probably supply this empty headed lout,' replied Sydney, pointing towards Michael.

'Now look here Sydney, don't push me. I've just about taken as much as I can this week,' said Stillion through gritted teeth.

'Don't threaten me! I'm a JP and a councillor. I'm not one of your mobster friends. You really are a disgrace. Unlike this fool organist you had every chance in life at your posh public school. It's a good job your father isn't alive to see the shame you've brought upon your family. They say you're about to become a father. Well I say it would be better for everyone if your wife never gave birth to a child created by yo—'

Sydney couldn't finish as in a second he was lifted from the ground by his throat and his head was banged against the adjacent wall with such force that the cloak above fell to the floor, hitting Sydney on the head on the way down. There he hung, suspended, gasping for breath.

'I'm probably going to get into a lot of trouble for this and for once I'll deserve it, but it'll be worth it. With that Stillion swung his free left fist.

Michael jumped forward and grabbed it. 'No Stillion! No, that's what he wants. It's not the answer for you, and anyway Mr Gridley was complaining about me.'

Sydney was still suspended three inches from the ground as Stillion said: 'Never mention my father, wife or child again.' Then he let go.

'Gentlemen! Enough!' At last, Loftus had summoned enough courage to speak. 'Mr Gridley, you have a family waiting to leave. Mr Sloane you have one waiting to go in. Michael get back to your organ. I will see you later.'

Then all four men left the office as if nothing had happened. Loftus accompanied a shaking Gridley to the garden of rest where his loaded limousines were waiting. Michael walked with Stillion to the chapel entrance where the chauffeurs stood by their closed limousine doors awaiting Sloane's nod.

Reverend Price was ready, Michael was playing, Sloane was nodding and the limousine doors opened to release the mourners. They lined up two by two, the chauffeurs joined Arthur Kemp at the rear of the hearse and Stillion took the head of the coffin and held it steady as the bearers lifted it onto their shoulders. The coffin was then turned so it might proceed foot first into the crematorium chapel to Michael's 'Onward Christain Soldiers'. The lad had a sense of humour, even when playing the correct music.

When all were seated or kneeling in prayer (a time referred to in the trade as 'eyes down for a full house'), Michael slipped out via the glass door and joined Stillion.

'What in hell's name was all that about?' was Stillion's obvious question.

'Gridley accused me of playing "Smoke Gets In Your Eyes".'

'Very perceptive of him. No doubt you were.'

'Very well, and nobody knew.'

'Incorrect. Obviously *he* did.'

'Well . . .'

'Well nothing. I don't like Sydney Gridley much and I do

172

like you. But I've warned you that this might happen. You must cut this music out. I've told you before. You'll probably get away with it this time because he can't prove he was right, but next time you're a dead man.'

'No, I'm dead this time. You see, on top of that he got me on the laundry.'

'What?' Stillion couldn't imagine what on earth laundry had to do with anything.

'Well, my van broke down yesterday so I couldn't drive to the laundrette, but all my togs were dirty so I brought them in here today. Washed them in the vestry sink and put them on the big, black radiators behind the curtains after the second funeral knowing that there was an instruction for the curtains not to close on the third. Unfortunately I forgot all about them and of course a bloody Gilbert funeral with Gridley conducting was the fourth.'

'Never mind Gridley. If it had been a Sloane funeral I would've been furious. I mean fucking hell, Michael, a bereaved family is entitled to more than that!'

'Oh man. You're right but it was an accident and you wouldn't have tried to get me and Loftus the sack just like that. Would you?'

'Probably not.'

'Anyway, I'm dead meat now.'

'We'll see. If I can help you or Loftus, let me know,' said Stillion genuinely.

'I'm sorry about the press. It must be shit just now,' said Michael, changing the subject as his brain registered Stillion's kind offer despite his lack of sympathy for what had happened, and his own problems which could so very easily bring public ruin to him.

'Thanks. You'd better get back in there, and don't even *think* about playing "Nowhere Man" for Sydney.'

At about eleven o'clock Jimmy turned up at Terri's to collect the cash from the previous night's take. The money she had taken was not good and he wasn't pleased. Without his drug dealing income he relied more heavily on Terri and the two other girls under his management.

The other two meant nothing to him and therefore he had pushed them hard over the last two or three days since the trouble with the Wilkes had blown up. He had threatened violence and they had responded by considerably increasing their income. On the other hand, Terri was the one who had got him into this mess and despite him asking her nicely to up her bonk rate, it had fallen. Thus he felt aggrieved and that his caring attitude was misplaced. He told her so.

'Caring attitude? What? Caring Attitude! What caring attitude? You live off moy immoral earnings sambo.'

He grabbed her red, curly locks hard and drew her face close to his. 'Don't you ever call me that mon, or I'll beat the shit out of you.'

'OK. OK. I'm sorry. Yow're 'urtin' moy. Let fuckin' go or I'll scream.'

'I mean it mon, and I don't care. Scream if you like.'

'OK. OK. Just let go.'

He let her go. They were facing each other, both breathing heavily with emotion rather than exertion. His emotion was sparked by the pain of being let down by one he thought liked him; hers by the anger of having to obey this man whom she despised, not only for being her pimp and all that entailed, but also because he was weak and not even good at it.

He didn't want to go. He wanted to make up with sex. She wanted him to go. She certainly didn't want sex. She hated sex with the punters but at least they paid, whereas this bastard, having taken most of that money, then expected sex for nothing. If he wasn't going to volunteer to leave then she would. 'I gotta go out.'

'Why?'

'To meet a fella for sex all right? I mean it's what yow want ain't it? I mean, one minute yow want to beat moy brains out 'cos I ain't earned enough bread, the next yow don't want moy to go to work. I can't win can I?'

174

There was no arguing with that, so Jimmy nodded and she left.

She looked back over her shoulder every now and then to make sure Jimmy wasn't following her. She knew he wouldn't stay in the flat for long but she had managed to leave without giving an address and she didn't want to be followed because she had no appointment and, what's more, no intention of making one. She needed time on her own – she needed to think, and then she needed to plan.

Her mind was clear about so much. She knew what she disliked and she was certain about a lot of what she liked and wanted, although that was more difficult, as for most of her life she had had so very little of what she desired.

She knew she didn't like: being a whore, Lozells, having no clothes, Jimmy, being poor, her grandfather, most men, sometimes and increasingly herself, and the Wilkes and their hold on people like her. She knew she wanted to be taken away from Lozells to Streetly, Solihull or, best of all, Edgbaston. She wanted a man to love her and for her to love him back. A man to respect, to look up to, who would provide for her, be kind to her and make real love to her. A clean-smelling man who would take her gently with his fragrant sex. Unlike the evil, cheese-smelling, crabby willies that she had to get her mouth round as some unwashed man of whatever race thrust her head into his lap.

So far so good. She knew with her head what she wanted and what she didn't. She could even try to concoct the most unlikely plans of how to get out of the Lozells ghetto and into an Edgbaston mansion. It may never happen but she could plot a course there. Why not? Her dreams kept her going and had done so since she used to lie awake at night listening to her dad beating the fat out of her mum, or her mum beating the gristle out of her brothers and sister. Her head was fine and so were her dreams, because they were, after all, only dreams.

Now she had a major problem. Her heart. She thought she was in love. This ocean of emotion, which had broken over her for the first time in her life was both wonderful and frightening, and therefore to her must be love. The terrible life she had led

175

had given no space for tender thoughts or emotions. They only happened in her dreams. But now, at the age of nineteen she, who was so mature for her years in the hard experiences of life and yet so immature emotionally, was having her first schoolgirl crush and it was biting her hard. It had in a few hours infected her mind and body so badly that she could not concentrate on anything physical or mental which was not related to it.

It was cold. She did not feel it. Time passed but to her it stood still. She repeatedly started her brain but it just broke down within seconds and wandered off on its own.

The worst of it was that the man who had stepped out of her dreams and into her life, causing her such delight and pain, would probably never notice her in that way. He was married and about to become a father. Even worse, her brother had come up with a plan at her instigation which had made his life terrible and might damage his business and reputation for years to come.

She pretended to herself that she was walking anywhere, so that she might be alone with her thoughts. But she knew the truth — she was walking the two miles to Sloane House in the hope of getting a glimpse of Stillion Sloane.

The rest of Stillion's working day went as planned and was hence quite out of character with the previous events of that week. However, a man on the fourth funeral had asked, jokingly, if Stillion was going to hand out free samples of cocaine. Unfair? Certainly. Poor taste? Of course, but nevertheless only to be expected given the newspaper coverage of that morning, and Stillion would have certainly settled for that as the only incident when the day had started and he had read the press.

Meanwhile, Fred Gilbert had tried everything he knew to get the final seal of approval for his deal out of Charlie Williams. Williams was friendly. Williams was pleasant. Willaims remained enthusiastic but nevertheless elusive when it came to giving his final agreement to sell. Then came the breakthrough. Fred, unhappy and without consulting his bank, upped his offer by

£50,000 to £850,000 and then £50,000 again to £900,000. He was now within £100,000 of Sloane's offer and could boast that his was definitely deliverable and not dependent upon the results of an exhumation which could ruin Stillion Sloane and would almost certainly make it impossible for Sloanes to continue with any idea of buying the Williams business.

Charlie Williams was now sorely tempted. Fred Gilbert certainly looked the better bet given Stillion's problems. Moreover, there would be no ongoing scandal attached to a deal with Gilberts, whereas there certainly could be in the case of Sloanes, even if Stillion could still find the money to complete the acquisition in the first place. And with the difference being reduced to only £100,000 a bid in the hand might well be better than a bid in the bush.

'So you agree? It's ours for nine-hundred grand?' pushed Fred.

'Well . . .'

'Come on, Charlie, mate. I can't go higher than nine-hundred grand, but at least you're certain of getting all of your money with no scandal and uncertainty hanging around.'

'Well, we are perhaps there,' answered Charlie weakly.

'Perhaps? What does that mean old man? Surely we're either there, done and dusted, or we're not.'

'Well, can I give you my final answer on Monday?'

'You could but I can't promise to buy at that price then. Just say the word and we have a deal now,' declared Fred robustly.

'I can't. I still need to consult members of my family and my solicitor. What about close of business Friday?' asked Charlie vaguely.

'I'll have to consult my advisers. I'll phone you back.'

Fred's advisers were not in this instance his solicitors, bankers or accountants. His advisers, or to be more precise his adviser, was Sydney.

He located Sydney in the garage as he returned from Perry Barr Crematorium still shaking with rage and indignation over the antics of Michael Russell and Stillion Sloane.

'Ah, Sydney, a word in your ear regarding that little matter we were discussing this morning,' Fred boomed out across the garage floor before whispering as he approached, 'I think we're nearly there with Charlie Williams, but I need to know when that exhumation is going to take place. Charlie has said yes but wants to have until close of business Friday before giving his final word. If the exhumation takes place at first light Friday then by virtue of your argument Sloane still has a chance of getting back into the race. If the exhumation isn't on Friday morning then Sloane is still embroiled in his crisis and we can win for sure.'

'Leave it to me. I'll see what I can find out,' replied Sydney, who not only hated Stillion Sloane more than ever, but needed to ensure that Elton had the same information in order to put the original plan into effect, and in addition a new little plan that Sydney had just dreamed up on his way back from Perry Bart Sydney made for the mortuary in order to find Elton, who as usual just had a fridge full of stiffs for company.

'When's the exhumation then?' queried Sydney.

'I don't know.'

'Well shouldn't you find out? Doesn't it occur to you that with all of this publicity in the press it's going to happen any day now? I mean, your plan is useless if you don't know when the actual exhumation is. It might be tomorrow for all you know, which means carrying out your work with Jimmy tonight. How were you intending to find out?'

Elton stared back blankly for a second and then looked at the floor as he always did when he was about to get a good bollocking.

'My God! That Nick Smith must have been stupid allowing a fool like you to run up a grand's worth of debts,' sneered Sydney.

'Well it just didn't occur to moy, and neither did it yow. I mean, I thought it would be in the papers,' defended Elton.

'Well it isn't, is it? And it *did* occur to me but I was stupid enough to think that even a complete idiot like you would have worked that one out. Obviously I was wrong. So what are you going to do about it? I mean time is short. You had better find out and report back to me within the hour. Get your grand-

178

father to find out or even you or that crazy little sister of yours. You're all family. You have a right to know.'

'Yow're right. I'll phone now.' And with that Elton phoned Hooper from the garage phone. Hooper informed Elton that he had already told his grandfather that unfortunately they had decided that an exhumation would be taking place first thing on Saturday morning. Elton replaced the receiver and returned to Sydney in the mortuary. 'It's first thing Saturday morning.'

'Good. Now listen to this. When the police find nothing they'll appear stupid and will try to find a scapegoat. That could be you. They don't know who the informer is but they do know who you are. I have a plan that leads them away from you. It is this. When you recover the ring, don't reseal the coffin and don't replace the soil properly.'

'Why will that help?' asked Elton.

'Because the police will think that either Sloanes or the drug gang have broken into the coffin overnight and taken away both the gun and the drugs. Whereas if you replace everything neatly they won't realise anyone has been in the grave and therefore they'll just think there were no drugs and no gun in the first place and the only person they know who suggested there could be was you. Wasn't it, you idiot? And as long as Jimmy and you don't leave any fingerprints they're bound to reach the conclusion that the gang got a tip-off when the exhumation was to be and rescued the drugs just prior to it.'

'OK. I see that. But why do yow suddenly want to 'elp moy? We both know that yow 'ate moy bleedin' guts?' asked Elton with a degree of logic.

'Because I hate Sloane much more than even a half-witted fool like you! You help yourself and keep that public schoolboy twit under pressure and I won't like you but I will leave you alone here in future. It's up to you. Do we understand each other?'

'We do Mr Gridley,' nodded Elton. For once someone was asking him to do less and get more.

Sydney left Elton Field to finish preparing the bodies for tomorrow's funerals and returned upstairs to the offices. He knocked on Fred Gilbert's door and put his head round it. 'The exhumation will take place on Saturday morning. Therefore Mr Stillion Sloane cannot possibly get out of the mire by Friday evening. So you can let Charlie Williams have until then.'

'Well played Sydney. But tell me old man, how did you find out so quickly?' jollied a grateful Fred.

'I asked your embalmer Elton Field. Remember the deceased was his grandmother,' purred Sydney.

'Good, good, good,' responded Fred, who wasn't really listening as he dialled Charlie Williams. He couldn't get through. Charlie's private line was busy. He was on the phone to Joyce Higgins.

It was already dark when Terri found herself approaching Sloane House. The Soho Road was busy. On the pavements the shoppers picked their way across the ice and slush and round the fruit and veg stalls of the Asian shopkeepers. It was cold and the shops looked well lit, warm and inviting. To her they seemed to be a shelter not just from the dark and the cold but from life itself. In there, there were families. Families shopping, families serving, families browsing and probably families stealing. Families. She was excluded. Bloody well outside in the cold on her own and excluded. Always the bloody same.

At the end of the Soho Road the shops petered out and Sloane House stood on one side and a petrol station on the other. After these buildings both sides were darker as the properties became either offices or warehouses with the occasional church.

Terri reached the pavement in front of the garage forecourt. It was wide there, just where Holyhead Road met Soho Road. From this vantage point she could gaze across the road and watch Sloane House which was a blaze of light and activity.

The lights beamed out brightly from the reception, as they did from the upstairs offices. Downstairs the lights of the chapels of rest were more subdued. Off to her left hearses and limousines came in and drove down the side drive heading for the garage to be washed. Coffins on wheel biers were coming up the same drive in the other direction. They were heading for the chapels and the evening's viewing which would start at six.

She felt very excluded. She also felt very insecure. The cocky little vixen wasn't so sure of herself away from her home game on the Lozells Road, where she knew the people and what was expected of her. It was a common life, cheap, with no expectations. It was only made bearable by the illusion of short-term kicks.

Now she had walked, as if in a dream, off her patch into a different place that was really the same place. The only real difference was that the few miles distance just changed the streets and the faces. Other girls worked this part of town. The real change was the mental state that had made her take that walk in the first place. She had walked away from the Lozells Road and all that it stood for, and the Messiah that had brought about this transformation was Stillion Sloane. And now she was worshipping at his temple. The mouthy, young whore of Lozells standing in the cold evening air hoping to catch a glimpse of her god, braced against the cold as the promised snow began to fall.

She was transfixed. She hadn't the courage to approach this temple for fear of rejection, and yet she didn't want to leave. So her indecision rooted her to the spot and she just whiled away the time watching Victoria Thomas go from her office to Stillion's and back again. How she envied that woman. She must spend as much or even more time with Stillion than he did with his wife. What an opportunity. One that Terri would not have wasted. Surely if you were with him all the time you would lose the tongue-tied feeling that she had.

Across the street, upstairs in his office and just out of Terri's view, sat Stillion Sloane. He tried very hard to busy himself with checking the garage orders for tomorrow. John was talking and he was listening but his mind kept drifting away. It had seemed better when he had a funeral to conduct – at least his professionalism had distracted him. He felt so hollow and empty. Powerless to prevent a gross injustice from ruining his father's name, his

181

business and the future of his wife and child. The weight of such stress and depression was so very heavy that he almost found it hard to stay awake. He felt that the very effort of leaving his desk to go downstairs to check the chapels to be almost too much for him. This was indeed a stern test of his character. He must not be found to be lacking.

Occasionally John and Stillion were interrupted by calls from journalists who were either trying to pick up new developments, get a different angle or even catch up. Such calls were always fielded by Vicki first but Stillion took them all in the conviction that he had nothing to hide.

Then the phone rang again. Instantly Stillion was alerted to a different ring. It was in his head, an urgent ring, and even before he picked up the receiver he knew who was phoning. He was correct. It was Stephanie and it was urgent.

'Darling the pain has been getting worse all afternoon and now they're every few minutes and I think my waters are breaking. My bag's packed. I'm ready. Shall I call an ambulance?'

'You'll do no such thing. I'll be there in minutes. Hang on old girl.'

'Yes, but if you're tied up with all that trouble.'

'Oh shit to the trouble. I'm coming now. I love you darling, just hang on.'

'I love you too.'

The phone went down. John would check the chapels with Keith Jones. Vicky would clear his desk. Arthur ran his car up onto the forecourt and Stillion took off down the stairs, leaping five at a time.

Terri had noticed the change in activity. She had noticed Vicky take off from her office and arrive in Stillion's. Then the bald back of John Palin's head had appeared as Stillion came into view and he crossed his office for the door. At the same time Stillion's Jaguar had arrived at the front. Oh no, he was leaving. This must be decision time. Without her mind being certain of what she was doing or what whe would say when she got there, her legs propelled her across the busy main road and delivered her safely on the other side. Stillion was now in his car. She half walked, half ran to the right exit, where he was heading. He got there first but had to stop due to the traffic. This gave her a chance. Her hand started upwards in a wave and her mouth opened to say she didn't know what but in that second he was gone. He hadn't even noticed her. Excluded again? Naturally.

5

Friday

Thursday night turned into Friday morning and still the snow, which had fallen on ice and had begun at around six p.m. on Thursday evening, continued to fall heavily. Over a foot made transport arrangements in the city most difficult, and the reaching of bereaved families up uncleared side roads almost impossible.

Not that Stillion Sloane had noticed the snow. He had collected Stephanie and delivered her safely to Birmingham Maternity Hospital. There she had been placed in a private labour room and together they had monitored the baby's heartbeat on the screen and timed her contractions.

This was her first baby, and therefore as is often the case, labour was a long and hard-fought battle. Stephanie was very brave and Stillion very attentive, calm and supportive. The hours passed and still the baby did not come. Eventually morning came and with it the announcement that Stephanie was unlikely to give birth for at least another twelve hours. It had been a false alarm after all. But they were assured by one and all that this was quite normal and Stillion was packed off home so that he might shower, change and then make his way through the snow to work.

John Palin and co. were surprised to see him. Indeed, John and Graham Stone had just started to alter the garage orders as he arrived. They looked expectantly at him.

'No, nothing yet. Mother and baby well, but baby doesn't want to come out,' announced Stillion stoically.

'You can't blame him, looking at the weather,' said John.

'Or the bloody events surrounding his or her family,' added Stillion before asking, 'What about the press today?'

'I've got all the papers for you,' chipped in Vicky as she arrived behind him laden down with various daily rags. 'There's not so much. I suppose because there's nothing new. Most just have small pieces which run on from yesterday saying that an exhumation will be granted but not when.'

'It'll be Saturday morning. Hooper told me yesterday. It won't be in the press though. They won't want the press muscling in on that,' mused Stillion.

'No, especially as they'll have red faces when there's nothing found,' added John.

'Well, let's hope so,' said Stillion, almost to himself.

'There can't be . . .'

'I know John, I know, but I'm beginning to wonder how this nightmare got started; who on earth fanned the flames and when and where will it all finish?'

'You know, I know, Vicky knows, even the bloody dog knows . . .' burst out John.

'Thanks a lot John,' interrupted Vicky.

'. . . that Elton Field, Sydney Gridley and Fred Gilbert are all in this somewhere,' continued John.

'We might like to suppose that. We don't know that and while all three have motives, Elton's granddad is against an exhumation, his sister is on our side and whatever you think of Fred Gilbert or that nasty little piece of work Gridley, they're hardly likely to get involved in murder or drugs or face the wrath of the police or the drug barons by making such a story up. I could see them trying to take advantage of the situation now that it's occurred but that's very different from suggesting that they, either with or without Elton, started the whole thing. It's the sort of thing Harry Wilkes would start. But he'd be murdering and drugging not reporting the same to the police. I mean, Harry Wilkes wants the police crawling round the drug community like a hole in the head.'

'Maybe. But I still think . . .'

'I think I'd better get out early on the first job. The roads are in a terrible state and the first funeral is up a mountain in Kingstanding.'

'Right you are but . . .'

'John, not now. Make sure Arthur and Walter have placed two buckets of grit on the hearse lower deck and one in each limo boot.'

It was still snowing as the first 'A', 'B' and 'C' fleets pulled off the forecourt simultaneously. Graham Stone and the 'B' fleet were going to a Handsworth address and then on to Handsworth Cemetery. Colin Miller and the 'C' fleet were due at a Handsworth Wood house before ending up at Witton Cemetery. Stillion and the 'A' fleet had drawn the short straw – Kingstanding, which was high, mighty cold and twenty minutes away even on a clear, snowless day.

Walter drove carefully and while the main roads were bad, a combination of gritting by the corporation and the morning rush-hour traffic had kept them just about passable. He was silent. He quite rightly guessed that the boss was not in a talkative mood. He could just catch the odd glimpse of Mr Stillion out of the corner of his eye. He seemed miles away and only returned to the job in hand occasionally when he glanced into the wing-mirror on his side to ensure the following limousine and hearse were still in tow.

It was true. Stillion's mind was in complete turmoil and concentration was difficult. A cocktail of mixed emotions had him in its grip. His mood changed by the minute as one emotion flooded in and another ebbed away as his brain danced like a dragonfly from this funeral, to Stephanie's labour, to the exhumation and who or what had started the crisis that had almost certainly cost him the Williams acquisition and could even cost him much of his current business and his reputation. For the thought had not been lost on Stillion that this awful, unfair and unwarranted publicity would distress his friends and please his enemies at the bank's regional office. It would help his enemies carry the day and that could mean the withdrawal of the funds for the Williams acquisition and possibly even bring

186

a demand to clear the existing overdraft immediately. If that happened the bad publicity would almost certainly prevent him from going to another bank and therefore he would be stuck at the mercy of his current bankers, which would mean having to sell off most of his acquired firms and maybe even Sloanes itself in order to meet the bank's demands. And who would buy Sloanes with the prospect of falling funeral numbers due to the scandal?

The thought of Fred Gilbert getting control of the growing Sloane empire at a knocked down price as a result of a forced bank sale was appalling and was made no better by the prospect of Sydney Gridley dancing on the Sloane grave as it happened. Stillion wished he had been a little more humble in his dealings with the little tin gods up at the regional office. But it was too late now and no good crying over spilt milk.

How had he got into this mess? Where had this story come from? Why had the newspapers jumped on it so quickly? Why had the police taken it so seriously? Could there be any truth in it? Who could have placed drugs and a gun in that coffin? Surely the bearers would have noticed the extra weight – wouldn't they? What was this story of protection money about? He only knew one gangster and thanks to a baseball bat with his blood and Wilkes' fingerprints on it that man shied well away. So could it be the Vance gang? But if it was them why had it been said he had been paying protection to them? He had never met any of them.

All of these questions and many more besides went round and round in his head, as did the imminent birth of his first child and the safety of his beloved Stephanie. He wanted this child so very much. He wanted him, or her, to be the first of many. He wanted to provide a secure family and financial background for them and leave them a strong business that perhaps they would leave to their children and in turn they to their children and so on.

He had worked hard to re-establish the Sloane name and business following the years of his father's illness. Now, on the very eve of his first child's birth, just when things had been going so well, it had, if not quite in the twinkling of an eye then in a couple of days, all turned sour.

Instead of rejoicing at the acquisition of Williams he was facing a crisis of survival and feeling like an inadequate father even before fatherhood had embraced him. The potential danger of Joyce Higgins didn't even warrant a thought and was therefore temporarily forgotten.

Yes, Walter was right not to talk as they rode along together, for Stillion was so far away, lost inside his own head, that the words would probably not have been heard.

The vehicles made a slight detour in order that they might arrive at the house facing down the hill. Considering the conditions excellent progress had been made along the main roads. Sloanes were also very fortunate that the client's residence was only one road away from the large and busy Kingstanding Road and therefore, despite a difficult last 500 yards, they arrived at the house bang on time.

Stillion pulled himself together, ordered Walter to call the hearse through and removed his top hat. The hearse, with Arthur Kemp's face a study of concentration, slithered passed before coming to rest on the right side of the road at the top of the hill.

Stillion may have been somewhat distracted by the week's events but not so much that he had led his cortège into the road from the other end. If he had it would never have made it up the hill. The road was littered with private vehicles which were either attempting in vain to get up the hill or had been abandoned in the attempt.

Stillion stepped from the limousine on the road side and found it impossible to make his way to the pavement without clinging onto the bonnet for support. The heavy fall of new snow on top of frozen ice had made the conditions underfoot most treacherous. Eventually Stillion led his troop of bearers across the pavement and up the short garden path to the front door of this recently acquired council house.

'Good morning, my name is Stillion Sloane of Sloane & Sons and I shall be conducting the funeral for you this morning,' opened Stillion, with right hand extended as he reached the man standing in front of the closed front door. 'Would you be so kind as to introduce me to Mrs Edith Barlow?'

'Sure mate. Follow moy. We're all surprised to see yow lot what with the roads and all.' He rang the bell and upon its opening entered with Stillion following. Arthur, Walter and the others waited in the front garden. Soon Stillion returned with Mrs Barlow, the deceased's daughter, and the family flowers were quickly collected before Stillion and Mrs Barlow disappeared again into the warmth of the little house in order that Stillion might arrange the seating in the two limousines while Arthur and co. arranged the flowers in the hearse. This done they returned to their vehicles and waited.

A few minutes passed, as Stillion explained the funeral's procedure to the mourners, before he arrived at the front door and nodded to Arthur, who then moved the hearse off, left across the road and two limousine lengths down the hill. It was very slippery and Arthur's experience told him to turn the front wheels in leftwards so that they rested against the kerb and thus prevented the hearse from taking off without him. He walked back as Walter pulled into place and was therefore on hand to open the limo's door as Stillion assisted the first car's mourners down the path and across the pavement.

'Do mind your head as you go madam. Would you like to take a seat on the far back? Do mind your head as you go sir. Would you like to sit next to your wife?' and so on. Polite, efficient and effective. A well-oiled team that was clearly a cut above its competition. In time the second limo was loaded in the same fashion and Stillion, having thanked the gawping crowd for taking the trouble to pay their respects, made his way to the front of the hearse as Arthur got back behind its wheel.

Stillion, as with his first funeral yesterday, decided against a long walk. Then it had been due to the vicious attitude of the crowd in Lozells. Today it was due to the fact that walking on

189

this hill in Kingstanding might be even more dangerous. One slip and he could be having his next ride in the back of the hearse instead of the front.

After only a couple of steps he stood to one side and let the hearse pass, slipping into the front passenger seat as it did. 'OK, nice and gently. No more than a couple of miles an hour down the hill. Turn left at the T-junction at the bottom. Right at the main road and then put her on eighteen to Perry Barr as we've got bags of time.

'Right you are,' responded Arthur.

Halfway down the hill the hearse started to gather pace.

'Gently. Gently. I said only a couple . . .'

'I know yow did but she's broken away on the ice! My foot is 'ard on the bleedin' brake,' panicked Arthur.

'Ease it off!' commanded Stillion as he knocked the automatic transmission out of 'D' and into 'I' which he hoped would have the effect of slowing the vehicle.

Soon the hearse was at the T-junction. Arthur was turning the steering wheel left but the hearse was going straight on and heading for a lamppost on the other side of the adjoining road. The vehicle ignored the halt sign and entered the road. Luckily nothing was coming in either direction but still it headed for the lamppost which seemed to be just at the end of the bonnet.

Stillion and Arthur both instinctively closed their eyes, but the crash did not come. Instead the wheels gripped the road and the hearse veered a little to the left before stopping.

'Phew. That was bloody close,' exhaled a relieved Arthur.

'Move it. For fuck's sake move it,' snapped Stillion.

'What?'

'I said move it before . . .'

Bang. The two men bounced in their seats.

'What the . . .?'

Bang. It happened again but with less impact this time.

'. . . before the two limos hit us,' finished Stillion, for he had worked out that if they had lost control on the ice and snow

190

then it was logical that the two following limousines would do so as well.

'It's hard to believe that this bloody week can get any fucking worse,' exclaimed a distraught and by now almost suicidal Stillion as he got out to ensure no mourners had been injured. Luckily there were no following private cars or matters could have been worse.

No mourners were hurt and all understood the danger of these conditions. They even seemed most grateful that Sloanes were doing their best in very difficult circumstances and were happy that the funeral hadn't been postponed until Monday as a result of the weather.

Stillion managed to sneak a look at the damage to the vehicles before taking up his position once more in the hearse.

'What's the damage boss?' enquired Arthur.

'No one hurt,' replied Stillion.

'I meant the motors.'

'I thought you might. It appears they all met bumper to bumper and what damage there might be is not visible. I think we got away with it.'

Indeed Stillion was correct. The advantage of having a modern matching fleet was more than just aesthetic. The shock-absorbing bumpers which had met each other upon impact had saved the day and thus Sloanes had been spared the damage which Elton Field had inflicted upon the Richards & Gridley fleet some thirteen months previously on another cold Friday morning during the funeral wars.

'Right at the main road and then eighteen will still do fine,' reminded Stillion as the cortège got going again. Despite its little shunt it managed to arrive at the crematorium two minutes early.

James Loftus met Stillion at the chapel entrance.

'I didn't expect to see you yet. Neither the eight-thirty Co-op nor the nine o'clock Gilbert funerals have arrived,' he said without reference to yesterday's near punch-up between Stillion and his sworn enemy Sydney Gridley.

The service took place with a borrowed minister, who was waiting for the eight-thirty Co-op funeral. He had arrived while they hadn't, whereas Sloanes had arrived while their minister hadn't.

Michael Russell played nothing that vaguely sounded like 'It's All Over Now', and when the committal took place the closing curtains did not expose any drying underpants. Then Stillion led his grateful family to the garden of rest to view the flowers before leaving just as the eight-thirty Co-op was arriving at nine-fifty. Still there was no sign of the Gilbert funeral, which was apparently being conducted by Sydney Gridley. It might only be small crumbs of comfort but Stillion couldn't help but be slightly warmed on this very cold day by the idea that Gridley was stuck somewhere with a cortège and his blood pressure rising.

All three Sloane fleets had five funerals each. This was indeed a lot, but not unusual for a Friday in January, especially a January caught in the grip of a cold winter. Stillion was fortunate that four of his five funerals were service and committal at Perry Barr, because such funerals were quick and did not require laborious and bitterly cold trips to a graveside. The other funeral was both long and laborious. It was long because it was a West Indian Baptist funeral at Winston Wylde's church, and laborious because as usual the service would be followed by a burial in Handsworth Cemetery, the scene of the proposed exhumation. There, after the committal service, the men would mould up the grave, the West Indian term for filling it in, as the women sang.

Stillion didn't mind. The West Indian community had always been very loyal to both Stillion and his father before him. And of course Winston Wylde was a good and trusted friend. But most importantly it was all part of the job. Don't be a funeral director if you can't stand the cold of the cemetery.

Sloanes returned to the crem at ten fifty-eight for their eleven o'clock second funeral and still the nine o'clock Gilbert job had not arrived.

On 'A' fleet's next funeral, gritting, pushing and even rocking the hearse from side to side had to be employed, as did some smart detours to avoid upward routes. Stillion was grateful to enter the chapel at the crematorium by twelve thirty-three instead of twelve thirty. Not perfect, but brilliant given the obstacles. The Gilbert funeral still hadn't arrived.

The next funeral, that of the West Indian Baptists, was not easy, but at least it had stopped snowing and the cortège did not have too many side roads to negotiate from the family's house to Winston's chapel before entering the cemetery five minutes early.

The journey from the hearse to the graveside was fraught with danger. The hill was steep, the snow was deep and there had been no respite in either the weather or the cemetery staff's workload to allow for a path to be cut up to the grave.

The procession was led by the foreman followed by Winston Wylde, Stillion Sloane, the casket carried by eight large black men and then, in between it and the mourners, came Arthur Kemp and Walter Warburton. They were on hand to catch the casket should disaster strike and the bearers slip, thus dropping the casket and causing it to take off like a toboggan in the mourners' direction.

It was indeed a long and difficult walk, which took some eight minutes to complete. A period of pain that in particular the bearers would not forget for some time as the casket handles cut deep red grooves into their freezing pink palms.

Once the committal service was over and dirt was being flung, (along with more than a little snow) into the grave by the male mourners, Stillion and Winston had a chance to exchange a few words.

'Do you know when it will be?' asked Winston.

'Yes. Tomorrow morning, early.'

'Well then, your pain will be over and your innocence proved.'

'Maybe. I know I didn't do anything wrong, but then again this whole episode defies belief. There has to be some reason for all of this happening. Did you find out anything?'

'Not yet. Questions have been asked and now we must wait. And talking of waiting – the baby?'

193

'No, nothing yet. Steppie's in hospital as you know, but now they say perhaps this evening or tomorrow morning. They'll induce her if necessary on Sunday.'

'Give her our love and tell her we're thinking of her.'

'I will.'

'By the way Stillion, I should mention, well I mean, I don't want to add to your problems and I don't wish to talk ill of anyone, but you should be careful,' said Winston slowly.

'Careful of what?' interrupted Stillion abruptly, immediately angry at the prospect of any more trouble.

'Well, that girl, Terri.'

'You mean Elton Field's sister? I don't think she has anything to do with this. She's been very supportive. Her brother, well that could be different, but her—'

'No, no, I'm not talking about that problem. I don't know anything about that, but my questions on your behalf have revealed that she works as a prostitute for a Jamaican lad I used to teach and she's heavily into drugs. Moreover you must have noticed the way she looked at you.'

'I didn't.'

'Well you must be blind.'

'Don't be silly Winston, you just said she was a whore. Everybody knows whores don't fancy men just like that, especially ones they don't know.'

'I repeat you must be blind. You were the only guy in the room she took any notice of. And I'm saying she's known to be bad news. Anyway did you get hold of her brother?'

'No. I've left several messages for Elton to phone me back both at work and at home over the last two days, but nothing. He's always out on a funeral or a removal or just not in. I'm going to call at his house tonight if Stephanie's situation allows.'

'Anyway, I'm with you. You're my friend and a good man and what's more I'm sick and tired of all this drugs business. It's destroying my people and the police either can't or won't do anything to bust it up.' With that Winston wished Stillion good luck with both the birth and exhumation and got into the waiting hearse so that Arthur Kemp could take him home.

The nasty turn in the weather had meant that Fred Gilbert had taken little self-persuasion to leave himself off the funerals for the day. After all, he should concentrate on the Williams acquisition, so he called Charlie Williams on his private line. No reply. He left it a few minutes and tried again. Engaged. A few minutes later – still engaged. He tried the Williams switchboard and was told that Mr Williams was engaged but would call back.

'Just remind him about our deal,' blurted out a frustrated Fred.

'I will,' replied the telephonist politely, not knowing what on earth Mr Gilbert was on about. However, she duly relayed the message to Mr Williams, who was furious with the cavalier comment as the whole matter was supposed to be confidential. Even though Fred hadn't said what the deal was, the mere mention of the word might spread a rumour around his garage in a matter of minutes. Charlie, like any other selling proprietor, did not want his staff to know that the business was up for sale until the deal was done and they were, as a result, someone else's responsibility. He mused on this and the conversation he had had with Joyce Higgins about Stillion Sloane.

During the morning Inspector Hooper put in one last call to Harry Wilkes.

'Look 'arry, I know yow told moy that it ain't got nothin' to do with yow. I 'eard yow. But I got to warn yow if yowa blokes got finger prints or stuff like that on that gun or those drug packets, I won't be able to 'elp. It's all 'appening now. I couldn't stop it if I wanted. Yow said go ahead didn't yow. But if any of yowa blokes was on that job I'd tell 'em to scarper now all right?'

'Look, I told yow already, it's nought to do with us. Relax and just do your fuckin' job straight for once, OK?' Harry

195

slammed down the phone and sent for Alf so that they could run through the night's plans for operation 'Nick the Ring'.

Meanwhile, Hooper was awoken from his reflections upon how he hated having to deal with the impossible Mr Wilkes by a call from Bill Woodall.

'So it's tomorrow is it?' asked the old man.

'Yes and yow can come and watch if you wish, but please keep this information confidential,' responded Hooper.

'Watch!' exploded Bill. 'Why yow bloody indecent . . .'

'Now look Mr Woodall, I've been about as patient with yow as I'm going to be. I know yow don't want your wife disturbed but I've already explained she's got to be.'

'No she don't – leave 'er be is wot I say. Leave 'er be.'

'Yow will 'ear from us in due course.' Hooper finished the conversation abruptly. If Harry could kick him about he could always do the same to old men like Woodall.

Terri's previous evening had been further soiled by making up the money she hadn't made while standing outside Sloane House. Then when work was done, or done enough to be able to give Jimmy something which wouldn't send him mad, she had retired alone to her dirty little bedsit. She was in a state. She wasn't getting enough coke or crack or smack or anything; she didn't have the money. She daren't spend all of Jimmy's. Some, perhaps, but all would be stupid and would almost certainly get her the beating she had been trying so hard to avoid.

Moreover, Sloane had now totally taken over her mind. He was meant to be hers. She was convinced that it had been him who had been sent to her in a vision day after day, night after night since puberty. He was the knight in shining armour that was to bend from the saddle of his white charger and pluck her from the hell that was her life.

She had never had a chance. She had been born in hell, caged in a lousy house with awful parents, filthy brothers and a piteous sister and not given, or at least not taken, education. And yet she knew she was both pretty and bright. Rip off her clothes and those of any posh Edgbaston girl and underneath the wrapping it would be her breasts, her pert bottom, her flat tummy and perfect legs that would turn the head of any toff like Stillion Sloane. What's more, she might not have a snotty, middle-class accent or know about the Tudors and the Stuarts or even domestic science but she was streetwise and they weren't. Moreover she could stiffen a whole man's body in bed when she got really into it. She could paralyse a Stillion Sloane in bed if given the chance. He would never want another if he could be persuaded to have her.

'But he couldn't be persuaded could he?' she thought. 'He's got a beautiful, pregnant wife, who's posh, talks posh and bleedin' well looks posh, probably fucks awfully posh too. Poor man. Just forget it,' she told herself. But she couldn't. Something deep down kept telling her that this was her chance and if she spurned it then her dirty bedsit would be the high point rather than the low point of her ghastly life. Drink, drugs and whoring would age her fast and thus allow her to slip even further down life's greasy pole. A day would quickly come when even a naked Terri couldn't pull the punters or even fool herself, and then what would life hold? What hope would be able to shine into such a black abyss? No, she determined, this was it. It was now or never. God, if he bloody well existed, had shown her the route. The route was Stillion Sloane and she must risk all on this one throw of the dice.

Such thoughts had raced round her pretty head as her red curls lay on the dirty grey and white-striped pillow that hadn't had a case on it in years. Her pale ribby body shivered under the unwashed army blankets.

She didn't sleep. She couldn't sleep. She wouldn't sleep until a decision was made. In the end and despite great personal risk to herself and the selling of her companions for her own ends, she determined to meet Stillion and tell him the whole story. Thus she would save his reputation and business and at the same time become his responsibility. Decency and gratitude would prevent him from throwing her back into a pool where pikes like Jimmy or sharks like Alf could eat her alive. He would have to get her a flat in a nice part of town. He would visit. She would seduce him. Her sex would blow his mind and thus little by little she would win him over. She could wait. It would be a pleasant flat, much better than this dump and the only tricks she would have to perform would be for him, and she actually fancied him. She could do it. Eliza had in *My Fair Lady*. She had liked that film. She could be Eliza and Stillion could be the professor. It could work. The more she thought about it the more she thought, 'It could work, and if I don't try I'll be stuck 'ere or fucking worse for ever.'

Elton? Jimmy? Well the first had been a poor brother since she could remember, while the second was a black bastard who had lived off her faked orgasms and the sex she had given to every shape, size and colour, that had, once its owner had parted with the cash, been forced upon her. Let them swallow for a change. To hell with them.

But what if Stillion, once he had been told the story, just went straight to the police and turned them all in, her included? Well, for one he couldn't because unless the police caught Elton and Jimmy in the act the exhumation would just go ahead and doubt would always remain, especially as she would then deny that she had told him the story in the first place and nothing could be proved unless she told the truth and the boys were caught in the act. Moreover she would demand, and get, his word. Men like Stillion didn't break their words. She knew this from the movies. She had seen plenty of men who looked and talked like Stillion in the old black and white movies and such men, unlike Jimmy, Elton, Alf or Harry Wilkes, only gave their word in order to keep it.

She determined to phone Sloane in the morning, and then fell asleep.

When she awoke the plan had been cemented in her mind. She showered, dressed and made for the one public telephone on the Lozells Road which had been in working order on the previous day. Thankfully, if unusually, it still was. She phoned.

Her call was taken by the telephonist, who put her through to Victoria. Terri asked for Stillion but was told he was out on funerals all day. Terri declined to leave either her name or a message but said she would phone back around a quarter to five.

'He's avoiding moy,' she thought, before realising that he couldn't be as he didn't know that she was going to phone and now that she had, his secretary didn't know her name. Or perhaps she did. Perhaps Stillion had seen her on the previous evening outside the funeral home and just ignored her and then told his secretary not to put her calls through.

This would be most illogical to a rational and balanced person but Terri had never really been either, and just now she was completely irrational and totally unbalanced. She wandered across the Lozells Road to buy a coffee, have a fag and wait with one eye on the clock and the other watching out for her money-sucking employer – Jimmy.

Stillion's last funeral of the day took him back to Perry Barr at four o'clock. It was still bitterly cold and the dark day was turning into a black night. However it was no longer snowing and the traffic thus had a chance to wear down the snow. consequently the main roads were greatly improved from the morning.

James Loftus had been troubled all day. First, he was still concerned about Sydney Gridley's threat to report him and Michael Russell to their employers. He wasn't that concerned about Russell – it would be annoying to have to find a replacement, but that was it really. He was naturally much more concerned about himself. He could be fired as a result of Russell's stupidity and at his age another job, let alone a cushy number like his, would be hard to find. He was sixty and had managed to stay on in the army after the war right up until 1970 when he had retired as a major at the age of fifty and come to manage the crematorium later that year. Naturally he had an army pension, but this job made the difference between what the pension paid and what his bitching wife expected. If he was to lose it, a sixty-year-old like him with few qualifications could only really expect to find employment in one of life's more menial roles such as hotel doorman or self-employed gardener. Roles reserved for old men who were humble, polite and inexpensive. Therefore a future of possible humiliation at work and humble pie at home was staring the troubled manager in the face.

Second, with the exception of the most professional Sloane & Sons, most of the other funerals had arrived at various stages of lateness due to the weather and thus disrupted the smooth running of his military-style operation. Indeed the nine o'clock Gilbert funeral, with that dreadful Gridley fellow as its conductor, had still to arrive. No doubt when it did Gridley's temper would be such that he would find fault with anything and everything. Gridley was known not to be a man to let anyone off lightly when he got his claws into them. He had been an arrogant owner and now he was a bitter employee. His change in status and fortune had done nothing to create humility and understanding within him as far as James Loftus was concerned.

Reverend Fred Price was ready. Michael's organ could be heard from within the chapel, the coffin was on the bearers' shoulders and the mourners stood with Stillion behind it, when Loftus, who was standing in his customary position in the chapel's porch, noticed a cortège pull through the entrance gates. It wasn't the Co-op's last running early; no, he wished it were, but it wasn't. It was the late, indeed unbelievably late, nine o'clock Gilbert funeral.

Loftus froze with fear. The time was one minute to four and he knew Sydney Gridley well enough to know that given half a chance he would claim that as it wasn't four o'clock yet his funeral should be allowed in first. He had witnessed just yesterday how Gridley and Sloane hated each other and now a confrontation, which Sloane wouldn't seek but Gridley might, in front of both sets of mourners, would mean he might as well start writing his part-time gardener advert for his local post office's shop window.

Loftus nodded urgently to Fred Price, who turned and started to walk with the words, 'I am the resurrection and the life sayeth the Lord.' The shouldered coffin, followed by Stillion

Sloane and the mourners, followed him into the chapel, where the coffin was placed on the catafalque while Stillion seated the mourners in the pews to the right.

Meanwhile the Gilbert cortège came to rest and a furious Gridley came steaming across the snow-covered driveway towards the porch with Loftus firmly fixed in his glare.

'It's not yet four o'clock,' he blurted out.

'Ssh,' whispered Loftus, and indicated the same by putting a finger to his lips and pointing with his other hand to the open chapel doors.

'Don't you "ssh" me you incompetent clerk. It's not yet four o'clock and my funeral should have gone in before Sloane's,' shouted Gridley.

'Mr Gridley, it *is* four o'clock by my watch. Your funeral is seven hours late and please keep your voice down,' pleaded Loftus.

Michael Russell, whose organ was placed just to the right of the door, heard Sydney's voice and played louder to drown it out.

Steam was almost coming out of Gridley's ears as he went on. 'Loftus, I have already reported you and that drug addict organist to your head office regarding yesterday. Now get that funeral out of that chapel this instant or I will report you again.'

'Mr Gridley, I don't wish to upset you but what you ask is impossible because . . .'

At that moment Stillion arrived on the scene, having closed the chapel doors and caught the intent of Sydney's request.

'It's the late Mr Gridley I presume,' mocked Sloane.

'Why you cheeky little bastard. How dare you, a friend of the underworld and the toast of the tabloids, speak to me like that!' spat back Sydney.

'Gridley, you know those stories aren't true. The exhumation will prove that and if I ever find out that you had anything to do with spreading these rumours in the first place I'll . . .'

'Threaten violence like yesterday I expect. Well don't trouble yourself. I'm a JP and a councillor and I don't mix with the underworld like you,' taunted Sydney.

201

'No violence. If I ever find out that you had anything to do with this I will drag you through every court and newspaper until the city's population know exactly what a bitter and twisted old man you really are.'

The confrontation was over and Stillion turned away to ensure the hearse had taken the flowers to the garden of rest and that the limousines had pulled forward to accommodate the departing mourners. Gridley returned to his hearse with the words, 'Neither of you have heard the last of this,' before reluctantly leading his own cortège to the rear of the crematorium to await Sloane's departure.

Once Stillion's mourners had left the chapel Gridley's cortège pulled into place. Its original minister had given up the ghost hours ago and so Loftus had arranged for the Reverend Price to stay on after the Sloane service and take this one. Price was happy to oblige as the money would come in handy. Nevertheless he was happy to see the Gilbert funeral arrive as Loftus had originally asked him to come in for three o'clock, the time when the original 'sky pilot' had to leave for a Women's Institute tea party and he, like Loftus had begun to wonder if Gridley was going to show up at all.

Michael Russell had wisely decided that discretion was the better part of valour when he realised that Loftus and Sydney Gridley, and then Stillion Sloane, were facing each other in the porchway just on the other side of the glass chapel doors. However he did strain to hear what they were saying and managed to pick up on the fact that Gridley had already reported Loftus and himself to head office. The crematorium owners were very traditional and strict disciplinarians. They would not like what Sydney would have told them. Russell knew that meant he was dead in the water.

'Well I might as well go down with all guns blazing,' he thought to himself, and then played a hardly disguised 'Out of Time' singing the lyrics to himself with Chris Fallow's voice in his head as Sydney passed the organ. A perfect tribute to Gridley's timekeeping.

'I said, baby, baby, you're out of time. I said, baby, baby, you're out of time. Yes you are . . .'

But neither the tired mourners nor the angry Mr Gridley seemed to notice. This was perhaps because all their senses had been seriously dulled by the experience of the journey from the farmhouse near Barr Beacon to the crematorium. Under normal circumstances such a journey would only take some twenty minutes. Today was different. The cortège had arrived nearly three and a half hours late at noon, having battled its way bit by bit up the Beacon. Then on leaving the farmhouse, the hearse had slid into a ditch on the side of the descending country lane and everyone had to wait in the limousines while a local farmer could be located in a nearby pub. It was hard to persuade him to leave his bar stool by the blazing fire in order to fetch his tractor and haul the hearse out. Indeed Sydney had only achieved this by slipping him a fiver which Sydney would make a tenner on the account and then claim the larger amount back from petty cash. This haul out took nearly two hours, as did the rest of the journey as the cortège slipped and slid its way down to Great Barr and then on to Perry Barr.

The strain upon conductor, bearers and mourners alike had been immense and if Michael Russell had played a bog standard version of the 'Stripper' it wouldn't have made much of an impression.

Sloane House had been like a five-star hotel putting on a major corporate function all day. In other words, serene in the public areas and like a madhouse behind the scenes. The bad weather was causing the death rate to spiral even higher than a busy January month would normally realise and therefore the reception, hall and even landing were fully occupied by small huddles of recently bereaved families with one member clutching the green disposal certificate. They were waiting their turn to go into one of the three arrangement rooms. In these sat families discussing the funeral arrangements of their late relative. In one arrangement room was John Palin, in another his assistant, and in the third sat Victoria Thomas. She didn't usually make funeral arrangements but today was an exception.

A receptionist ferried families by turn into the next vacant room and discretion and timing were employed by Palin and co. to get their families from an arrangement room into the selection room, as Stillion insisted only one family be in the selection room at a time in order that they might select the coffin or casket of their choice in private.

Neither Victoria nor Palin's assistant June Reynolds were allowed to actually book times – these had to be booked by Palin himself and then pencilled into the day book temporarily until they could be written up fully later on.

Palin always insisted that he controlled the booking of all funeral times, including arrangements being phoned in from the Sloane branches and subsidiaries so that he could maximise fleet usage and avoid unnecessary double bookings. This he did to the benefit of the company, its clients, shareholders and staff and normally without difficulty as everything could easily be accommodated in this fashion on a normal working day.

But this was no normal working day, and Victoria and June were delayed even further by arrangement details flooding in from all the branches. Palin's desk was a sea of funeral arrange-ments, partial funeral arrangements, first call instructions, green certificates, completed cremation application forms and B, C and F cremation papers. All would have to be married up, put in a folder with the completed arrangement form stapled to the outside and the details written into the day book before the folder could be placed in a tray relevant to the day on which the funeral would eventually be conducted.

Laborious, but efficient and a very far cry from today when a sympathetic young lady might arrange a funeral by punching the information into a computer which would then not only provide the day book print-out but also produce the coffin order and body label as well as request the removal, and in the case of a crematorium, order the doctor's papers.

Elsewhere in the building other Sloane staff were busy on

death's production line. There were ambulances to be manned and snow and traffic to be battled against so that next week's bodies could be moved into the mortuary. There were coffins to be fitted, plates to be engraved, bodies to be embalmed, bodies to be boxed, coffins to be moved up to the chapels for viewing, and, now the fleets were finishing their gruelling day on the highways of human combat, there were vehicles to be washed and muddy interiors to be cleaned.

At such times it has always been traditional in the honourable funeral profession for staff to rise to the occasion, just as Londoners did in the Blitz, and of course Sloanes' staff were no exception. But today was special because every last man and woman who worked for the company had felt the unfairness of this week's accusations and were both pleased and relieved to be busy. Rightly or wrongly they believed that it showed that the surrounding communities supported them, and were not going to make any judgement until after the exhumation proved things one way or the other.

Unless you've ever been at the centre of such stressful, immediate activity, the sense of which is heightened by being always aware that the client is bereaved, unhappy and therefore not always patient or rational, then it is hard to imagine what it is like.

This was the case with Terri. Her world was in slow motion as she waited for Sloane to return to his office. Every minute seemed like an hour as nothing could distract her from her one thought of how Stillion Sloane, the man from Edgbaston, was going to become her father, lover, protector and provider for now and perhaps more in the future. She wasn't that mad that she was sure of the future – after all to dislodge a pretty young wife with a small baby would not be easy, so for now mistress status would do. She kept telling herself that mistress status was possible if she took the opportunity of helping him now when he really needed help. That would then present an opportunity to seduce him.

So when four forty-five eventually came and the lonely, excluded and thoroughly mixed up Terri trudged through the snow and black slush on the Lozells Road, she had no picture in her mind of what was really happening at Sloane House. Instead she imagined Stillion sitting in his office, sipping a cup of coffee, reading the newspaper and thus available to take her call.

Therefore it was both a shock and a disappointment to be told by Jones' old mother, who had been drafted in to man the phones during this mayhem, that Mr Sloane couldn't take the call because he was on another line. The old girl asked Terri if she wanted to leave a number. Terri thought 'Be brave, it's now or never' and said, 'My name's Terri Field. Mr Sloane knows moy quite well. I got some very important information for 'im. He should phone back straight away. Moy number is – ' And she read out the number of the phone box. Old Mrs Jones assured Terri that the message, which she had written down, would be passed to Mr Sloane as soon as he got off the phone. Terri replaced the receiver and punched the kiosk glass. As she squeezed her eyes shut, tears fell onto her cheeks.

'Why oh why does nothin' ever go right for moy?' she moaned. 'It's like I'm cursed. I wait all day for 'im and now 'e's on the bleedin' phone and I'm stuck 'ere in this fuckin' phone box.'

At that moment an old Brummie woman opened the kiosk door and asked, 'Could I use the phone duck?'

Her question was met with the full force of Terri's anger. 'Get the fuck out of 'ere grandma before I knock yowa lights out all right?'

The old lady retreated, bemoaning the behaviour of today's generation and shaking her head with the words, 'I blame the parents I do. No discipline. Shouldn't be allowed.' Terri watched her go as she waited for Stillion's call but it didn't come and it wouldn't, because old Mrs Jones was looking after five lines, answering calls and scribbling all the time. In her confusion not only did she completely forget about the call but she also managed to knock the scrap of paper with the message on it off the desk, and unfortunately for Terri (and perhaps Stillion also) it fell straight into the waste-paper basket. So now

Terri was standing in a cold, dark phone box awaiting the most important phone call of her life from a man who had no knowledge of what she wanted to say, how she felt or that she had even phoned in the first place.

At half past five, the front door bell of Sloane House rang and Victoria Thomas descended to answer it. Everyone else had been seconded to John Palin, so that he might get this rush of death under control and consequently ensure that the ensuing funerals turned out to be exactly what was ordered.

Victoria opened the door and said good evening to an elderly man in an old mac, who entered.

'I'd like to see Mr Stillion Sloane, please.'

'Of course. And who might I say is calling?' answered the ever correct Vicky.

'Alan Bater of the *Birmingham Post* and *Mail*.'

'Do you have an appointment?'

'No I do not.'

'Please take a seat while I go and find out if Mr Sloane can see you now.'

'Thank you.'

Bater sat down and Victoria disappeared back upstairs. She returned very quickly. 'Mr Sloane is terribly busy. He's been out conducting funerals all day and has returned to an epidemic of funeral arrangements . . .'

'. . . so the publicity hasn't hurt you,' Bater interrupted.

'Apparently not,' answered Victoria, with some satisfaction before continuing, 'However, if you will be kind enough to understand that his time is short due to this and the fact that his wife is expecting a baby at any moment, he will see you now. Please follow me.'

Bater thanked her and followed her up the stairs and along the landing to Stillion's office.

Stillion needed to see a journalist like a hole in the head. However, he thought that to send the man away might be regarded as a sign that he had something to hide, and so he had agreed to a short meeting.

'Good evening, Mr Sloane, my name is Alan Bater,' said the

journalist as Vicky showed him in. Stillion stood up, shook Bater by the hand, offered him a seat and sat down again.

'What can I do for you then Mr Bater?'

'I've been covering your story,' Bater began.

'You mean the alleged drug and gun story. It is not *my* story and is total rubbish as far as I'm concerned. The exhumation will prove it, one way or the other.'

It was now Bater's turn to interrupt. 'But I think you might be right. I'm not here to crucify you. I've watched your people, and you, and now I'd like to spend some time with you so that I can understand death from a funeral director's perspective.'

'Well, perhaps next week or the week after . . .'

'I would prefer now.'

'But I'm terribly busy. It seems that half of Handsworth has died this week and to each family, understandably, their funeral is the only one that counts, and all have got to be conducted perfectly. On top of that, Stephanie, my wife, is about to give birth to our first child.'

'That's perfect. You just go about your business and I'll tag along and keep out of your way. I promise you won't notice me.'

Stillion thought for a second and then nodded. 'OK. If you're sure you won't mind seeing some of the sights I'm going to see in the next hour.'

'I did mortuary duty in Normandy during the last contest with the Boche,' answered Bater. This was a bit of an exaggeration, as guarding the field mortuary at night didn't mean he got to see the gruesome sights inside and thus his inner self was somewhat nervous at the prospect of a mortuary visit. He hoped it didn't show.

Stillion got up and Bater followed him round on his tour of the death factory. First stop was the brightly-lit but bitterly cold garage. There the chauffeurs, with their smart livery now hung in their individual metal lockers, were putting the fleet to bed. The three hearses, six limousines and any available ambulances were being sprayed, sponged, sprayed again, leathered and their interiors cleaned.

'It's very bright in here,' commented Bater.

'It has to be,' answered Stillion. 'When the dust-sheets come off these vehicles on Monday morning, they must appear as new. You need very bright lights to ensure you can see every finger-mark on the panels and interior windows, and be able to hoover every grain of mud off the mats and carpets.'

From there they proceeded to the fitting shop, where Walter Warburton, having already finished his limousine and all of Monday's coffins for weekend viewing, was laying Tuesday's coffins against the left-hand wall. He would be in all Saturday and Sunday to fit out all of these and as many of Wednesday's and Thursday's that time and stocks allowed. Because of the burst in the death rate that day, which hadn't even hit the fitting shop yet, this was essential from the company's point of view, and Walter didn't mind. First, two day's double time was almost a week's extra wages, and second, with him being on the premises Keith Jones was bound to call him out first for any house or coroner removals which came in over the weekend, and the pay for these was excellent. Indeed, four would equal a week's wages. Therefore if it remained as busy over the weekend as it had done during the week, Walter could look forward to earning two, three or even four weeks' money over two days. This level of business only happened a couple of times a year and funeral wages were not good, so Walter would grab this opportunity with both hands.

Bater noted that the fitting shop was Dickensian but efficient. In particular he was interested in the Taylor Hobson engraving machine on which the breastplates were engraved. He looked at this as Stillion and Walter discussed the stock shortages that would occur given that the high death rate was now becoming even higher.

From there Stillion led Bater next door into the mortuary. Here Bater could see a bank of fridges at the far end of a large and cold room. They appeared to be able to take three trays in height per door and there were five doors. Off to the left was a line of silver-painted mortuary trolleys. Perhaps twenty in total. Each trolley had on it a body beneath a clean white sheet.

Bater assumed that all the fridges, like the trolleys, were occupied and thus calculated that the room currently housed some thirty-five deceased people.

In addition, and off to the right, were lines of obviously occupied coffins on wheel biers. Two men kept coming and taking one at a time up to the main funeral home where they would be placed in one of the chapels of rest.

Like the garage, the lights were bright and everything appeared to be white and very clean. Bater remembered how one was never supposed to see either hospital laundries or the kitchens of great restaurants, and was impressed.

He followed Sloane down the line of mortuary trolleys as Stillion lifted each foot and read a tag attached to the toe. Then he checked the fingers of each hand. Bater asked what he was looking for.

'This ticket is placed on the body the moment we come into contact with it at the hospital. It conatins all the vital infor- mation: name, age, date of death, religion, type of coffin, funeral details and jewellery instructions. I'm checking that all these bodies have tickets and that the jewellery instructions have been followed.'

'But they all have their name written on the soles of their feet as well. Why's that?' queried Bater.

'Because tickets can fall off, and usually my staff don't know the deceased and therefore couldn't identify them if that hap- pened. Once the body has been prepared and embalmed and the coffin fitted out the deceased will be placed in the coffin and the ticket removed from their toe and attached to the coffin handle until it is placed in the hearse. That way we know that we have the right body in the right coffin going on the right funeral.'

Stillion completed the line and then moved on to do the same with each body in the fridges. Bater accompanied him. He wasn't feeling as squeamish as he thought he might. Once finished Stillion walked back down the mortuary and into the embalming theatre. Bater followed.

'Oh for fuck's sake,' thought Bater as his tummy churned

210

and his head turned away. There on the centre slab was a full autopsy case. A woman slit open from underneath her chin straight down to her pubic hairline. A piece of her skull was in a nearby sink with a cold tap pouring water over it. A man in a white mask, gown and boots was embalming the body. He stopped when he noticed them and pulled down his mask to address Stillion.

'This is Mrs Burton, the old canon's wife. The butchers at the hospital have left me very little to work with but I'll manage. I'm afraid we're going to have to "top and tail" in the fridges and on the trollies over the weekend as we're full down here and God only knows how we'll manage when all today's arrangements come in next week. I'm running out of clean white sheets and I'll be forced to put new removals on the floor at this rate.'

'Ask Victoria to order you two dozen new sheets and borrow some coffin boards from Walter. Place them on spare trestles to save anyone's mum being placed on the floor.'

Bater still felt sick but he was most impressed by the conversation. The public didn't see these places but they were clean and the attitude seemed to be as caring and professional as it had been on the children's funeral in the full gaze of the public.

They returned to the main building and Bater accompanied Stillion and Keith Jones as they checked each chapel to ensure all would be perfect for the visiting families over the weekend. Jones read out all the details on the ticket while Sloane checked off the same.

Then it was back to Stillion's office and a conference with Palin about the day book before going through Monday's garage orders with Graham Stone, Colin Miller and Lawrence Kemp.

Bater was amazed. He had had no idea that so much work went into the arrangement, administration and conduction of a funeral. He had suspected that Sloane & Sons were innocent as charged by the press. Now he was almost certain. But he must be sure.

Stillion phoned the hospital. Stephanie was comfortable and there was no sign of an imminent birth. He would go and sit with her anyway when he had finished work. He was about to say goodbye to Bater when Victoria called him from her office. It was Winston Wylde and it was urgent. She put him through.

'Stillion, it's Winston. You must come quick. I'm at the Happy Valley children's home. I was called here to help. A child is on the roof and won't come down. He wants to talk to you. His name is Luther and he says you know him.'

'Yes, I do. Where's the home?'

'Halfway down Cornwall Road on the left.'

'Right, I'm on my way,' finished Stillion, and replaced the receiver.

Graham Stone would ensure all was finished down in the garage, while John Palin would stay on to tidy up the day book. Victoria offered to go and sit with Stephanie, which Stillion gratefully accepted as he flew out of the door for the second night running.

'I'd like to go with you if I might?' asked Bater.

'Sure,' replied Stillion, and the two men took off down the stairs, across the hall, through the reception and into Stillion's XJS which Lawrence Kemp had brought up from the garage for him as ususal.

Cornwall Road was just over a mile away and the Soho and Rookery Roads were much clearer now that it had stopped snowing and the evening rush-hour traffic had beaten its way through. The fact that both roads were on major bus routes had obviously also helped. Therefore it was only a matter of minutes before the Jag pulled up by the flashing blue lights of the two police cars already in attendance. Sloane and Bater got out. Winston and a police sergeant greeted them.

'Hi Stillion,' greeted Winston. 'The boy is up there, at the apex by the end. He threatens to chuck himself off the roof if anybody goes near him. He asked for you.'

'OK. How do I get up there?' asked Stillion as Bater scribbled furiously on his note pad. This was better than he had bargained for.

'Allow me,' answered the police sergeant, and led the way.

'Just keep that prat out of it,' demanded Stillion as he

noticed the young policeman who had upset both him and Luther so much on Monday evening.

'I won't have moy officers called prats,' declared the sergeant.

'Well don't employ them then,' answered Stillion, his bright blue eyes burning back into the sergeant's glare. Neither man blinked and it was only Winston pushing from behind Stillion which refocused both men to their quest.

They climbed up to the third floor of the old Victorian building where they were met by a Happy Valley staff member who led them up a ladder into the loft. Here there was a skylight which led onto the roof. It was already open and the wind was blowing some of the snow down into the loft where it coated the rafters.

The staff member gave Stillion directions. 'Go through the skylight and left. That'll take you up to the apex. Then face right. He's crawled to the very end near the front of the house. In fact right at the last inch before the drop.'

'How long has he been up there?' demanded Stillion.

'Don't know, but we discovered him about three quarters of an hour ago.'

'I have to warn you that you're going up there of your own free will and that the police cannot and will not take any responsibility for you . . .' The sergeant's words petered out as he caught Stillion's withering stare in the half light.

Stillion removed his coat and jacket and placed his hands in the snow on the roof either side of the skylight before hauling his torso through and into the bitingly cold night. The temperatures had fallen as the snow clouds had cleared and the stars now shone in a freezing, clear sky. Stillion pulled the rest of his body through the gap and knelt in the snow. He faced left and ascended on all fours to the apex.

'Fuck me. What kind of a week is this?' he wondered once again as he clambered up to the top. Once there he sat astride the apex and focused right. At first he could not determine anything. He called out, 'Are you there Luther?'

213

'Is that you Mr Stillion?'

'Yes,' replied Stillion as he noticed a little dark blob, some fifty feet away.

'Why did you send me here? You promised me good food and kind people. My momma ain't yet buried and you put me in a place where the man wants to do dirty things and then there is the big guys in here who want me to shoplift for them so they can have money for drugs. Yer is no better than the rest and I believed in you. The first white guy that I believed in.'

'Steady Luther, I'm your mate.'

'That's what you said before. I trusted you then and look what happened.'

'Well I don't know what did but I promise you that nobody is going to abuse you or make you steal. I promise. Now if these things have happened . . .'

'Happened?' interrupted an angry Luther. 'Why you think I'm up here Mr Stillion? Why? 'Cos I like it? No, 'cos the man threatened me with the belt if I don't let him do bad things with me. He does it with all the small boys. They is just too scared to talk. Then the Rastas from Lozells Road come at night to collect what we stole for them and if we ain't we get a beating from them.'

'OK I hear you. We'll sort it out. Just walk back along the top of the roof to me. Put one foot on each slope like this.' Stillion stood up to demonstrate.

'I ain't coming anywhere unless you take me away from here,' answered Luther.

Meanwhile Winston Wylde had left the sergeant by the skylight and returned downstairs, grabbing three blankets on the way down. He gave these out to a staff member, a policeman and an onlooker, asking them to take a corner along with another three people in each case. This done he then stationed one set behind Luther at the front of the house and two more on either side of that part of the building so that if Luther was to slip the outstretched blankets might, along with the deep snow, soften his fall. This would have to do until the fire brigade, which had not been called originally, arrived.

Winston returned upstairs and found a young woman standing by the skylight with the sergeant, who now had his head out of it straining to hear the ongoing conversation between Stillion and the boy. Winston knew the woman. It was the arrogant, if well meaning, woman from social services that he had come into contact with several times, and who had taken such an instant dislike to the capitalist funeral director Stillion Sloane on Monday.

'Why is a bloody untrained man out there? There's no profit in it for him. He should leave it to the professionals. I mean, what does he think he's doing?' she demanded.

'Your job,' came back Winston's flat but most effective response.

At about that moment Terri passed the end of the road. She had waited and waited for Stillion to return her call. In the end and out of desperation she had plucked up courage and phoned again. On this occasion the phone was answered by Keith Jones. He had told her that Stillion had had to rush out but may return later.

She didn't know what to believe. Was this man telling the truth? Or was Stillion avoiding her? Or perhaps she just wasn't that important to him? On the other hand, she had said that she had important information for him.

'Did he get moy message?' she had asked.

'Oh I'm sure his secretary would have passed it on,' answered Jones, unaware that it was not Victoria but his own mother who had answered the call and then lost the message.

Terri had put down the phone so bitterly disappointed that she forgot how cold she had become while waiting there. She knew what she had to do. This was her only chance and by tomorrow it would be gone. Almost as if on automatic pilot her legs began the long and icy walk to Sloane House. There was nothing for it, whether he was there now or returning later, she would have to meet him face to face.

As she passed Cornwall Road she could see the police-car lights flashing and these were now joined by those of an ambulance and a fire engine. She walked on. She didn't like the police and anyway it had nothing to do with her.

Stillion had decided that, while he hated making promises which were not within his power to keep, that he had no other choice. 'I promise you Luther that if you come back here and inside then you will never have to spend another night in this place.'

'Promise?'

'I promise. Now please come back.'

'I can't. I'm too cold and I'm too scared.'

'OK. Wait there. I'm coming over to get you.' Stillion stood up again and began to move slowly along the apex of the roof. He moved one foot at a time very gently across the down-slopes either side of the apex. The roof was high enough and the weather cold enough for him to imagine that he was crossing some ridge on Mount Everest. The top snow of the previous night and the day was deep and had fallen on the frozen ice that had been there for three weeks or more. This meant that conditions were very treacherous.

Stillion realised this and moved with great caution. But his care did not prevent his left leg from suddenly slipping away from beneath him and down the slope. He waved his arms in a large circle in an attempt to regain his balance and for a split second he looked to have succeeded before the leg went altogether with such force that his whole body followed, and suddenly snow was avalanching down the roof and cascading over the gutter and down the sixty feet or more to the ground, where it caught the upturned faces of the people below. As the snow went down the roof it was accompanied by Stillion's rolling body. Instinct made him grab for the gutter and there he now hung, with his legs kicking against thin air as the snow fell on down to the ground. He had cheated almost certain death – but for how long? Within seconds his freezing fingers were rebelling against having to hold onto the sharp and rusty gutter, and his

216

arms, at full stretch, ached while his kicking legs could find no support.

'Hold on Mr Stillion! I'm coming!' called out Luther.

'No. No. Stay there,' cried out Stillion in a manner that reflected both his pain as well as his authority.

The sergeant, still looking from the skylight on the right side, had seen Stillion stumble and then disappear over the left side of the apex. 'Shit, he's a gonna,' he yelled out.

'What? Get out of my way!' barked Winston. He pushed the policeman to one side and hauled himself through the skylight before crawling on all fours up to the apex and then along it to the point where it was obvious that Stillion had departed from his intended course.

Alan Bater was below with pen in one hand and pad in the other. But he couldn't write. Like everyone else he just stood looking up, transfixed by the moment. Somewhere in the back of his mind he thought his feature could become an obituary.

'Hang on Stillion! Hang on!' shouted Winston firmly.

'I'm doing my fucking best!' replied Stillion, trying to hide the fear in his voice while forgetting not to swear in front of the child and a man of the church.

'Can you get the ladder from the engine up to him?' yelled down Winston.

'No, there are trees in the way,' was the reply from a leading fireman.

'Can you catch him?' was Winston's next question.

'It's too dangerous, but I've sent men up with ropes. They'll be there any second.'

'Hold on Stillion. Hold on,' begged Winston.

'I don't think I can old man,' said Stillion quite calmly, having resigned himself to the fact that death was staring him right in the face and there wasn't a damn thing he could do about it. How unfair not to see his baby and not be able to say goodbye to Steppie and the rest of the family.

He felt his fingers start to slip.

Winston recognised Stillion's resignation and knew he must

217

act now. He ripped off his jacket, hooked the top of his feet to the apex and lay face down in the snow with his arms outstretched, having thrown the jacket towards Stillion while still holding onto one sleeve.

'Grab the jacket!' he commanded.

'I can't!'

'You can! Come on. Stillion Sloane never gives up his wicket. Come on!'

Stillion let go of the gutter with his right hand and his legs swung left as the crowd below gasped. The jacket's sleeve was still about three inches beyond his grasp. Winston unhooked his right foot which allowed him to move fractionally nearer to Stillion. He quickly retrieved the jacket and threw it again. This time Stillion got it at the second attempt with his right hand and let go of the gutter with his left as he did so, dropping a few inches as the jacket took his full weight. Again the crowd gasped. Luther turned away. He just couldn't look any more.

'That's better Stillion! Now just hang on,' urged Winston.

'I hope you didn't get this jacket from one of those bring and buy sales.'

Then three firemen appeared on the roof and with much professional speed roped a chimney breast which was then connected to them and Winston. A second rope, with a stirrup loop in the end, was thrown to Stillion.

'Transfer your right hand to the rope and try and find the loop with a foot,' commanded one fireman, who was kneeling in the snow on the other side of the apex, while a second next to him was holding onto the rope which had been attached to Winston's waist. The third had proceeded further on and was recovering Luther.

With his left hand clutching the jacket sleeve and his right the rope, Stillion got his right foot into the stirrup more by luck than judgement and they hauled him back over the rusty gutter. For the first time in what seemed like a lifetime he felt safe and not just about to meet his maker. He exhaled a steamy breath

218

from his exhausted body as he arrived back at the apex. The exhumation scandal didn't seem so serious now.

'Thanks Winston. You saved my life old man.'

'No, you and the jacket did it really. I just helped. Anyway I know God didn't want white trash like you up there today,' joked Winston.

First Stillion had sworn and now Winston was poking fun at the Almighty. Unusual, but perhaps understandable.

Then Stillion threw his arms around Winston's neck and kissed his cheek, with the words, 'Thanks anyway.'

Luther, now crying for the first time since his mother's death, joined them before all three were assisted back to the skylight.

'I'm so sorry. I'm so sorry,' Luther sobbed uncontrollably.

'It's OK. It's OK. It's over now,' said Stillion. He hugged the little boy before passing him down through the skylight.

'You is a brave man Stillion Sloane,' said Winston quietly.

'You too,' answered Stillion, who glanced back at Winston and detected that the minister was fighting to prevent his eyes from welling up with tears. 'And a good one,' he added.

Once through the skylight the two men and the others present were confronted by the young woman from social services.

'Why wasn't I called sooner?' she demanded. 'Why was an untrained undertaker sent out on the roof? He could have killed the boy as well as himself. Indeed he very nearly killed himself and could have killed the reverend here.'

Winston Wylde answered on behalf of all and as he was black his answer was the most effective. The young woman's political persuasion which had been so keenly defined only recently at university, meant she would not have heard a word that either the police or a capitalist undertaker could have uttered. Whereas a minister of the black people was quite different.

'What on earth are you talking about woman? The boy would only talk to Stillion here and that's probably because he's the only one to have shown him any real kindness of late.

219

You should be asking yourself why this boy or any boy or girl is in this place. It has been suggested tonight that this home is a house for theft, drugs and sexual perversion and I, for one, am not surprised.'

'I resent that remark greatly,' said the home's long time principal, who was standing next to the social services woman. He addressed Luther. 'Luther come with me. It's past your bed time.'

The boy didn't move. Winston placed his hands gently on his shoulders.

'The boy is coming with me,' he declared. 'Stillion has promised him he won't have to stay here tonight. I am the pastor of this parish and my family and I will care for the boy in the short term. I will sign whatever papers you want and take full responsibility. The boy has made some very serious allegations and they must be looked into without delay. I must add that this is not the first time I have heard such allegations about this children's home.'

'Now just a minute . . .' began the principal, before being interrupted by the social services woman.

'Everybody just hold on. This boy is the complete responsibility of the local social services office and I will . . .'

'. . . have a private word with moy, miss. If you don't mind.' Now the sergeant interrupted and led the social services woman a little distance away for a private conversation.

When they returned the young woman declared, 'I accept the pastor's kind offer.' The sergeant, motivated by keeping the powerful Winston Wylde on side, had pointed out that the lad, if left at the home, could and probably would repeat the trick or even think up something worse, and if that were to happen and he was to be hurt as a result then all fingers would point at her and a promising career would be over before it had really begun.

Everyone returned to the ground floor, where the ambulancemen checked over Luther, Stillion and Winston, while they in turn thanked the firemen. The police took notes as did Bater. Everyone could tell that the young social services woman was

220

flushed with anger but nobody noticed that the principal was white with fear.

Matters were all tidied up quite quickly after that and it was soon time to leave. Winston took Luther with him, while Bater was set to return to Sloane House with Stillion so that he might collect his own car. It was seven twenty-five p.m. when Winston drove the short distance home. He felt angry at what the drug culture was doing to his people. It was not just the damage and deprivation that drugs did to the users, but how the misery caused by the resultant theft, violence and prostitution spilled over into the lives of uninvolved innocents, young and old alike. He resolved that the Jimmy Gimmes of this world had to be stopped now, so that in five years' time Luther and his generation weren't as hooked or as depraved. He had tried the pleasant civilised approach and look where it had got him. Now it was time for a change and his anger would give him the strength to see it through.

As Stillion's Jaguar sped back up the Soho Road it passed a lonely girl trudging through the slush and snow. It was Terri. He didn't notice her, but she noticed him.

It was just past seven-thirty when Stillion's car pulled onto the forecourt. He turned off the engine but the two men didn't get out of the car immediately. Instead they remained seated and talked.

'That was a very brave thing you did back there,' commented Bater.

'To slip, brave? No, I cocked up really. It was lucky that Winston was there and acted so quickly.'

'He's a good man,' said Bater thoughtfully. 'And he likes you. So does the boy and you know what they say about children.' His voice trailed away as he noticed the main reception door open and Keith Jones come running out towards the car.

'Mr Stillion! Michael Russell is on the phone for you! he says it's most urgent.'

Both men leapt out of the car and ran for the reception, the young Sloane leaving the much older Bater behind. Once in the reception Stillion went to the desk and switched the call to that receiver.

'Hello? Michael? What's the problem?'

'I've just got to Reverend Wylde's house with some sheet music for Sunday and his wife is very distressed. She says that Reverend Wylde arrived home about ten minutes ago with a little boy who he has left with her and has gone off to the Lozells Road to confront one Jimmy Gimme about drugs. She says that she's never seen him so mad and I think she wants you to stop him before something terrible happens.'

'OK. Look, he may well head for the Villa Cross Café. That's where all the local pushers hang out. We've got to try and head him off before he goes in there. Minister or not they'll rip off his balls and stick them in his ears in that place. You're nearer than me so go for it. I'll meet you there, Whatever you do, *don't* go inside. Wait outside for me.' Down went the receiver. 'You still with me?' he asked Bater.

'You bet.'

Stillion raced back to his car. He desperately wanted to phone the hospital and find out about Stephanie but he just couldn't spare the time. At least she was in good hands. If he didn't hurry Winston could be in very bad hands.

'You've always denied any drug involvement, so how do you know where the pushers hang out?' asked Bater slightly suspiciously.

'Everybody who works this area does. Winston does. Do you seriously think he's involved with drugs?'

'Of course not. I'm sorry,' replied Bater genuinely.

'Forget it,' said Stillion as the car sped out of the drive and down the Soho Road, almost running down a solitary girl as it went.

Terri stamped her feet and burst into tears. Why was the bastard doing this to her?

Winston Wylde had had enough. He had taken Luther to his house just before seven-thirty, and having introduced him to his kind and friendly wife determined to act now while his fury burned in him and fuelled a courage which time might extinguish. He had driven straight to the Villa Cross Café and parked his car right outside on the double yellow lines – something the law abiding Winston would never normally do.

He strode into the café. It was unusually quiet for a Friday evening. As he looked round there was only a small West Indian lad in a dirty white apron behind the little counter in the far left corner and a couple of tarty looking black girls watching four guys playing pool on the far table. One was Jimmy Gimme.

'Jimmy, in the name of God I enter this evil place because I am going to put a stop to you and your kind!' boomed Winston's strong voice.

'Oh for Christ's sake, what now?' exploded Jimmy, who was fed up with people entering the café and threatening him. His humiliation at the hands of Harry Wilkes' white trash on Monday evening hadn't done his street cred any good and now the bloody local pastor was about to give him a public bollocking. He should hit Wylde, that was the only way to deal with it. But he didn't, first because Winston Wylde was a big and very strong man and second because a bit of him still remembered the frightening Sunday School teacher that he had once respected and even admired.

'Empty your pockets. I want all the hash, coke, crack or whatever on that pool table NOW!' Wylde yelled at them all.

Flicky, so called because of his love of knives, who had had his back to the entrance until now, slowly turned round and stared coldly at the pastor.

'Now listen to me, creep. You want to talk to Jimmy, find another place. But don't you dare enter this place yow voodoo bastard and never raise your voice to me or I'll stick this pool cue right up your arse you motherfucker.'

'Why you . . .' stammered out an enraged Winston, starting foward in blind rage.

'OK Virgin Mary fucker. You want it, you got it,' snarled Flicky. A huge flick knife appeared from beneath his black leather jacket and shot open to reveal a nine-inch blade.

'There's four of us,' continued Flicky – Jimmy had no option but to line up with the other three – 'and just you and your mother fucking God.'

'Not quite correct old man,' came a familiar voice from behind Winston's back. Winston turned his head for a second and there, coming through the door, were three crazy, idiotic and yet wonderful fools. It had been Stillion's voice and he was accompanied by Alan Bater and Michael Russell.

The four pool players could not believe their eyes. Here in their holy of holies, where only Harry Wilkes' men dared step, and then only in force, were three white men challenging them. Yes, challenging them right here in their own back yard. A posh public-school funeral director, some old man in a mac and a scruffy hippie in a cassock. Quite unbelievable.

'Stay out of this Stillion,' Winston called back over his shoulder as his eyes locked onto Flicky's again.

'I will not,' answered Stillion. Bater wished he could take notes. This would be one hell of a story if he ever lived to write it down.

'Peace man,' added Michael, because it was his usual greeting and because he didn't know what else to say. He really didn't expect anyone to heed the advice.

'Listen you honky shit you don't dare come in here if you knows what's good for you. If you're not gone in a twinkling of an eye I'll have to cut your guts out and sell them to the Delhi Moon Restaurant for tonight's late suppers – starting with you, old man,' threatened Flicky, pointing his knife in Bater's general direction.

'I'm not frightened of you,' responded Bater stoically, determined to show to his younger colleagues what he was made of. 'I fought in France in the last contest and killed much better men than you in Korea before your father had even thought of poisoning your mother with you, boy.'

Flicky's eyes narrowed with anger. 'I'm nobody's *boy*, old man.'

'I'm sure nobody would want you to be,' replied Bater with

224

a bravado that was bound to cause him and probably the others great physical pain.

'Why you . . .' Flicky advanced round the pool table towards the uninvited guests. He was automatically followed by his companions, who were armed with pool cues.

Then, from nowhere, a shot rang out and everybody froze except the small guy behind the counter who ducked out of sight. Seven of the eight men looked around to establish what had happened. The eighth knew.

'No violence,' commanded the pastor.

'I think you'll find this prevents it,' responded the man with the gun. 'Empty your pockets on the pool table please gentlemen,' said Michael Russell as he struggled to keep, and sound, calm. He was waving a pistol in the direction of Jimmy and his friends. 'The next one has your name written on it,' he added, addressing Flicky. 'I haven't taken to you, I've had a long, hard day behind the ivories, and just give me one excuse and I'll happily fill you full of lead.'

Suddenly Flicky didn't seem so tall and not half as threatening. He, along with the others, meekly obeyed. Winston moved forward and ran his hand through and his eyes over the belongings.

'This is nothing. No keys, no cigarettes, no money and no drugs. You expect me to believe that this pile of rubbish is the sum total of what you four are carrying?'

There was no reply. 'OK then, if that's the way you want it, we'll do it another way. Strip.'

'What?' all four replied in indignant unity.

'You heard, man. Strip and be smart about it,' commanded the pastor.

'You don't want all of us man,' blurted out the smallest of the four. 'It's just Jimmy if it's drugs.'

'Shut it!' hissed Jimmy.

'We'll soon see, won't we? Chuck your clothes onto the pool table NOW!' barked Winston as Michael waved the pistol once more.

Soon the four tough guys were standing there just dressed in their white boxer shorts and not looking very tough at all. In particular they didn't appear tough to the two tarts who sat there with their mouths open in disbelief. Their heroes had been reduced to little boys without a punch being thrown or a kick lashed out, and by a pastor, the local funeral director, an old man and a sort of church-type hippie brandishing a pistol.

Stillion assisted Winston in emptying all the pockets of the discarded clothes, and sure enough, among the keys, knives and coins, there was plenty of grass.

'You're busted,' said Winston.

'We just smoke it, pastor. Honest. We're not selling it and it's only Jimmy involved in this cemetery thing,' insisted the smallest.

'What cemetery thing?' asked Stillion.

'Shut it or I'll fuckin' kill you,' threatened Jimmy to his little mate.

'I think we should go now,' interrupted Michael as he was suddenly struck by the thought that any number of these guys' mates could arrive at any moment and turn the tables on him and his chums. Moreover he knew something they didn't.

'OK. But we take him with us,' insisted Stillion, pointing at Jimmy.

'Come out from behind that counter,' commanded Winston. The little guy in the dirty apron, who had been peeing his pants, stood up.

'Do you have a stock room?'

The little guy nodded.

'Can it be locked?'

The little guy nodded again. Stillion held out his hand. The little guy reluctantly handed him a key.

'OK,' said Stillion, 'you three with me.'

'What about our clothes and belongings?' asked the only lout who hadn't spoken so far.

'Later. Move,' ordered Stillion, and proceeded to march them round the counter and into the back. He soon returned with just the key.

'Tell him to pick up his clothes and follow us,' said Stillion to Winston, as if Jimmy wouldn't understand the order from Stillion directly.

'You heard him,' said Winston to Jimmy.

'What about them?' asked Michael, pointing at the two black girls.

'Just leave them here. They won't steal any of the guys' things. Will you girls?'

The girls shook their heads violently.

So the four of them left with Jimmy, who gingerly crossed the freezing pavement in just his shorts while clutching his pile of clothes. He was seated in the front of Winston's car. It was decided that Michael should travel in the back to ensure Jimmy behaved, and that Bater, who suddenly felt quite faint now that the realisation of what had just happened was catching up with him, would drive Michael's car. Stillion would bring up the rear in his own car.

'Handsworth police station?' queried Winston out of his driver's window to Stillion as the latter threw the stock room key as hard as he could across the Lozells Road.

'No mon. Please Pastor Wylde. No police,' begged Jimmy, who hadn't been slow to realise that an evening spent talking to the police might not result in charges against him but would certainly mean missing his appointment in the cemetery – and the consequences of that might prove fatal. 'I could tell you a lot. But I won't tell the police.'

'OK. But you'd better not be wasting our time,' said Stillion.

'We'll go to my place,' said Winston. 'Tell your friend to follow me.'

Jimmy dressed as Winston drove the short distance to his house. Michael sat in the back and relaxed. Thank God they were out of that dreadful café. He knew things could have gone terribly wrong in there, but now this Jimmy seemed like a big kid listening to his old Sunday School teacher giving him a stern lecture as he drove.

Winston pulled into his drive and the two following cars parked in the road. Winston got out as did his two passengers on the other side of the vehicle. Jimmy knew it was now or never. He went for it. He kneed Michael in the cassock, in what he hoped was the right place. It was. The organist groaned, doubled up and dropped the gun, which disappeared into the snow on the drive. Jimmy galloped towards the pavement with Winston in pursuit. Stillion and Bater heard the commotion as they locked the cars in the street and Stillion gave chase while Bater went to the assistance of the organist.

Jimmy was a lot younger than Winston but he was out of condition, whereas the pastor was a fit man. Winston soon caught up with his ex-pupil and his anger spurred him to make a flying rugby tackle which brought both men crashing into the deep snow. Jimmy was underneath, face down, with his right arm forced up his back by his captor.

'Jimmy, may God forgive me but you make me so angry.

'I can't talk. I can't talk to you and I can't talk to the police. I'm a dead man if I do,' pleaded Jimmy.

'Well, if you won't talk to us then it becomes a police problem. That's their job and it's my duty to help them stop drug trafficking. And, I haven't even mentioned all the fornication and prostitution which I know you're involved with as well. But I will, to the police.'

By now Stillion had caught up with them and was listening to the conversation. Naturally he agreed with every word that Winston was saying. He was, after all, a good citizen. He shared Winston's desire to clean up the area and stop the drug parasites from keeping the folk of Lozells in their grip. He knew there could be no real prosperity until the yoke of the drug barons had been broken.

However, Stillion could not forget what one of Jimmy's colleagues had said in the café. The word 'cemetery' had been used in connection with drugs. It had been said that Jimmy was involved and to Stillion that only meant one thing. Jimmy must know something about the supposed existence of drugs, and perhaps even a gun, in the buried and soon to be exhumed coffin of Elizabeth Woodall.

Stillion knew that he must not let this opportunity slip. He also knew that the information could not be beaten out of Jimmy because Winston wouldn't do that and nor would the police. Jimmy knew this and he also knew what the price might be for informing. Hence, they needed to give Jimmy an incentive to talk.

Winston pulled Jimmy and himself to their feet without letting go of Jimmy's arm, which was still firmly pushed up his back. 'Well Jimmy, it's the police then.'

'I got an appointment to keep pastor, and if I don't I'm dead meat. You might as well kill me here and now as take me to the police.'

'Jimmy, if you don't talk to us and tell us about this trouble, then we can't help you.'

'I can't talk! I can't . . .'

'Well, then there's no alternative,' said Winston with a firmness which was just as much about him having no alternative as it was about his desire to be tough.

'Wait. I have an idea,' said Stillion. 'Winston, let's rejoin the others and go inside your house for a few minutes. I need to talk to you while Michael and Mr Bater look after Jimmy.'

Meanwhile, back in Winston's drive, Alan Bater, who had enjoyed more journalistic adventure in the last two hours than he had done during his whole career in Birmingham, had helped the damaged organist to his feet, and while the latter had recovered his breath and made the decision to live, Bater had groped around in the snow for the lost pistol. Eventually he found it, and picking it up shook the snow off it before inspecting it.

'Bloody hellfire,' he exclaimed. 'This is a bloody starting pistol.'

'I know that. It belongs to my dad. He used to be involved with Birchfield Harriers. The point is that *they* didn't know that.'

They were now joined by the others.

'I don't care for guns,' commented Winston, nodding at the pistol in Bater's hands.

'Well, this one is harmless pastor. By the way, I'm Alan Bater of the *Post* and *Mail*. I don't think we've had the opportunity of being introduced. Anyway, this pistol has only one real purpose and that's to start athletic races.'

'What!' exclaimed Stillion and Winston in unison as they both realised the significance of the statement.

'Fucking hell!' sighed Jimmy under his breath and almost to himself.

The grip on Jimmy was relaxed as all five men went inside. Once there, Jimmy was locked in the downstairs toilet as neither Stillion nor Winston were confident that either the hippie pianist or the old man could contain a man like Jimmy now that he knew that he'd been held up by a starting pistol.

Winston took the other two to the kitchen so that they could chat over a cup of coffee with Mrs Wylde, who had just finished bathing and putting to bed an exhausted Luther, who had been made most welcome by her own children.

Winston then led Stillion into his study so that they could speak privately. However, their conversation did not take place until Stillion had phoned the hospital and established from the ever-loyal Victoria that Stephanie was fine and giving no indications of an immediate birth.

Having assured Winston that Stephanie was doing well, Stillion came to the point. 'Look, Winston, that boy out there is a mine of information. He could tell us everything we need to know about the drugs racket, and judging by what one of his mates said he also knows about what went into that Woodall coffin, if anything, and if it did, how it got there. However, neither the police nor us are going to get any sense out of him while he is so clearly petrified of what will happen to him if he talks. You might make him fear God – I doubt it, but you might. The police might make him fear prison. I guess they have a better chance than you. I could beat the shit out of him, if you'd let me, which you wouldn't, but even if you did, I bet I'd stop a long way short of what the drug barons would do, and he knows that. So, we must give him a big incentive to *volunteer* the information.'

Winston thought for a second before replying. 'Yes, all of that makes sense, but what could we offer him?'

'Well, I could offer him money if that was OK with you,' said Stillion slowly. He was unsure how Winston was going to react to his suggestion. Such uncertainty was made much worse by the fact that a positive reaction from Winston was what Stillion desperately needed.

'No that would be bribery. On the other hand remember on Wednesday we conducted Jessie Nicholls' funeral. I told you that she had left me the whole of Peter Baker's estate for the benefit of my church and the salvation of its members. Well, Jimmy is or at least was a member of my church. I taught him at Sunday School. Surely a plane ticket to his native Jamaica and a cheque for a thousand pounds to get started with, provided he got a home, a proper job and gave up both drugs and drug dealing, would qualify as using the money for his salvation? We could then make all of this conditional on him telling us everything he knows. But how would we know what he was telling us was the truth?' reflected Winston.

'We wouldn't. But you're right – we're offering him a great way out in exchange for information which really helps us, and if he lies, he knows that we know where he's gone and that we could put it about where we got our information from. He has to trust us too. It's all about trust.'

Winston thought for a long while. Finally he said, 'OK. Let's do it. I don't know where the money's coming from, as we don't get anything from the estate until after probate . . .'

'Don't worry, Sloanes will give the church an interest-free loan and that's not bribery,' interjected Stillion.

'Well that's it then,' smiled Winston. 'Let's go and see the boy.' It was now eight forty-five p.m.

It was at about the same time that Terri arrived at the Villa Cross Café. It had taken her more than an hour and a quarter to tramp her way through the slush and ice back down the Soho Road and onto the Lozells Road. She had tried to thumb a lift

231

or even catch a lift and a little business on the way, but there were no takers. The roads were still very poor and the pavements worse. Therefore any kerb-crawling male looking for business would be driving straight to the known pubs, whore-houses or massage parlours rather than thinking any girl would be silly enough to be on the streets.

She had cried, mostly out of sheer frustration, nearly all the way back, and therefore with red eyes, runny make-up and a puffy face, she didn't quite cut either the beautiful or tough image that she normally portrayed.

She took a seat, lit a Players No. 6 and waited to meet Jimmy as arranged. Like most West Indian young men he wasn't very punctual and therefore she wasn't sure how long this wait might be. No doubt when he arrived eventually he would give her grief about her poor earnings. She would put this down to the dreadful weather. He wouldn't beat her in public, not even in this hell-hole. Anyway, hopefully he would be too worried and nervous about his little jaunt into the cemetery to trouble her too much.

She had looked around the room for him as she had entered and was surprised not to see him already there. That was strange. Not only did Jimmy play pool there with his mates every Friday evening before going to a club in the city centre, but she always had to meet him in the café at this time in order to give him any money she had earned. He had arranged to meet her there for that very purpose only yesterday morning.

Eventually the waiter, who could almost walk normally again as his jeans were nearly dry, came over to take an order. This was not because he was helpful but because the management would kick his arse if they discovered people using the place as a rendezvous without buying anything.

' 'ave you seen Jimmy?' she enquired.

'What? You not know? Pastor Wylde, the funeral guy with the blond hair and two other motherfuckers arrived here. Held the joint up and took Jimmy away. They used guns and locked the rest of us in the stock room. Everybody is raging about it man.'

'Wot the fuck is yow talking about? Pastor Wylde and Stillion Sloane acting as Butch Cassidy and the Sundance Kid? Don't be stupid! Yow're drugged up or wot?' answered a disbelieving Terri.

'Ask anybody, it's all over Lozells. I thought you knew. I mean, I thought that was why you was crying.'

'Well it ain't,' Terri said irritably. She went to find Flicky. He told her the whole story. Immediately she left for a phone box to call Elton. Of course she might be going to phone Elton and warn him that Pastor Wylde and Stillion Sloane had kidnapped Jimmy and probably frog-marched him down to the local nick. A good sister might have done this, but that was not Terri's style and the safety of Elton came way down her list of priorities.

She realised that her chances of finding Stillion and making her latest plan work were now fading fast, so the original plan *must* work or she might yet be thrown into Mo-Mo's stark naked. Therefore she put the man from Edgbaston to the back of her mind and concentrated on survival. She must ensure that brother Elton went to the cemetery and retrieved the ring as planned. She must warn Elton that Jimmy wouldn't be meeting up with him or he might wait for him before chickening out himself. On the other hand, if she were to tell him that lover boy was down the cop shop and might be spilling the beans, then wild horses wouldn't drag Elton anywhere near the cemetery. So she phoned Elton and told him that she had just been told that Jimmy had taken off to Brighton with a white girl who looked after the coats in the Elbow Room Club.

'I'll fucking kill him! What am I going to do now?' moaned Elton.

'Yow still got to go. Yow is dead. I'm dead. We both is dead in the water if we don't get that ring. And I can't take any more!' Terri began to cry.

'OK. OK, sis, don't cry. I'll not let yow down. I'll phone Alf. That bastard will 'ave to 'elp moy. I can't do it on me own, 'e'll 'ave to 'elp 'cos 'e needs the ring too.'

*

233

Stillion followed Winston out of the study and back into the hall where Jimmy was retrieved from the toilet. Michael Russell and Alan Bater left the entertaining company of the serene Mrs Wylde and found the other three in Winston's lounge. All, Jimmy included, were offered seats in the messy but spotlessly clean room. Once everybody was comfortable, Winston opened the discourse.

'Look Jimmy. I've known you for many years. Nearly all your life. You've turned your back on your parents, some of your old friends, your church, your learnings, your cricket and anything else that was good. The happy, smiling face that we saw at church or on the cricket field has been replaced by the haunted face of a man who lives on immoral earnings and money made from helping people get drugs. These drugs cause addiction and are expensive. Thus the addicts must steal to pay for the drugs that feed their habit. What have you done? Look at the misery. Misery for addicts, misery for the robbed, misery for parents, their children, and the general misery as you and people like you have continued to drag Lozells and my people down.'

'Is that the end of the lecture?' interrupted Jimmy under his breath in an act of semi-defiance.

'No it is not, and you had better listen and listen well because you is going to make one almighty decision in a moment's time Jimmy. One hell of a decision which could determine the rest of your life. Now are you listening to me boy?'

'Yes,' answered Jimmy in a quiet, sulky voice.

'Good. Now I need things from you. Mr Sloane here needs to know things from you. You help us and we'll help you.'

'You can't help me man. I talk to you. I squeal on people. I is dead. Oh shit, I is dead!' Jimmy rolled his eyes and blew out his cheeks.

'Not if you're not here,' interjected Stillion. 'Look, we know you have a passport and we know you have relatives in Jamaica. Winston tells me you went there to visit them last year or the year before. Anyway, what if we knew of a trust, a legacy that wanted to help you? A kind of charity that believed you were

234

worth saving and would pay your ticket to Jamaica and then give you a thousand pounds to start again without the drugs, without the prostitution and without the threat of violence that keeps you so frightened now? A clean start. A second chance. If we knew such people wouldn't you want to meet them and take them up on their offer? Wouldn't it get you out of the hole you're in?'

'Well sure man. Of course I don't want the bastards to cut my willie off. But then why should I believe you? Why would a charity want to help me. You? Sure you two, I see that. But why a charity?'

'A Mrs Jessie Nicholls left the church a lot of money to help people like you Jimmy,' answered Winston. 'You might even remember her. A large lady who would come down from Great Barr every Sunday.' Jimmy shook his head. 'She left money for me to help people like you and therefore it's me who will make the decision. But I'm only going to save you if you help me save Lozells. Therefore I want to know all about the who's-who of the drug network. I want to know the people, the drugs, the places and the times . . .'

'And I want to know everything about the drugs and the gun that are supposed to be in Mrs Woodall's coffin,' added Stillion. 'And before you even think about why you should help me, let me tell you that it is I who will have to find the cash to fund you until Mrs Nicholls' will is cleared.'

'Well, there it is Jimmy. The choice is yours. A visit to the police station with the drugs that I picked off the pool table or a chance to get the drug barons off your back and get a new start. What's it to be?'

'Would I have to stay away forever as part of the deal?'

'No. But I wouldn't come back for a while if I were you, and if and when you do it must only be as an honourable citizen that I see on my front pew every week,' replied Winston.

'How do I know you'll keep your word?' asked Jimmy.

'You don't,' answered Stillion. 'But you should know that Mr Bater here is a journalist, and I suppose there must be a bit of

him that hopes we don't as it would make such a great story.'
This perverse piece of psychology did the trick.

'A ticket when?' asked Jimmy.

'Monday,' replied Stillion.

'Money?'

'Same day.'

'Flight?'

'Next week.'

'Safe house until then?'

'Here or somewhere else of your choosing,' answered
Winston.

'And if I wanted to take my girlfriend?'

At this point Stillion looked to Winston who nodded and
Stillion replied, 'No problem.'

'OK man, deal. I'll tell all, but you must get me and my girl
away or we is both dead.'

Then Jimmy told them everything he knew about the drug
network. The people, the places, the times, the drugs, the prices.
Everything. Bater and Pastor Wylde made notes while Stillion
and Michael Russell sat and listened.

'Well that's it. He won't use my actual name in the paper?'
finished Jimmy as he pointed at Bater.

'No I won't,' Bater answered for himself.

Stillion had been very patient. He had played the game and
let Winston obtain and document the evidence and information
he needed to help the police, nail the pushers and maybe even
scare the barons a little. But now it was his turn. 'OK Jimmy,
now tell me all about the drugs and gun that are supposed to
be in Mrs Woodall's coffin.'

'OK. Well it's like this,' commenced Jimmy, who was finding
it easier to talk now. A confession always gets easier once it's
started. He began his tale. He told them about his debt to the
Wilkes and how it was really Terri's fault. He told them about
the car trip and the meeting in the pub. He told them about
Elton's plan and how Alf bought it, but at what price to Elton
and Terri. And then he told them about the old man sitting
next to them all in the pub – a Mr Sydney Gridley, and how he

had taken over after Alf had left and made some adjustments to the plan.

As he spoke Bater, Russell and Wylde sat there in complete disbelief. Stillion was intrigued, amazed and bloody angry but he did not struggle to believe because he knew Harry Wilkes, Elton Field and Sydney Gridley much better than the others.

Now all the pieces to the jigsaw fitted, with Sydney Gridley's involvement confirmed – no doubt he had wanted to gain favour with Fred Gilbert as well – Stillion could even see how Fred Gilbert would have used the story against him with Charlie Williams and that it was either Gilbert or Gridley himself that had leaked the story to the press. Yes, Stillion was there, well nearly there, because neither Jimmy nor Stillion knew about the relationship between Harry Wilkes and Inspector Hooper.

'And that's about it man. But when your willie is going to be snipped, it's got to be self-preservation that's the thing really.'

'You said you're to meet Elton tonight? Where? When?' Stillion asked.

'Ten past ten, halfway up the road which runs up the old side of the cemetery. There's a small gap in the railings. I was to climb through and wait behind some bushes there for him. I'm glad not to be there; I hate cemeteries and I've never been to one at night.'

'Well it's ten to ten now. I've got twenty minutes to get up there and catch the little shit in the act,' said Stillion, looking at his watch.

'Shouldn't we call the police and let them handle it?' asked Winston.

'There's no time, and if they go crashing in there with size ten boots and Elton is alerted then Jimmy's tale is just a story. It would be his word against theirs.'

'I ain't giving no word. That wasn't the deal. You said Jamaica with my woman and a grand next week. I ain't talking to the pigs. That wasn't the deal,' bleated a panicked Jimmy.

'Quite so,' said Stillion, to Jimmy's surprise. 'I must go or I might miss him.'

'Correction. We must go – you'll need a witness,' said Winston as Stillion rose to go.

'Better with two. I'm going to the end of the line,' added Bater, and then asked: 'May I use your phone?' He dialled without waiting for a response. 'Hold the front page. No, hold pages one and two and tell that Yorkshire twit that I've got a story which will blow his socks clean off.'

It was decided that someone must remain at the house to protect and keep an eye on Jimmy. Jimmy would probably be as good as gold now, but even his mere presence there could attract trouble and Winston needed to know that his wife, children and guest, little Luther, would all be safe. It would not be a good idea to take Jimmy to the cemetery, so someone had to stay and it was quickly decided that it would be best if Winston himself remained behind as the custodian of his own home. Michael Russell was relieved. He thought the job might have been given to him. He wanted to be in on the kill, especially if it meant getting back at Sydney Gridley.

As they left, Stillion turned in Winston's porch and shook Winston's hand. 'Thanks Winston. Thanks for this and thanks for the roof.'

'Shut it. Thanks to you and these fellows I'm here – otherwise I might now be on a hospital ward or even in a hospital mortuary. Now take care, do this thing and then go and see your wife man.'

Stillion led the way with Bater. Michael Russell followed in his own car as they made their way across Handsworth to the cemetery.

Having put the phone down to his sister at five past nine, Elton set about finding Alf. He did so with a heavy heart. He knew Alf would be his only salvation. He daren't approach anyone else. Nobody else knew about the scam except Sydney Gridley and Nick Smith, and neither of them would go down into a grave with him. So Alf was the answer. Either Alf would come himself or at least order one of the boys to.

Alf needed the caper to be successful as much as he did. Oh sure, Alf could inflict pain on him if it went wrong but then Harry Wilkes could inflict even greater discomfort upon Alf if things didn't work out to his satisfaction. None of that worried Elton. His problem was how to get hold of Alf at such short notice on a Friday night.

Elton knew Alf and the boys pulled in the club protection money on Thursday and Friday nights. The threat of wrecking the joint and thus the weekend trade as well acted as a little added incentive for the owners to use Wilkes' security exclusively and always pay on time. But which club would he be at? Elton phoned round the venues and managed to get Alf at the fourth attempt.

'What the fuck do yow want toe-rag? Yow is supposed to be on yowa way to the bleedin' cemetery ain't yow?'

'Well that's just it. I got a problem . . .'

'Problem! What problem? You had better not have a problem 'cos if yow and Jimmy don't do the business I'm going to 'ave both yowa willies chopped up and served as calamari in Gino's Italian.'

'Look it ain't moy fault. That bastard Jimmy 'as run off to Brighton with some tart.'

'So, we'll find 'im, snip 'is balls off, put them in a pickle jar and display them to show what 'appens if yow upset moy OK? And if yow don't want to end up the same way I'd get up to that fucking grave if I were yow.'

'Of course I'll go but I need 'elp. I can't 'old the torch and unscrew the lid, open the coffin and find the ring on my own. You'll 'ave to come and 'old the torch for moy.'

'I ain't going in any fuckin' cemetery at night mate,' said Alf, horrified at the suggestion. On the other hand, Elton had a point, and careless use of the torch might be spotted by an occupant of one of the houses situated on the other side of the road. In a more composed voice he continued, 'I can't 'elp yow. Mr Wilkes would be most angry if I didn't finish my security rounds for 'im. But I see yowa point. I'll send Frankie to meet yow at the original place and at the same time. But then don't yow dare fuck up. Mr Wilkes will not be pleased if this goes wrong and yow know what that means don't yow?'

'Yeah I do,' replied Elton in a resigned fashion.

Alf replaced the telephone receiver behind the bar of 'Open Lock Club' and turned to face his small army of assistants all suitably dressed in black tie. 'Er Frankie, a word in private my son . . .'

Stillion, followed by Michael, approached the cemetery from the road which led directly to the main gates. Then, instead of turning left and up to the proposed rendezvous of Elton and Jimmy he turned right into a small estate of 1960s houses and parked his car among those of the residents. Michael Russell did the same.

'Why do you think they chose this time?' Bater asked Stillion.

'Well, probably because it's late enough and dark enough but not too late. I mean, if they had chosen midnight or even one in the morning then while they might have been OK in the cemetery they would have been most conspicuous once they left. I honestly don't know, but I would hazard a guess that's why.'

They walked towards the main entrance gates. Suddenly Stillion stopped and whispered to Michael, 'You keep KV.'

'What?'

'Watch out,' answered Bater for Stillion.

'Yes, just make sure the coast is clear while I help Alan over this fence.'

'But over the fence is a garden,' pointed out Michael.

'Trust me.'

Stillion helped Bater up and then it was up to the old man to negotiate the spikes on top of the five-foot fence and let himself down the other side into the deep snow of the garden. Then Stillion helped Michael to achieve the same before joining his two companions in the garden.

'This is the garden of the lodge house by the main gates.

240

We'll cross it to the other fence which is only a small wooden one. Once over that we're in the cemetery. Be careful where you tread. The lodge is occupied by the cemetery registrar. He has a large German shepherd dog that lays dog turds six inches high and there'll be hundreds of them under the snow.'

'Fuck the dog crap, it's the dog that I don't want to come into contact with,' muttered Michael.

'Well, keep your voice down, hope that it isn't put out to take a crap and let's get out of here,' replied Stillion.

'I'll drink to that,' said Bater, who still wasn't quite sure if he was dreaming all this.

Once they were over the small wooden fence they were standing in the cemetery, 'Follow me,' ordered Stillion. 'And follow *directly* behind me. Don't stray to the right or the left because we're crossing a public section and there'll be some open graves here which could be deep and hard to see in the dark.'

'Jesus Christ,' exclaimed Bater in a whisper.

'You don't get any of that at Perry Barr,' said Michael in a serious voice.

'Why not?' asked the ever inquisitive journalist.

'Because it's a crematorium,' sniggered Michael.

'Shsh!' insisted Stillion.

They passed across the packed ice in the main drive with great care. Then Stillion led them left along the snow-covered verge back towards the main gates.

'I thought the grave was up there,' whispered Michael, pointing up the hill to the night.

'It is, but we'd be noticed long before we got to our hiding place if we took that route. Follow me.'

Stillion led them down to the gate and then up a small path to the right which ran along that side of the cemetery. Bushes just inside the perimeter fence hid their presence from the road and the houses, while a line of trees and the hundreds of large Victorian gravestones kept them well concealed from anyone like Elton who might already be in the cemetery. They proceeded slowly and silently up the hill. Stillion counted off three pathways to the right. He stopped at the fourth.

'This is Hodgson Walk. It's so named because some descendants of Cecil Rhodes called Hodgson are buried in that posh section to the right. The Hodgson grave has a large white marble monument on it. It's about halfway down. We'll hide behind it. The Woodall grave is across the path on the left. We'll be able to see and hear Elton. As long as we remain still and quiet he'll never know we're there. Follow me. Absolute silence from now on please.'

They proceeded until they reached the Hodgson monument.

'Don't step on the actual grave because it has marble chippings on it beneath the snow,' whispered Stillion. The other two obeyed without a word. They took up their positions and waited.

Sydney Gridley had experienced an exhausting and stressful time. A near punch-up with that bloody boy yesterday had been followed by the funeral from hell today. More amazingly the boy seemed to be standing up to the bashing the tabloids were giving him better than anticipated. Either he wasn't feeling the pain as much as Sydney had hoped, or if he was then, to Sydney's great displeasure, he was good at hiding it. Sydney hated Stillion so much that he wanted him not only to suffer enormously but be forced to show it – to be humiliated by his public despair.

At the end of a long and frustrating day, Sydney had withdrawn to his small lonely flat. He had intended to have a bath and go to bed but his mind couldn't shake off Elton's night work in the cemetery. The money would come in useful. He liked the idea of taking so much so unfairly from Elton. But most of all he liked the idea that if Elton followed his instructions correctly and left the coffin open, then the finger of suspicion would point at Stillion. Thus his plan would continue the uncertainty and would thus prevent Sloane & Sons from expanding and may even ruin what they had.

So there was no bath. The cemetery was a magnet and Sydney was drawn to it. At nine forty-five he put on his coat and left home.

He approached the cemetery by the country lane which wound across the snow-covered Sandwell Valley from the Newton Road. He did this on purpose as he didn't want Elton to know of his presence. He knew the point and the time where and when Elton and Jimmy had agreed to meet and enter the cemetery. As a result he determined to enter unnoticed right at the top end where a car accident had bent the railings and thus caused a gap which his small frame could get through. Thereafter he would creep the considerable distance through the snow to near the Woodall Grave and ensure the two incompetent idiots did the job he wanted.

Sydney didn't really believe in God and he certainly didn't believe in ghosts, so a trip through Birmingham's second largest cemetery on a dark and moonless night posed no problem to him whatsoever. He wanted to protect his investment and ensure his instructions were carried out. He would remain out of sight and observe. If they got it right, then fine. On the other hand if they got it wrong, he would be there to put them right.

He slipped quietly over the ice and down the sweeping main drive from the top gate, crossed in front of the beautiful gothic cemetery chapel, avoided some naked tarmac for the sake of silence, passed between the brick graves of some important nineteenth-century industrialists and one most treasured child and climbed up the section behind. Then he turned left and inched his way down through some very deep snow and onto the section where the Woodall grave was. There he hid behind a large headstone. He was some thirty-five feet from Woodall's opened plot which was further down the hill. Sloane and co. were another twenty-five feet or so beyond. All had slipped so silently into place that Sydney was unaware of the Sloane party's presence, as indeed they were of his. Therefore in blissful innocence everyone waited in silence. It was now ten past ten.

*

Frankie had blown a fuse when told he must go with Elton and refused point blank to do so.

'Look Alf, mate, yow do it if yow want or get another silly fucker,' he said, pointing at the little black-tie army who all looked away. 'I ain't going down a fucking grave mate. I ain't. Wild horses won't drag moy down there, OK! I mean, you get another idiot. Who yow phoning?'

'Mr Wilkes,' answered Alf before continuing, ''ello 'arry. I 'ave a little problem. That little gardening job tonight, well the little git needs 'elp cos Sambo's done a runner and now Frankie's refusing to take the coon's place.'

'Is he?'

'Is he what?'

'Is he refusing to go, yow fuckin' thick prat! Ask 'im from moy!' screamed Harry.

'Mr Wilkes asks yow if yow is refusing to go,' passed on Alf in a slow and deliberate fashion.

Frankie shook his head.

'What does that mean, turd 'ead? Is yow going or not?'

'I'll do it,' answered a deflated Frankie. Going down a grave to rob a decaying body in the pitch black might be horrible but it was a lot less dangerous than crossing Mr Harry Wilkes.

'He'll do it. Thanks. Goodbye.'

But Harry hadn't finished. 'Not so fuckin' fast Alf. I don't want any fuck ups. Yow go and supervise them. Let Frankie do the work. Keep a low profile. Yow know what I mean. Keep out of sight but ensure the job is done. I wouldn't be in yowa shoes mate if it ain't done right. Yow understand moy cock? I want the money and I want it all. OK?'

'But what about the collections?' whined Alf.

'Do this and then finish them. Right?'

'Sure boss,' replied Alf. Now as crestfallen as Frankie, he put down the phone and stood there in silence.

'Well?' questioned the others.

'Well what?' replied one aggravated Alf.

'What did the boss say?' they asked.

244

'He said we must all go and make sure that the little four-eyed turd and Frankie do a good job.'

'What! Yow must be fuckin' jokin'?' answered one in disbelief.

'Yow know full well that I ain't fuckin' Joseph King and shut it, or would yow like moy to speak to Mr Wilkes about it?'

'No thanks,' was the response. And all six of them left for Handsworth Cemetery.

They arrived by the bottom gates at eight minutes past ten and parked their car in the small bus terminus which was a little to the right of the gates, not far from the lodge whose garden the Sloane party had crossed only minutes earlier. Then they crossed over and proceeded past the stonemason's and up the snow-covered road to where they were to meet Elton.

If any householder had torn themselves away from *News at Ten* and its weekly Friday-night job survey that was used to beat up the country's first woman prime minister, they might have noticed six big fellows in dinner jackets trudging through the snow. But apparently they didn't. Or maybe someone did and sensibly thought, 'Leave well alone,' and had gone back to the TV set. Either way the little army arrived at the gap in the railings and climbed through at ten-fifteen.

'What the fuck is all of this?' whispered a cold Elton as he squinted at Alf through his thick glasses. 'I thought yow weren't coming and now yow bring all these guys dressed like club bouncers. Talk about attracting attention. There's only snow and mud in here you know. These guys will freeze dressed like that and I only need one to help moy.'

'Shut it four-eyes. Mr Wilkes' orders, OK?'

'OK,' answered Elton, who couldn't believe Harry Wilkes could have been that daft but thought he'd better get on with it before the next Wilkes order was to take all their wives as well.

In fact, Elton had been quite astute for once. Harry Wilkes had only ordered Alf to go with Frankie. The idea of bringing the others as extra protection against whatever monsters lurked in the cemetery at night was Alf's own idea. Alf couldn't have gone down the grave for sure, but neither did he want to wait in this snow-covered graveyard on his own while the other two did the deed. He might be big and strong but all of that counted for nothing when dealing with ghouls and ghosts.

They were about to proceed down the same perimeter path that Sloane had come up and then head along Hodgson Walk to the grave when another body pulled itself through the railings.

'What the fuck?' exclaimed Alf.

'It's me. Nick Smith.'

'What the fuck is yow 'ere for?' demanded Alf.

'Yow don't think I'd trust that little four-eyed, spotty shit did yow? I'm 'ere to protect my money.'

'Yeah, well we're 'ere for that.'

'So I see. But I didn't know Wilkes was sending half his army,' replied Smith in a whisper.

Smith had kept a low profile all week, preferring to let Wilkes' boys do the job they were so very good at. But the original plan had been for only Elton and Jimmy to go to the cemetery and therefore, just like Sydney Gridley, Nick Smith had been drawn to this eerie place in order to protect his interests.

Elton led the way, followed by Frankie. Then came Alf, his guards and then Nick Smith. They were quiet, but not quite as quiet as Sloane or Gridley had been before them. Both Sloane and co. on the far side of Hodgson Walk and Sydney just up the hill from the Woodall grave could hear them coming. They couldn't see them and had no reason to think that there were more than two of them, but they could hear them.

As they walked down Hodgson Walk, Elton noticed footprints in the snow. Whose were these? He worried for a second and then noticed there were lots of them leading to and from his gran's grave. Of course, the bloody thing had only been reopened that afternoon in readiness for tomorrow's exhumation. He relaxed and proceeded towards the grave.

Some forty feet short of the grave, Alf stopped and raised his hand so that those behind him also halted. Then as Elton and Frankie proceeded on to the grave, he led the rest to the left just of the Walk and signalled for them to crouch behind a large black marble headstone.

So, as Elton helped the reluctant Frankie down into the grave he was being watched by Stillion and co, Sydney and Alf, Nick Smith and the others.

Elton knew that there would be only a small amount of soil above the coffin, so he had no need for a large spade. Indeed he had only brought a small coal shovel, which he had kept under his coat along with a screwdriver and a torch. He wore gloves and intended to dispose of his tools and the torch in the canal the next day. He gave a shivering and unhappy Frankie the torch.

'Point the fuckin' thing down into the grave before turning it on. Then point it at whatever I'm doing so I can see,' he commanded. The boot was on the other foot for once. He was entitled to give the orders as he knew what he was doing and was also the brave one that was going to put his hand inside the coffin and wrestle the ring from the skeleton, or worse the decaying corpse.

They were several feet down, as the grave had originally been bought for two and therefore room had been left to inter old Bill Woodall on top of his wife when the time came. This might have posed problems for them in getting out, especially Elton, who was only around five and a half feet tall, which meant that his height was about the same as the grave was deep. However, wooden supports had been left in the grave overnight to prevent the sides from collapsing, and these provided a climbing frame to the surface.

Elton began to scrape away the soil. 'Hold the fuckin' torch steady mate,' he whispered in frustration. 'Yow're shaking the bleedin' thing all over the place. There's no need to be so terrified, they're all dead in this place. My gran wouldn't 'urt yow any road. She never would 'ave, when she were alive neither, so yow can stop shakin' with fear.'

'I ain't shaking with fear,' lied a thoroughly miserable Frankie. 'I'm shaking with cold. I only got this poxy dinner jacket on yow know.'

'Stand with yowa feet apart and right up against the sides of the grave like moy,' instructed Elton.

'Why?'

'Cos yow 'ave a good chance of going through the fuckin' lid if yow don't. It were only a veneered oak on chipboard and it's been down 'ere a bit. If yow want to get friendly with moy gran, just keep standin' as yow are and I'll wager yow'll be in the cowin' box with 'er any minute.'

Frankie jumped and pushed his legs as far apart as the grave would allow.

'Remind moy to leave the grave so it looks like someone's been in.'

'Why?'

''Cos the pigs will believe it were the Vance gang or Sloanes trying to get the gun and drugs of course, and then they'll never know any better. That's good for moy boss and yowas ain't it?'

'Suppose so,' answered Frankie, who really couldn't give a shit. He just wanted Elton to get on with it.

'But remind moy to churn up any footprints,' went on Elton as he worked away.

'Why? I mean, if yow want to make it look like somebody has been 'ere?' asked Frankie as he had nothing better to do other than hold the torch and wait.

'Because the footprints belong to yow and moy silly! God! Yow ain't going to get a degree in being a crook is yow?'

'Watch it four-eyes! We won't always be down 'ere yow know.'

'We will if yow don't shine that fuckin' torch over 'ere,' answered Elton as he located the two head screws and set about them with his screwdriver. Then he dug away some wet and heavy soil beyond the head-end of the lid. He did this so that he might get his hands down below the lid's moulding.

'Get right down to the foot end. I've cleared all the soil away and unscrewed the head end and now I'm going to try and lift the lid. Hopefully the leverage will pull the screws out of the chipboard on the foot end and the lid will be free to come up. When it does, yow pass moy the torch and hold the fuckin' lid while I try and find the fuckin' ring. Got it?'

'Yeah,' replied Frankie, who had to admit that Elton did seem to know what he was doing. He was also cheered by the prospect that, as he was holding the lid from the outside while Elton went into the coffin, he would not be required to see the corpse.

Elton chucked away any remaining soil that was in his way up and out of the grave, got his feet either side of the lid and then bent down so that he could get his fingers under the moulding. He pulled up. The lid came up some two inches and then stopped. He tried again – the same thing happened.

'Shine the torch all around the edge of the lid,' he commanded.

'What's the matter?'

'The fuckin' thing won't come up. I'll have to dig out some more.' And with that he used the shovel to remove more soil from around the edges.

It was now ten-forty and Stillion and co. hadn't moved for thirty-five minutes. None of them had known they would be spending any time that evening outside, let alone in a very cold cemetery standing in deep snow that had their feet both wet and freezing. Bater, who was a lot older than the other two, was now very cold but wouldn't have missed being there for all the tea in China.

They could see the torch flickering in the grave. They had seen something they assumed was soil come flying out of the hole and they could hear muffled voices.

On the other side of the plot, up the hill. Sydney's observations had been the same. He was also very cold, even though he had come dressed for the occasion. The headstone he was hidden behind wasn't big enough to allow him to stand. His joints were too stiff for him to crouch so he had had to sit down in the snow and now his arse was truly frozen. Sydney, ever the gaunt little man, thought his haunches were about to burst through his thin little bottom.

But neither Alan Bater nor Sydney Gridley were as cold as Alf and his boys. Although they had been crouching down for only about eighteen minutes, the lightweight nature of their suits meant that they were now very cold indeed.

'What the fuck is going on with those two?' whispered Alf to Nick Smith.

'I don't know, but it takes time.'

'Yeah. Well it's OK for yow mate in yowa fuckin' big coat,' replied Alf, who was envious of the great coat that Smith had wrapped himself up in.

After another five minutes of patient work Elton made a second attempt at lifting the lid. This time it came up some four inches and then with another tug the foot-end screws broke away from the chipboard and that part of their mission was accomplished. He was in.

'Right, pass moy the torch and hold the lid up as high as yow can,' ordered Elton as he bent forward.

This was the ghoulish bit. He poked his head under the lid and shone the torch. He looked down the length to the foot end and could see the gown and frill were still amazingly white. He was surprised by the dank, damp, earthy smell. He had expected the stench of rotting flesh. There was none, or if there were, it was less powerful than this musty, earthy odour.

He looked back up the coffin. Immediately below his own hand was the rotting head of his grandmother. She wasn't a skeleton, but she wasn't really recognisable. Then he caught sight of her white, crinkly hair and he knew it was her and a shiver ran down his spine. At last, perhaps, a flash of conscience. It lasted but a second as he pointed the torch back down to the left with his right hand and used his left to yank up the left sleeve of the shroud. Up popped a rotting hand. He focused the beam on it. Praise the Lord. There were two rings. The gold wedding ring that old Bill Woodall had given his doting Betty all those years ago and a diamond ring which was there to save the hides of Terri and himself.

He rested the torch on his grandmother's chest and used his gloved right hand to remove both rings. The wedding ring might be a nice little bonus for him. Just his little secret.

The rings came off easily enough. There wasn't the fat on

250

the fingers that there once was. He dropped the sleeve and the decaying digits disappeared once more. He placed the wedding ring in his trouser pocket, but held onto the diamond ring.

Then he resurfaced from beneath the lid with the words, 'Got it.'

'Fuckin' great mate,' spat out a relieved Frankie in a loud whisper.

'Ssh. Yow'll wake the dead. It ain't much to look at is it?' Elton showed Frankie the ring by shining the torch on it, before putting it into his coat pocket.

They then replaced the lid and Elton scraped away any footprints with the shovel. They shone the torch about to see if all was OK. It seemed so. You could tell the grave had been tampered with, but not by them.

'Shine the torch on these planks. I'll get out. Then yow pass moy the torch and I'll guide yow out,' whispered Elton cheerfully. It was nearly over now.

Elton had climbed halfway up the planks and thus had his torso above ground level when a figure stepped forward onto Hodgson Walk.

'I'm making a citizen's arrest . . .'

'Aah, aah, aah!' screamed Elton who, having failed to recognise the voice of his old boss Stillion Sloane, thought a spirit of divine retribution had come for him, and in complete panic and shock he fell back in the grave and onto Frankie, whose right foot as a result went through the coffin lid and got stuck there.

Elton was struggling to his feet while Frankie attempted to free his foot as Stillion continued, 'I charge you with grave robbing and giving false information to the police. Do not resist. I am not alone.'

'No yow fuckin' ain't mate, whoever yow might be,' boomed Alf's voice as he led his army of dinner jackets down Hodgson Walk to rescue Frankie, and hopefully Elton with one important ring on him.

Stillion, now joined by the other two, turned to see their advancing enemy.

251

Suddenly a strong Brummie voice commanded, 'Everybody stay exactly where yow are. Yow're all under arrest.' Then in a flash the grave and the immediate area around it were lit up by the large arc lamps that had been placed there in readiness for tomorrow's exhumation.

The voice had come from the right of Stillion. Alf and his lads couldn't see the man behind the voice as he was behind the lights. They didn't know if he had company, or if he did, how many. But to them it was definitely the voice of a copper. They just knew it and they also just knew that it was time to go.

'Run for it lads! It's the pigs!' Suddenly the dinner jacket boys were off. Alf hesitated for a second. So close and yet now, so far. Then he scarpered too as the boys in blue appeared from behind gravestones and rushed past a shocked Stillion as they gave chase.

Alf, Nick Smith and the boys dispersed. Alf made for where they had entered the cemetery, the others did not. As a result he had a chance of escape while they had none.

Elton had got back to his feet and looked up.

'Yow're nicked mate,' said a copper, peering down at him. The grave had become a pit and he and Frankie were captured in it. Frankie obeyed the first rule of the Wilkes gang when confronted by the law: deny, deny, deny.

'What yow on about officer? Moy and moy mate 'ere was taking a short cut across the cemetery when we fell in 'ere. And now I got moy foot stuck in this bleedin' coffn.'

'Course yow 'ave,' replied the officer as he bent down and removed something from underneath one of the top planks. 'And this microphone will have picked up all yowa chat about 'ow unlucky yow was to fall down a grave won't it?'

The police, who were out in force to deal with just this situation, were now galloping over graves and rounding up Nick Smith and the dinner jacket boys.

The officer in charge approached Stillion, unsure of his role in all this. After all, his commanding officer, Inspector Hooper, had organised the trap, expecting to snare Sloane and the

Vance gang. The officer therefore hadn't expected Sloane to be attempting a citizen's arrest of Wilkes' people – which he now knew them to be having clocked Frankie's well-known mush in the grave.

Alan Bater, who was well-known to, and respected by, the police, stepped up and soon all was made clear. As he told his tale Elton and Frankie were hauled from the grave and handcuffed. Then at various intervals policemen returned with their prisoners. Eventually all the captives were lined up. There were seven in total: Elton, Frankie, Nick Smith and four dinner jacket boys. Alf had got away. He might soon wish he hadn't. He would have to explain to Harry Wilkes how five of his heavy brigade had been arrested in the pursuit of a diamond ring which was now, along with Elton and Nick Smith, in police custody. Oh, Harry wouldn't like any of that one little bit. Not only had the ring gone, and the day's debts remained unpaid, but Elton and Smith couldn't be relied upon to keep their mouths shut. Worst of all, Harry had lost the majority of his hard men that kept all of his various customers in line. And on top of all this disastrous news, Alf would have to explain how four more of Harry's men came to be in the cemetery than were supposed to have been there.

The prisoners were cautioned and then marched away down Hodgson Walk to the main drive where police vans had arrived for their transportation. Stillion, Michael, and Alan Bater were free to go, provided they promised to attend the Steelhouse Lane police station at eleven a.m. the next day to make statements. Two policemen remained behind to guard the grave. The exhumation would be carried out as planned tomorrow.

As they walked down the drive Stillion expressed his gratitude to Michael and Alan.

'Guys, you're heros. Without you two tonight, well, who knows what would have happened.'

In all the excitement time had flown by and it was eleven-fifteen when Michael rushed Bater away so that he might collect his own car at Sloane House before dashing into town to post his blockbuster.

'I'm too late for the first one but if I race I'll make the late edition. Good luck with the birth. Thanks for everything. I've had the time of my life,' shouted Bater, waving out of the window as Michael's car sped away.

The two remaining policemen were now on their own and after all the excitement were sufficiently off guard not to notice the slight and frozen Sydney Gridley slip away. The further he got the more his fear turned to disappointment and then anger, before fear returned as his thoughts turned to what Elton might be telling the police. Sydney realised that Elton had no incentive to keep Sydney's name out of it. On the other hand, Elton had no proof and it would be just his word, the word of a liar and a thief, against the word of a councillor, JP and Rotarian. He suspected Terri wouldn't come forward as that would incriminate her and he had noticed that Jimmy was not standing under the arc lights as one of those arrested, so maybe he had got away. Either way, Sydney needed to get back home. He shuffled his feet through the snow to disguise his prints.

He was a most miserable man. He could only be distracted from the thought of Sloane being hailed as a wronged man who had heroically cleared his own name by the thought of what the inside of a prison might be like for an old JP who had been so judgemental while on the bench.

Ever since his defeat by Sloane, life had held out little prospect of hope. He had, after all, lost the business and his family in a week of madness caused by his blind hate of Sloane, and now in the space of another week that same hatred might have cost him his dignity, and his freedom as well.

Stillion made his way from Handsworth via Smethwick, Bearwood and Harborne to Selly Oak where he hoped Stephanie was still waiting in the hospital to have their baby.

He drove as fast as the roads would allow. The events of the evening, his heroics and the joy that should result from the lifting of the depression caused by such false and public accusation were hardly evident to him. He would savour them later for sure, but for now he was consumed by a passion for his wife and a great need to be with her. He played Paul McCartney's 'Maybe I'm Amazed' several times over on the car's stereo as he went. The lyrics seemed so apt.

He dashed into the hospital and down the corridors which he had trod more sedately with Stephanie twenty-four hours earlier. He occasionaly sped past a nurse or a white-coated person who would then call after him, 'Can I help you?' He ignored them and pushed on.

He stormed into the room. She was gone. Victoria was there. So was his mum, and of course Stephanie's. But no Stephanie.

'Where is she?' he pleaded as he gasped for breath.

'They've been taken into the delivery room,' said his mother-in-law softly.

'Straight down the corridor. Double doors at the end,' added the practical Victoria. 'You'll need to get gowned up. Ask the nurse on the desk in the corridor.'

'I won't put up with this cavalier attitude to our girl. I'll see you about this later,' was his own mother's contribution to the welcoming speeches.

Stillion glared back defiantly for a split second before retreating into the corridor to find the nurse. He was still joining all the ties of his green gown and mask as she showed him into the delivery room.

The gynaecologist, the midwife and two nurses were present and appeared concerned. All were posted around the bed. Mr Johnson was at the foot, the nurses either side of Stephanie while the midwife was relaying heartbeat times from the monitor off to the right.

'Ah, Mr Sloane. So glad you could make it,' smiled Mr Johnson in an ever so slightly sarcastic tone, which Stillion ignored as he raced to Stephanie's side and relieved one of the nurses of his wife's hand.

'Darling you made it!' She smiled. Her forehead glistened with perspiration.

'Yes darling. I'm so sorry I'm late but I'm here now.'

'Is the little boy safe?'

'Yes he's fine. Winston is fine. The exhumation is fine. The business is fine. Just relax because it's you and our baby that we have to think about now,' soothed Stillion as he stroked her damp hair.

'Oh darling. I'm such a lucky girl. I love you so very much.'

'And I love you.'

'Do you darling? Really? Like I love you?'

'Probably more.'

'Impossible.'

Mr Johnson, who was trying his best not to listen to their conversation but concentrate on the imminent birth instead, could not help but feel a slight sense of nausea. 'This man,' he thought, 'has just been paraded on the pages of every newspaper this week as someone in collusion with the drug barons. He can't even be bothered to get back here after work and now within two minutes of arriving very late and only just before the birth he has his beautiful wife eating out of his hand.' He didn't have time to dwell on his thoughts.

'Come on Stephanie. I can see the baby's head. Come on, one more big push. There's a good girl. One more big push. Come on, keep pushing.'

Stephanie's beautifully shaped and smooth legs tensed every muscle as her feet pushed against the stirrups. Then in a flash, less than a blink of the eye, it happened. There was a baby, there was a cry, there was a cord, there was a tiny manhood and there was a son for them.

Stillion gripped her hand so hard he nearly crushed it. He stared in disbelief as this most beautiful thing of things was placed on his mother's tummy and the cord was cut before her son was given to her to hold.

The boy had a full head of quite dark hair. He even had a fringe. His eyes were open and he looked like Beatle Paul. He was truly the most beautiful thing that Sloane had ever clapped eyes on.

For a moment he was stunned, then, as the nurse took the baby away to weigh and clean him before wrapping him in a blanket, the week, the pool, the four dead kids, Luther, the scandal, the pressmen, the newspaper articles, the fear, the snow, the roof, the café and the cemetery flashed in front of him and he fell on his wife's neck and wept silently.

Stillion was an empire boy, a British, middle-class lad who had rarely cried since he was about ten years of age and never since then in public. Indeed Stephanie had never seen or heard Stillion cry and she had known him since she had been a small girl. Now she could feel his hot tears run off his cheeks onto hers and roll down into her mouth where she could taste their salt.

'Darling what's the matter?' she whispered.

'Nothing Stephanie. Nothing at all. Thank you. Thank you a million times for our baby. He's wonderful. The son I've always wanted. You're so clever. Life is so very wonderful. It's only just beginning. There's so much hope and so very much to look forward to. You and me together, nothing feels so good. I love him and I love you.'

'And the problems?'

'They're all gone, but not now. I'll tell you about it all tomorrow. Just rest now.' Then his voice broke and wavered as he got up from his knees and added, 'I wish the old man was here to see this.'

Stephanie nodded as she squeezed his hand. He smiled at her through his tears, which he brushed away with his fingers as the nurse returned. 'He's a fine boy to be sure, eight pounds, two ounces, and you my girl such a slip of a thing. You must have been all baby.' She passed Stillion his son. 'Now you go to your daddy a bit.'

'Are you sure this blanket's not too tight?' asked Stillion.

'You may well be right. But it is my fourteenth birth this week young man. How many have you been after doing now?' smiled the nurse.

'Good point. Can I show off my son to our family?'

'You can, but please come straight back,' answered Mr Johnson, who had softened his opinion of the father having discreetly witnessed his very private moment with his wife.

Stillion turned to Stephanie. 'Are you still happy with the

257

names?' Stephanie smiled as she nodded. Stillion then strode with his son in his arms back down the corridor. He beamed down on the expectant and nervous trio.

'May I present Stillion Arthur George Sloane.'

All jumped up and laughed and giggled and wept.

'Congratulations,' said his mother-in-law through tears of joy.

'Well done dad,' giggled a very happy Victoria.

'Never mind you. What about Stephanie? How's she?' asked the predictable Mary Sloane, who was busy trying to control her own emotions.

Then they all admired little Beatle Paul before Stillion returned him to his exhausted mum, who was by now very sleepy. From there he accompanied her on her bed-wheeled procession to her private room but not before they both said goodbye to little Stillion who was whisked away to join the other newly-borns in order that his mother might get some badly needed sleep.

Stillion sat with Stephanie until she slept, and then returned downstairs to collect the mothers. Victoria, having done her duty and more besides, was now on her way home. Stillion would thank her tomorrow. He took the 'old girls' as he irreverently called them to see young Stillion just once more before they left the hospital at twelve-forty a.m. They drove their own cars the short distance to Stillion's where they wet the baby's head with a bottle of champagne, which was mainly drunk by Stillion as the 'old girls' both insisted on driving home despite Stillion's invitation to stay.

Phone calls were made by them in turn around the kingdom and even around the world to every possible relative and close friend. The 'old girls' did the calling and Stillion was only required to receive the congratulations.

Eventually Stillion's mother-in-law left at ten past three and was followed at twenty past by his own mum who hung back so that she might kiss and hug her son with a rare display of emotion. Indeed so rare and so unexpected was it that it took her son completely by surprise, but he enjoyed it none the less.

Then he sat alone with just a new bottle of champagne for company. He poured himself a glass, saluted the picture of his father above the mantelpiece and thanked God for his son, the happy state of his wife and his own deliverance from a week of hell. He gulped down most of the glass, placed it on the coffee table and leant back to rest his eyes before going up to bed. However his physical and mental exhaustion meant that within seconds he had fallen into a deep sleep.

Alf had known that the secret exit and then a mad dash down the road to his car was his only hope of escape. Making for the exit was a sensible move. Luckily for him no one latched onto him as he ran back up the parameter pathway to the gap in the railings.

Nevertheless, it would have only been a matter of time before a patrol car would have picked him up if he hadn't made it back to his car. But he had made it and then had the sense to drive away slowly. Indeed the two police vans that had arrived within minutes of the balloon going up had passed him driving away while on their way into the cemetery. Then he had driven around in a blind panic. Instinct had made him escape but now he realised he might have been better off as a guest of Her Majesty. At least he would have been a victim. At least he would have gone down with the ship. At least he wouldn't have to face Harry Wilkes with what had happened. And worse, he knew how Harry's mind worked. Harry would not only be brutally angry that the mission had failed and caused him so much damage, but he would question how it was that Alf had managed to escape. He would wonder whether or not Alf had done a deal with the police.

Harry's brothers, who wanted more say in the business away from the scrap metal bit, were jealous of Alf. They hadn't Alf's bottle and could never be relied on to manage either drugs or protection. Harry had tended to keep them back on the acceptable face of scrap metal and second-hand cars but now with this cock up and most of Alf's team under arrest, Alf's days as a

259

trusted top man could be numbered. Worse, if that were to happen, his very days may be numbered. Men like Harry didn't put men like Alf out to grass.

What was Alf to do? He drove around. Then he drove over to Harry's house, but frozen with fear he couldn't get out of the car. He just listened to 'Night Ride' on the radio and kept telling himself he would approach Harry's front door at the end of the next record.

After more than an hour there he eventually told himself that he had no choice but to throw himself upon Harry's mercy and in so doing try and push as much of the blame as he could in the direction of Elton, Nick Smith and even Frankie.

He got out of his car, which he had parked some way from Harry's new and very splendid Edgbaston home, which was only situated half a mile from Stillion's, and walked. It was twelve-thirty a.m. when he rang Harry's bell.

The two Rottweilers that Harry kept in his garage went mad and lights went on upstairs. Alf could hear Harry's wife, Lottie, shouting to Charlotte and David, the couple's two children. His luck was really out. The two teenage children were known party-goers and he had expected them still to be out. Moreover he had kidded himself, while waiting in his car, that perhaps Harry or even Harry and Lottie, who got to go out a lot more with Harry since her one night stand with Stillion Sloane, would still be on the town or at least having a nightcap. Whereas he had clearly woken the others and he may well have woken Harry as well.

Someone fetched the dogs from the garage and suddenly they were leaping up at the other side of the front door. A voice said 'Who's there?' It was Harry's voice. 'Oh fuckin' 'ell,' thought Alf.

'It's me, Harry, Alf.'

'What the fuck do yow want? Have yow no idea about what fuckin' time it is?'

'I need to talk to yow Harry, now. It's urgent.' There was a pause.

'Wait a moment.'

Three large bolts thundered back to reveal Harry Wilkes in a bright-red silk dressing-gown, pale-blue silk pyjamas and lambs-wool slippers. Each of his hands were placed inside the studded collars of his guard dogs, both of whom strained to get away from him and at Alf as they growled and gnashed their large white and very sharp teeth. Alf didn't like dogs and he hated these.

'Yow had better come in,' said Harry, and motioned his head for Alf to enter. Alf stayed frozen to the spot. 'I said, come in,' repeated Harry.

'Eh, it's the dogs Harry,' answered Alf weakly.

Harry looked at Alf disdainfully and with some trouble got the dogs into the kitchen and shut the door.

Alf then entered, even though he was now terrified of the noise the dogs were making while leaping up at the kitchen door.

Harry flicked some switches and the ground floor lit up to reveal its opulence. He led the way to his own private snug, barking up the large staircase on the way that everyone else should go back to sleep as it was only Alf.

Harry entered. Alf followed. Harry shut the door and turned to Alf. 'Now what the fuck is this about? Yow 'as fucked somethin' ain't yow?'

Alf stammered and stuttered out the story.

Harry couldn't believe his ears. Each second got worse. No ring. Jimmy gone with all debts owed. Untrained, unreliable and unloving Nick Smith and Elton in police custody where they could talk, and most of his bully boys, who wouldn't talk, with them.

'Do yow realise what yow 'ave done? Do yow?' And then before Alf could answer, Harry went on, 'Yow 'ave cost me the money, the ring and yow 'ave got five of moy best guys locked up, God only knows for 'ow long. How the fuck can I run the fuckin' business without them? Yow fuckin' incompetent bastard. People won't pay protection. We won't be able to control

261

the drugs. Vance and his gang will move in. The police . . .'
Harry stopped his ranting and thought for a second before
continuing, 'The police now know it was us and not Vance.
Hooper will 'ave to 'elp us. Wait a minute! How come yow got
away? I mean, 'ow do I know that yow ain't sold out to the pigs
eh? Well, answer that.'

' 'Arry.'

'Don't yow fuckin' 'Arry moy. My brothers warned me about
yow. I should 'ave listened to them shouldn't I?'

' 'Arry!'

'Yow come 'ere. Oh for fuck's sake, yow fuckin' little bastard.
They could 'ave followed yow 'ere.'

'No 'Arry. They didn't. I sat away down the road for a good
hour before I walked up to the 'ouse. Look, I'll make it up to
yow. I will 'Arry I promise.

'Why did we 'ave six men in the cemetery? I said two.'

' 'Cos I thought . . .'

'I don't fuckin' pay yow to think, shit 'ead.'

'I'll put it right, 'Arry. I promise.'

'Too fuckin' right yow will Alf. Too fuckin' right yow will.'
Ironically Alf's greatest cock up, the loss of the major part of
Harry's army, was the one thing that was to save Alf, as Harry
had come to realise that at this point in time, due to acute staff
shortages, he needed him.

'Yow'll do the following, all right?'

'OK! Of course, 'Arry, anything yow say.'

'First yow'll go on half pay until the full value of the ring,
not our share, but the full value, is repaid to me. Second yow
will get word to those two toerags Field and Smith that they had
better keep their traps shut. Third yow will get word to Frankie
and the boys that I'll get them out as soon as I can get moy brief
on it and to stay quiet in the meantime. Fourth yow will find
out where that Jimmy fucker is. Then yow will castrate 'im. I
want his cock and balls on moy desk in seven days. But before
any of this yow will go and find Field's fuckin' whore of a sister
and yow will bring 'er to the office at eight in the morning. Is
that clear? Fail once more and yow will never even imagine in

yowa wildest nightmares the trouble that yow will be in. Now get out.'

Alf left.

Terri had returned to the café after her telephone call to Elton in the hope of seeing Jimmy. She didn't love Jimmy, she didn't even like Jimmy, and there were times when she knew she hated him, but he was protection. A bloodsucker who lived off her whoring and who of late had bullied her. A person she spent most of her time avoiding because she hadn't earned enough money to make him happy, or if she had, avoiding him so that she might spend some of it.

But just now, in her darkest hour, she had a feeling that Jimmy was at least vaguely on her side. After all the bastard had given her the drugs she had demanded. She had broken all promises to pay. He had got into terrible trouble because of her. He hadn't really beaten her. A bit perhaps but nothing like Flicky would have done if she had been his whore. And however bad he was or however much she didn't like him at least she wouldn't be on her own just now. Just now, as that utter bastard Stillion Sloane had rebuffed all her attempts to contact him. How crazy she had been. The man from Edgbaston was no better than the bastards who paid for her sex. No, he was worse because at least those unloving bastards lusted after her. The high and mighty Stillion Sloane didn't even do that.

She had a coffee, lit a cigarette and waited. She looked a mess. Her hair was bedraggled, the eye make-up which had run earlier as a result of her constant crying had now dried in streaks down her blotchy cheeks and her eyes remained red and puffy. She wished Jimmy would arrive. Where was he? If Pastor Wylde and that bastard Stillion Sloane had taken him to the police then she would be in trouble if he talked. But he wouldn't talk would he? No of course he wouldn't, because the price the Wilkes gang would extract for talking would be so much worse than anything the police could do to him. But what if he did a deal with the police and they let him go up north or something?

Shit, that would be bad for her. She could become one penniless whore with an acid scarred face and no future. No, Jimmy wouldn't do that to her would he? She wished she had earned the bastard more money now instead of wasting time on silly schemes about the man from Edgbaston. She wished she had been a little nicer and above all she wished she hadn't called him sambo.

She glanced at her watch. It was now ten thirty-five p.m. Elton and Alf must be in the middle of their mission. 'Please God, if yow bleedin' well exist, let them be successful,' she prayed as she waited. It didn't occur to her that if God did exist it might be better to pray without swearing and doubting his existence. Nor did it occur to her that God might not wish to assist those robbing a grave.

The time dragged. She was shaking with cold, depression and cold turkey. She needed something to get her up, but she had no money. She had wasted so much valuable time pining after that public schoolboy bastard that she hadn't filled her purse since Jimmy had last emptied it. She was on her last cigarette and didn't even have enough cash for another coffee.

She looked around. The café was pretty empty. The pushers, the thugs, their molls and their whores had all pushed off for the city-centre discos and work. It was Friday night after all.

There were no business prospects in sight. Just Ian, the little black waiter. She tidied her hair and face and called him over.

'Yow want sex?' she asked casually.

'Me-ee?' stammered the little kid who was everyone's whipping boy. A lad who was treated with such contempt that he had never even dared to ask any of the whores for sex, safe in the knowledge they would have laughed in his face and then ridiculed him in front of the whole place.

'Yes, yow silly. How much money yow got?'

'Er, four quid,' he replied.

'That's no good. Take some from the till.'

'I can't. They'd kill me. Sorry, I daren't,' he apologised and turned to go.

'Wait. Give moy the four quid and go to the loo and take yowa trousers down. Yow'll only get an 'and job for this mind,' she instructed as she grabbed the cash.

Ian did as he was told. She finished her cigarette and followed him. She pushed open the unlocked door and squeezed into the narrow, dirty little room. Between the toilet and her stood little Ian. She was taller than him and she was not a tall girl.

Ian had removed his dirty apron and dropped his now dried jeans around his ankles as instructed. He stood there, looking quite frightened and holding his shirt up with both hands. She looked at him contemptuously before saying, 'Yow've still got yowa underpants on.'

'But I've never shown a girl my thing before.'

'Get them down,' she commanded. He obeyed. 'Well, yow should 'ave,' she commented in a kinder tone as her gaze sized up the job at hand. 'Yow're quite a big boy really ain't yow?'

Ian didn't reply. His small frame was shaking and his engine, which nearly reached his belly button, was throbbing.

Terri looked at her quivering client and thought, 'This won't take long,' as she moistened the thumb and fingers of one hand and then stroked his black helmet while lightly tickling his balls with the other hand.

Almost immediately the throbbing engine started pumping and hot, thick cream splashed across her hand before splatting down onto the dirty floor.

'Yow needed that, didn't yow? Now shut it or I'll never do it again. Right? Keep quiet and maybe I will. But a fiver next time, right?' And with that she was gone.

However, the four pounds didn't do her much good. She couldn't find a supplier of anything on the Lozells Road. Those going to town had gone. Those who weren't were off the street due to the weather. Moreover the licensing laws for bars and public houses meant that even the avenue of alcohol was cut off to her as ten-thirty had come and gone.

Where could she get a fix or a drink even? She couldn't really afford to go to town and even if she could, by the time she got there it would be time to return and link up with Elton as planned. Even her craving didn't distract her from the conviction that she must watch what happened to the ring. She didn't trust Elton much and she didn't trust Alf at all. Especially now that Alf had had to go to the cemetery and help retrieve the bleeding ring. She knew Elton would be the one to actually rescue it from her gran's finger and that he should then give it to her so that she could take it to the valuer as planned. But that was when Jimmy was going to the cemetery with Elton. What, now that it was Alf instead, if he demanded to have the ring. She knew Elton would give it up rather than face a beating. And then once Alf had the ring the Wilkes could keep all the money and there would be nothing she could do about it. Oh why oh why hadn't she thought about that before, when Elton had told her he was going to ask for Alf's help?

She looked at her watch. It was now eleven o'clock. She wished the time would pass. Waiting for them without distraction was almost as bad as being there, she told herself. Where could she get a drink? Then she had an idea – granddad. He always kept a drop of Scotch on the sideboard. She could distract him and nick the bottle. Good idea.

She made her way once again down the hill, past the burned out house, to his place. 'Blimey,' she thought. 'Trips to granddad is almost a daily event nowadays.' She rang his bell and waited. He would, of course, be in bed. He would, naturally, be very annoyed, but with a bit of blubbing she could probably get him to put the kettle on and while he did she could nick the whisky.

To her amazement he answered the door almost straightaway. What's more he was dressed. He even had his hat and coat on.

'What yow want now? I ain't got any money if that's what yow want.'

'No. Granddad I ain't come for money. I . . . I . . . I just come for a cuppa and a chat.

'Well I ain't got time for that. Goodbye.' And Granddad slammed the door in her face.

She rang the bell again. He didn't answer. She was shocked. She knew he didn't like her, let alone love her. She knew she was a great disappointment to him. But he had never before refused her entry.

She turned to go and had only walked a couple of paces when a taxi drew up outside granddad's and the driver got out and rang his bell. Granddad obviously thought it was Terri again and at first didn't reply. The taxi driver then knocked on the door and yelled 'Taxi!'. What on earth was going on? Why was granddad dressed to go in a taxi? He never ordered taxis.

She walked back to his front door and came face to face with her grandfather who had a suitcase in each hand.

'Granddad,' she exclaimed, 'where are you going at this time and with all that luggage?'

'None of yowa business moy girl,' came back a defensive response.

'Yow can't leave. What about the exhumation in the morning?'

'To 'ell with that. Let 'er be is what I say, let 'er be.'

'But where yow going?'

'Mind yowa own business.'

'I'll scream.' With Terri, blackmail or bribery nearly always began with a scream or a cry.'

'All right! All right yow little busybody. If yow must know I'm off on the two o'clock flight from Elmdon to Palma, Majorca for a winter break.'

'But yow ain't got a passport.'

'Well not for the first time yow're wrong. I got a visitor thing from the Post Office. I got the tickets and moy luggage. I'm off away from this bloody weather and yow. Goodbye.'

And with that he gave the taxi driver the cases. He put them in the boot and they left, leaving Terri standing there with her mouth open and no drink to put in it.

There was nothing for it. She would have to go round to Elton's place ahead of time. They had arranged to meet there at midnight. It was now about half eleven and so, as his house was only a few minutes walk away, she would be early. This was unfortunate. There would be no drink in the house and she would have to put up with talking to Doreen, Elton's wife. This was only just preferable to waiting in the cold.

The two girls had little in common, didn't see each other often and therefore had nothing to talk about. Terri was a single, free-spirited girl, tough, streetwise, selfish but a little organised and physically clean. Her denim shirt, jeans, sheep fleece jacket and old white sneakers told you that. Doreen, six years older, was a timid, placid and plain looking housewife who just couldn't cope with anything. Her two children were undisciplined, dirty and rude. Neither were toilet trained and both often stank of urine, especially first thing in the morning. They always seemed to have streaming colds which was hardly surprising as they ran around constantly barefooted. The house was filthy dirty. Washing up, laundry and cleaning never seemed to get done as Doreen was always about to start on one of them when something else distracted her. Elton had even taken to doing his own shirts, just to ensure he had one.

Doreen's dress also reflected her circumstances. She usually wore a dirty, lime-green twin set over an old, tight black skirt, which wouldn't do up at the top, due to her failure to get her figure back after the birth of her second child. There were no tights to cover her unshaven legs and on her feet she wore a revolting pair of old slippers which had once belonged to Terri's mum.

As Terri walked she thought how Doreen hadn't been any help to Elton. On the other hand it could be said that Elton's debts had always deprived Doreen and the kids of carpets, furniture, clothes and toys and so perhaps a stronger woman would have walked out by now.

Did Elton gamble because she was such a pig? Or was she such a pig because of Elton's gambling? A fine question which could be asked about drink and drugs as well and then posted through nearly every letter-box around the Lozells area for an answer. A little bit of the selfish Terri understood what Pastor Wylde was up against; it was just that she didn't think any of it had anything to do with her.

There was another reason why it was a close-run thing between standing in the cold and risking freezing to death and going to Elton's early and having to talk to Doreen. Doreen and her domestic chaos reminded Terri most uncomfortably of her own terrible childhood. It was too much *déjà vu*. Doreen could have been a younger and thinner version of her mum. Perhaps this was a little harsh as there was no evidence that Doreen had even failed to feed her brats, and she was never seen down the pub. Doreen lived for *Coronation Street* and her ambition was to save enough money to start renting a video machine so she could record each episode and watch them over and over again.

It was just after eleven-thirty when Terri knocked on Elton's front door. Doreen answered.

''Ello Dor. I've come to meet Elton. Is 'e back yet?'

'No. Yow'd better come up and wait. 'E said 'e would be back for midnight. I'm watching the late movie. It's 'umphrey Bogart. Casa something or other. Anyway come in. The kids 'ave just gone down.'

Terri was pleased about that. After the threats, violence and rejection of the week she needed two little bastards caked in urine crawling all over her like a hole in the head.

She followed Doreen inside and plonked herself down on the cheap, worn and slashed PVC covered settee. The only other piece of furniture in the room was a wacking great TV set rented from Granada. Doreen might not waste what little money she was given on fags and booze like Terri's mum, but Terri suspected that the TV rental was the first item on the family budget each week.

They watched *Casablanca* together in silence. Doreen didn't know what to talk about, while Terri enjoyed the film. She didn't get to see much television and this film was up her street until the rejection in Paris reminded her of her own at the hands of the man from Edgbaston. Then she turned off mentally, jumped up and said, 'That's not too interesting is it? Let's talk while we wait. I don't get to see you that much for some reason.'

The placid Doreen was too weak to object and so turned to look at Terri as she sat down again.

What could Terri talk about? They couldn't discuss the ring because she knew Elton would never have mentioned any of that business to Doreen. What else? They had so little in common. She couldn't talk about drink, drugs, whoring, pimping or the size of willies to Doreen and she didn't want to hear about the rent man. She was struggling, and then the word 'granddad' just popped out.

'Granddad?' queried Doreen.

'Yes. Granddad. I've just come from granddad's and 'e's gone on 'is 'ols. Yow wouldn't believe it would yow?'

'I would. I took the nippers to see 'im this afternoon and 'e 'ad two cases in the 'all. Where yow going? I said. To Majorca for four months 'e said.'

'Four bleedin' months!' exclaimed Terri. 'Four bleedin' months!'

'Yeah. Well, until sometime in May any road.'

'Well the tight fisted fuckin' bastard. That must 'ave cost a bleedin' fortune.'

'Yeah. I said that'll cost yow a fortune and 'e said 'e'd 'ad a little nest egg for a bit but 'e was going to blow some of it before yow and Elton got to 'ear about it.'

Terri could say no more. Inside she was on fire. 'Bloody old bastard! Four months in Majorca! Jesus!' She had thought the old git had booked a cheap out of season special for pensioners lasting one or perhaps two weeks. But four months . . .

'It's a lovely hotel called the Villamed. I remember the name 'cos of the Villa. I said, oh I bet yow chose it 'cos of the Villa. 'E said na, it were 'cos of the four stars.'

'Four fuckin' stars! No. Dor, yow got that wrong.'

'I ain't got it wrong. Everybody thinks I'm dim but he showed moy the brochure and even I can count four stars yow know.'

'What a selfish old bastard!' Terri would have liked to have gone on to point out that if granddad had that sort of money then he could have easily paid off both Elton's and her debts

270

and therefore neither of them would have been subjected to the events of the last week.

That conversation exhausted they put the TV back on and waited for Elton's return.

6

Although Harry Wilkes had returned to the marital bed once Alf had left he found it impossible to sleep. Thanks to the bad tidings that Alf had brought there was simply too much on his mind. He rose again at three a.m. very agitated by the events of the evening and the difficulties that the future now held as a result.

'Where are you going at this time?' asked Lottie.

'To murder yowa public schoolboy lover. Now shut it and go back to sleep.'

Lottie knew not to discuss matters further with her husband when he was in such a mood and so said nothing as Harry put on his dressing-gown once more and descended the great staircase to his den.

Once there, he sat at his desk, flicked through his private phone book and dialled a number. It rang for some time before there was an answer.

''Ello 'ooper, that yow?'

'Inspector Hooper speaking,' replied a sleepy voice.

'Yow let moy down. Didn't yow? Yow bastard.'

Hooper, now fully awake, realised that he was talking to Harry Wilkes. He had known he would be at some point, from the moment he had been informed that his trap had worked brilliantly, but had caught an ex-Sloane employee and half the Wilkes' gang. Harry was a very unhappy man.

'Look yow can't blame moy, 'arry. Yow told me to go ahead with the exhumation. Yow told me that yowa people wasn't involved. I just did what yow said. Yow can't blame moy, Christ almighty be fair.'

272

'I never told yow to set a trap.'

'Yow told moy to get on and do moy job and that's what I did.'

Harry couldn't really argue with that so he changed tack slightly. 'Any road what are yow going to do to release moy lads?'

'Nothing.'

'Nothing?' boomed Harry so loudly that it started his dogs barking.

'I can't do anything. Elton Field has confessed and made a full statement. We'll release 'im on police bail in the morning; 'is story is that 'e, with others whom 'e won't name, hoaxed the police and caused a sensation in the press which forced an exhumation order to be made. He'd planned with his accomplices to remove a valuable ring from the grave the night before the exhumation in the knowledge that the grave would be all but reopened in readiness. 'E said 'e was doing this because 'is sister and 'im 'ad debts. 'E wouldn't say who these debts were with. Moy officers suspect they were to Nick Smith the bookmaker and your gang. As yow no doubt know Nick Smith was also arrested. To date 'e 'as refused to make a statement. Yowa blokes are saying they were just taking a short cut across the cemetery on their way for a drink in the Hawthorns up by the Albion ground. Frankie says 'e fell in the grave by accident. But we 'ave a tape which suggests that ain't the case. We bugged the grave. Clever really.'

'Look, it won't be clever if I 'ave to let it be known what yow been up to for the last few years. Fancy going down with moy guys do yow? Yow know what they do to coppers inside don't yow? Clean out yowa arse with a bog brush made of razor blades don't they!'

'Look 'Arry, be fucking reasonable mate. I'll do what I can. At least Frankie doesn't mention you by name on the tape and we need each other. Sure I want to go up, not down. The better I do the more I can help. If it weren't for the trap I'd look pretty stupid 'ere 'cos you lied to moy. You pushed moy to get the exhumation order 'cos you knew the truth but didn't bank

273

on the trap. But I set the trap to catch your enemy Vance and Sloane, not yowa blokes. You let moy believe the stories. You told moy to do moy job. I did.'

'OK. OK. Just get moy guys out and destroy the tape.'

'I can't do that. It's evidence and there'll be more than one copy by now. Frankie is done for. Provided Nick Smith or Elton Field don't upset the applecart, I may be able to let the others go on the grounds of insufficient evidence. You 'ad better ensure they stick to their story and that the other two don't blow it.'

'Alf will see to it in the morning.'

'I suppose 'e was the one that got away.'

'What?'

'Moy men said they were sure one got away up the 'ill.'

'No comment. Just deliver at least four of moy blokes to moy. OK?'

'I'll do moy best, and please understand this weren't moy fault. I was only doing moy job. I'd better go and get some shuteye before I 'ave to get up for the fucking exhumation.'

'Is that still going ahead?'

'Sure. A crowning moment of glory for young Mr Sloane no doubt. Not only will all of this 'ave the police and press falling over themselves in the rush to apologise to him, but he'll appear a complete hero having rescued some kid off a roof in Handsworth last night before attempting to arrest yowa blokes in the cemetery with the journalist Alan Bater and some hippie just before we actually did.

'What!?' roared Wilkes. 'Sloane was in the cemetery? 'Ow the 'ell was 'e there?'

'Don't know. 'E'll give us details in the morning. But Bater told a story at the graveside which matched up to Field's and implicated your gang in general and Alf in particular. However, unless we find some black kid called Jimmy then that bit will remain hearsay. Neither Bater nor Sloane seem to know where this Jimmy is.'

Harry put down the phone. It was clear that the lousy black

274

bastard Jimmy had spilled the beans that had cost him thousands and his best men, and had allowed Sloane to bounce back once more. My God he hated that little son of a bitch but still not half as much as that privileged prick whose filmstar face would now be appearing all over the press as a hero.

If Harry and Sydney Gridley ever got to hold hands and concentrate on Stillion Sloane then the force of hate would surely lift both of them off the ground.

Terri and Doreen, uncomfortable in each other's company and with little to talk about, became mesmerised by the TV and fell asleep. They were awoken at four o'clock by the telephone. It was Elton making the one telephone call a prisoner is allowed. A sleepy, and therefore more stupid than usual, Doreen answered. Soon she was screaming hysterically like a demented idiot. Terri grabbed the phone. 'Elton, what's happened? Where are yow?'

'I've been arrested. They bugged the grave. They know everything. They got the ring. I'm so sorry sis. I got to go now. Tell Dor I'm sorry. I'm so sorry. Give my love to the nippers won't yow? Bye.'

'What did 'e say?' sobbed the heap of dirty clothes on the settee.

'Not much. 'E just fucked my life up completely that's all,' replied Terri coldly, and made to leave.

She headed for her flat. She would have to pack a few things and make for town. From there she would have to hitch to the big smoke. London would have to hide and feed her. There was no Jimmy, no Elton, no granddad and certainly no man from Edgbaston to keep her in Birmingham. Moreover, now Jimmy had gone and the plan had failed someone would have to be sacrificed at the high altar of Harry Wilkes' temple, and she knew that she would be that sacrifice.

She walked briskly and by four-fifteen had arrived at her flat. She opened her front door, flicked on the light and walked in.

She stopped dead in her tracks. She knew she wasn't alone even before a voice said, 'Fine time of night to come 'ome ain't it?'

She knew the voice. It struck terror. It had threatened her with Mo-Mo's earlier in the week. It was Alf's voice. She turned round. He was sitting in the room's one comfortable chair in the corner.

'I wouldn't be in yowa shoes for all the gold in the Bank of fucking England girl.'

'Why?' she asked weakly as her eyes darted back to the door.

'Because . . .' He leapt to his feet in time to prevent her dash for freedom. She screamed. He gave her an almighty backhand slap across her face and threw her down on the mattress. He dived on top of her and covered her mouth with his large hand.

'Scream again and I'll finish yow 'ere and now bitch, all right?'

Her eyes nodded agreement. He lifted his hand a couple of inches. She did not scream. He took his hand away and stood up. She tried the crying game. 'Please let moy go,' she whimpered.

'Sorry it's more than moy life's worth. Get ready, yow is coming with moy.'

'Look yow can have moy. I throw myself upon yowa mercy,' she said, turning from tears to sex in an appeal to his penis. She ripped open the studs on her denim shirt to expose small but perfectly formed breasts. Alf hesitated. She undid her belt and pulled apart the metal buttons which ran down the front of her jeans. She was wearing no knickers and Alf could see the top of her red crop. His ageing engine was aroused and his Y-fronts were bulging but he resisted the temptation. This had not been part of his instructions and he had got into enough trouble already by taking matters into his own hands.

'Get dressed I said. Yow are coming with moy. We can go there nice and civilised or I can beat the shit out of yow. The choice is yowa's.'

Terri chose to go quietly. She was frightened by what lay in store for her and annoyed that in this week from hell she couldn't even help herself by tempting this fat lout.

They walked the little way to his car. He bundled her in and drove off to Wilkes' main offices which were still situated in the scrap metal yard in Nechells.

They arrived at four-fifty and Alf made Terri safe from escape and his own temptation by locking her in a broom cupboard. To be certain he then locked the room in which the cupboard was situated. He made himself a cup of tea and waited for Harry.

At about five-fifteen Jimmy woke in a cold sweat. Something had come to him in his sleep which was clear as anything and yet hadn't occurred to him with all the emotion of the previous night. Harry Wilkes would go for Terri if the ring wasn't recovered. He had known that. Sure. That was why he had wanted to take him with her. But what if Harry got to her before Wylde? She could be in real danger. Jimmy would have been even more fearful if he'd known the actual scale of the problems his actions had caused Harry Wilkes.

He got up, dressed and knocked on Pastor Wylde's door. Winston got up.

'I'm sorry to wake you and Mrs Wylde, pastor, but I'm worried for Terri.'

'Who?'

'Terri Field. She's my woman.'

'Yes, I know.'

'Well I'm worried that Wilkes' people will get there before us man.'

Stillion had already spoken to Winston to announce the birth of his son and explain what had happened at the cemetery. Therefore, unlike Jimmy, Winston knew the scale of Stillion's victory and the depth of Harry Wilkes' problems. The boy was right. They must collect the girl now.

'OK Jimmy. I'll dress. We'll fetch her now.'

Within minutes they were on their way. It was only a two-minute drive to Terri's flat. Jimmy let himself in and then returned quickly. 'She ain't there Pastor. She ain't there!' he yelled, showing genuine concern.

'OK. Calm down. Where could she stay?'

Jimmy thought and they drove round to Terri's grandfather's home. No reply. From there they drove on to Elton's and were told by an hysterical Doreen that Terri had been there but had left about an hour and a half ago.

They cruised the area cautiously. They needed to find Terri while not being discovered themselves. Eventually they returned home empty handed and Winston phoned Stillion, who was awoken from the deep sleep he had slipped into. It was now seven o'clock.

'What do we do now?' asked Winston.

'Well, we should keep our word to Jimmy and therefore we can't tell the police about him. They seemed to lose a lot of interest in him last night once they had Elton, his bookie and half the Wilkes gang. If we tell the police about Jimmy and Terri then we would have to give up Jimmy, and he doesn't deserve that given that he kept his side of the bargain.'

'Agreed. So what do we do?' asked Winston again.

'Look, as you know, I've been invited to attend the actual exhumation at nine o'clock.'

'Will you still bother to go?'

'Sure. I'm going to the end of the line on this after all the accusations which have been flying around this week. Inspector Hooper will be there and I'll talk to him about Terri. In the meantime you should get Jimmy hidden, somewhere away from your place. It won't take the Wilkes gang long to get round to the Villa Cross Café this morning and that'll lead them straight to you.'

'You're right. I'll take him to my sister's in Dudley. That's off Wilkes' patch.

'What about little Luther?'

'He's still asleep.'

'Great. I'll call you after I get back. Tell Jimmy that Terri is probably lying low somewhere and I doubt if the Wilkes would dare harm her now that the police have got Elton. It's just too close to home for them.'

At seven-fifty Harry Wilkes' Rolls-Royce drew up outside his scrap metal yard in Nechells. He unlocked the corrugated iron gates himself and drove through before locking them again behind him. He entered the reception. The lights were on and Alf sat there with a mug of sweet tea in one hand and a ciggie in the other.

'Yow got the girl, I 'ope?'

'She's locked in a cupboard in the next office, Harry,' answered Alf.

'Good. Bring the whore up to moy office,' said Harry. He walked through reception and up the stairs to his own palatial office which was quite out of keeping with the rest of this dirty little office block.

Alf quickly obeyed and soon Terri was pushed up the stairs and thrust into Harry's room.

'So yow is the little bitch who started all of this trouble. I understand yow owe moy a lot of money and now, largely thanks to a crazy scheme which yow and yowa daft brother dreamed up, I got five of my blokes banged up by the pigs. That makes moy very angry, yow know.'

'But Mr Harry, sir, it weren't moy idea. It were Elton's.'

'Shut it!' roared Harry. 'This ain't a discussion. Yow speak when I tell yow. Right?'

Terri nodded.

'Right. Just remember if yow hadn't had the drugs off that thick sambo without giving him the dosh for them then none of this would have happened. Right?'

Terri failed to answer.

'Right!' screamed Harry.

Terri nodded.

'Right. So yow owe moy money and yow cost moy money. Money to get moy boys out. Money on legals. Money perhaps to 'ire new staff. Yow cost moy lots of money girl, and that's without any missed payments due to moy staff shortages being taken into account. There's still half last week's payments to be collected thanks to some fucking idiot taking half moy security staff on yowa brainless caper. Right?'

Alf looked at the floor and Terri nodded.

'Good. So I reckon yow owe moy twenty-five grand.'

'What?' blurted out Terri, who knew that she wasn't supposed to say anything but just couldn't help herself. 'I only ever owed yow two grand. I mean on Monday morning Jimmy told moy I 'ad to find two grand by the weekend. Now it is the weekend and yow tell moy that I owe yow twenty-five grand. It just can't be.'

'I wouldn't argue if I was you girl. I want the full eighteen grand for the ring and I want seven grand due to all the trouble yow have caused. Yow've got one year to pay it all off. It must be in weekly instalments of five-hundred quid, paid to Alf every Friday night at six o'clock at yowa flat.

'Five-hundred a week. That's thousands and thousands,' cried out Terri, and promptly burst into tears.

'Actually it's twenty six grand. Now shut your blubbing girl. It won't wash with moy,' said Harry coldly.

'But it's impossible. I can't. I can't earn that in a good week let alone every week. It's true. Please understand,' wailed Terri.

'Shut it!' roared Harry, slamming his fist down on his desk violently. 'Stop crying, you whore. I'm going to show yow what will happen if yow don't make up the money in any one week.' He reached into a drawer and produced a small bottle. He opened it and then poured some of its contents into an empty inkwell on the desk. 'Take yowa jacket off,' he commanded. Terri obeyed. 'Now take yowa shirt off.'

'What?'

'Yow 'eard. I said take yowa shirt off, whore. Don't play the shy bitch with moy. Nearly every Mick, Pat, Singh and sambo 'ave 'ad a butchers at yowa tits. Move!'

Terri pulled open her denim shirt, tugged the bottom of it from within her jeans, pushed it off her shoulders and let it fall

280

to the floor. Automatically the vulnerability of her predicament made her fold her arms across her chest to cover her breasts.

'Forget that. Put yowa 'ands behind your back, now,' barked Harry, who did not intend to have the girl – Christ no, she'd been had by far too many Irish, Indians, Pakistanis and West Indians for racist Harry's liking. Nevertheless her now exposed bosoms were exquisite and he could not but help notice that his old willy was stirring. Alf, who had remained passively behind the girl during the meeting, moved to one side so that he could catch an eyeful.

'That's better girl. Obey moy and save yowaself some trouble. Right?'

Terri, who was now standing to attention in just her jeans and dirty old sneakers, nodded.

'Now watch this,' said Harry in a more reasonable tone as he picked up an old biro and dunked it into the inkewll. He held it there for a few seconds before pulling it out. The biro was melting as the liquid bubbled over the part that had been sub-merged. 'Amazing, the power of acid, ain't it? I *said*, ain't it?'

Terri nodded.

'Now if yow fail to find five-hundred in a week, any week, yow will 'ave a little bit of yow put into acid. Maybe a finger, maybe a toe, maybe an ear. It'll 'urt a lot and soon yow'll be scarred so much that yow won't earn, and that'll be the end of yow, won't it? Now just so that yow know that I'm not joking I want yow to put yowa right nipple in this inkwell. The pain will remind yow to get it right in future, won't it?'

'Aaaarrrgh!' screamed Terri, and instinct had her running. Alf caught her by the elbows and moved her back towards the desk where Harry had picked up the inkwell and was holding it out towards her. 'Would yow rather do it yowaself or should Alf 'ere do it for yow?' He smiled.

Now she was crying genuine tears. 'Look, I'm sorry about the two grand but it weren't moy fault that yowa blokes were nicked. If Jimmy hadn't gone off with Pastor Wylde and Stillion Sloane then yowa blokes wouldn't 'ave been there, would they?'

'What did yow say?' demanded Harry.

'I said it weren't moy fault,' sobbed Terri, now with her spirit truly broken.

'No, about Sloane and Jimmy.'

'I meant that Pastor Wylde and Stillion Sloane and an old man and some hippie kidnapped Jimmy last night and because of that yowa blokes went instead 'cos Elton said 'e would 'ave to ask Alf to 'elp 'im if Jimmy couldn't go.'

'But Elton said Jimmy had run off to Brighton with a girl,' interrupted Alf.

'I told 'im that 'cos I was scared that if I told 'im anything about Pastor Wylde and all he'd not go. I just wanted to get the job done. That's all. I just wanted to give yow yowa money Mr Wilkes and 'ave done with it.'

'So Sloane had Jimmy. That's why Sloane was in the cemetery,' said Harry, almost to himself.

'What boss?' asked Alf.

'That bloke who stepped forward in the cemetery was Sloane. Didn't yow fucking recognise his bloody posh voice?'

Alf shook his head.

'That bastard public schoolboy twit has really turned the tables on us. That fucking la-de-dah snob has cleared himself, wrecked the plan, cost us the money and got moy blokes banged up!' seethed Harry.

Terri had no idea why Harry Wilkes hated Sloane so much. She had thought all of this was about money and that Sloane's reputation was just an unfortunate casualty of the original plan, but now she sensed an escape route.

'I 'ate the man from Edgbaston, yow know.'

'What?' both Alf and Harry asked at the same time.

'Yeh. I 'ate 'im.'

'Who do yow 'ate? Who the fuck are you talking about?' demanded Harry.

'Stillion Sloane. 'E jilted moy. 'E was moy way out of Lozells and 'e cut me dead.'

'Stillion Sloane was yowa lover?' asked Harry in total disbelief.

'Yeh,' she replied as she began to edge back from the precipice and invention was working overtime in her pretty little head.

'When?' demanded Harry.

'When Elton worked for 'im,' she lied. 'I would exchange moy life for 'is with yow.'

'Now look 'ere,' began Alf, who didn't like the way this conversation was going. He was on the ball enough to immediately suspect that she might set up a murder for him to commit and get out of her debt while that bastard Harry would still deduct half his wages for the next year or so. Therefore he could end up being wanted for murder and on half salary just because he didn't want to stand in a cemetery by himself for half an hour.

'Shut it,' overruled Harry before turning to Terri and addressing her almost kindly. 'What exactly are yow saying?'

'I'm saying if yow wipe the slate clean with moy I'll 'ave a go at killing Sloane for yow 'cos I 'ate 'im too.'

Harry's brain went into overdrive. Hooper would probably get four of the five boys off. The debt was really only two grand. The actual cost was a lot less. Sloane's murder could be achieved because when Harry arranged for the girl to be suspected and subsequently caught she would have done it and there would be a motive. So the old baseball-bat blackmail that Sloane had relied on for the last year or so would be useless. Revenge could be achieved and this silly bitch could pay the price. However, the underworld would really know what had happened and the message would be clear – you can't mess with Harry Wilkes.

Harry liked it. Harry also knew that he must strike while the iron was hot. 'Put yowa shirt on and get out of 'ere. Yow 'ave twenty-four hours. Don't do a runner. 'E's dead by tomorrow and yow owe moy nowt. Fail and yow owe moy twenty-six grand. Do a runner and I'll 'ave yow killed. Get caught and yow is on yowa own. Try to implicate us and yow're dead. Understand?'

Terri nodded. She was back in the land of the living. At least Mr Wilkes had given her a chance – that was more than Stillion had ever done. If the man from Edgbaston couldn't become

283

her saviour by being her lover then it was his own fault that he would have to do so by becoming her victim.

'I won't let yow down, Mr Wilkes,' said Terri positively as she dressed.

'No. I don't think yow will,' smiled Harry as he thought, 'This bloody ring saga might not be so bad after all.'

She asked for a lift and Alf was instructed to drive her to Edgbaston at nine-thirty after she had had a chance to go home for a shower and a change of clothing.

When Stillion finished his telephone conversation with Winston, he stretched, yawned and fell back onto the comfortable sofa. A combination of alcohol and little sleep, added to the stress and strain of the week, meant that he still felt exhausted. Moreover, his back and neck ached.

On the other hand he was able to quell his immediate feeling of wanting to vomit with nerves by telling himself that it was over. His son was born, his wife was well, his enemies defeated and his name cleared. My God the world was a better place this morning than it had been twenty-four hours previously.

He told himself to calm down but was nevertheless close to tears and shaking with emotion as he climbed the stairs to shower, shave and dress for his trip to the cemetery.

His usual Saturday casual jeans and sweatshirt were discarded in favour of a smart dark blue suit, white shirt and black tie as a mark of respect for the late Mrs Elizabeth Woodall.

He left the house at eight-fifteen. His first stop was the newsagent opposite to the White Swan pub at the bottom of Richmond Hill. He bought all the newspapers. The Asian proprietor smiled at him in marked contrast to how he might have greeted him, having picked up on the late edition headlines.

Stillion flopped back behind the wheel of his Jag and flicked through the papers as he indulged his passion for ice-cream as a breakfast delicacy. He was looking for the *Birmingham Post*.

It was the late edition. The front page had a large photograph of Stillion under a headline which blasted: 'Sloane Cleared as Police Trap Drug Ring in Cemetery.' The whole of the front page was given over to Bater's story of what had happened and was splendidly written in the first person by a man who had actually been there. Modesty had forbidden him to play up his own part too much but there were starring roles for Michael, Winston, and of course Stillion. Moreover Bater had been most generous about the ingenuity of Inspector Hooper.

The article picked up the story from the previous day and then traced its progress through Friday evening: Bater's visit to the funeral home, the dash to save Luther, the race to save Winston, the sprint to the cemetery and the successful apprehension of seven men – one of whom being a funeral worker who was related to the deceased whose grave was being robbed.

Most of page two continued the story and had other photographs which included one of Winston Wylde and another of Inspector Hooper. Bater had been as good as his word and kept Jimmy's name out of it. On page six Johnny Titmarsh's editorial claimed the scoop of the year and praised his paper for unearthing the truth. Naturally there was no pubic apology for the earlier articles – just a bashing of the national press for getting it wrong.

Stillion had been found innocent and been portrayed as a hero. Thanks to Bater it had all been done in a frank yet spectacular way. For once there was a public putting right which was as visual as the public getting it wrong.

Late editions of the nationals got the story to varying degrees and Stillion's photograph was in most. It would take them a few hours to catch up, but they would surely do so. The story was far too good to pass over.

Stillion turned off Paul McCartney and tuned in the car radio. He flicked from station to station. Every national and local station was running the story. Some were even reporting it from radio cars outside Sloane House and one even had a reporter in the maternity hospital. 'Thank God they haven't got our home address,' Stillion thought, but he knew it would only

285

be a matter of time. 'They'll have it by lunchtime. They always do,' he concluded.

He finished his ice-cream and drove off through the dark grey early dawn to Handsworth cemetery. He arrived at the bottom gate at eight-fifty as planned and the Jag was waved through by a policeman. He drove up the main drive to where it met Hodgson Walk. There he parked and walked to the grave.

The dawn allowed those present a view of the cemetery at its dramatic best: black, leafless trees and dark Victorian grave-stones all covered in snow. It was cold and the clouds above threatened worse weather. However, there had been no snow overnight and therefore the previous commotion by the grave and beyond was apparent.

Hooper had taken great interest in the various footprints in the snow. He could relate all of them to the information he had received. All of them, that is, with the exception of a set that ran down the hill above the grave to within some thirty-five feet off it and then away again. These prints could not be accounted for. Very strange.

Inspector Hooper and Stillion had never actually met. They had only ever spoken on the phone, such had been the speed with which the exhumation order had been obtained. Hooper had expected to catch Sloane in his trap. If he didn't he had expected to interview him thoroughly once the exhumation had taken place. Last night had changed all of that. However, they knew each other by sight as a result of their pictures featuring in so many newspapers.

They nodded at each other, shook hands and stood side by side under the arc lamps as the exhumation got underway at nine.

'The granddaughter, Terri Field, said she would be here. But she isn't. I know Pastor Wylde is worried abut her. I don't suppose you've heard anything?' asked Stillion.

'No, we 'aven't.'

'Could you make some enquiries?'

'We'll 'ave to if it appears that she were part of the con-spiracy to rob this grave. If she weren't, then someone will 'ave to report 'er missing first,' replied the inspector. Then he added, after a pause and with a smile, 'If she *were* involved you can bet yowa bottom dollar that's why she ain't 'ere now. Any road she ain't the only one gone missing. Mr Woodall has vanished. Gone abroad. I stopped this morning at 'is place to see if 'e 'ad changed 'is mind and wanted to attend. There was no reply. I knocked up a neighbour who told moy he'd gone abroad for four months. I know 'e were against the exhumation but that's ridiculous.'

'Four months?' queried a surprised Stillion.

'Strange ain't it? And there are more strange goings on. Firstly, look up the hill at those footprints. They tell me somebody came and went last night without actually going to the grave. None of moy men saw or 'eard anybody and they couldn't have been involved in the chase as they don't connect up. Did you see or 'ear anything?'

'No I didn't,' answered Stillion honestly, although he suspected who it could have been.

'Secondly, we found two rings on Elton Field. A wedding ring and a diamond ring. What were the actual instructions regarding 'er jewellery. Do you recall?'

'I do. John Palin and I looked over the original arrangement form earlier this week when all of this blew up. There were four rings. Two small diamond rings which were to be removed, and a wedding ring and a much larger diamond ring which were to be placed in the safe and then back on Mrs Woodall just before viewing on the evening before the funeral.'

'Are you certain? Do you know if those instructions were carried out to the letter?'

'I do. All chapels are checked by the caretaker and myself each evening before viewing and that includes jewellery instructions. Anyway, if we'd got it wrong Mr Woodall would have had our guts for garters. The viewing book shows that he was the only one to visit his wife. I suppose Elton could have as well, because he was on the staff and wouldn't therefore have been recorded in the book. I don't know. Why are the jewellery instructions suddenly so important?'

'I don't know. It's just very strange. I've got seven men in custody for robbing a grave of a wedding ring worth peanuts and a diamond ring worth about fifty nicker, seventy-five at the most.'

'What! But the information that Alan Bater and I came by said that the ring was worth eighteen-thousand pounds!'

'Yeah, I know, but our blokes say it's the only thing in Mr Field's story which doesn't add up. We'll get a professional opinion today but our boys 'andle this stuff all the time. They couldn't be that far out. Very strange.'

The ravaged coffin of old Mrs Woodall was hauled from her resting place and placed inside a large casket which was then closed and removed to the awaiting hearse.

'I'll be in touch, Mr Sloane. Thanks for your 'elp and I'm sorry you got caught up in all this. We was only doing our job, you understand?'

'Sure,' replied Stillion with as much politeness as he could muster – he knew that Sloanes and the police would have to go on working together for many years to come.

'By the way, congratulations on the birth of your son. Yow needn't make a statement today. Go and see yowa wife and baby and drop by Steelhouse Lane on Monday,' smiled the inspector.

'Thank you, inspector. Thank you very much,' replied Stillion with genuine gratitude this time.

Stillion drove home quite slowly as he pondered all that Hooper had said. When he arrived he phoned Sloane House and spoke to Palin.

'Hello Stillion. Congratulations to you and Stephanie on the birth and congratulations for sorting out all the problems! I bloody told you Elton Field and Harry Wilkes were in it. I bloody bet that bastard Sydney Gridley is too.'

'Yeah. He's supposed to be, but you won't read that in the papers as there isn't any proof yet.'

'I knew it. By the way, this place is under siege. Every radio and television station in the country wants to interview you, as does every newspaper and magazine. I've got stacks of numbers here for you to call back. It's just a matter of time before they

288

get hold of your address and I understand that some are outside the hospital. Oh, and I hear Bill Woodall has disappeared.'

'Yes I know. Look, are you certain that Mr Woodall was the only person to visit Mrs Woodall in the chapel?'

'Well, as certain as I can be. Only George Brown would really know because he recorded the names in the visitors' book and he's dead. On the other hand I can't ever remember him getting it wrong. Why?'

'Because someone switched the ring worth eighteen grand, which Woodall wanted keeping in the safe secretly along with her wedding ring until just before viewing, with one of the two cheap ones. Now it could only be either Elton Field, Bill Woodall or George Brown. It couldn't be Elton Field because he wasn't there when the coffin was closed, he didn't have any idea of the ring's true value and he wouldn't have risked going to jail by digging up a grave for a ring worth fifty quid. Neither could it be George, God rest his soul, as not only was he an honest soldier but Bill Woodall would have noticed the rings had been switched when he was in the chapel and George sealed the coffin in his presence. I suppose George could have returned later from his flat and reopened the coffin but I doubt it. Anyway, he died poor. Whereas George would have given Bill Woodall a packet containing the two returned rings just before Bill Woodall was shown into the chapel of rest. He would have then been left on his own. He could have made the switch and old George would never have noticed.'

'But why would he do that?' demanded Palin.

'I suppose because he knew the value of the ring and wanted to sell it and keep the proceeds,' replied Stillion.

'But as her husband he could have done that anyway,' insisted Palin.

'Sure, but Elton and his sister Terri would have known he'd have kept it and might have even come to know the value. They would have been inventing schemes by the week to get it or the cash off him. He knew they didn't know the real value so he let them think it had been buried. Then he made his one mistake. Terri went to him for money. He gave her none but said she

289

could have one of the cheap rings left by her grandmother. Unfortunately she took the ring to be valued to the very same jewellers that her grandmother had used, and that's how all three diamond rings' value became known to her and in turn to Elton. Given the value of the expensive one that was supposedly buried, they made their plans to get both of them out of serious debt problems.'

'And that's why old Bill Woodall was against the exhumation I suppose. He knew he would be found out.'

'Correct.

'Bloody hell! Stillion, do you realise this whole fucking week has been for nothing then?'

'Well a fifty-quid ring actually! Do you want my season tickets to the Villa today? If we beat Liverpool this afternoon the championship's ours I bet.'

'Why, aren't you going?'

'No. Important as it is, I've got a young man to go and explain the game to instead. Do me a favour. Phone Winston or Ellen Wylde and see if it would be OK for you to take our little friend Luther with you.'

'You mean the little black lad? Thanks, I will. Do you want to write these telephone numbers down now?'

Stillion did and finished the call. The phone immediately rang again. It was Father O'Rourke. He wanted to say that he never doubted Stillion for a second, and angled for a drop of the hard stuff to wet the baby's head with. Then it was Reverend Freddie Price who wondered if Stillion would like to read the lesson in his church the following Sunday now that he was such a local hero. He might also consider sponsoring a new stained glass window to celebrate the birth of his son.

The phone never stopped. Victoria Thomas, Arthur Kemp, Walter Warburton, friends, family, suppliers and other clergy. Indeed everyone and anyone who had his home number, which was fortunately ex-directory.

Then came the icing on the cake. Charlie Williams phoned to say that he had never thought for a second that there was anything in the rumours. He was sorry that he hadn't been returning calls but this had been done on the advice of his solicitor. Anyway, even before this morning's wonderful news he had sought independent advice as to whom he should sell his business. He had taken it upon himself to ask someone who knew Stillion well and who had sold to him. Joyce Higgins. She had said that without any shadow of a doubt Stillion was a brilliant funeral director and a decent and honest man that she liked.

As a result he was inclined, if Stillion's offer was still on the table, to accept. He would let Fred Gilbert know.

'Should I disappoint Mr Gilbert, Stillion?' he asked.

'Indeed you should,' was Stillion's reply, and he laughed as he put the phone down again. His winning streak had not been broken after all.

The doorbell rang. It was flowers for Stephanie and young Stillion. The phone rang again. It was Gillian Weston bubbling with support. The doorbell rang again. It was a telegram which read, 'One all. So far. I'm off to Spain. Congratulations on everything. I'll get you next time. Love Joyce.' Stillion smiled. The phone rang yet again. It was John. The press had definitely got his address. At least three had just phoned Sloane House for confirmation. He had better watch out. Now the doorbell rang. He opened the door. More flowers? Another telegram? Press? He could see no one. He wandered out of the door and through the brick porch. That was funny. Nobody. He turned to the right. Crack!

The man from Edgbaston lay in the snow in his drive, blood oozing from his head. Was he dead? She didn't know. She turned the claw hammer round in her hand. She had better make sure. She stood there for a second transfixed. He was so beautiful. His sleeping face so saintly in the snow. So smart in his blue suit. She noticed how clean his shoes were. Why had he let her down? She would have loved him so well if only he had given her a chance. Still, it was too late now. She raised the hammer again. But it was snatched from her hand. She turned round to see a woman. She ran off down the drive in a daze. She felt as if she were floating on air.

291

She didn't notice the press car coming as she ran into the road. They met in a hurry. The car to come. Her to go. Now she was also lying in the snow.

The other woman bent over Stillion Sloane.

'It's a good job for you my bedroom is at the front of our house,' she told an unconscious Sloane as she bent down and felt his pulse. Elizabeth Ripley had repaid her debt to Stillion. It hadn't taken forever either – just five days.